LOVE OF A STONEMASON

Family Portrait, Book Two

LOVE OF A STONEMASON

Family Portrait, Book Two

Christa Polkinhorn

Bookworm Press

Bookworm Press
1223 Wilshire Blvd., #1054
Santa Monica, CA 90403

Cover design: Diane Busch
Cover images: Sanjeri, istock.com

Author photograph: Diane Busch

ISBN: 978-0-9600135-5-5

Printed in the United States of America

This book is dedicated to the memory of my mother, Anna Umiker, my father, Heinrich Umiker, my sister, Rosmarie Spiegel-Umiker, and my brother-in-law, Luigi Spiegel.

PART ONE

MONTE SOSTO

Chapter 1

Karla Bocelli hated the painting. She had worked at it off and on during the past year and never managed to finish it. But no matter how much she disliked it, she couldn't convince herself to destroy it. It seemed to haunt her.

It was warm and muggy in early June in the south of Switzerland. Patches of mist hugged the mountains behind Lago Maggiore. Karla clasped her artist's portfolio under her arm and brushed a strand of hair from her damp forehead. She was on the way to the old part of Locarno, thinking, once again, of the troublesome picture.

She saw the car just as she stepped into the crosswalk. An old beat-up Fiat screeched to a stop a few inches away from her. Karla jumped back and dropped her portfolio, spilling its contents onto the pavement. Her heart thudded and she took deep breaths, trying to calm the queasy feeling in her stomach. *That smell. Burnt rubber.*

A young man got out of the car and stared at her, stunned. "Are you all right?"

Karla, still dazed, nodded. She bent down and began to pick up her drawings. A few pedestrians stopped, but when they realized that nothing major had happened, they walked on.

The driver's dark voice rose to an angry pitch. "Jesus Christ. What's the matter with you? You practically threw yourself in front of my car. I could've killed you. Are you suicidal or what?"

"I'm sorry, I wasn't watching." Karla slid the papers back into her portfolio.

"Yeah, well, that's obvious. Wake up, for heaven's sake."

3

His belligerent voice angered Karla, who was gradually regaining her composure. She stood up, flipped her long dark hair back over her shoulders, and faced him. "I said, I was sorry."

He was tall, broad-shouldered, and sturdy, with longish dark tousled hair and green eyes, which now glowered at her. He must have been her age or a little older, perhaps in his mid-twenties. As Karla continued to pick up her drawings, he approached and bent down to help her.

"You're an artist?" he asked in a friendlier tone as he looked at one of the charcoal sketches.

"Yes." Karla snatched the paper out of his hand.

"I hope your pictures aren't ruined."

"What do you care? Why do you have to drive like a maniac?"

"Great," he shouted. "Now it's my fault?"

"This is a pedestrian zone, in case you haven't noticed." Karla grabbed her portfolio and stepped back onto the sidewalk. Her heartbeat had slowed to almost normal, but her knees still felt wobbly.

"Do you always jump in front of moving cars without looking?" He turned around and walked away. "Airhead," he mumbled. He shot her a last angry look, got into the car, and slammed the door. The engine revved and then died several times. Finally the car started and he drove off, leaving a cloud of stinking smoke behind.

"Jerk. Perhaps a new muffler would help. Never heard of air pollution?" Karla crossed the street after carefully checking the road for traffic. Still shaken, she made her way through the old part of Locarno toward the art store to drop off her drawings to be framed for the upcoming opening.

Karla was a young artist whose first exhibition of her paintings and drawings opened the following Friday. The gallery belonged to a friend and patron of hers. Silvia and her husband were art lovers, and devoted some of their time and money to help fledgling artists show their work.

Having recovered somewhat, Karla was able to take in the sights of the old part of this city she loved: the boutiques and small shops along the narrow cobblestone streets; the quaint houses painted in ocher, orange, and pink; the piazzas with their pots of cornflowers and red and white geraniums; the small, simple Romanesque and the more ornate Baroque churches. Karla inhaled the mixture of scents so familiar to her from her childhood when she came here often with her mother and grandmother: the smell of espresso, of grilled meat and fish as well as herbs and spices from the restaurants, stores, and coffee bars.

When Karla arrived at the gallery after dropping off her drawings at the art store, she looked through the tall shop window at the row of paintings on the wall. It was only now that the momentous event began to sink in. She was overcome by a surge of pride and excitement. *My first exhibition.* She knocked on the window. Silvia, who was already in the gallery moving chairs and folding tables, turned around and waved at her.

"So what do you think?" Silvia stepped back and motioned at Karla's paintings. She was a woman in her fifties with a wild mane of graying hair. Her outfit was a mixture of femme fatale and hippy—low-cut, tight, black top and long, flowery skirt.

"Great. I like the way you arranged them." Karla studied the row of pictures. There were a few watercolor and acrylic landscapes with a calm, Zen-like feel, while many of her oil paintings exploded in fiery reds, yellows, and browns with a volcanic intensity. In addition, Karla had chosen a few experimental pictures: landscapes that clashed with foreign objects, such as scrap metal, a computer sticking out of a flower. She wanted to strike a balance between paintings that might appeal to regular visitors and those that would receive attention from art collectors.

5

"I hope somebody shows up." Karla sighed. "I've been looking forward to this, but now I'm getting nervous. Do you really think I put the right paintings up?"

"Sure you did, they're great. Relax."

"The last few of my drawings should be framed and ready by Thursday," Karla said.

"Good. I left space on the back wall for them. I ordered the snacks and the wine. So we're ready. Don't forget the bios. And don't worry, the opening will be fabulous." Silvia gave Karla a hug, enveloping her in a cloud of patchouli perfume.

By the time Karla arrived at the stone cottage she rented in the small village at the beginning of the Maggia Valley, the air had thickened. In the direction of Saint Gotthard, the mountain that divided the south from the north of Switzerland, towering heaps of dark clouds were churning, the first sign of a thunderstorm.

Karla filled the espresso pot with water and finely ground coffee and set it on the stove, then went into her studio, a room with a skylight and a window facing south. The owner, an artist himself, had the skylight installed since the windows in this typical southern Swiss house were small and the lighting wasn't good enough for painting. Sitting in front of her easel, Karla began to mix her paints. The picture she was working on was the one she had been thinking about earlier that morning when she almost got hit by the car.

The half-finished oil painting was different from her intensely colorful landscapes. It was a stark, somber picture, almost devoid of color. It showed the stylized outline of a woman in black, a dark, lonely figure standing at the edge of the canvas, who covered her face with her hands. The rest was empty space, except for a glowing spot of color at the right upper corner.

Karla had started the painting after the unexpected death of her aunt the year before. She had been Karla's only remaining blood relation aside from her father, who lived in Peru and whom she barely knew. Her aunt had raised Karla since she was five years old, after her mother and grandmother had been killed in a car crash. She and Karla had been very close, and her death had been a devastating blow. The year before her aunt's death, Jonas, her aunt's boyfriend and Karla's dear friend and mentor, had died after a heart attack.

Scanning the picture with half-closed eyes, Karla picked up a brush, dipped it in a mixture of gray and green paint, then stopped to examine the painting again. The slender, dark figure looked forlorn and lost. Not even the color in the back was comforting. It was orange-red, the sun of the evening, which had lost its warmth.

Why do I even bother with this thing? Frustrated with the timid and self-effacing woman in the painting, Karla tossed a sheet over it and put the picture, once again, into the storage room next to her studio.

The espresso pot hissed on the stove, and the scent of fresh coffee filled the room and dispelled the smell of paint. Karla poured herself a cup and decided to drink it black; perhaps it would ease the tension in her head. The slight headache she had woken up with had intensified during the day, in part due to the change of air pressure before the storm, and in part, perhaps, because of her tumultuous morning with the young man.

Karla stood by the kitchen window, sipping her coffee, savoring its slightly bitter taste. She tried to picture the man again, his muscular figure, his longish, dark hair and, particularly, his expressive green eyes. Too bad they hadn't met under more pleasant circumstances. In spite of his angry outburst, she felt a certain curiosity about him.

A breeze kicked up and shook the azaleas in front of the house. The large creamy-white-and-red flowers of the horse-chestnut trees swayed back and forth. Karla stepped outside. It smelled of rain, damp and musty. The meadows in front of the house were filled with blue, purple, and yellow wildflowers, and down the hill the birches, ashes, and tall hazels along the river Maggia leaned into the wind.

Karla went back inside and prepared a canvas for a new painting. She pulled the cloth tightly across the stretcher bars with the help of canvas pliers and fastened it with staples. After covering the canvas with a base layer of gesso, she set it aside to dry. She turned on her computer and printed out a stack of bios for the exhibition.

Outside, daylight was fading fast as smoky-gray storm clouds began to darken the sky. After a quick dinner of soup and bread topped with cheese, Karla tried to do some sketching, but nothing came of it. She was tired and her head still ached. She took an aspirin and went to bed early. Listening to the wind whooshing through the trees, she fell asleep.

Later in the night, Karla woke up drenched in sweat. The bursting of broken glass and a woman's desperate scream for help were interrupted by claps of thunder. At first, she was unable to distinguish between the noises in her dream and the sounds of reality. A whiff of burnt rubber and acid hung in the air.

Karla peeled back her down comforter and sat up, pushed herself to the edge of the bed, and lowered her feet to the floor. She brushed a tangle of hair from her wet forehead and took a deep breath. It had been the same nightmare she had suffered from since childhood, but the thunder and lightning were real. The grandfather clock in the next room struck eleven times. She must have just fallen asleep when the thunder woke her.

Karla got up and looked out the window. Lightning lit up the sky, and the shadows of clouds swept across the meadows. The trees bent over and swayed in the gusts of wind. She went into the kitchen and poured herself a glass of water, then sat by the window. Sipping the cold liquid, she tried to squelch the shreds of troubling images her dream had left her with: the mangled bodies, the blood, the broken glass, the fire.

"Mama?" Karla whispered into the dark. Her eyes filled with tears. "All I have of you is a scream for help. I barely even remember what you looked like."

There was no answer, only the thunder in the distance. Karla got up and opened the door to the patio. She stepped outside as it began to rain. First, large individual drops hit her arms and face, then the clouds burst. She bent her head back, closed her eyes, and let the rain pound on her face for a few seconds, enjoying the harsh cleansing sensation. The water soaked through her T-shirt. She began to shiver and went inside, pulled off her top and grabbed a towel to dry off. Back in bed, she listened to the now steady and peaceful-sounding rain and fell asleep again.

Chapter 2

The sky was a clear blue after the thunderstorm of the past night, with only a few fleecy white clouds in the north and streaks of sulfur-yellow etched on the horizon in the south. The air felt fresh and clean. It promised to be a beautiful early-summer day.

Karla stepped outside and inhaled the sweet scent of the wisteria in the courtyard. However, no matter how hard she tried to enjoy the day, she felt out of sorts and depressed. Her nightmare, her inability to finish the painting she struggled with, and the unsettling feelings after her near accident the day before all seemed to have banded together and attacked her, full force, in her sleep.

Painting didn't help, either. She wanted to go back to her colorful landscapes, to drown her dark mood with globs of fiery paints, but the newly stretched canvas merely stared back at her. It was glaring in its whiteness, hostile. Finally, Karla gave up trying to work. She would pay a visit to Lena and get some roses for her mother's grave.

Lena cultivated and sold roses, and was known all over the valley and the nearby cities for her beautiful rose fields. She had been one of Karla's closest friends for many years. Having known her mother well, Lena had often babysat Karla when she was little. Karla had spent the first five years of her life in the Maggia Valley and had moved north to live with her aunt after her mother's and grandmother's deaths. After Karla's aunt had passed, Lena encouraged her to move back to the Vallemaggia and invited her to stay with her until she found a place of her own. Lena and her husband, Luigi, and their four children had become like a family to Karla.

On the way to Lena's, Karla passed by the rose fields, which were in full bloom, although some damage from the thunderstorm was visible. A few of the bushes had been knocked to the ground, and the field was strewn with rose petals, which looked like big confetti. But even so, the flowers were dazzling. Shades of red, from crimson to purple to mauve, different hues of orange, multicolored roses as well as the simple white and yellow ones, all sparkled in the sun and formed a pleasant contrast to the dark green of the pines in the background and the vineyards on both sides.

Normally, Karla couldn't walk by the rose fields without stopping to admire the abundance of colors. Today, though, she barely glanced at the flowers, although their sweet fragrance was almost overpowering.

Karla found Lena in the large shed next to her home, busy preparing for the upcoming market. She was putting roses on the conveyor belt of a machine that separated the flowers by length, so they could be arranged into bouquets more easily. Lena was a stout, motherly woman in her late forties, with lively blue eyes and thick brown hair streaked with gray.

"Hi there." Lena gave Karla a quick smile, then continued to watch the roses glide by. She occasionally picked one up and set it aside, then turned off the machine. "How are you?"

"I don't know. I got up on the wrong side of the bed." Karla blinked as the tears rose in her eyes.

"Oh?" Lena peered at her, then took her by the arm. "Come on, the coffee is still fresh. I need a break."

They went inside and Lena poured them each a cup. She sat next to Karla and put her arm around her. "So, tell me, what's bugging you?"

The motherly gesture broke the dam that held back Karla's tears. All the pent-up emotions of the past couple of days flooded her. Lena waited patiently until Karla was able to stop crying. She hugged her and gently patted her back, as if to comfort a child. "What's the matter, Karla?"

"I just had one of those miserable dreams again, and yesterday I almost got run over by a car," Karla finally managed to say between sobs. She told Lena of her near accident, her inability to deal with one of her paintings, the nightmare. "It all just brought it back again. I'm lonely. Anna and Jonas are gone. I have no family left and ..." She burst into tears again.

"Honey, I know, it's hard. But why don't you come to us when you feel bad? You know you always have family here. You're not alone."

"Thanks, Lena. I know. It's just one of those days."

"Talk about family. Have you heard from your father lately?" Lena gently brushed a strand of hair out of Karla's face.

"Not in a while. It's my turn to write. I just haven't been up to it. I've run out of things to write to him about. Problem is, we haven't seen each other in ten years, and you start to lose track."

"I understand. Perhaps you should plan a trip to see him."

"Yeah, I know. I should." Karla wiped the tears from her face. "I've been busy saving my money for painting, but I guess I could stay with his family. He even offered to pay for my plane ticket. It

11

would be great to visit Peru again." Karla hugged Lena. "Thanks for listening to me. It does make me feel better." She managed a weak smile and got up. "I actually came down here to get some roses for Mama's grave."

"Pick as many as you want. And take one of the vases here." Lena reached for a vase on the kitchen cabinet and handed it to Karla. "And if you're up to it, come and help me bake this afternoon. Luigi is with the lambs, and the kids are in school. I could use some help. I'm making a few loaves of braided bread. Unless you've painting to do?"

"No. Baking sounds wonderful. Just what I need to get my mind off my problems."

Karla walked the short distance to the cemetery. The sweet aroma of her bouquet of roses brought a smile to her face. *It's going to be a good day,* she tried to convince herself.

The river Maggia on the other side of the street roared with gusto, spilling its waters in swirls and rapids toward Lake Maggiore. The noble chestnut trees in front of the graveyard were in full bloom, and their long yellowish catkins exuded a strong, pungent scent. Scattered by the wind, the abundant pollen of the male blossoms covered the ground and graves with a film of fine golden dust.

As Karla climbed the few steps to the graveyard, she brushed against an overhanging branch of a wet hazel bush that showered her with a rivulet of water. She spotted two men working on the plot next to her mother's grave. One of them was in the process of leaving. He loaded a cart with tools and pushed it toward the exit. The man who stayed behind was crouching before a freshly planted plot, wiping off what seemed to be a new gravestone. A shock of dark hair hung over his face. When Karla put down the vase filled with the roses on her mother's grave, he stood up.

They stared at each other.

"You?" Karla asked.

"Oh my god, it's the woman who jumps in front of moving cars." A sarcastic smile teased his lips as he glared at her with his green cat eyes.

"It's the maniac who ignores pedestrian zones. What are you doing here?"

"I'm your local stonemason. I put up one of those." He brushed a strand of hair from his forehead and pointed at the newly planted stone.

The gravestone stood out somewhat from the others. It was made of polished gray-green gneiss. The top edge, however, was left in its original unpolished shape, giving the tombstone an artistic flair. The text was carved in a simple italic font, and the only decoration was a bunch of grapes chiseled into the stone.

"That's beautiful," Karla said.

"Thanks." He pointed at the stone on her mother's grave. "Someone close to you?"

"My mother."

"Oh, sorry." He squinted his eyes and looked at the stone more closely. "That was a long time ago, you must have lost her early."

"Yes, I was five when she died. A car accident."

"A car accident? Jesus. Seems to run in the family."

Karla glared at him. "I don't think that's funny at all. You sure have a warped sense of humor."

"I'm sorry, that was stupid. I didn't mean it that way. It just struck me as a strange coincidence. I almost ran you over, and now ... I apologize. And I'm sorry I yelled at you yesterday. I was wrong. I was driving too fast." He stretched out his arm.

Still angry, Karla hesitated. But seeing his imploring look, she gave in and shook his hand. It was large, but in spite of the rough work, his palm felt soft. "It was my fault, too. I should've been more careful," she admitted.

She was struck again by the unusual color of his intense green eyes. They changed from verdigris to shades of blue according to the way the sun touched his face. He was handsome, in a rough kind of way. *I'd like to paint him.* Realizing she was staring at him, she quickly averted her gaze. A breeze kicked up, buffeting the leaves in the trees and tugging at her hair.

"Look, we started out all wrong. Can we just forget about yesterday? And go out for coffee or a movie or dinner or something? My treat."

"You sure move fast. Yesterday you called me an airhead, and now you ask me out?"

He gave a guttural laugh. "Well, yesterday was yesterday. I'm glad I didn't run you over, a beautiful girl like you. By the way, I'm Andreas."

"Karla."

"So what do you say?"

"I don't know. I'm really busy this week. I'm preparing for an arts exhibition on Friday, but if you're interested, here is an announcement." Karla pulled a card out of her purse and handed it to him.

"Oh, that's right, you're an artist. Great, I love paintings. Had to do quite a bit of drawing as part of my training." He studied the card, which showed a couple of Karla's paintings. "Interesting work."

Karla liked the sound of his voice, deep and throaty, even a little tender, now that he wasn't yelling or making sarcastic remarks. "So what do you do aside from making tombstones?"

"All kinds of stonework, but also some metal sculptures. I just can't make enough money with that kind of stuff yet. So it's mainly tombstones for a living. Talk about making a living, I better get back to work. I have to plant a few more of these at another cemetery." He pointed at the gravestone. "Three people died the same week."

"Oh? Well, you should be pleased." Karla chuckled.

He raised an eyebrow. "What's that supposed to mean?"

"Good business for you. More tombstones."

"And I'm supposed to be the one with the warped sense of humor, huh?" He laughed, then picked up the rag with which he had wiped off the gravestone and stuffed it into the back pocket of his tattered jeans. As they walked toward the exit, Karla noticed his beat-up Fiat parked on the other side of the road.

"Okay, see you Friday." He lightly touched her arm.

Karla nodded. "Drive carefully. Don't run over any pedestrians," she called after him.

He turned around and opened his mouth as if to say something, then shook his head and grinned. He waved at her as he got into the car. The engine started right away this time.

Karla looked after him as he drove away. *He must have had his muffler fixed.*

Lena's rustic kitchen looked like a bakery. The heavy cherry-wood table was covered with pans of dough and a thin layer of flour. On the walls hung black iron pots and the typical copper bowls and pots popular in the south of Switzerland. Lena was busy kneading the dough for braided bread.

"It smells delicious." Karla inhaled the warm, yeasty scent.

"Cut yourself some. I made this one earlier." Lena pointed at one of the finished loaves. "There is butter and jam over there, and I just made fresh coffee."

"You don't have to tell me twice." Karla cut a thick slice of the freshly baked honey-colored loaf. The inside was buttery yellow and soft, and Karla gave a sigh of pleasure as she bit into a piece slathered with Lena's homemade blackberry jam. "Heavenly."

Lena gave her a cursory glance while kneading the dough vigorously, occasionally slapping it onto the table to make it smooth and springy. "You seem to be feeling better."

"Yeah, I am." Karla licked a drop of jam from her finger, then put on one of Lena's aprons. She picked up a slab of dough and began to knead. "Guess what? I ran into the guy who almost hit me with his car yesterday."

"You're kidding. Where?" Lena divided her piece of dough into three equal parts and began to braid them.

"At the cemetery. He was putting up a gravestone. He's a stonemason. His name is Andreas."

"Andreas O'Reilly?" Lena looked up, then dipped her hands into the flour and continued to pull and punch the dough.

"I don't know his last name. You know him?" Karla stopped kneading and stared at Lena.

"Yes. He made a few gravestones for our cemetery. In fact, he carved my grandmother's stone a couple of years ago. He does beautiful work. So he is the guy who almost hit you? Strange. He doesn't seem like the careless-driver type."

"I think we were both at fault. At first, I thought he was a real jerk, but today he seemed more pleasant. What do you know about him?"

"Not that much, just the little bit he told me or I heard about him. Some problems with his family, I don't know any details. He was raised by his aunt and uncle. He's quite an accomplished sculptor, considering how young he is. He was hired to put up some stone sculptures in the area."

"He said he was coming to the opening on Friday. He asked me out," Karla said.

"You must have made quite an impression on him." Lena chuckled.

"I don't know." Karla stopped kneading again and glanced out the window. "I've had more than my share of questionable dates. I'm not too eager to get involved with anybody. I don't have much luck with men. Anyway, we'll see if he shows up on Friday."

"You're not paying attention, Karla. Come on, let me finish." Lena smiled and shook her head. She grabbed the hunk of dough that Karla had been working on. "Why don't you apply the egg wash instead?"

"Sorry, Lena, I'm not much help today." Karla sighed. She removed the towels from the loaves, which had risen to full size. She gently poked one of the plump, smooth braids with her finger, then picked up a baking brush, dipped it into the mixture of water and egg, and glazed the tops of the breads with even, generous strokes.

"Nice job." Lena pointed at the loaves Karla had just finished. "You definitely have more talent handling a brush than kneading dough." There was a cracking sound outside. Lena looked up. "Another thunderstorm?"

Karla watched through the window as the wind carried off a small branch of the apple tree behind the house. She felt the familiar pressure in her head. "No, not a thunderstorm. The wind is changing."

Chapter 3

"How do you feel seeing all these people admire your work?" Silvia handed Karla a glass of white wine.

"It's exciting. A little scary ... it makes me feel exposed." Karla looked around the gallery, where friends and strangers had gathered. Some of them were examining her paintings; others stood around and chatted, sipping their drinks and picking at the appetizers. A couple of Karla's artist friends talked animatedly. A girl dressed in black, wearing high dress boots, with strands of purple in her short hair, waved at Karla, who went to join her.

"Hey, great stuff." The girl with purple hair and pierced nose and eyebrows motioned at the paintings. "How did you manage this? I mean, getting this venue? I'm looking for a place for my own work."

"Geez, Sarah, don't waste any time congratulating Karla on her success. Be your usual pushy self and only think about Number One." A gangly young man with a ponytail shook his head and sneered.

"Oh, Jason, don't be such an ass. Karla knows I'm happy for her." The girl gave Karla a hug. "I didn't know you did that kind of thing." She pointed at Karla's more experimental paintings. "That's cool. I love that one with the PC sticking out of the flower. I'll get us some wine. Don't go anywhere, I need to talk to you." Sarah pointed her finger at Karla, then marched over to the table with the snacks.

Karla wondered how Sarah managed to walk in her tight miniskirt and high-heeled boots. At that moment, she spotted Andreas, who was looking at her paintings. He must have come in as she was talking to her friends. At first, she barely recognized him. He was wearing slacks and a jacket, and had evidently made an attempt to comb his unruly hair. "Listen, guys. I'm sorry, but I have to say hello to someone. Later, Sarah." Karla waved Sarah off, who returned with two glasses of wine.

"You look distinguished tonight," Karla said as she walked up to Andreas.

Andreas appeared to feel uncomfortable dressed up. The outfit had seen its better days. The jacket seemed too tight for his muscular body, the sleeves were a little short, and the slacks bulged slightly at the knees. He gave the impression of a caged tiger.

"I don't feel distinguished at all. In fact, I feel rather foolish in this monkey suit, but I thought I couldn't very well attend an opening in my torn jeans." He pulled at his poorly knotted tie.

"Oh, it suits you very well," Karla tried to reassure him.

"I love your art." Andreas squinted his eyes as he studied one of Karla's oil paintings. "The luminosity in this picture ... it reminds me of an exhibition I saw not long ago, of paintings by Giovanni Segantini and others."

"Yeah," Karla said, excited. "He is one of my favorite painters of that era. I love the Swiss and Italian divisionists. The way they created the illusion of light emanating from the canvas. I kind of play with their technique sometimes."

Andreas motioned at Karla's scrap-metal landscapes. "Interesting. Very different from your other work."

"I'm still experimenting. I'm not sure yet where I'm going with those."

"What's wrong with that? Why limit yourself? That would be boring." Andreas peered at her. "I like painters, and artists in general, who have the guts to experiment. Art is a constant search for new ways of expressing yourself, isn't it?"

"I guess you're right." Karla nodded.

"Hey, Karla, aren't you going to introduce me?" Sarah, who had come up behind Karla, poked her lightly in the back and gave Andreas a flirtatious look.

Karla was getting annoyed at her friend. Sarah could be irritating sometimes, but today she was outright obnoxious. Not wanting to create a scene, she introduced Andreas.

"So what do you do, sexy?" Sarah winked at him.

Andreas kept a straight face, folded his arms in front of his chest. "What do I do? That should be obvious. I'm here to look at Karla's art."

Sarah gave a toss of the head. "I don't mean that. What do you do for a living? Are you an artist or something?"

"If you want to interview me, you have to make an appointment. But I warn you, I charge a lot." Andreas still kept a straight face, but there was a gleam of amusement in his eyes.

"Okay, you want to be that way. Knock yourself out." Sarah turned around on her heel and marched to the other side of the gallery.

"Your friend obviously doesn't appreciate my kind of humor, either." Andreas gave a quick, throaty laugh.

"I guess not." Karla smiled.

19

They walked over to where Karla's watercolors hung. Andreas studied them quietly for a long time. "You really caught the effect of the light. They're fascinating."

"Thanks." Their eyes met, and Karla felt a tingling sensation somewhere between her throat and stomach. *I guess he can be sensitive.*

"That mountain." He pointed at a painting of Monte Sosto, a mountain in the Blenio Valley, a side valley of the Leventina just south of Saint Gotthard. Karla had forced herself to get up early one morning so she could catch the special quality of the sunlight piercing through the mist at dawn. It was one of her favorite aquarelles.

"I used to live in Olivone and looked at Monte Sosto almost every day," Andreas continued. "I got so used to it that I didn't even see it anymore. This painting brings out the mystical quality I noticed when I first saw it. I believe that art makes us *see* things we normally merely look at."

"Monte Sosto has always fascinated me, because the minute I saw it, it reminded me of Machu Picchu in Peru," Karla said.

"Really? You know, I think you have a point. I've seen pictures of Machu Picchu. Yes, there is a certain similarity. So you've been to Peru? Fascinating. I'd love to go to Peru. They're famous for their ruins and stonework—uh-oh, here is your friend again. I think she's in trouble." Andreas motioned at someone behind Karla.

When Karla turned around, Sarah was walking unsteadily toward them, followed by Jason, who tried to hold her back. "I'm sorry, guys, I'm plastered." She stumbled and fell against Andreas, who caught her. Sarah threw her arms around him and started to cry. "My life is a mess. It's going nowhere. Nobody loves my art. I'm going to kill myself."

Andreas tried to hold her away from him. "No, you're not. It'd be a real pity if you did."

"Do you really ... think so?" Sarah's face was a mess. Her black eyeliner was running down her cheeks.

Andreas, still holding her at a little distance, spoke vehemently. "Yes, you're a very pretty woman, once you wash that stuff off your face. And don't let anybody make you doubt your artwork."

"Oh, you're such a sweetheart." Sarah tried to embrace Andreas again.

Leave it up to Sarah to create a scene and steal the show. Karla was peeved.

Jason pulled Sarah back. "We're going home. Sorry, guys, this is really embarrassing." He shook his head. "She's had a rough time."

"I'm so sorry." Sarah began to weep again and hugged Karla. The mixture of alcohol and a sweet-smelling perfume was overpowering.

Karla patted her back, trying not to inhale. "It's all right, Sarah. I understand. Let's talk when you feel better."

Sarah nodded. She was still crying when Jason led her away. People were staring at them.

"Poor girl. What's her problem, anyway?" Andreas asked.

Karla shrugged. "She's had all kinds of problems, mainly with money and trying to promote her art. She's actually an interesting artist. She makes these huge papier-mâché sculptures, but so far she hasn't been able to find anybody who would give her a chance to exhibit them." Karla watched as Sarah stumbled outside with Jason holding her up.

"Is Jason her boyfriend?" Andreas asked.

"No." Karla shook her head. "Jason is gay, but he's Sarah's closest friend. I'll talk to Silvia. Perhaps she'll be able to help. Silvia is the owner of the gallery," Karla explained. "Just makes me realize how lucky I've been."

Andreas, who watched as Sarah left, shook his head. "It's not just luck. It's also hard work, talent, insistence, and patience, and yes, I guess lots of luck." He motioned with his head toward Sarah. "She's quite young, and if she's already that disillusioned, she is in the wrong field. Art is a tough business. And if she keeps drinking like this, she'll end up ruining her life or killing herself."

"That sounds pretty negative," Karla said.

"It's not negative, just realistic." Andreas narrowed his eyes. "Believe me, I know what alcohol can do to a person." He paused. "My father was an alcoholic."

"'Was'?"

"He doesn't live with us anymore. I don't know where he is or if he's still alive. I have no contact with him."

"Sorry."

"It's all right. Let's not talk about it."

Karla remembered Lena mentioning something about problems in his family.

"Sorry, Karla, I've come to kidnap you. The press is here." Karla smelled Silvia's patchouli perfume before she felt her arm around her. "A man from the local newspaper wants to talk to you."

"Oh no," Karla said. "What am I supposed to say?"

"Come on, Karla. You better get used to this." Silvia chuckled. "You're on your way to fame and glory."

Chapter 4

The day after her first exhibition, Karla got up earlier than usual, eager to paint. The opening had been a success. Several of her paintings had sold. To her pleasant surprise, Andreas had bought the aquarelle of Monte Sosto. In addition, Karla had an appointment with the person in charge of buying works of art for one of the major banks in the area. He liked her large, colorful canvases, and he wanted to order some for his bank subsidiaries.

Karla pulled on a pair of shorts and a work shirt, tied her long, black hair into a ponytail, and stepped outside. A thin veil of early-morning mist hovered over the fields and the part of the river Maggia she could see from her house. The pines were a rich green, and the leaves of the birches along the river quivered and sparkled in the sun. The colors seemed particularly vivid this morning.

Aside from the mild climate, it was above all the quality of the light and the colors that drew Karla to the south of Switzerland. Each season had its own special coloration, ranging from the diffuse tones of winter with its elongated shadows to the lively hues of spring to the fiery reds and purples of a summer sunset to, finally, the shades of mist and the mellow light of fall.

Karla sat in front of her easel and squeezed globs of oil paints onto the palette. This was one of those moments when it became clear to her, once again, why she painted. The empty canvas, when everything was possible and nothing was decided yet. The excitement in the beginning, when her hand first felt the texture of the canvas or paper, the smells, the colors, the sensation of the brush gliding through the paint on the palette. Then the first creative impulse when the brush touched the canvas, the initial few brush strokes, perhaps hesitant at first, then more and more determined, taking control, then letting the painting guide her, taking control again, until she was so absorbed that she forgot time. When the doorbell or the phone rang, she looked up briefly, shook her head, and went right back to painting, ignoring the disturbance.

At noon Karla took a break. She showered and dressed, and got ready to drive to Bellinzona to do some shopping. Bellinzona, the capital of the canton Ticino and a city with an interesting past dating back to Roman times, was about a thirty-minute drive from the Maggia Valley. Its three castles on the hill above the town dominated its skyline and gave the city a distinct medieval flavor.

For Karla, the castles had a more personal significance. They reminded her of a happy time during her childhood, when her mother and grandmother were still alive and took her on outings to the castles. She had been fascinated by the thick stone walls, the narrow windows, the steep stairways. Her mother had told her stories of knights and damsels in distress, of ghosts haunting the castles, and Karla had spent hours drawing and painting those scenes. Now, she looked at the castles with a feeling of nostalgia.

Just as she got ready to drive home, she remembered that Andreas's studio was in Bellinzona. At the opening he had told her he would call her to show her some of his sculptures and other stonework. Karla pulled out his business card. His workshop was in a former factory building in the industrial area of Bellinzona. On an impulse, she took the freeway exit toward the south of the city. It didn't take her long to find the place. She parked the car nearby and walked toward the square, yellowish brick house. The door to Andreas's part of the building was open, and she heard the grinding sound of a machine. There was a sign above the door: *Andreas O'Reilly – Scultura*. A few stone and metal sculptures in different stages of completion stood outside.

Karla stopped at the corner, feeling uncomfortable. She didn't want to give Andreas the impression she was so eager to see him that she couldn't wait for his phone call. She decided just to take a peek to find out what his workshop looked like. He probably wouldn't even hear or see her with the machine running. She advanced to the open door and carefully looked inside. A light smell of stone dust and a whiff of exhaust drifted her way.

Andreas was sitting on a low stool with his back toward her. His face was covered by goggles and a mask, and he was holding some kind of power tool with which he polished the surface of a piece of rock in front of him. He was dressed in blue workpants and a yellow undershirt. Karla watched him for a while, and couldn't help but admire the play of muscles on his tanned arms and shoulders as he held on to the grinder, which slightly vibrated in his hands. Andreas turned off the machine, removed his mask and goggles, and wiped his forehead. As Karla stepped back, she realized that she cast a shadow next to his chair.

Andreas wheeled around on his stool and looked at her, puzzled. "Hello. What a surprise. What are you doing here?" He got up and wiped his hands on a towel and dried his face. There were goggle marks around his eyes.

"I ... I was in the neighborhood and remembered your workshop, so I thought I would just drop by." Karla, caught in the act of snooping on him, felt the heat rise to her face. "And I wanted to thank you for buying a painting," she quickly added.

He gave her a wide smile. "Welcome. You're actually the second woman who dropped by today. I didn't know I was that popular with the ladies."

"Oh? Who else dropped by?" *Gee, this isn't really any of my business.*

"Your friend. The one who got tanked at your exhibition."

"Sarah?"

"Yeah, that's her."

Karla was stunned. "Really? That's odd. What did she want?"

"She was probably just overwhelmed with me and couldn't keep away." He chuckled. "Just kidding. She apologized for being a mess the other day. She said she wanted to see my workshop and invited me to check out her artwork."

"Are you going to?" It was out before Karla could stop herself.

"Don't you want me to?" His grin widened. He obviously enjoyed her discomfort.

"I don't care." Karla was getting irritated, not just because she was making a fool of herself but because she suspected that there were reasons behind Sarah's visit other than a casual meeting between artists. *It wouldn't be the first time that Sarah stole one of my boyfriends. But he isn't my boyfriend. So why should I care?*

"You look upset. What's the matter?" He peered at her with a serious face.

"Nothing." She tried to sound casual. "I guess I better go."

"You just got here. Come on, I'll show you the studio. Want some coffee?"

Karla nodded and forced a smile. "Coffee sounds great."

While Andreas washed two cups and turned on the small espresso machine next to his desk, Karla looked around. Along the walls were shelves with stone samples of different types of granite, gneiss, marble, serpentine, verrucano, and many more, in shades ranging from black to blue-gray to sea green to orange to red to terra-cotta to muted gold. On the other side of the room was a shelf with all kinds of stonecutting tools as well as goggles and masks to protect from the dust and stone splinters. Another machine stood in the corner next to a half-finished tombstone.

Karla touched some of the rocks, feeling their different textures, the smoothness of a piece of green alabaster, the rough surface of granite. "I didn't even know there were that many kinds of stones. Where did you get them all?"

"This is just a small sample of what's out there. Some of them I bought, some of the smaller ones I collected while hiking." He picked up a piece of blue-speckled marble and caressed it with his hand, then gave it to Karla to hold. It was polished and smooth on one side and left raw on the other.

"How beautiful. I always thought of marble as being smooth. But it's actually quite rough," Karla said, brushing her hand over the unpolished side.

"Yes, in its natural state. It takes some work to make it smooth and polished. Just like with us humans, huh?" He put the stone back on the shelf.

"I think I like the unpolished side better," Karla said.

"Stones or humans?" Andreas winked at her, then walked over to the coffee machine.

Karla shrugged. "Both, I guess."

"Good, that gives me some encouragement. Not much polishing here." He handed her a cup of espresso. "It's quite strong, you might want some sugar."

"No, I like it strong, thanks."

"Well, that's me. Strong and unpolished." Andreas had a mischievous spark in his eyes.

Karla laughed and felt the heat rise to her face. She knew she was blushing. She took a sip of coffee and pointed at a group of small stone fountains, some plain, others with elaborate carvings. "These seem to be very popular these days."

"Yeah. That's the kind of stuff that sells. Just like gnomes or frogs, which I refuse to make. Too kitschy." Andreas lifted one of the heavy fountains, seemingly without effort, and moved it out of the way. "But let me show you some of my other stuff." He led Karla into the second room, which contained several stone and metal sculptures. There were a few stone mandalas of gray-black or greenish granite with fine carvings, green and purplish stone figurines, a rounded shape made of bronze, and several other delicate metal sculptures as well as a combination of wood and metal. Each work was unique. Form and material of the sculptures fit together perfectly. There was no doubt, Andreas was extremely talented.

Karla walked around for a while looking at the different works of art. She gently touched one of the small stone mandalas. "How beautiful. ... So delicate and yet so powerful."

Andreas smiled. "Thanks."

"Do you ever show your work?"

"I've been in a couple of group shows. I'm going to be in one in August. It's an exhibition in Ascona of students from the *Scuola di Sculptura di Peccia*."

"You studied at the sculpture school in Peccia? That must be an excellent school. I heard they attract students from all over the world."

"Yeah, I took a few workshops there as well as in Carrara, Italy."

Something tickled Karla's nose and she sneezed.

"Bless you ... it's the stone dust," Andreas said. "There's always some around after I use the grinding or polishing machine."

They stepped outside, where the late-afternoon sun was just about to disappear behind the tall building on the other side of the street. The last sunrays bounced off the metal roof.

Karla touched one of the granite slabs sitting next to the door outside, which felt warm, having absorbed the heat of the day. She looked at her watch. "I guess I should get going, otherwise I'll hit rush-hour traffic." She turned to face him. "Thanks for showing me your work. That was a real treat. I'd like to see more."

"Glad you liked it. Most of my work is in someone's garden or in a park. I can give you a guided tour of O'Reilly's artwork, if you're interested." Andreas laughed his typical throaty laugh. "How about next Saturday?"

Karla nodded. "Yes, that would work."

Andreas gave her a warm smile. "How about if I pick you up?"

Karla handed him one of her business cards. "Okay, here is my address. I live just up the hill from Lena's place. It's called *Casa di tre Angeli*. You can't miss it."

"'Tre angeli'? Three angels, huh. Any connection to you?" The humorous glint in his eyes was back.

"None at all ... though I could use one once in a while." Karla smiled wistfully.

Andreas followed her to the car. "Karla." She turned around. He pulled her close and kissed her. His breath smelled of coffee, smoky and slightly bitter. "See you Saturday."

Before Karla could do or say anything, he turned and walked back to his workshop in his leisurely wide-legged swagger. Karla opened the door and got into the car. She waited for a while before starting the engine, then slapped the steering wheel.

"Damn. I don't want to fall in love."

Chapter 5

A gust of wind swept into the yard, shaking the leaves of the chestnut trees and the rhododendron plants.

"Not again!" Karla exclaimed. She held on to her easel and canvas.

The *Nordfoehn*, a dry northern wind, had been blowing on and off all night. This wind was the only disadvantage in the otherwise ideal environment. Once in a while it had an invigorating effect on Karla, but most of the time it made her feel irritable, anxious, even depressed, and gave her a headache.

"All right. I guess I wasn't meant to paint outside this morning," she muttered, as another blast swept down on her. She gathered her painting tools and put them into her studio. She didn't feel like finishing the painting inside, so she grabbed her sketchpad, sat by the window, and thought about what to draw. She made several attempts, but was unable to concentrate.

It wasn't just the annoying wind. Ever since yesterday she had been thinking of Andreas, his sculptures, his kiss. It had been more than a kiss between friends, and it had stirred up emotions she didn't care for. After a series of unsuccessful short-term relationships, Karla had decided to stay away from men for a while. And then this fierce, irritating, but oddly endearing guy with his biting humor had to turn up and unsettle her again.

And the thing with Sarah. What was the real reason behind Sarah's visit? Was it really just to apologize and talk about art?

Sarah and Karla had had an on-and-off friendship for several years. They exchanged ideas about art, went to museums and galleries together, and sometimes critiqued each other's work. The friendship, however, had cooled when Karla caught Sarah sleeping with one of her boyfriends.

Was Andreas attracted to Sarah? He had shown concern for her, but Karla didn't think he had more than friendly feelings for her. But then again, you never knew. *And why should I even care?* Karla tossed her drawing pad aside.

The wind was blowing fiercely now, howling around the corners of the house and slamming one of the shutters closed. When Karla stepped outside to fasten it again, she saw that the sky was a deep, clear blue, the wind having wiped away all the clouds.

Karla sat down again and forced herself to get at least one drawing done. She picked up her pad and a piece of charcoal. Almost automatically, she began to sketch Andreas, as she remembered him sitting in front of the stone slab. She realized she was out of practice drawing human figures, having focused mainly on landscapes. After several attempts, she ended up with a sketch she liked. It depicted his muscular body bending over the stone, a strand of hair hanging into his face. She left out the mask and goggles, wanting to show his face in profile.

Perhaps she would give it to him on Saturday. Feeling more at peace again, she was ashamed of her anger at Sarah. She was her friend, after all, and Karla hadn't even called her to find out how she felt after her breakdown at the opening. She picked up the phone and dialed Sarah's number. It took a while before she answered.

Sarah's voice sounded tired. "I'm trying to take a nap."

"Sorry. I didn't mean to disturb you, I just wanted to know how you were," Karla said.

"I'm okay."

Sarah's distant and cool voice irritated Karla. *You make an ass of yourself at my first opening. You could at least apologize.* "I heard you went to see Andreas."

"Yes. I did. I wanted to apologize."

"Oh, I see. Was that the only reason? You were all over him at the opening."

"So? What do you care? Are you two an item or something? How did you find out I went to see him?"

Karla felt anger rise in her like bile. "He told me. He's my boyfriend, Sarah." *Gee, what a lie.*

It was quiet for a while at the other end. Karla could hear Sarah's breathing. Then her voice again, friendlier now. "Karla, look, he's great. I felt really low the last few days. Just talking to him made me feel better. I have no intention of interfering in your relationship. You're lucky to have him as a boyfriend."

Karla started to feel ashamed, but she still distrusted Sarah. "It wouldn't be the first time."

"Oh, Karla, why bring up that old stuff. You weren't even interested in the guy anymore."

"Yeah, but you didn't know that when you jumped in the sack with him."

"Karla, you know what? You're so fucking petty."

"Sarah, let's not fight." It was too late. Karla heard the click at the other end.

Why can't I keep my mouth shut? Karla lowered her head onto her arms and sighed. Not only had she lied to Sarah about her relationship with Andreas, she had begrudged her friend the little encouragement he had given her as an artist.

Perhaps Sarah was interested in Andreas. At least she was honest about her feelings. Karla, on the other hand, had appropriated Andreas, although she wasn't even sure how she felt about him or how he felt about her. He had kissed her, he wanted to meet her again, but that was all. And Karla's feelings for him? She liked him, she was even attracted to him, but she wasn't sure she was ready to get involved.

The following morning it was raining, the Nordfoehn having collapsed the night before. The rain felt soothing after the harsh, dry northern wind, and the sky was a lively display of towering dark clouds. The mountaintops were hidden behind layers of white mist. *Stormy landscape, Rembrandt,* Karla thought as she scanned the horizon. It had cooled off somewhat, and the air smelled of burning wood from the neighbor's oven.

Later that day, Karla made an effort to clean out the storage room, which was overflowing with canvases of half-finished and finished paintings as well as sketches on paper. She resisted this periodic chore. It forced her to decide which pieces she considered worth keeping and which she wanted to discard or paint over. Not an easy task; it required ruthless honesty and a discerning eye.

Karla kept pulling paintings out of storage, putting them back in, pulling them back out again. In the process, she came across the canvas with the dark woman she had been struggling with. She glanced at it, shook her head, and decided to hang on to it. One day, perhaps, she would be able to finish it.

In the evening, there was a pile of discarded sketches in the recycling bin and several canvases that could be reused. The cleanup gave Karla a feeling of freedom. She took a deep breath and stepped outside to watch the evening settle in. It had stopped raining, and the heavy clouds had thinned. The southern sky was pink with tints of purple, and the evening breeze brought a whiff of wet grass.

Chapter 6

When Karla woke up on Saturday, she was surprised how quiet it was. The previous few mornings she had been roused from sleep by the patter of rain on the stone roof, the swooshing of tree branches, or the wind howling around corners.

She pushed back the shutters and was greeted by a clear blue sky with only a strip of haze on the horizon. A mild breeze from the Maggia River brought the resinous scent of pines. The dewdrops on the chestnut leaves in the courtyard glittered in the sun.

Karla opened the door and stepped outside barefoot. She skipped across the courtyard, taking big steps since the stone slabs underneath the chestnut trees were still cold, and sat on the low granite wall. Hugging her knees to her chest, she bent her head back and let the sun warm her face. *Summer, finally.*

Inside the house, it smelled of paint and turpentine. Karla opened all the windows and put the espresso pot on the stove. After taking a shower, she stood in front of her closet, sorting through her clothes, trying to decide what to wear for her "tour of O'Reilly's artwork," as Andreas had called it. She picked out a pair of jeans and her favorite top, and checked herself in the mirror. Karla had inherited her mother's tall, slender figure and the reddish highlights in her shiny black hair. Her Latin father's influence was visible in the high cheekbones, wide-set dark eyes, full lips, and bronze hue of her skin.

After a light breakfast, she put on her painting apron, lugged her easel out onto the patio, set up a large canvas, and started to mix her paints. She tried to paint one of the colorful pictures the representative of the bank had ordered. She began to outline the scenery in front of her, then filled it with blobs and dots of yellow, red, and blue to suggest the meadow of wildflowers.

Boring, she thought and shook her head.

She added a row of oak trees with gnarled branches to make the composition more interesting. After a while, she put her brush down and sat back. Commission painting proved to be a lot more difficult than she had thought. She felt constrained and hemmed in, and her picture seemed lifeless to her.

A couple of hours later, she stepped back and examined the painting again. It wasn't bad; the colors of summer—red, orange, and cornflower blue—were pleasing. The contrast with the twisted branches of the oaks was, well, somewhat interesting. *Colorful but still boring,* she mused with a sigh. Then again, it might just be the kind of painting that would enliven the sterile atmosphere of a bank. *If it wasn't for the money, I wouldn't bother with it.*

She heard the sound of a car engine. A Fiat drove up the hill and parked in the driveway. It was Andreas. Her first reaction was to hide the painting, then she changed her mind. Just the fact that she wanted to hide it showed her how dissatisfied she was with it. Perhaps Andreas could give her some ideas.

Andreas took out a package from the backseat of his car and put it on the granite table. He greeted Karla with a hug and stood next to her, examining the painting. She liked the delicate scent of his after-shave.

"Tell me what's wrong with it," Karla said.

He looked at it without saying anything, then put his hand on her shoulder. "You don't like it?"

"No."

"Neither do I."

Karla glanced at him. "You sure are direct."

"You asked for my opinion." He shrugged. "You're a talented painter, so I can be honest. This painting isn't you. It's too tame, it lacks energy."

"I agree." Karla sighed and got up. "This is going to be a problem. I've never painted anything on commission." She told him about the contract. "He wants colorful paintings for his bank subsidiaries."

"I assume he saw your other paintings."

"Yes. He came to the opening."

"Did he give you any specific instructions as to what to paint?"

"No, not really."

"Then he likes the way you paint, so why are you trying to paint differently?"

"I don't really know. I was just thinking bank, what would be appropriate for a bank, you know, something ... for everyday people."

"Well, well, Ms. Snooty. You mean for those dummies who don't understand art?"

"I didn't mean that. You're terrible." *Here he is again with his biting humor.*

"Karla. He picked you because he liked the way you paint. That's what he wants, not some dumbed-down version. Just because he's a banker doesn't mean he doesn't have a feeling for art." Andreas's green eyes sparkled with mirth.

"You're right, I guess," Karla admitted, then shot him a roguish look. "But you sure can be irritating."

Andreas laughed out loud. "I've been called worse. But let me try to make it up to you." He pointed at the package on the table. "I think you liked this one."

Karla peeled off the wrapping. It was one of the mandalas she had admired. "That was my favorite. Thanks a lot. It's great." The mandala was of gray granite speckled with white and black mica. Karla traced the delicate carvings with her finger.

Andreas looked around the courtyard. "Nice place. Do you live here by yourself?" He pointed at the group of stone cottages that bordered the yard.

"I'm just renting one of the houses. The rest of the place belongs to the landlord."

"I love *rustici*. I wouldn't mind living in one myself," Andreas said. "Problem is, they are usually small, too small for me to work in. Which means I'd have to rent two places, and that's too expensive."

"Where do you live now?" Karla asked.

"I have a makeshift apartment in the back of my workshop." Andreas shrugged. "It's convenient for right now."

"I know what you mean. It's a little cramped here, although I don't have that many tools and the kind of machines you have. One day, perhaps, I'll be able to rent one of the other rustici and use as a studio."

"I'd love to own one before the damn German Swiss buy them all up," Andreas sneered.

Rustici were former stables in the south of the country that had been renovated and converted into living quarters. With their walls made of natural stones, their granite roofs, and their rustic flair, they were the all-time favorite vacation homes for the people from the north of Switzerland and Germany.

"Be careful what you say. I'm part Swiss German myself." Karla laughed.

"That's all right. I'll focus on your Peruvian heritage. It's the Latin element that gives you that special something."

"Thanks. I take that as a compliment. Talk about heritage," Karla said. "You have an unusual last name. O'Reilly? Are you of Irish background?"

"Yeah, on my father's side, but that was several generations back. I think my great-grandfather emigrated from Ireland to the United States. Then my father moved to Switzerland."

"So you're American?"

"No, I'm a Swiss citizen. I was born here and my mother is from here." His tone was dismissive, slightly abrupt. He picked up a piece of stone lying next to the chestnut tree and turned it over in his hand, then put it down again.

Better change the topic. "Well, let me show you around," Karla offered. She picked up the stone mandala, which turned out to be quite heavy. Andreas took it out of her hand, carried it inside, and set it up on the mantelpiece above the fireplace.

Karla's house had two stories. On the lower floor was her studio, and next to it a living room, kitchen, and bathroom. The living room was long and of irregular shape, sparsely but tastefully furnished with an oak-wood table, a couple of chairs, and a sofa. Next to the fireplace stood a large, old wooden closet with beautiful carvings. A few of Karla's paintings hung on the wall. The sofa was covered with a patchwork quilt Karla's grandmother had made for her.

Andreas lightly tapped the wooden closet door with his knuckle. He brushed his hand along the granite surround of the fireplace, looking at it closely. "Nice work. Real granite. In some of the newer places, they use imitation rock. It's cheaper, but it seems so fake."

He pointed at two pictures above the sofa. They were painted in a traditional realistic style and showed a winter landscape and a scene next to a lake. "Who painted those?"

"My grandfather."

"Hmm. So you inherited his talent."

"I don't know about that. But he has always been an inspiration to me, particularly the way he portrayed light and shadows. Unfortunately, I never met him. He died before I was born."

"Is your grandmother still alive?"

"No. She died in the same car crash as my mother."

"Good lord."

"Yeah. I was in the car as well, in the back, strapped into my booster. By a miracle I wasn't hurt at all, at least not physically."

"That must have been horrible. You must have had a shock."

"Yes, I did. I went into shock." Karla cleared her throat. "In fact, to this day, I can't remember anything of the actual accident. It surfaced more later on, when I started having nightmares."

"And your father?"

"My parents weren't married. My mother met my father as a young woman when she was traveling in Peru. I've only seen my father twice."

"I'm sorry. And I thought I had a difficult childhood." Andreas embraced Karla and held her close.

Overcome by the loving gesture, Karla swallowed as tears welled up in her eyes. "Fortunately, I still had Anna, my aunt. She was great, I owe her a lot. She really supported me in my artwork. Thanks to her, I have some savings and am able to take time off to paint. ... But she, too, died last year."

"That must be the aunt mentioned in the article. Have you read it?"

Karla surreptitiously wiped away a tear and tried to steady her voice. "You mean the article from the journalist who interviewed me at the opening? No, I haven't received my copy yet."

"I have it in the car. I'll get it for you," Andreas said. When he returned, he handed her a copy of the local newspaper. "It's really good."

The article was on the second page, next to a photo of Karla.

Exhibition by a Peruvian-Swiss artist. The young and talented painter Karla Bocelli had her first exhibition in a gallery in the old part of Locarno. The dynamic and colorful oil paintings, inspired by her Peruvian heritage, and her mystical Zen-like aquarelles make Karla Bocelli one of the contemporary young artists to be reckoned with. ...

Karla blushed, then put the paper down and smiled. "He writes a lot better than I talk. But let's go. I'd like to see more of your artwork."

They first drove to Peccia, a village of fewer than one thousand inhabitants at the end of the Maggia Valley, where one of Andreas's sculptures was exhibited. Peccia was best known for its vast marble and granite quarries, its sculpture school, and its *sentiero delle sculture*, a sculpture trail leading through the village. Each year, works from different artists were displayed at the piazzas and along the road through and around the village.

The narrow street to Peccia led through a picturesque landscape, with vineyards and small dairy farms, and past waterfalls cascading down cliffs.

"Be careful, the road ahead is winding and kind of dangerous," Karla warned Andreas.

"Don't worry." Andreas gave a quick smirk. "In spite of what you might believe, I do know how to drive." He shifted down and steered his car skillfully around the tight curves.

They stopped for a farmer who led a herd of goats across the road. It was quite a chore; the skittish animals bucked and jumped back and forth, but eventually, with some begging, shouting, and prodding by the goat herder, they ended up on the other side. Karla rolled down the window, inhaled the scent of fresh grass, and waved to the farmer.

Andreas chuckled. "See, that's why I drive carefully. I learned my lesson the other day. You can't trust those cute animals, neither the four-legged nor the two-legged ones." Karla punched him. "Ouch." He rubbed his arm.

When they approached the turnoff to the Peccia Valley, the road narrowed and became steeper. Andreas's car complained with a loud roar but made it up the hill.

As they walked along the sculpture path, Karla, who had never been there before, was surprised at how some of the sculptures were so well integrated into the landscape that they were almost indistinguishable from the countryside. Others formed an interesting contrast to their environment. In a field outside the village, she discovered a wooden structure next to a series of blooming trees. The color of the sculpture was the same as the tree trunks, whereas its angular form set it apart. Next to one of the churches stood a longish oval shape of white sandstone, which, though beautiful by itself, also emphasized the elegant shape of the church tower.

"Isn't it amazing?" Karla said and pointed at a sculpture Andreas had carved, a tall obelisk-like structure of black and white marble, which stood in front of a tall, plain stone building. "I wouldn't even have noticed that house without your sculpture in front of it. Together with the sculpture, it becomes much more interesting."

"I think that's one of the reasons why the people of Peccia love the sculpture path," Andreas said. "It's not just because it makes their small village up in the mountains a little bit famous, but because they see their environment in a new way. They discover things they didn't notice before or took for granted. That's what's great about art." Karla had never seen Andreas so animated. He waved his hands and his eyes shone with excitement.

"The people here may not 'understand' a sculpture the way an art critic or expert does. But they know if they like something or not, and they're not squeamish about expressing their preferences." Andreas chuckled. "I don't know what they say about my marble pillar. But, hey, if it makes them appreciate the building behind it more, it's worth putting it up. I think works of art shouldn't be stuck in museums or galleries. They belong in our everyday environment."

"Even in a bank," Karla said.

"Particularly in a bank." Andreas smiled and put his arm around her.

After leaving Peccia, they drove to Locarno. Most of the sculptures Andreas had carved stood in private gardens of rather well-to-do people. Some were in churchyards, one in the garden of a hospital, and one in a schoolyard.

"I love this one." Karla touched one of the sculptures in a small park in Locarno, made of Andeer gneiss, a green stone sprinkled with white and gray. It showed a smoothly polished animal-like shape on a rugged base. "It reminds me of something, but I'm not sure of what. Some creature stuck in stone, struggling to escape but unable to get away."

"Very perceptive," Andreas said. "I called it *Trapped*."

"Interesting." Karla gently stroked the stone. "What prompted you to create this particular shape? Sometimes when I paint I have a general idea of what I want to paint, and sometimes I just let the painting evolve on its own and I am surprised by what comes out. It often tells me something about myself I wasn't conscious of before."

"I know what you mean. That happens to me, too. In this case, it was a dream." Andreas hesitated, then continued. "I used to have nightmares when I was little. They often had to do with my father and my fear of him. I'd see a man approach and try to run away but couldn't. I was usually in this in-between state, when you know you're dreaming but no matter how hard you try you can't wake up. I guess I was trying to express that feeling." Andreas brushed through his hair.

Karla detected a touch of pain in his face. She was taken aback by Andreas's unexpected remark. "You were afraid of your father?"

Andreas hesitated. "Yeah. He was a real bastard."

"I'm sorry. I don't mean to intrude, but since you brought it up ..."

He nodded. "I know, it's okay. Want to walk for a while, down at the lake?"

They walked down a narrow cobblestone street, toward the lake. The promenade was busy with local people and tourists strolling along Lago Maggiore and enjoying the balmy evening. They eventually found an unoccupied bench, where they sat and watched as the sun slid behind the mountain range bordering Italy, pouring its last light in a river of silver across the lake.

"My father ..." Andreas cleared his throat. "My father is ... or was—I don't even know if he's still alive—a former member of the U.S. Navy, who kind of got stuck here when he met my mother. He never managed to assimilate. He was an alcoholic and abusive to both me and my mother. She finally divorced him. He moved back to the United States. I don't have any contact with him."

"I'm sorry."

Andreas turned his hands with the palms facing up in a that's-how-it-goes gesture. "That was long ago. Fortunately, I have a very loving aunt and uncle on my mother's side. Once they realized what was going on at home, they took me to live with them."

"And your mother?"

"After the divorce she came to live with us, as well. Still lives with my aunt and uncle, never got married again. I guess one time was enough for her. So I sort of grew up in an extended family. I owe a lot to my aunt and uncle. Without them, I don't know where I'd be today." He stopped talking and looked down at his large hands.

Karla watched him quietly. She was moved by his vulnerability, so unlike his normal cocky self. She noticed a thin scar on his cheekbone, and gently touched the spot below his right eye. "Did you get this while cutting stone?"

He took her hand and held it. "Yeah. It's from a stone splinter. When I was younger I didn't always wear protective gear. I probably felt it wasn't macho enough. I learned fast, though."

"Lucky it didn't hit you in the eye."

He nodded with a quick smile, then put his arm around her and pulled her close. He kissed her, first leisurely, then with increasing intensity. Karla felt the heat spread to her chest and abdomen. She pulled back. They looked at each other. His eyes had a brownish tint in the fading light of the evening. She smelled again the faint scent of his after-shave.

"Karla?" His voice was tender.

She felt he was going to make some kind of declaration about their being together, perhaps about making love. She turned away and looked out onto the lake.

He took his arm off her shoulder and lightly touched her hand. They sat next to each other for a while, gazing at the water, which by now was a mass of dark indigo blue with only the flickering reflection of city lights along the shore and a narrow strip of brightness above the mountains.

"It's getting late. Want to have dinner somewhere?" He sounded matter-of-fact, but not unkind.

Karla nodded. "Yes." She breathed a sigh of relief and felt disappointed at the same time. She had spoiled the moment of intimacy. Normally she wasn't shy or inhibited when it came to sex, and there had been quite a few men in her life. With Andreas, however, she felt something deeper stirring in her, something she had no control over, and it scared her.

Chapter 7

When Karla came home from shopping, there was the typical laconic message from Sarah on her answering machine: "Call me." Karla called her back, but Sarah seemed to be out again, so she left a message.

Afterward she tried to paint, but she had a difficult time. Her mind wandered. She was thinking of Andreas, their outings, the kiss down at Lago Maggiore, the dinner. Since the day of the sculpture tour, they had been to an art exhibit at the local museum and to a couple of movies.

Andreas, having noticed her hesitation at the lake the other day, had pulled back somewhat. He was kind, kissed and hugged her, but not with the earlier intensity, and she herself hadn't initiated any further intimacies. She had to admit, though, that she liked him more and more, and her determination not to get too deeply involved was waning with each subsequent visit.

Karla was torn. Her heart and body wanted him; her mind cautioned her. *You'll just get hurt again.*

She applied a few brush strokes, dipped her brush into paint, and stood there gazing out the window, until she realized the paint was dripping on the floor. Shaking her head, she picked up a rag and wiped the floor clean, knocking over the bowl with paint thinner as she got up. She cleaned up the mess just as the phone rang. It was Sarah.

"Listen. I ran into Andreas the other day and invited him so he could take a look at my sculptures. I told him to bring you along. Just so you know. So you don't blame me again for trying to steal your lover," Sarah said with a sneer in her voice.

"Sarah, please. I'm sorry for what I said. And as far as Andreas and I are concerned—"

"Sorry, Karla, there's someone at the door. Got to go. See you on Wednesday." Sarah hung up.

Karla picked up the brush and got ready to paint, then put her brush down again, opened her portfolio, and pulled out the drawing she had made for Andreas. She wanted to give it to him as a gift. She chose a steel-blue mat, cut it to the right size, and carefully mounted the drawing, then wrapped it in silk paper. Smiling, she gently touched the package.

Back at painting, she forced herself to concentrate. When the sun was about to set, she was almost done with one of the large canvases for the bank. She stepped back and nodded. "This is going to be good."

There was a knock at the door. She saw him through the window. Having been concentrating on her work, she hadn't heard him drive up the road. She opened the door. "What a surprise, I didn't expect you."

Andreas shrugged. "I was in the neighborhood, and I went to see Lena." His voice was cool, and he didn't smile or hug her.

Karla was startled by his cold behavior. "Come in. Want something to drink—coffee, wine?"

"No. Nothing. Thanks." He looked around. "You've been painting?"

"Yes. I've been working at one of the paintings for the bank." Karla motioned at the canvas.

He nodded, gave the painting a cursory glance, but didn't comment on it. Karla started to feel uncomfortable. His odd behavior dampened the joy of seeing him. She made another attempt to pull him out of his strange mood. "Sarah called. She wants us to visit her on Wednesday. She must have told you."

"Yeah, I know."

"Andreas, what's the matter with you? You seem upset."

He had been looking out the window. Now, he turned around and faced her. "So, we're lovers." His lips curled into a sardonic smile.

For a split second Karla thought he was talking about Sarah and him. She felt a stab in her chest. But no, that couldn't be. "Who are you talking about?"

"About us, who else?" Andreas glared at her. "Funny thing is, I didn't even know about it. I must have had a blackout when all this happened. I mean, us being a pair, having hot and passionate sex, you know, whatever belongs to a relationship."

Karla finally understood. "What did Sarah tell you?"

"What did *you* tell her? That's the more appropriate question."

"Andreas, I'm sorry. I told her something I shouldn't have, but I never went into any detail. Sarah tends to exaggerate. I only told her you were my boyfriend."

45

"Yeah, right. At a time when we barely knew each other. I mean, I wouldn't even mind if I had known about it."

"Andreas, please let me explain. When Sarah was all over you at the exhibition—"

"She was drunk, Karla. It didn't mean anything."

"Let me finish. Then the next day she came to visit you, and I was afraid ... I liked you, too ... and Sarah once slept with a boyfriend of mine. Oh, this is all ridiculous. I'm a complete idiot. I don't even know how to explain this."

Andreas folded his arms in front of his chest and glowered at her. "Well, let *me* try to explain. So you thought she wanted to snatch me away from you, although we hadn't anything going between the two of us, so there was nothing to snatch. But you figured, just to be on the safe side, in case you eventually wanted us to get closer, you kind of put a 'reserved' stamp on me, or something like that. You know the kind of thing, when you go to a store and you pick out a suit or a dress and you aren't quite sure about it, they can put it on layaway for a while."

"Andreas, please. I admit, it was dumb."

"You know, what I really don't get, if you want us to be a pair, why can't you let me know? Why play games? I think I made it pretty clear during the few times we were together that I liked you. But you kind of hemmed and hawed, got hot and cold on me. And just to make something clear, I'm not interested in Sarah. But I do respect her as an artist. You, on the other hand, turn me on. But now ... I don't know ... you don't seem to be the person I thought you were.

"Anyway"—he brushed through his hair—"once you make up your friggin' mind how you feel about me, then let me know. In the meantime, don't come around and confuse me with your stupid games. Good night." He walked toward the door.

"Andreas." Karla was shocked at the intensity of her scream. She lowered her voice. "Please don't leave. Not like this." She began to tremble.

Andreas turned around and looked at her, surprised. "What's the matter?"

"Don't yell at me like that and then just walk off. I admit, it wasn't the smartest thing to do, but you're blowing it all out of proportion. It wasn't as if I'd called you something nasty behind your back. Calling you my boyfriend may have been premature, but it meant I liked you. What's so terrible about that?"

"That's not what makes me mad. It's saying one thing and doing the opposite. I'm allergic to people who play games, who aren't honest with me." He came back and stared out the window.

"Andreas, I've been hesitant to get closer to you not because I don't like you but quite the opposite. I felt I was falling in love with you, and I was afraid."

"Afraid of what?" His tone was less aggressive.

Karla pressed her hands together, trying to stop them from trembling. She tried to swallow. Her mouth felt dry. "I'm afraid of ... I don't know. It seems that whenever I love somebody, they leave or die ..." A sob rose from deep in her chest. She sat on the sofa and covered her face with her hands. "And I'm so tired of it all." Her voice broke.

Andreas sat next to her. She felt his arm around her. She leaned her head against his chest and let the tears run down her face without bothering to wipe them away. Andreas didn't say anything, just held her close. Finally, Karla lifted her head.

Andreas put his hand on hers. He sighed. "So you're afraid, if we get involved, I'll die or leave, as well?"

"I know, it's irrational." Karla grabbed a wad of Kleenex and blew her nose.

"Well, I guess it's possible. I may leave one day for whatever reason. I may die. Or it may happen to you. How do we know? But to go through life without love because you're afraid of people leaving you, of being hurt. You can't be serious?" Andreas brushed a tear off her cheek. "We're talking about living without love for fifty, sixty, seventy years, depending how long you live."

He wrinkled his forehead. "That's an awful long time. Think about it."

Karla had to smile at his attempt to make her see the absurdity of it all. "I know."

"Look, I don't have the magic love potion. I'm no expert when it comes to relationships. I haven't had the most encouraging experiences in that department, either." Andreas put his hand on Karla's shoulder. "All I know is that I'd like to go on seeing you. I like you a lot. I'm not exactly the romantic type, but—"

Karla gently put her hand on his mouth, then kissed him.

He took her face into his hands. "Is that a yes?"

Karla nodded and sighed. "I guess. Yes. I'll give it another try."

Andreas gave a little smile. "Not the most enthusiastic response."

"Andreas. I really like you. You just have to give me time."

"All right, but no more games."

Karla shook her head and hugged him.

Chapter 8

Karla didn't know where she was when she woke up. Her head was pounding. She was lying in bed in her underwear. When she tried to get up, she felt nauseated and fell back on the pillow, moaning.

What happened last night? She looked around the room. The dress she had worn the night before hung neatly folded over the back of the chair. All she could remember was that she had been at a party with Andreas at the house of a friend of his who was a musician and had his own band. They had been listening to the music and dancing. There had been all kinds of food and different types of drinks. Karla usually didn't drink much alcohol, but there was some kind of concoction of fruit, sugar, and red wine that she really liked. She drank quite a lot. Then everything became hazy. The last thing she was conscious of was that she felt very unsteady on her legs, her head was spinning, and she asked Andreas to take her home.

Now, she had no idea how she got home, how she got undressed and into bed. The effort of trying to remember made her head throb. She gave a resigned sigh, closed her eyes, and fell back to sleep.

When she woke up again, she smelled the aroma of fresh coffee. She forced herself to get up and went downstairs, holding on to the wooden railing of the staircase. Someone had filled her coffeepot with the automatic-brew feature and set it for ten o'clock. She looked at her watch. It was five past ten.

In the bathroom, she splashed water on her face and glanced at herself in the mirror. She looked deathly pale, and her hair was a mess. She went back into the kitchen and poured herself a cup of coffee, took a sip, and sat next to the window. The sun was up, and she heard the daily noises: the rattling of the garbage truck, a car driving up the hill, the neighbor calling her dog. These otherwise familiar and comforting sounds now seemed to worsen the pounding in her head.

The phone rang. When she answered, her voice sounded hoarse, as if it didn't belong to her. It was Andreas. "Hey, wild woman. How are you this morning? Feel any better?"

Karla groaned. "I feel terrible. I have a splitting headache, and I can't remember a thing. What happened last night?"

Andreas chuckled. "Well, you got tanked and ended up dancing naked on the table. It was quite a sight and—"

"Andreas. Stop it. This isn't funny. Tell me what happened."

"Okay. It wasn't quite that bad. You drank too much of that sangria and then some *nocino*, and I think that's what did it. Dangerous combination."

"Darn it, why didn't you warn me? I hardly ever drink more than a glass of wine, but that sangria ... it tasted so good."

"Sorry about that. I didn't realize how much you drank. I was too busy dancing with you and kissing you."

Karla could just imagine the smirk on his face. "And then what happened?"

"You asked me to drive you home. You fell asleep in the car, and I had a hard time waking you up. Finally I got you into the house and up the stairs to your bedroom. I saw your automatic coffeemaker in the kitchen, so I filled it up and set it for ten o'clock in the morning. I didn't think you'd wake up any earlier."

"And then?" Karla asked.

"Then I left. I had to leave the door unlocked since I couldn't take the key with me, but I felt it was safe to do so in your neighborhood."

"So ... nothing else happened?" Karla asked, still suspicious. "I mean, between us?"

There was silence; then Andreas guffawed. "You don't remember?"

"No, of course not. Else I wouldn't ask, would I?" Karla was getting irritated. The heat rose to her face, and her mouth felt parched.

"Oh, boy. Too bad you don't remember anything. It was quite a night. You were incredible."

"This isn't funny. I'm not in a joking mood. My head is killing me, and you're starting to piss me off."

"*Calma, calma*. Calm down. Of course, nothing happened between us. What do you take me for? I don't take advantage of passed-out women. Not that I wouldn't have wanted to. You are beautiful, even when you're drunk. However, I'd like you to at least be conscious when we make love." Andreas laughed out loud again. His booming voice aggravated Karla's headache.

"Not so loud, please. My head. Tell me, seriously now, and stop making stupid jokes. Did I do anything embarrassing?"

"It wasn't too bad. After you dumped a glass of sangria on the host's pants, you stumbled toward me and asked me to take you home." He sniggered.

"Andreas. Please."

"All right, I won't torture you any longer. No, you didn't do anything embarrassing. It was a great evening."

"What about my car? Where is my car?"

"Your car is safe. I had to take it back with me, since I wouldn't have had any other way of getting home. Remember, we went in your car to the party? If you don't need it during the day, I'll bring it tonight. Stop worrying. Take a nap and sleep it off. I'll see you tonight."

"Okay. Thanks." Karla put down the receiver and let herself fall on the sofa with a sigh. *I can't believe it. Never got that drunk before. And then to ask if we had had sex. Idiot.*

Finally, Karla dragged herself to the bathroom, took a shower, and got dressed. After another cup of coffee, she started to feel a little better and decided to go outside and get some fresh air. She sat on a stone bench in front of the house, looking toward the mountains. It promised to be a clear day. A bank of benign white cumuli hovered on the horizon.

Karla stretched out on the granite bench and closed her eyes. She thought back to the evening, to the part she still remembered. The sun on her face and the hardness of the stone reminded her of Andreas's firm body and his kisses. *I should invite him for dinner,* she thought as she was dozing off.

There were a few people at the grocery store chatting with one another and with Gabriela, the owner of the store. The couple of stores and the few inns, called *grotti*, were the meeting places of

51

the villagers as well as the tourists who came here to swim and camp along the river Maggia.

"You look a little pale today," Gabriela said. "You're not feeling well?"

"I had too much to drink last night," Karla admitted.

"Oh, I see." Gabriela smiled. "Try a spoonful of honey. I heard that helps. Never tried it myself, but it can't hurt."

"Thanks. I'll give it a try." Karla bought the groceries and a bottle of wine. Although she couldn't possibly stomach any alcohol that day, she thought that Andreas might like some.

At home, she unpacked the groceries and stacked the fireplace with wood, in case they would want a fire in the evening. Then she began to prepare the sauce for the spaghetti. She sautéed onions and garlic; added tomatoes, fresh basil, oregano, spices, and a shot of red wine; and let it simmer.

Karla put on a CD and stretched out on the couch to relax. When the clock struck seven, she realized she had fallen asleep. The house smelled of tomatoes and spices. Karla got up and turned off the stove, then sat at the window to wait. Although it was still light, dark clouds had begun to gather over the mountains.

Just as it started to rain, Andreas pulled up in Karla's car. It was only now that Karla realized that he had no way of getting back to his place unless she drove him, since he didn't have his own car with him. Andreas brought her a big bunch of roses.

"What beautiful flowers. Thanks a lot. They look like Lena's."

Andreas smiled. "I got them from her. But how are you, wild party girl? You look lovely tonight. You must be feeling better." Andreas kissed her, then looked up and sniffed. "Something smells very good here. Are you cooking?"

"Just some spaghetti sauce. I thought you might be hungry. Would you like a glass of wine? I'll pass for today, for obvious reasons, but you're welcome to one."

"Actually, I can do without. Some water will do. I drank enough last night myself."

"Would you mind lighting the fire?" Karla gave him a box of matches. "It's getting cool with the rain." She went into the kitchen and brought out some appetizers—salami, olives, and mixed pickles—and a bottle of mineral water.

When she came back, Andreas had taken off his jacket and was kneeling in front of the fireplace, lighting the newspaper and rearranging the logs with his bare hands. Sparks were flying, but this didn't seem to bother him.

"Don't burn yourself," Karla warned him.

Andreas laughed and gave a last tug to one of the logs, then rubbed his hands and sat back. "That should do it." He flicked a spot of soot off his forearm. The flames shot up high, and soon the fire was burning full force.

Karla sat next to him on the soft, padded rug, putting the plate with the appetizers between them. Andreas picked up the plate and set it aside. He put his arm around her and pulled her close. "Now, what were you dreaming we were doing last night?" He looked at her with an impish glint in his eyes.

Karla tensed inwardly. She was anxious. *I feel like a virgin.*

Andreas kissed her, then pulled back a little. "Nervous?"

Karla nodded. No use denying it.

He brushed her hair out of her face, kissed her throat, then moved his lips to her ear, nibbling her earlobe. "So am I," he whispered.

Karla was surprised at the change of mood in him. The teasing smile was gone from his face. The expression in his eyes was deep, tender, and vulnerable. She embraced him, and they sat quietly for a while, their arms entwined, looking at the fire, listening to the rain slapping the windows and the hissing of the wood. They kissed.

Andreas pulled off his T-shirt. Karla touched his broad, almost hairless chest, moving her hand over his muscular arms.

He took her hand in his and kissed her palm, then brushed his lips along the inside of her arm to her elbow. He helped her slip off her top, pulled her bra aside, and kissed her breasts. They undressed quickly, and in the dim light of the candle and the fire, they explored and tasted each other.

Andreas moved slowly, caressing her, flicking her skin with kisses, waking every nerve in her body, making her quiver with desire. Karla, used to hurried sex with her short-time boyfriends, was overwhelmed by his care and sensitivity. She pulled him down on her, impatient, wanting more of him.

Andreas reached for his pants and pulled a condom out of the pocket.

Karla shook her head. "You don't need this. I have an IUD. Besides, I hate these. They smell awful."

Andreas looked at her, surprised. "I'm not crazy about them, either, but are you sure it's safe?"

"Positive."

"All right, here it goes." Andreas got ready to throw the still-wrapped condom into the fireplace.

Karla grabbed his hand. "Don't. I can't stand the smell of burnt rubber. It makes me sick."

"Oh? Okay." Andreas put the condom aside and kissed her again. He gently lowered her onto the padded rug and moved on top of her. A tangle of hair tickled her face. His breath had a warm, malty scent. "God, you're sweet." His eyes were dark with desire.

Karla pressed herself against him. When he slid into her, she gasped.

He paused for a moment. "Am I hurting you?"

Karla shook her head. "No, go on, please," she whispered.

As Karla adjusted to Andreas's steady strokes, she gave in for the first time with a man to a part in herself where gales of lust mingled with the gentler waves of love and compassion. After she came, her face was wet with tears.

Andreas kissed her, then touched her face. "Are you all right?"

Karla nodded and stifled a soft sob. "I feel great."

Andreas slid off her and put his arm around her. They lay quietly next to each other, listening to the rain tapping on the stone roof. Andreas raised himself on his elbow and looked down at her. The light of the flames from the fireplace danced across his face. His eyes were olive green in the half dark. "Tell me," he said in his deep, throaty voice, "do you always cry when you come?"

Karla brushed through his hair and shook her head. "No. This has never happened before. I've never made love like this. It was overwhelming ... in a good way." She paused. "Before, with other men ..." She searched his face and hesitated to continue.

"Yes?" he asked.

"It's been kind of disappointing, just physical. With you, it's different. It makes me feel alive, fulfilled ... and a little scared. I don't know what to call it." She felt a knot in her throat and turned her face toward the fireplace.

Andreas put his hand under her chin and forced her to look at him. "Why not call it love?"

Karla nodded and blinked, tears welling up in her eyes. "I guess it is."

A gust of wind splashed more rain against the western windows. The pine logs crackled and popped in the fireplace, and the room smelled of burning wood.

Andreas got up and put another log on the fire. After he lay back down, Karla gently stroked his belly. He put his arm around her and pulled her on top of him. He kissed her breasts, then gave her a mischievous smile. The flickering flames reflected in his eyes. "Were there many? Other men, I mean."

Karla laughed. "You had to ask." She paused. "Only a few ... and you? What about you?"

"Nope. No men at all. Only a few women."

"You're impossible." Karla gave him a playful pat on the rump, then straddled him.

"Oh, Jesus," he groaned.

Karla shivered when she woke up. While asleep, Andreas had pulled the blanket off her. She heard the grandfather clock chime nine times. The sun shining through the small window in the east of the living room spilled onto the mantelpiece above the fireplace and created a mosaic of light and shadow. The smell of burnt wood and cold ashes reminded her of the scent of a certain kind of black tea whose name she couldn't remember. Karla tried to pull the cover toward her.

Andreas woke up. "I'm sorry. I'm hogging the whole blanket." He yawned and covered her, then stretched and yawned again loudly.

"Your yawning sounds like the growl of a bear." Karla laughed and brushed through his tussled hair.

"Well, I'll tell you one thing. I'm hungry like a bear. Do you realize we haven't eaten since lunch yesterday? At least, I haven't. I hope you have some food in the house, or I'll have to eat you up."

"You're right. We forgot to eat. I have eggs in the refrigerator. I can make us an American breakfast."

"Sounds good to me, whatever that is." Andreas got up and stretched again, then bent down to pick up the still-wrapped condom on the floor. He looked at it and put it aside, then glanced at Karla. "What's this thing about the smell of burnt rubber?" He sat again and stroked her hair, letting the strands glide through his hand.

Karla sat up. "Ever since I was a child, I get nauseated when I smell something that reminds me of burnt rubber or latex or something similar, like the smell of tires after a sharp braking. It must have to do with the car accident I was in. The car started to burn, and from what they told me, they pulled me out of the wreck just in time." Karla pulled her legs up to her chest and wrapped her arms around her knees. "That's the worst part of the nightmare I occasionally have, the smell of burnt rubber. That and my mother's screams and the fears ..." Karla's voice gave out. "Sometimes, I'm afraid of waking up one morning and absolutely nobody is around anymore," she whispered.

Andreas embraced her. "I'm so sorry."

Karla nodded and gave him a weak smile. "It's all right. I don't have the nightmares as often as I used to."

"Have you ever had professional help?" Andreas asked.

"Yes, right after the accident, of course. Since then I've seen several shrinks. It helps for a while, but then I stop. For one thing, it's expensive. And so far none of the analysts were able to help me recall what actually happened. According to them, it's kind of a survival mechanism. A child who experiences a trauma only remembers as much as she or he can deal with. That makes sense, but I'm an adult now. I think remembering would be a great relief. Perhaps my nightmares would disappear ... and my feelings of guilt toward my mother or my fear of being abandoned again, all this irrational stuff."

"I understand." Andreas took Karla's hand and kissed it.

"Well, now at least you know you're involved with a crazy person."

"That makes two of us, considering my wonderful past." Andreas gave a snort.

Karla took a deep breath and smiled. "Anyway, what about that breakfast? By now, I'm kind of hungry, too. Even crazy people have to eat."

After showering and dressing, Karla prepared a meal of eggs, bacon, bread, butter, and jam, and soon the smell of fried bacon and freshly brewed coffee filled the small kitchen.

"Wow. That's food for a hard-working peasant. Do you eat like this every day?" Andreas asked as he picked up a piece of crispy-fried bacon and dunked it into the egg yolk.

"No, just once in a while, when I have guests. It reminds me of the United States." Karla poured him a cup of coffee.

"United States, Peru. You've been all over the world, haven't you? I feel very provincial next to you, world traveler."

"That was a long time ago. My aunt used to live in New York when she was young, and she took me along for a visit once."

"Is that the aunt who passed away?" Andreas asked.

"Yes."

"Hmm. So many deaths." Andreas looked at Karla thoughtfully, then continued to eat.

"What?" Karla asked.

"Nothing." Andreas shook his head.

"Come on, you wanted to say something."

"Well ... okay. It's just kind of ironic. You experienced so many deaths in your life, and now you're dating someone who makes tombstones for a living."

"It's odd, isn't it?" Karla smiled.

Andreas looked at her pensively. "Sounds like fate to me." He scraped up the leftover egg with a piece of bread and licked his fingers. "This is excellent, by the way." He pointed at his plate. "I could get used to this."

"I'm glad you like it." Karla was amused by his appetite.

Chapter 9

In early fall Andreas took Karla to meet his family. His aunt, uncle, and mother lived in a small village in the Blenio Valley. Andreas had told Karla quite a bit about his aunt and uncle, but rarely had mentioned his mother. Karla, who had always wondered about that, was curious to meet her.

Aunt Maria and Uncle Alois greeted them warmly. Andreas's uncle was exactly the way Karla had pictured him: a short, jovial, portly man with a booming voice who embraced and kissed Karla enthusiastically. His aunt was an equally plump, hearty, and vivacious woman.

"So you're the beautiful girl my nephew has kept hidden from us all this time." Uncle Alois slapped Andreas on the back. "He was probably afraid I was going to snatch you away from him."

"Yes, you'd love that, wouldn't you?" Maria smiled and shook a finger at him.

It was only now that Karla noticed a third person in the room, a thin, quiet, unassuming woman, probably in her fifties. Andreas introduced her as his mother. She greeted Karla with a shy smile. After saying hello, she seemed to disappear among the other people. Karla was amazed how little mother and son resembled each other.

Aunt Maria had prepared a typical dish of the area for lunch—*coniglio* and *polenta*, rabbit stew with slices of corn mush fried in olive oil and topped with parmesan cheese—as well as vegetables and salad. It was a very tasty meal, but Karla, who by nature wasn't a big eater, constantly had to stop Maria from putting more food on her plate.

"*Cara*, you're much too thin, you have to eat." Uncle Alois tried to put another piece of meat on Karla's plate.

"Leave her alone, for god's sake," Andreas finally intervened. "You know, Alois, not everybody can eat as much as you do. You could actually do with a little less yourself. You must be twice as fat as when I saw you last time."

"Don't be fresh, young man." Uncle Alois grinned. "Here, have some more wine." He poured Andreas another glass.

After lunch, Maria suggested they have coffee on the patio. While Andreas turned on the espresso machine, Karla stepped outside and sat at a large granite table under a pergola covered by a trellis of grapevines full of plump ripe grapes. Not used to drinking alcohol in the middle of the day, she was getting sleepy. She sat with her back against the granite wall behind her and closed her eyes.

All of a sudden, Karla heard Andreas's angry voice from inside the house, followed by his mother's quiet, subdued one. She opened her eyes and looked around. Maria and Alois brought out cups and liquor glasses.

Maria shook her head. "He's at it again. Why can't he leave her alone?"

Andreas stepped outside, his faced flushed from anger. "She drives me crazy."

"What's the matter?" Alois asked.

"Why doesn't she just kneel down in front of that damn photo and pray to it? Stupid woman."

"Andreas, she's your mother. You owe her some respect." Maria faced him squarely. "Go get her, and apologize while you're at it. You should be ashamed, making a scene in front of your guest."

"I can't help it, she just—"

"Andreas, please. Come on." Alois touched his arm. "Go get her."

Andreas shook his head, but turned around and went inside.

"Don't mind them," Maria said to Karla. "Andreas and Emilia just have to fight once in a while."

Andreas came out again, followed by his mother. His face was still flushed, while Emilia's was pale. Andreas sat next to Karla. He exhaled deeply, put his arm around her. "I'm sorry."

Although the mood was subdued for a while, Alois and Maria managed to cheer everybody up again with jokes and stories. After finishing his coffee, Alois opened a pouch of tobacco, stuffed his pipe, and lit it. He closed his eyes, sucked at the pipe, and blew the smoke toward the sky. Karla watched the small ritual, fascinated.

Alois winked at her. "My little vice."

When Maria began to collect the empty cups and glasses, Emilia and Karla got up to help. "You sit down and relax," Maria told them, then motioned at Andreas. "He can help."

"Yes, ma'am." Andreas gave a cursory smile.

Emilia sat on a chair at the end of the patio. Karla, feeling sorry for the quiet woman who seemed out of place among her vivacious and short-tempered relatives, went to join her. "I love Monte Sosto," she said, as they both looked at the mountain. "I got up early one morning and drove to Olivone to paint it."

"Yes, Andreas told me you were an artist." Emilia gave her a warm smile.

They continued to gaze at the mountain. Then Emilia did something that took Karla by surprise. She took her hand and squeezed it. "I'm happy he met you." Emilia's eyes lit up for a moment. It was the first time Karla saw any similarity between her and her son. It wasn't the color of her eyes, which were blue, but their brilliance, emphasized by dark eyelashes, and the expression of tenderness she sometimes saw in his eyes, as well.

"If you hadn't told me she was your mother, I would've never guessed," Karla said to Andreas as they were driving home. "You two are so different."

"True," Andreas sneered. "I have my father's looks, although not his character, at least I hope not."

"Your mother is so shy and quiet ... you almost feel sorry for her."

"Yeah, you're right. If you can believe it, though, she's a lot livelier now than she used to be. When I was a kid, she was practically a nonentity." Andreas sounded bitter.

"That's a harsh thing to say about your mother."

"Well, it's true. It took me many years to halfway forgive her for letting my father brutalize us the way he did."

"Didn't she try to protect you?"

Christa Polkinhorn

"Yes, but she wasn't very effective. Whenever she tried to stop him from beating me, he just lashed out at her, as well. We both ended up with welts and bruises. It was horrible."

"Perhaps she was too weak. He must have been a strong man."

"Weak is right. I mean her character. Nobody expected her to stand up to him physically. However, she tried to hide the fact that he was beating us. That's what I blame her for. Do you realize that, after all this time and all the mean things he did to us, she still keeps a photo of him in her bedroom? She hides it whenever I come over, because she knows I get furious. I think in a way she still loves the jerk." Andreas hit the steering wheel with his hand.

"That sounds like the typical battered woman syndrome. Was that the reason you were arguing?"

"Yeah. I know, I should just shut up and leave her alone."

Karla quickly changed the subject, not wanting to get Andreas upset again. "Your aunt and uncle are wonderful people. I hope they weren't insulted that I didn't eat more."

"Oh, no, don't worry. They always try to make people eat more than they are able to. It's their old-fashioned way of showing hospitality. No, they like you a lot." He glanced at her with a quick smile.

The next time they visited Andreas's relatives, Emilia showed Karla a few baby pictures of Andreas. They were alone in her bedroom, paging through a photo album. When Emilia put it back on the chest of drawers, Karla saw the photo. For a moment she thought it was a picture of Andreas, but when she looked more closely, she realized that it must be his father as a young man. She was shocked at the similarity: the same broad shoulders; the same dark, disorderly hair; and the same green eyes.

Emilia took the photo and shoved it into the drawer. "He probably told you about his father."

62

"Yes, it must have been a bad time for him ... I guess for both of you."

"Yes." Emilia sighed. "Andreas still blames me, you know. I don't think he really loves me. I mean, not the way a son loves his mother." Her voice trembled.

On the way home, Karla told Andreas of the incident in the bedroom. Andreas shook his head.

"Yup, that's my mother. She still has this victim mentality."

"Andreas, is it true you don't love her?"

"I love her in my own way." His voice sounded curt.

"Do you have any pleasant memories of your father at all?" Karla asked a while later. The moment she asked the question, she realized she shouldn't have done it.

"Please drop the subject, Karla."

"I'm sorry. I didn't mean—"

"It's okay." Andreas drove on in silence, then got off the main road and stopped at a parking lot next to the lake. "Let's get out for a moment."

They walked over to the boardwalk and looked out onto the lake. The afternoon breeze rippled the surface, and the water, reflecting the sunrays, shimmered like pearls. Andreas leaned against the railing and stared into the distance. He put his arm around her. "Look, Karla, I know you mean well, but please don't ask me about my father anymore. Perhaps one day I'll be able to tell you more, but right now I don't want to talk about it. All right?"

"Yes, of course. I'm sorry."

"And as for my mother. Yes, she's right. I don't love her the way she wants me to. I can't help it. To this day, she hasn't really accepted the fact that she failed me as a mother." Andreas stared down at the water, then glanced up at Karla from under his dark lashes. It struck her once again how much he looked like the man he seemed to hate so much.

"I won't mention your dad again, Andreas. But I can't help feeling sorry for your mother. It must be very hard for a mother to know that her child doesn't love her, or doesn't love her enough."

"She should've thought of that earlier," Andreas said with an icy voice. "She obviously didn't love me enough as a child, either, or she would've asked for help. It was more important to her what the neighbors thought than the fact that her son got beaten to a pulp. The whole time she kept pretending that nothing was wrong. My uncle had to threaten her to get the court involved before she finally agreed to let me live with them."

Karla felt him seething with suppressed anger.

"Damn." He slammed his fist down on the railing in front of him. The iron bars trembled.

He has his father's rage in him.

Andreas exhaled deeply, then gently touched her arm. "I'm sorry, Karla. Let's not talk about it anymore. It brings out the worst in me. Let's go."

They got into the car and drove on in silence.

I'm in love with a powder keg. That's just my luck. I heard that men who are abused as children often abuse their own children. Great prospects.

Chapter 10

Karla parked the car, and took the wrapped loaf of braided bread and the drawing she had made of Andreas out of the backseat. She heard the familiar noises from Andreas's studio, the chipping of the chisel against stone and the loud grinding of some kind of power saw.

Andreas was standing at his workbench in front of a granite rock. He was dressed in a full coverall and boots. Instead of his regular protective gear of goggles and mask, he was wearing a hardhat with a visor, which covered his whole face.

Karla watched him work from the entrance for a while. He was in the process of sawing through a rock, then put the saw down, picked up a hammer and chisel, and chipped away the loosened stone slivers. As usual, Karla was fascinated by the combination of strength, concentration, and tenderness with which Andreas handled stone. He hit the chisel with varying strength, cut and carved with great care, brushed the stone dust away, then took off his glove and caressed the stone with his bare hand, as if he wanted to apologize for hurting it.

When Andreas stopped to rest and removed his hat and earplugs, Karla went inside. He stood, opened his coverall down to his hips, and tied the sleeves around his waist. "Just the woman I was waiting for." He hugged and kissed her. She noticed the slightly musky smell of fresh sweat.

"That's heavy-duty gear." Karla pointed at his hardhat and visor.

"Granite splinters are very sharp. I hate wearing too much stuff when I work. It gets too hot, especially in summer, but you wouldn't want one of these in your face." He showed her the crusted scab of a cut on his forearm. "Or one of those rocks falling on your feet wouldn't be very pleasant, either. What's this?" He motioned at the packages Karla had put on one of the shelves.

"Homemade bread from Lena and something I made for you."

Andreas looked the drawing. "Hey, that's great. Thanks. I have to find a place to hang it."

"We'll find a spot when we get back," Karla said. "You better hurry. We're supposed to be at Sarah's in half an hour. Remember, she wants to show us her new set of sculptures?"

"Damn. I forgot all about it." Andreas slapped his forehead.

"Can you make it? Otherwise, I'm sure we can postpone."

"No, I want to get it over with. I keep promising to look at her stuff and then something comes up. I need to take a quick shower, but I'll be ready in five minutes."

Karla followed Andreas into the apartment. "Don't look too closely." Andreas waved his hand. "I haven't had a chance to clean up." He stripped out of his coverall and dropped it on the floor next to a pile of clothes. Karla smiled and shook her head. Andreas was immaculate when it came to personal hygiene, but his apartment was a constant mess. "Creative disorder," he called it.

While Andreas was showering and changing, Karla put the loaf of bread away and searched the wall for a spot to hang the drawing. When her cell phone rang, she was surprised to see Sarah's number. *I wonder if she's canceling. I wouldn't mind. I'd much rather spend time with Andreas alone than watch Sarah's flirtations.* However, it wasn't Sarah; it was Jason.

"I got your number from Sarah's cell phone. Listen, I have bad news. Sarah OD'ed on sleeping pills and probably something else. Could be attempted suicide. She's in a coma. Doesn't look good."

Karla held on to the back of a chair and sat down. Her heart pounded, and she started to feel dizzy. "That's not possible." But she knew it was very possible. Sarah had been drinking and using drugs, and she had been unhappy.

Andreas stepped out of the shower and pulled on his underwear. "What's the matter with you? Why are you so pale?"

It took Karla and Andreas longer than expected to reach the hospital. There was an accident and traffic had to be rerouted. When they finally arrived at the hospital, it was only to hear that Sarah had died. Her parents and a few friends were there. Jason was in tears. "I found her. I called the ambulance. I tried everything."

"It's not your fault, Jason." Karla hugged him.

After expressing condolences to Sarah's desperate parents, whom Karla barely knew, she asked her mother if she would allow her to see Sarah one more time. Her mother nodded and motioned to the nurse, who took Karla to the special room where the bodies of the dead were kept until burial.

Karla hesitated before entering. She had seen her share of dead bodies, but that first look at a deceased was something she could never get used to. The room was cold and absolutely still. It gave the feeling of a chapel. Sarah's body was lying on a bed, covered with a sheet. The nurse lifted the linen to expose Sarah's face, then stepped back to give Karla some privacy.

Sarah's face was pale except for the light bruising under her closed eyes. She looked surprisingly peaceful. Nobody would have guessed that the person whose lifeless body lay there had been miserable.

Seeing her vivacious and normally loud friend so still, Karla was overcome by sorrow and shame. "I failed you," she whispered.

Sarah had been a difficult person, but Karla, busy with her own life and desires, hadn't even noticed how desperate she was. "Sarah, I'm so sorry. Please forgive me," was all she was able to say. With tears streaming down her face, she left the room.

Andreas and Jason were waiting for her. Andreas put his arm around her. "Are you all right?"

Karla shook her head. "No. But there's nothing I can do now to make it right. It's too late."

Jason, who had regained his composure somewhat, suggested they have a memorial service for Sarah, together with her friends. Karla promised to help him organize it.

Back at Andreas's place, the mood was subdued. Karla couldn't settle down. She kept getting up, pacing the floor, walking up to the window, sitting down again, and wrapping strands of hair around her finger.

"I still can't believe it. Last time I talked to her she sounded cold and abrupt, but not desperate. How could I've known? But I should've known. I was a bad friend."

Andreas shook his head. "Come on, Karla, you have to stop blaming yourself for things you have no control over. Nobody could've foreseen this."

"I'm not blaming myself for her death. I blame myself for not supporting her more when she was alive. And I certainly had control over that." Karla got up and glanced absentmindedly at the drawing she had done of Andreas. "I was too busy with my own life." She turned around and faced him. "You've given her more encouragement in the short time you knew her than I did in all the years we've been friends."

"Karla, you're delusional. What encouragement? I told her I'd look at her work and never did. Too busy with my own life, as well." They looked at each other.

"I think she was in love with you," Karla said.

"She came on to me quite strongly. Even after she knew the two of us were dating. I wouldn't call that love. She was jealous of you, Karla. You had everything she didn't. Success. Boyfriend. I don't think she was a good friend to you. You don't need to feel guilty."

"It's ironic. *She* had everything *I* didn't. A wonderful family, a father and a mother who loved her. And she looked down on them, thought they were too bourgeois and provincial." Karla shook her head. "It's so sad."

Andreas hugged Karla. "We couldn't have changed Sarah's destiny. She was on drugs and alcohol. She had no self-confidence. She self-destructed."

"I still feel I didn't treat her right." Karla sighed. "I wonder if artists can ever be good friends. There's so much competition. So much envy and backbiting."

It took Karla a long time to fall asleep. She thought of the many things she still wanted to tell Sarah. Karla had talked to Silvia about a possible exhibition of Sarah's work, and Silvia had promised to look at her sculptures. She wanted to tell Sarah about it during the planned visit, but now Sarah would never know. *Why couldn't you have waited, Sarah? What a waste.*

Karla dozed off, then heard someone call her name, seemingly from far away. She was in a forest near a steep cliff. Two women, Sarah and another young woman who resembled Karla's mother, stood at the edge of the cliff. It seemed they were about to jump. Karla tried to run to hold them back, but she couldn't move. She opened her mouth to shout, but no sound escaped. Then the two figures were gone, and Karla finally managed to scream. Someone grabbed her from behind. She turned her head and looked into the face of a Latin man. Then it changed into Andreas's face.

"Karla, wake up. You're dreaming."

Karla sat up and gasped for breath. Andreas held her. "It's all right. Just a dream."

Andreas put two cups of cappuccino on the table and cut slices of Lena's homemade bread. The air smelled of fresh coffee. The sunrays hitting the crystal on the windowsill tossed a pattern of rainbow colors across the floor.

Karla sat at the table, her chin propped on her hand, thinking about her dream. It was hazy now, but she clearly remembered the face of the Latin man.

Andreas sat next to her and put his arm around her. "Feeling a little better?"

Karla nodded. "Andreas, I made a decision. I want to go to Peru. I need to see my father again, before he, too, dies. I want you to come with me."

Chapter 11

The red, orange, and ocher colors of fall were fading. Before Karla fully realized it, the farmers had finished picking the grapes and Lena gave her a bouquet of the last roses. The wind from the west blew the leaves off the chestnut trees in the yard. It began to rain, and a month later rain turned into the first snowflakes, and then winter came full force.

Karla and Andreas were on the way home from a walk along the river Maggia. It was a sunny but cold day. Their breath turned into thin white clouds, and with each step the snow crunched under their boots. It was late afternoon, and the sun was beginning to disappear behind the hills. The snow-covered branches of pines and ashes glimmered like glass in the light of the last sunrays. It was by far the coldest winter in years, and even the south of Switzerland was bearing the brunt of the polar air sweeping through Europe.

"I want to celebrate this year." Karla slid her hand into Andreas's coat pocket. "Last year was terrible—it was the first Christmas after my aunt's death, and I was distraught. Now, Sarah died, but I want to celebrate. I'm so sick of sorrow and grief. Sarah would've celebrated. She had a big bash each Christmas, got totally drunk, but she celebrated. My aunt always went to church on Christmas Eve."

Andreas squeezed her hand. "All right, let's celebrate. We'll go to Christmas Eve Mass in honor of your aunt, and we'll drink a glass of wine to the memory of Sarah. I'll pass on the getting-drunk part."

"Sounds great. We'll get a Christmas tree and bake cookies and the whole bit." Karla started to skip, and slid on a patch of ice. Andreas caught her in his arms at the last minute.

"Careful, or you'll spend Christmas in a cast." Andreas held her. White mist was gliding up in front of his face. "Your lips are blue." He kissed her.

When Karla woke up in the morning, Andreas was already dressed. He put a cup of coffee on the nightstand and sat on the bed.

"What time is it?" Karla asked, yawning.

"Six o'clock. I'm off. I have tons of work to do. If I don't finish Alfredo's gravestone by tomorrow, his relatives are going to put me into a grave. I should've done it weeks ago. I just didn't expect it to be that cold by now. Don't ask me how I'm going to plant the damn thing now that the ground is probably frozen. I might have to use an ice pick." Andreas grabbed his down jacket.

"Can't you stay a little longer?" Karla asked with a mischievous smile, sliding her hand under his sweater and trying to reach inside his pants. "It'll be easier to set the stone later in the day when it's warmer."

"I wish I could," he sighed, "but I really have to go. ... Karla, stop it. Don't. I can't. No. You're not being very helpful. ... Oh, what the heck." He laughed as he stripped off his clothes. "Now, I'm really going to be late."

After Andreas had left, Karla looked outside to check on the weather. It was snowing lightly; small, dry flakes twirled to the ground and dusted the roofs of the neighbors' houses. She opened the window a crack and inhaled the air, which smelled of burning wood. After a hot shower, she decided to go to Lugano and do some Christmas shopping.

The traffic was heavy. It seemed that everybody was out shopping. Andreas and Karla had decided not to give each other any Christmas gifts and save the money instead for their upcoming trip to Peru. Karla wanted to give him a little something anyway, something to put under the tree, and thought about getting him a music CD. Andreas liked operas, organ music, and bands of the sixties, particularly blues musicians, such as Ray Charles and B.B. King. Browsing through the music collection, she came across a CD of Andreas Vollenweider, a Swiss musician who played electronic harp and whom Karla loved. She bought it, thinking that the same first name might be a good omen.

Back home, her mailbox was stuffed full with Christmas cards. Karla groaned. It meant she had to send cards back, and that wasn't something she enjoyed much. There was a fat envelope from Peru. She opened it and found a short letter and, to her great surprise, two airplane tickets in it.

When she had called her father to tell him that she was planning to visit him and bring her *novio* along, Arturo had asked her for his full name. Now she knew why. In the short letter, her father told her that he had booked their flight for the approximate dates she had given him, but he would be able to alter them should their plans change.

How generous, she thought. *Is he trying to make up for neglecting me?* She shook her head. Arturo may not have been like a regular father to her, but he did try to help her.

As a child, Karla had been fascinated by this exotic man, whom her mother had called her *papá* and whose photo stood on the chest of drawers in her bedroom. He sent her presents, talked to her on the phone in a language she didn't understand. He never scolded or punished her like the fathers of her friends. He was special.

When she did miss him, occasionally—or rather someone like him, a father figure—she pulled out her crayons and drew him. A father and a mother, and in the middle, she herself, a little girl, holding her parents' hands. Later, Jonas, her painting teacher and boyfriend of her aunt, had become like a second father to her.

It was only when Karla got older that the shiny veneer of the mysterious man in Peru began to fade and her feelings toward him became more conflicted. When she was thirteen years old, she spent the summer with her Peruvian family in Cusco. She remembered that time as a fascinating experience.

Karla enjoyed being with Arturo's wife, Rosa, and her two half sisters and seeing a new country. Her father, however, remained a stranger. The relationship between the two was tense throughout the visit. Arturo was a kind but serious man and the typical Latin *pater familias*, and Karla resented his attempt to treat her like a daughter and put the same restrictions on her as he did with his other children.

A knock on the door interrupted Karla's musing. It was Andreas. Karla quickly put the tickets away. She would wrap his and give it to him as a present.

"Why don't we go and pick out the Christmas tree today?" Andreas suggested. "I have the pickup with me."

They bought a tall silver fir at a farm nearby. Andreas put it up, and they spent the afternoon decorating it. Afterward they went over to Lena's to help her bake Christmas cookies, which meant Karla was helping and Andreas was in their way, burning his fingers and tongue, because he couldn't wait until the cookies were cool.

On Christmas Eve Andreas and Karla went to an evening Mass in a small Catholic church in Bellinzona. The festive service was just enough to get them into the holiday spirit. The pictures of the saints along the walls flickered in the candlelight, and the room smelled of incense. Karla ignored most of the sermon—it was always more or less the same—but the sound of organ music brought tears to her eyes.

They spent the rest of the evening at Karla's, lighting the candles on the tree. Karla held a small twig into the candle flame, which filled the room with the scent of pine. She had prepared a meal of marinated vegetable salad with tomatoes, artichoke hearts, olives, and corn, topped with bacon bits as well as cold meat; lox; and different kinds of rolls. For dessert she prepared a dish called zabaglione, made of beaten egg yolks, sugar, and Marsala wine, which she served in high-stemmed glasses.

Andreas had his normal healthy appetite and polished off whatever she put in front of him. He licked the serving spoon for the zabaglione clean, then stood and groaned. "Too much food, I have to go on a diet."

As Karla had suspected, Andreas had bought her "just a small gift." It was a gold necklace.

"Andreas, we decided not to give each other anything, remember? This is much too expensive." Karla tried on the necklace and preened in front of the mirror. "Well, here is yours. If you don't like it, you can exchange it."

"Yeah, so much for not giving me anything, huh?" Andreas unwrapped the package. "I love Andreas Vollenweider."

"Great. Well, now for the big surprise." Karla gave him the plane ticket. "This is from my father."

Andreas glanced at the ticket, then at her. He looked stunned. "I can't accept this."

"Yes, you can. You must. If you don't, my father will be deeply offended. Besides, I've already called and thanked him."

Andreas shook his head and slapped the ticket on the table. "I don't even know him." His face was flushed, and he narrowed his eyes.

Don't get angry now. "Andreas, please, don't spoil it. My father owns a travel agency and probably got a big discount."

Andreas picked the ticket up again and looked at it. "I've always wanted to go to Peru," he said in a low voice. "All right, I accept it." He gave Karla a hug.

Karla was relieved. For a moment she had been afraid Andreas was going to blow up again.

PART TWO

THE STONES OF OLLANTAYTAMBO

Chapter 12

The plane flew a loop over the Pacific Ocean, then descended toward Lima.

"What do you see?" Karla asked, bending over Andreas, who was pressing his face against the small airplane window. She had let him have the window seat since he had never been to Peru.

"Nothing at all," he said. "Except for fog or smog, or whatever it is."

"Yeah, that's normal for Lima, particularly in the morning."

Although exhausted from their twenty-hour flight from Zurich via Madrid to Lima, Karla and Andreas were excited about arriving in Peru. After the plane landed, they stood in line to go through customs, picked up their luggage, and walked into the entrance hall.

Karla was surprised how much the airport had changed since her last visit. It was modern and clean, with lots of shops and eating places, most of them North American. There was Dunkin' Donuts, McDonald's, and Starbucks next to a couple of Peruvian fast-food places. A few stores offered alpaca sweaters and Peruvian pottery and jewelry, as well as sweatshirts with university logos from the United States, baseball caps, and European perfumes and liquors.

"I think airports and large cities all over the world are starting to look alike. Think how many McDonald's and Starbucks we have in Zurich and Lugano," Karla said. "But we better find our taxi driver."

Karla had ordered a pickup service from the hotel, since taking one of the many taxis in front of the airport was risky if you didn't know exactly which ones were official. "There he is." Karla pointed at a man who held up a sign with their names on it.

The driver, a middle-aged man with short black hair and a thin scar across his cheek, welcomed them enthusiastically, took their suitcases, and led the way to the outside part of the airport. The air was still cool and damp from the fog that early in the morning, and it smelled of a mixture of moisture and exhaust fumes.

In the parking lot they were surrounded by a horde of other taxi drivers who tried to lure them into their cars. One of them tried to grab Andreas's bag and got a scare when Andreas, who towered over the man by more than a foot, held him by the arm and gave him a threatening look.

"Talk about stiff competition," Andreas grumbled as he got into the cab.

They drove to their hotel in Miraflores, one of the wealthier districts in Lima, where the well-to-do *limeños* lived and many of the tourists stayed. On the way they passed dilapidated houses smeared with graffiti next to impressive colonial-style buildings and statues of Indian and Spanish warriors. An abundance of small mom-and-pop outfits—liquor stores, vegetable and fruit stands, toy and machine-part shops, seedy-looking bars, and restaurants—lined the streets. Merchants were hosing down the sidewalks and chasing away the beggars, who seemed to have spent the night in the doorways. The first business people in smart suits were hurrying on their way to work.

After about a forty-minute drive, the taxi driver pointed to the right.

"*El mar.*"

They peered out the window. Because of the fog, which still lingered over the city, there wasn't much to see except for a wide stretch of beach. "It'll clear up later on," Karla assured Andreas, who had never seen the Pacific Ocean.

Their hotel, called El Patio, was in the center of Miraflores and only a few blocks from the beach. It was a romantic guesthouse, which did its name justice. The entrance led into a courtyard, and the patios on the second floor were crowded with flowers and plants. Although the hotel was small, it was easy to get lost in the maze of hallways, staircases, and unexpected turns and corners. The hotel may have been a private home once, and additional parts had been added somewhat haphazardly later on.

Their room on the second floor was small but clean and, to Karla's great relief, faced the inner courtyard and not the noisy street. At least they would be able to get some sleep.

"I need to take a shower. I feel terribly grubby after the long flight," Karla said. She stripped off her clothes and stepped into the bathroom, hoping the water would be hot. As she remembered from her past visit, hot running water was a luxury in Peru. Fortunately, things seemed to have improved since then, at least in the better hotels in Miraflores.

Karla sighed with pleasure as she felt the warm water ease her stiff muscles. Andreas joined her. They kissed and lathered soap on each other. "Try not to swallow the water, or you might get sick," Karla warned Andreas.

After a quick breakfast of papaya juice, tea, and rolls, they went to explore the city. They walked the few blocks to the boardwalk above the Pacific Ocean, trying to cross the streets without getting hit by a car. The drivers didn't seem to know or care about the concept of a pedestrian zone.

"This is worse than Italy," Andreas grumbled. He held Karla back as she was just about to step into the street and a car came racing toward them. "That guy would have run you over."

Karla snickered. "Hmm. I know of some Swiss drivers who—"

"Geez. How long are you going to hold that against me? It only happened once, and I'm normally a decent driver." Andreas glared at her.

"Calm down. I'm only kidding." Karla patted his arm.

When they reached the boardwalk, the sun was able to penetrate the fog and the Pacific Ocean slowly emerged in all its grandeur. Andreas was overwhelmed by its expansiveness. "This makes the Mediterranean look like a big lake," he said, snapping pictures.

On the cliff high above the sea was an elegant outdoor shopping mall, filled with North American, European, and a few Peruvian shops and restaurants.

"I need a cup of coffee. After twenty hours with hardly any sleep, I'm starting to fade," Karla said.

To Andreas's dismay, Starbucks was the only coffee shop open that early. "I didn't come here to drink gringo coffee," he protested.

"Come on, Andreas, it's only a cup of coffee. You wouldn't like regular Peruvian coffee anyway. It's usually instant, not very tasty. Why do you think Starbucks and the European coffee shops are popular here? And not just with the tourists."

They went inside, where young, friendly Peruvian baristas served them cappuccino. Karla inhaled the strong smell of coffee beans. "It's not so bad. This may be a North American outfit, but it provides good jobs for local people."

Andreas wasn't convinced. "Oh, yeah? How do you know how much the *peónes* here get paid? I bet you the people in charge, who make the big money, are gringos."

After drinking their coffee, they walked along the boardwalk, watching the surfers catch the waves and paragliders swoop across the sky. They went to see *El Beso*, the famous sculpture at El Parque del Amor.

"There it is," Andreas exclaimed. He pointed at an enormous sculpture that depicted a man and a woman engaged in a passionate, everlasting kiss on a pedestal high above the ocean. The work of the well-known artist Víctor Delfín was sculpted in clay and surrounded by low, wave-like stone walls covered with colorful mosaics and inscriptions. Some of the walls snaked along the cliff, which dropped down perilously toward the sea.

Karla and Andreas sat on the stone steps next to the sculpture. On the stairs and along the low walls, young couples were sitting in the sun, kissing and snuggling. The fog had finally lifted. It was warm, and the pale-blue ocean glimmered in the sun. It smelled of salt water and algae, and the breeze brought an occasional whiff of exhaust fumes from the highway below the cliff.

"This is marvelous." Andreas pointed at the sculpture. "I read somewhere that the artist was once arrested for kissing a girl in public. If that's true, this sculpture must have turned into his ultimate revenge. There are more couples hugging and kissing here than there would be police to arrest them.

"I also read that lovers around here compete for who can kiss the longest. Let's see if we can beat the lovers in stone." After kissing Karla for a long time, he glanced up at the sculpture again and shook his head. "I guess they always win."

They leaned back on the stairs and let the sun warm their faces. "You know what the best thing is about being here, aside from all this beauty?" Andreas waved his hand in a sweeping gesture at the ocean and the sculpture.

"No. What?"

"Being here with you." He smiled and gave her a hug.

Karla brushed through his hair, which was still moist from the shower. "I'm so glad you came with me. It would've been tough to face my family alone."

"I know. Family." Andreas rolled his eyes.

"Let's go to the art gallery near our hotel," Karla suggested. "I saw a sign about an exhibition I'd love to see."

The Galería de la Municipalidad was a small gallery that exhibited paintings by contemporary Peruvian artists. The current exhibition was by the painter and illustrator Cynthia Capriata, a Peruvian artist living in New York, whose abstract, detailed, and colorful mixed media Karla had always admired.

"Interesting," Andreas said, as they stood in front of a large oil canvas. "Her style is different from yours, but look at the intense colors. They remind me of some of your paintings. It must be the Peruvian element the journalist was referring to in his article."

Karla nodded. "Strange. I never even realized how much I am influenced by a country I hardly know."

Andreas pointed at a picture. "I like your paintings better than hers."

"You're just saying that to make me feel good."

"No. That's not true. I don't lie when it comes to art. She's good. I like your stuff better. That's a fact." Andreas squeezed Karla's arm.

After spending the rest of the day looking at a few additional museums, they returned to their hotel to change for dinner. There was a restaurant right across the street from the hotel, which served typical Peruvian food. It was small and beautifully decorated with colorful tablecloths, paintings, and clay figurines in the few alcoves around the walls. It smelled of roasted meat and sweet and pungent herbs. Although it was early, there were already quite a few tourists who weren't used to the late dinner hours of the Latin Americans.

Tired of Andreas's constant complaints about "gringo food," Karla decided to introduce him to one of the most famous indigenous meals: guinea pig. The menu, which was written in Spanish and English, listed the meal as *cui*, the Quechua word for guinea pig. She hoped Andreas wouldn't know what it was. "Why don't I order us something truly Peruvian?" she suggested.

"Sounds good to me." Andreas put the menu aside. "I'll leave it up to you, as long as it's not hamburgers or bratwurst or something."

"Don't worry." Karla suppressed a smile. *We'll see how adventurous you really are.*

Karla ordered another typical Peruvian, although less exotic, dish for herself: *truta,* baked trout with herbs. If Andreas didn't like his dish, they could always switch.

When the waiter brought their food, Karla could barely keep a straight face. As expected, the guinea pig was served in traditional fashion, with head and paws attached, next to a generous portion of vegetables and several different types of potatoes, the staple of Peru.

"What the f ... heck is this?" Andreas exclaimed. "It looks like a rat." His mouth was wide-open, and he looked as though he had seen a ghost.

"Psst, Andreas, not so loud." Karla burst out laughing.

A middle-aged German couple at the next table chuckled. "I had the same reaction when I first saw it. It's actually very tasty if you can get past the way it looks," the woman said.

Andreas stared at his plate in disbelief, then at Karla. "What did you order, for heaven's sake?"

"This is cui, or guinea pig, one of the most famous dishes in Peru. Didn't you read your guide?"

"Yeah, but ... I certainly didn't realize they served it head, feet, and all. I'm surprised they didn't leave the fur on as well." Andreas started to poke at the piece of meat with his fork.

The waiter came over and asked, with a concerned face, if something was wrong. Andreas looked at him, then at Karla, then shook his head. "No, everything is fine." His features relaxed, and his facial color was back to normal.

Relieved that Andreas didn't have a major temper tantrum, Karla put her hand on his arm. "Honey, try it, and if you don't like it, we can switch. That's why I ordered trout, which I know you like."

"You did this on purpose, didn't you?" Andreas gave her a punishing look.

"Well, yes, kind of. You've been wanting the real thing all day. It doesn't get any more Peruvian than this."

"Thanks a lot. Couldn't you have started me out on something a little less exotic?" Andreas cut a small piece and put it in his mouth, chewing it carefully. He shrugged, then took another bite. "It's not bad." After a few more bites, he seemed to actually enjoy his meal. "Not bad at all. And the vegetables are excellent." Andreas polished off his whole meal and then started to pick at Karla's plate.

Karla smiled. "Well, now you're a true Peruvian. You've passed the test."

Chapter 13

The following day Karla and Andreas flew to Arequipa, a town in the southern part of the country, where they planned to spend a few days. It was at an elevation of 7,500 feet and was a perfect place to become acclimated to the altitude of Cusco, which was over 11,000 feet above sea level.

Surrounded by majestic mountains, Arequipa, also called the *la Ciudad Blanca*, the White City, was a dazzling sight. According to most travel guides, Arequipa got its nickname from the buildings, made of an off-white volcanic rock called sillar, which glistened and sparkled in the sunlight. However, as one of the taxi drivers told Karla and Andreas, there was another reason for the name. It was called the White City because it was originally settled by "white" people of European, mostly Spanish, origin.

Karla hadn't been to Arequipa on her former visit to Peru, so it was a new experience for her as well. Both she and Andreas fell in love with the place. One of their favorite spots was the sixteenth-century convent, Santa Catalina, which was almost a city of its own. The many colonial-style buildings were connected by courtyards and cobblestone streets. Paintings adorned the walls, and even the sparse living quarters of the nuns were tastefully decorated and comfortable. It was obvious that the convent used to house the daughters of well-to-do Peruvians. Only girls of European immigrants were allowed; indigenous girls were not accepted. Nowadays, only a small part of the convent, inaccessible to visitors, was still inhabited by a few nuns.

Santa Catalina was a painter's and photographer's paradise. The vibrant colors of the buildings and patios—different shades of red and brown, from orange to salmon to maroon, as well as yellow and a deep indigo blue—and the bright flowers in the gardens were a feast for the eye. Karla and Andreas spent a few hours walking around the property and admiring the subtle play of light and shadow as the sun moved across the sky and its rays fell on the buildings at different angles.

"I've always admired the way my grandfather handled tone, or value, in a painting." Karla squinted her eyes and studied a blooming bush lit by the sun. "If I stayed here long enough, I might discover how he did it."

"But that's exactly one of your strengths, the play of light and dark in your pictures," Andreas said.

"Not good enough yet." Karla shook her head.

"Perfectionist," Andreas teased her.

While in Arequipa, Andreas and Karla took a day tour to Toro Muerto, an archaeological site in the high desert that consisted of hundreds of carved rocks. The origin of the carvings was uncertain. Archaeologists believed they had been created over a thousand years before by the Wari people, a pre-Inca tribe.

Aside from the driver and the guide, there was only a small group of people in the van. Toro Muerto was not as popular a tourist place as the famous Colca Canyon with its condors. Visitors of Toro Muerto were mainly people interested in archaeology or stone art. Their guide explained the significance of some of the designs, then gave them free time to explore on their own.

The petroglyphs were spread out over a fairly large area. Andreas, who was fascinated not just by the carvings on the vast boulders but equally by the shapes and textures of the rocks, walked all over the place, taking pictures of the fissures, bands, and striations in the stone.

Karla was equally captivated by the mysterious carvings, and even more so by the otherworldly luminescence of the desert. The bright light made her eyes water. It was hot and dry, and soon Karla had a hard time keeping up with Andreas. She finally sat on one of the rocks and pulled a drawing pad and acrylic pens out of her backpack. "I want to draw some of the symbols on these rocks and capture the different colors. Why don't you walk around on your own for a while? Don't stray too far, though. We'll have to meet the others soon."

 "Good. But don't try to follow me or we may lose each other. Wait here. I'll be back." Andreas waved at her and disappeared behind a boulder.

Karla began to sketch the shapes of the rocks and drew a few of the symbols and figures, such as the Inca cross and the picture of dancing people. She tried to sketch the different shades of the rocks, which ranged from eggshell white to orange to pink to deep purple. The sky was a brilliant blue. In the distance, rich green rice fields formed a beautiful contrast to the glimmering white and yellow of the sand and mountains.

Karla got so absorbed, she almost filled her entire sketchbook. When she heard people calling, she checked her watch and realized that it was already past the time they were supposed to meet back at the van. She quickly gathered her things, and struggled to climb one of the larger boulders. From the top, she could see the van in the distance. She pulled out her jacket from the backpack and waved it in the air. One of the people waved a piece of cloth; they obviously had seen her.

But where was Andreas? Karla called his name. There was no answer. She was getting concerned. She didn't dare to go look for him, or they might miss each other, so she waited and tried to be patient. She knew Andreas had a tendency to forget time when he was captivated by something. He had missed meetings with clients and showed up late for their dates because he had been working on one of his sculptures. She was familiar with the feeling of total absorption and normally didn't hold it against him.

After about twenty minutes, Andreas still wasn't back and Karla began to worry. What if something had happened to him? He was strong and athletic, but he may have fallen and hurt himself, or perhaps there were poisonous snakes around. There were snakes in the desert, weren't there? But he would've called. He couldn't be that far away. She called again. No answer. What if Andreas didn't come back?

A wave of fear and dread flooded Karla. This was just like her nightmares about her mother. She would be all alone, abandoned. Perhaps she would find Andreas injured, bloodied, dying, or dead and she wouldn't be able to help him.

"No," Karla screamed. She pressed her hand over her mouth, trying to stifle the panic. Her heart pounded, there was a humming noise in her ears, and her breath came in spurts.

"Andreas," she called again. She burst into tears, sobbing uncontrollably, rocking her body back and forth. She knew she was about to snap. With the last of her willpower, she jerked herself out of her frenzy. "This isn't real, he'll come back, this is just my old fear, this isn't real," she kept saying out loud, repeating it over and over like a mantra. Slowly, she got hold of herself enough to climb the boulder again.

The van was still there, but she didn't see any of the tourists or the driver standing around. They must be inside; they were probably about to leave. *I must find Andreas.* As she tried to climb down from the boulder, she slipped, fell, and scraped her arm. It wasn't serious, but it hurt, and the pain together with her fear brought the tears back.

At that moment Andreas emerged from behind a boulder and waved at her. At first, Karla felt a great sense of relief. Seeing his smiling and unconcerned face, however, she started to scream as her fears turned into rage. "Where have you been? How can you be so selfish and inconsiderate?"

"What's the matter with you?" Andreas stared at her with unbelieving eyes. "And what happened to your arm?"

"I tried to find you. I called you. You didn't answer. I fell. I was so afraid. The others have probably left by now. We'll die out here." Karla burst into tears again. In her fury, she hit Andreas's chest with her fists, pummeling him.

Andreas caught her hands and bent her arms behind her back, then pressed her against him, hugging her. "Calm down, for heaven's sake. I told you I'd be back." He held her until she stopped squirming. "Karla, it's okay. I'm back. Drink some water. The heat is getting to you." He handed her his bottle.

Karla pushed it away, sobbing. "We were supposed to be back over half an hour ago. It'll take us at least twenty minutes to get back to the van. If there is still a van. Can you tell me where we're going to spend the night without water and food and anything out here? In the middle of nowhere?"

"Karla. You're hysterical."

"I'm hysterical? How dare you? I begged you not to come back late. Oh, why do I even bother?" She picked up her backpack and started to march in the direction of the van as fast as possible, stumbling once in a while in the soft sand.

Andreas overtook her and put his arm around her. "Let me see your arm."

"Leave me alone." Karla punched his arm away.

Andreas held her back. "Karla, I'm really sorry. I agree, I should've come back earlier. But these carvings, this whole area, it's so fascinating. I've never seen anything like this. I may never come back here, and I just wanted to take it all in. Don't be angry, please." He gently touched her shoulder and looked at her imploreingly. His boyish face was flushed from the sun and the excitement.

When Karla saw him so contrite and animated, her anger deflated. "It's just ... I was so worried about you." She sobbed and leaned her face against his chest.

Andreas held her in his arms. He gently stroked her back and kissed her face. "I'm sorry. Everything is all right. They won't leave without us. And if they do, there are towns and people around here. We'd find another way of getting back. Don't worry."

"Let's just go," Karla said.

Andreas took her arm and supported her. They hurried back to the van in silence. When the driver saw them, he gave them a stern look, dropped his cigarette on the ground, and climbed into the van. The guide shook his head. "What happened to you?"

Andreas tried to explain. "I got carried away. I'm a stone and sculpture enthusiast, and this was a precious experience. Please forgive us." He opened his arms and gave the guide an entreating look. "You have an amazing country. It's a great privilege for me to be here."

Andreas's sugarcoated praise and his enthusiasm brought a smile to the guide's face. "You should be more careful. Being out in the desert without water is very dangerous."

The tourists inside were a little less forgiving. They booed as Karla and Andreas got in. Karla blushed, gave them an apologetic look, and sat by the window, trying to make herself as small as possible.

"We should've left you guys out there," one of the women said, glaring at them.

"I know, I know. It was my fault." Andreas hugged Karla and gave the woman a disarming smile. "I got carried away. I apologize. Can I make it up to you guys?"

"You can buy beer for everybody once we get back to Arequipa," one of the men, a history teacher from Lima, teased him.

Karla was exhausted and thirsty. She tried to soothe her parched mouth with the last drops of her water. Andreas gave her the rest of his bottle, claiming he wasn't thirsty. He kept hugging her. "I'm sorry I didn't realize I was gone that long."

Karla nodded and held his hand. Slowly, she started to feel like herself again.

"Look what I found out there." Andreas pulled a small, flat, purplish stone out of his pocket. It was round and had an indentation on one end and was pointed at the other end, which made it look like a heart.

"What an unusual form," Karla said. "It's pretty. Where did you find it?"

"A desert spirit gave it to me. He told me I'd need it to comfort a beautiful woman."

Karla gave a weak smile. "Oh, Andreas, don't do this again. You can't leave me alone in the middle of nowhere. I get frantic. I—"

"I know. I forgot. Please forgive me."

It was quiet in the van. Everybody was tired from the heat and the strenuous hike in the sandy desert. Karla leaned her head against Andreas, who put his arm around her. His shirt felt warm and smelled of sand, sun, and his body. It soothed her to sleep.

By the time they arrived in Arequipa, Karla had recovered enough to agree to go out to dinner. The other tourists, however, decided they were too tired to take Andreas up on his offer to buy them beer.

Karla and Andreas picked a restaurant on one of the colonnaded balconies above the Plaza de Armas, from which they had a view of the city, the brightly lit cathedral, and the mountains in the background. It was their last evening in Arequipa; the following morning they were going to fly to Cusco.

Love of a Stonemason

Admiring the almost twenty-thousand-feet-high volcano, El Misti, with its conical peak covered by snow, and the even higher Chachani Mountain as they slowly faded into the night, Karla took a deep breath. For the first time since arriving in Peru, she felt a stronger-than-usual kinship with the country of her paternal ancestors. The mountains looked a little bit like Switzerland, although the landscape was different: wider, more open, and more elusive. The country struck her at once as familiar and remote, much like her Peruvian family and, above all, the man she called her father.

"I'm nervous about seeing Arturo again." Karla sighed and took a sip of her bottle of Inca cola, a popular drink she remembered from her last visit.

"I can understand that. He's probably even more nervous than you are. He just got a little older, but you changed from a teenager to a lovely young woman." Andreas gave her a quick kiss.

"You know, I was just thinking, we probably won't be able to sleep together at his house. From what I remember, they are very strict Catholics," Karla said.

"What? You must be kidding. You're sure you're talking about the same guy who knocked up your mother and got her pregnant?" Andreas shook his head in disbelief.

Karla smiled. "He was a young man then, and I hope there was a little more involved in my conception than him knocking up my mother."

"I'm sorry, I didn't mean it that way. You can't be serious, though. After all, we are adults."

"I know, but we aren't married."

"That's ridiculous. I can't imagine not making love to you for … how long are we going to stay with them? Four weeks? Impossible!" Andreas slapped the tabletop with his hand and frowned.

"Don't get upset now. We aren't staying with them the whole time. We're going to take overnight trips to Machu Picchu and other places. And I'm not even sure. Perhaps I'm wrong. Perhaps they've become a little more liberal. I just wanted to forewarn you." Karla wished she hadn't mentioned anything.

I can just see it. I'll be stuck trying to negotiate between a Swiss hothead and a conservative Peruvian family.

"We'll have to figure something out," Andreas said, his forehead still wrinkled. He called the waiter and paid.

"But look at this." He pointed to El Misti as they stepped out into the street. They stood in silence, admiring the view of the snow-covered top of the volcano gleaming against the darkening sky.

Chapter 14

As the plane took off from Arequipa, the sky was a bright, clear blue and the snow-covered mountains glistened in the sun. It was April, the tail end of the rainy season in the Andes. The flight to Cusco took an hour, during which the flight attendants had barely enough time to serve a quick meal of sandwiches and *mate de coca*, a tea made of coca leaves to alleviate the symptoms of altitude sickness.

The captain announced the upcoming landing, and the plane began to descend toward the historic capital of the Inca Empire. Karla watched, terrified, as the pilot seemed to fly directly into a mountain, then realized, relieved, that he was heading for an opening between two mountains. She spotted the familiar sign, *Viva El Perú Glorioso*, imprinted on the mountainside above the city.

The airport of Cusco was fairly small. The planes didn't taxi directly to the gates but let the passengers off outside. As Karla and Andreas climbed down the stairs from the airplane, they noticed the air was clear, crisp, and very thin. While walking to the reception area, Karla had to slow down to catch her breath. Even Andreas, who was in better physical shape from all his hiking and lugging heavy stones, said he felt a little lightheaded.

In the airport hall they were welcomed by a group of Andean folk musicians with pan flutes and string instruments. As usual, when Karla listened to the joyous as well as melancholic melodies, her eyes misted over. Like many other things in Peru, the music felt both intimate and foreign to her. While they waited for the luggage carousel to start turning and their suitcases to arrive, Karla's heart pounded, in part because of the altitude, but probably more so because she was nervous about meeting Arturo.

Outside, Karla spotted him right away. He still looked the same: slim body; thick, straight black hair; high cheekbones; square chin; slight scowl on his face as he scanned the passengers emerging from the airport hall. She remembered him as being taller, but she had been a child back then. Now, they were about the same height.

Rosa, Arturo's wife, seemed to have gained a little weight over the years. She was still an attractive woman, with dark eyes and shiny auburn hair. Being of European descent, she was somewhat fairer than Arturo. It was she who saw Karla first. She came rushing toward them and embraced and kissed Karla. "Look how tall and beautiful you've become."

Arturo and the children followed behind. Being face-to-face with her father, Karla waited for that feeling of warmth and familiarity she felt she should have toward her only surviving parent. Instead, she felt shy and uptight. Her mouth was dry, and her voice almost failed her when she greeted him.

"Karla," Arturo said in a warm but quiet tone, and gave her a hug. He held her by the arms and stepped back a little to look her over. "You're all grown up. You've become a young woman." He sounded surprised, as if he had expected her to be a child still.

"Papá, this is Andreas," Karla finally said, her voice still hoarse and trembling a little.

Arturo shook hands with Andreas and welcomed him.

"You remember your sisters?" Rosa asked and motioned to the two teenage girls standing next to her. Manuela, the older of the two half sisters, who had been seven when Karla last saw her, was now a young girl of seventeen. She had inherited her mother's looks, the soft auburn hair and the fair skin. Maria, the younger one, was of darker complexion and had Arturo's mestizo features.

Karla hugged them, feeling more relaxed around her half sisters. "I've seen photos of you, but I still can't believe how grown-up you are. And this must be Antonio." She smiled at a little boy who was hiding behind Rosa. He watched Karla with dark, expressive eyes and a brash smile, but when she tried to hug him he pretended to be shy, hiding his face in Rosa's skirt.

"He is the newest addition to the family. Antonio, come say hello. Where are your manners?" Arturo grabbed the little boy gently and pushed him toward Karla and Andreas.

Antonio hesitantly shook hands, then looked at Andreas and asked, "Did you bring me a present?"

"Antonio!" Rosa said with a stern face. "That's not polite." Arturo pulled his ear a little. Everybody else laughed. Antonio, embarrassed, rubbed his ear and hid again behind Rosa.

"Well, well, here is my favorite niece. And what a gorgeous young woman she has become!" The loud thundering voice behind Karla belonged to a man who resembled Arturo but was older. He smiled broadly and hugged her.

"Uncle Guillermo," she exclaimed as she recognized him. She remembered him as a jovial, friendly man who had spoiled her with attention and gifts ten years before. "How nice of you to come."

"We had to use two cars, since everybody wanted to come to the airport," Arturo said. He picked up Karla's suitcase and started to walk across the parking lot to his car. Karla and Andreas went with Arturo and Rosa, while the girls and Antonio squeezed into Uncle Guillermo's VW.

"So, you finally have a little boy," Karla said. "I remember when I saw you last, Arturo used to complain about being outnumbered by women."

Rosa laughed. "Yes, he came somewhat unexpected. He is a handful, as you'll find out soon."

In the meantime, they had arrived at the Plaza de Armas, the center of the city, from which they drove up a steep hill toward San Blas, the artisan district of Cusco, where the Delgados had their home. Karla closed her eyes a few times, unable to watch as Arturo maneuvered his car through the uneven streets. Most of the roads were too narrow for two cars to pass. In addition, there were steps on both sides and the drivers had to keep the wheels of their cars from sliding over them.

When they arrived at their home, Karla breathed a sigh of relief. "How anybody can drive here is beyond me."

"You get used to it." Arturo shrugged. He opened the gate and parked the car in the large courtyard.

Inside, they were welcomed by Elsa, a relative of Arturo's, who lived with them and helped Rosa with the housework. She was a short, somewhat plump, and friendly woman. She had been the children's nanny when Karla had lived with them during her last visit. Judging from her shriveled face, Karla felt she was quite old. She hugged and kissed Karla. Then she patted Andreas's hand and complimented Karla on her *novio guapo*, her handsome boyfriend. She gave a wide smile that deepened her wrinkles and exposed a mouth with several missing teeth.

Arturo and his family owned a modest but fairly large two-story home. All the lower rooms had separate entrances to the light-filled courtyard, which donned a colorful flower bed in the center. The rooms on the upper floor were connected by means of an outside balcony that went around the whole building. Karla believed that the Delgados belonged to the somewhat loosely defined Peruvian middle class. Arturo owned a travel agency. In order to supplement their income, they rented out two of the rooms on the lower floor.

"I bet you're tired from your trip," Rosa said. "Why don't you relax for a while before lunch? Manuela will show you your rooms."

"Unfortunately, we don't have any guest rooms, since all the spare rooms are rented out at the moment. You'll have to share. I hope you don't mind," Arturo added.

"Oh, no, we don't mind at all." Karla gave Andreas a quick glance.

"All right, Karla you can stay with Manuela, and Andreas will have to share a room with Antonio. Don't worry, Andreas, Antonio is very quiet. He won't bother you. Right, Antonio?" He looked at his son with a stern face. Antonio nodded but smiled his naughty-little-boy smile.

"I told you so," Karla whispered to Andreas, as they went to pick up their luggage on the patio.

"Ridiculous," Andreas mumbled under his breath.

Karla carried her suitcase to Manuela's room. She hoped Andreas would get used to the arrangement. Although she, too, would have preferred to be in the same room with him, she also enjoyed being with Manuela. It would give her a chance to get to know her a little better. They would have a lot of catching up to do.

Manuela's room was small but light and airy. There was just enough room for two beds, a small table, a chest of drawers, and a closet. It was on the second floor of the house, and had a view of the mountains in the distance, unlike most of the other rooms that faced the courtyard.

Manuela had cleared a few of the drawers and part of the closet so Karla would have room for her stuff. She was sitting on the bed watching Karla unpack. "Papá is so old-fashioned," she said.

"How do you mean?"

"Well, you know, not letting you stay with Andreas."

"Oh, that. I guess they feel strongly about this, about us not being married."

"I was thinking"—Manuela lowered her voice and spoke in a conspiratorial tone—"if you want to, we can switch at night after everybody is asleep. I can stay with Antonio and Andreas can sleep here. We'll just have to switch again before they get up in the morning."

"I don't know, Manuela. It sounds tempting, but I'd be worried Arturo and Rosa would find out."

"Oh, they wouldn't notice. Their bedroom is on the ground floor at the other end of the house."

"I'll think about it. If we get too desperate, we might take you up on your offer."

"I know how it is." Manuela smiled with a roguish twinkle in her eyes. "I have a boyfriend, too."

"Really? Do Arturo and Rosa know?"

"Oh, no, they'd kill me."

Karla looked at Manuela, wondering how long she'd be able to hide this from her strict parents. "You'll have to tell me about him, but we better join the others now."

Downstairs, Andreas was playing with Antonio on the patio, helping him assemble the Lego house they had brought him as a gift. Karla sat next to Arturo and watched them play. She was happy to see that Andreas seemed to get along well with his roommate. She decided not to tell him yet about Manuela's offer, since she knew he'd jump at the idea. It didn't seem right to her to go against Rosa and Arturo's wishes. Although she was Arturo's daughter, she felt more like a guest in their home rather than a family member. She was afraid to do anything that might upset them.

My father is still a stranger to me. She glanced at the man next to her, whose serious, almost morose, face lit up with a smile every once in a while when he looked at her or his young son. As if he had guessed her thoughts, Arturo put his arm around her and gave her a quick hug, then got up.

"Go wash your hands, Antonio. I think lunch is just about ready. Antonio," Arturo said sternly, since the little boy was still involved with his game and didn't pay attention to him. "Did you hear me?"

"Let's go." Andreas took Antonio by the hand. "We can finish later."

He sure is strict. Karla glanced at her father's serious face. She went inside to help Rosa and Elsa carry the dishes to the table. To her surprise, she discovered the few drawings and paintings she had sent the family over the years. They were framed and hung in the living and dining rooms. "We love your art," Rosa said when she saw Karla looking at the pictures.

Rosa and Elsa had prepared a delicious soup made of quinoa, a native Peruvian grain, as well as potatoes and vegetables. After Arturo had asked Maria to say grace, they ate in silence. During lunch Karla was able to look around the dining and living rooms. As she remembered from last time, the colonial-style furniture was of solid wood, some with beautiful carvings. The colorful posters of Peru and her paintings on the walls lit up the rooms and formed a pleasant contrast to the rather heavy furniture.

After lunch, Arturo, who had taken the week off from work, asked Andreas and Karla if they were interested in going to see one of the ruins nearby. Karla asked to be excused. She was still feeling the effects of the high altitude and had a slight headache. "I'd rather rest for a while. Andreas, why don't you go with Arturo if you feel all right? I'll join you guys tomorrow."

After they had left, Karla went into the kitchen, wanting to help Rosa, Elsa, and the girls clean up, but Rosa told her to lie down. Karla gratefully obeyed. She didn't feel well. Rosa made her a cup of mate de coca to take to her room. She drank a few sips of the tea and took a pill against altitude sickness, then lay down on her bed. After a while, the medicine began to take effect and she fell into a restless sleep.

It wasn't the usual nightmare of her mother's bloody body during that accident eighteen years before. She just saw someone who she thought was her mother motioning to her. Karla strained to reach the woman's outstretched hand, and woke up sobbing.

The dream didn't upset her the way her nightmares normally did; it just saddened her. It made her aware that her mother was the missing link. She was the person who could have closed the gap between her and her father. Her mother, however, had become a stranger, as well, someone who had faded from memory with the passage of time. Karla turned around. With tears still sliding down her cheeks and soaking into the pillow, she went back to sleep.

The next time she woke up, Andreas was sitting on her bed. He kissed her, then gave her a probing look. "Have you been crying?"

"It's nothing. I just had a bad dream."

"About what?"

"About my mother." Karla sat up, hugged her knees to her chest, and sighed. "She was reaching out to me. It felt as if my mother wanted to take me to my father." Her voice quivered. "I don't know if I can ever feel really close to him."

Andreas hugged her. "Give yourself time. You haven't seen him in so long." After a pause: "He talked about you. He asked me how long we've known each other. Stuff like that. I think he is checking me out to see if I deserve you." Andreas chuckled, then he took her face between his hands. "He loves you. I can tell by the way he talks about you and looks at you."

"Perhaps you're right." Karla sighed.

Chapter 15

The train to Machu Picchu zigzagged slowly up the hillside of Cusco by means of a series of switchback turns. It passed so close by the houses and shacks that Karla and Andreas were able to see inside and catch glimpses of people's private lives. An old woman wrapped in a thick shawl was climbing one of the narrow, steep stairs; a few younger men were standing in a doorway, smoking and watching the train; a stray dog was digging through a heap of garbage at the side of the road.

"Look." Karla pointed at the sky, which turned crimson as the sun began to rise. The whole of Cusco and the surrounding hills and mountains were spread out in front of them, bathed in golden light.

At the small station of Poroy, the train stopped for a while, then descended toward the Sacred Valley and the foothills of the Andes. Before long, they followed the Urubamba River and passed through the varied landscape of lush green fields, agricultural terraces, and villages. Colorfully dressed *campesinos* were herding llamas, and women in traditional garb were working in the corn and vegetable fields.

The train ride to Aguas Calientes, the town at the end of the rail line, took four hours. At the few stations the train stopped at, peasants offered their wares to the tourists. Women with long, black braids and wrapped in multicolored woven blankets lifted baskets filled with papaya and corn with huge kernels up to the windows of the train. Men shook bundles of coca leaves. Small children were waving. A young boy carried a baby llama. Karla took a picture of him and handed him some coins.

Before Aguas Calientes, the valley narrowed and the mountains towered high on both sides. Below, the Urubamba, now a turbulent mountain river, splashed white foam and rushed over boulders and rocks.

Karla and Andreas spent the night in Aguas Calientes, a small but lively tourist town, from which the buses to Machu Picchu left. After a stroll through the city, a visit to the local museum—which gave them a virtual tour of the area and explained its history—as well as a dip in the hot springs, they went to bed early, since they wanted to be on the first bus to the ruins the following day.

There were already quite a few tourists at the bus stop at five thirty in the morning. When everybody was seated, the bus took off and made its way slowly up the steep and curvy mountain road leading to the ruins. Karla inhaled sharply as the bus crossed a narrow bridge, and she looked down the steep cliff above a seemingly bottomless canyon. The bus shifted gear with a clunk and jerked around a hairpin curve, and they had their first view of Huayna Picchu, the mountain above the ruins.

After showing their entrance tickets at the gate to the ruins, they hiked up a steep path to a small house with a thatched roof, called the Hut of the Caretaker. On the meadow next to it, a few llamas were grazing.

They sat on a stone slab and looked at the scenery in front of them. At first, the mountains were hidden in thick layers of fog. The air felt clammy and smelled of damp grass. Soon, some of the fog began to lift, exposing parts of Huayna Picchu, "Young Peak," and Machu Picchu, "Old Peak," after which the area was named. Shrouds of mist floated by the mountains and hovered over the ruins, giving the landscape a mysterious, otherworldly appearance.

"This is overwhelming," Karla said. "What must the Incas have thought when they first discovered this place?"

Andreas pointed to Huayna Picchu, the mountain in the background of the ruins. "I read a little bit about Inca mythology. Huayna Picchu has the shape of a crouching puma if you look at it a certain way. You have to relax your gaze, and then the shape becomes obvious. The three smaller rocks on the left form the wings and the head of a bird, a condor, as the Incas believed. The puma and the condor were sacred animals to the Incas. So perhaps they came here, saw those rocks and mountains, and decided this was the perfect place to build a city. Two of their sacred beings would protect it."

"Yes, you may be right," Karla said.

"Let's see if we can discover some other animals," Andreas suggested. "Doesn't that stone over there look like the head of a monkey?" Andreas pointed to a rock beneath them. "You know, I just realized something."

"What?"

"That's the way I create my sculptures," he said. "I look at a stone and try to discover what kind of a shape is hidden in the stone. Sometimes it's obvious. At other times you need a little imagination to see it. Once I know what it is, then all I do is take a chisel and hammer and get rid of the stuff around it. It's like freeing a prisoner. And it's those sculptures I like best, the ones that are already present in the stone. I sometimes don't a see a form in a rock, then I just try to give it one. But, somehow, those sculptures aren't as satisfying to me." Andreas shook his head. "I knew I was doing that all along, but it's only now, looking at these rocks, that I really became conscious of it."

"Like this?" Karla pulled out her sketchpad and drew one of the rocks Andreas claimed looked like a turtle. Then she took a green pen and drew the animal shape superimposed on it.

"Exactly." Andreas nodded.

By noon, the sun had burnt through the mist and the mountains were bathed in golden light, with only shreds of fog floating by.

In the course of the day, more tourists arrived with their guides, who told them the standard stories about the ruins in different languages. Karla and Andreas, who by then had seen most of the sights, walked up a hillside and sat on a slab of stone, relaxing and admiring the view of the ruins spread out in front of them. It was quiet in that spot, away from the main throughway. The calm was interrupted only once in a while by shreds of talk in different languages—Japanese, German, English—as groups of tourists made their way down a path nearby.

Karla leaned her back against a rock and closed her eyes. Andreas took her hand and held it against the stone they were sitting on. "Feel how warm it is. It's granite, it absorbs heat really well." Then, after a pause, "This reminds me of something."

"Of what?"

Andreas hesitated. "Of a rock near our house."

"In Olivone?"

"No." Andreas hesitated again, then continued. "It was when I still lived with my parents up north. Our house was near a river and a quarry, and there were lots of boulders and rocks along the river."

Karla sensed that Andreas was about to reveal something from his past. Knowing his hesitancy to talk about anything related to that time in his life, she didn't dare to interrupt him for fear he would close up again.

"One of the rocks caught my attention when I first saw it. It was large, smooth, and round at the top, like a dome. At the bottom there was an indentation where the stone had eroded. Probably by the water that might have flown underneath at one time. It was like a small cave, just big enough for me. I must have been about six or seven years old."

He was quiet again. Karla looked at him. He was gazing into the distance, then looked down at his hands and continued in a low voice. "That was my rock. I used to hide in the cave when I wanted to be alone or when my father came home from one of his drinking binges and brutalized us. I would lie in that cubbyhole all rolled up into a tiny ball. There I felt safe. That stone seemed to be the only stable place when everything around me erupted in violence."

Karla put her hand on his. He looked at her, and in his eyes she saw the child he had been: a small, helpless boy wanting to believe in the power of the stone to protect him from a cruel father. It made her heart contract in pain. She wanted to hug him, to tell him it was okay. Instead she remained silent, waiting for more.

"One day I was lying on top of the rock, just enjoying the warmth. I heard my father call me. It was one of the days he was sober and in a good mood. I wanted to answer, but then I remembered that this would give away my secret hideaway. I jumped down from the rock and hid in the cave underneath. I was hoping my father would give up looking for me after a while, but I heard him come closer and closer. I was terrified he'd find me. I skidded as far back as the cave would allow, making myself as small as I could. I shut my eyes, hoping he wouldn't see me. You know how kids are, thinking if you close your eyes the other people won't be able to see you, either."

Andreas took a deep breath. "It was very quiet for a while, so I looked up, checking to see if he had gone. There was my father, standing in front of the rock. He looked directly at the cave. I swear he looked straight at me. But he didn't see me. I held my breath and I prayed. I don't think I ever prayed that hard in my life. As if by a miracle, my father turned around and walked away." Andreas stopped, then gave Karla a quick glance. "I was convinced the rock had made me invisible and saved me."

Karla was waiting for him to continue. When nothing more came, she asked, "Do you still believe the rock protected you?"

He shrugged. The child in his eyes had disappeared, and he was the adult again. "About a week after this incident, I went to live with my aunt and uncle, and from that moment on my life turned around."

Andreas took a deep breath and hugged Karla. She held on to him, savoring the intimacy that the shared moment of his painful past had created between them.

In the late afternoon Karla and Andreas took the last bus to Aguas Calientes, where they boarded the train back to Cusco. They arrived after dark. As the train descended the hill above the city, the brightly lit Plaza de Armas, the cathedral, and the Iglesia de la Compañia de Jesús welcomed them.

"Home again." Karla picked up her daypack, and they made their way toward the exit. Outside, they were greeted by the shouts of taxi drivers, whiffs of exhaust fumes, and the smell of wood ovens. *Yes,* she thought, *it does begin to feel like home.*

Chapter 16

"If I ever catch you there again, I swear I'll beat you with a belt!"

Andreas and Karla looked at each other, shocked, as they heard Arturo's loud and angry voice. They were just coming home from listening to a band play traditional Peruvian music. It was close to midnight. They stood in the courtyard waiting.

They heard Manuela's shaky voice: "We were just having a drink at the bar."

"Don't you lie to me. That place doesn't even have a bar."

There was a hard slapping sound, and Manuela began to cry. Karla felt Andreas stiffen next to her.

"That's enough, Arturo." It was Rosa's calm but stern voice. "Manuela, go to your room."

"I don't know what to do with her anymore," Arturo screamed.

Then Rosa's voice: "Well, hitting her isn't going to solve anything."

"Then why don't *you* take care of her? *You* can deal with her when she comes home pregnant."

"Don't shout at me." Rosa's voice was still calm. "Isn't that just like a man. All you can do is scream and hit, but when it comes time to accept responsibility, you leave it up to me. Then somehow it's my fault."

"Por Dios!" Arturo stormed out of the living room and rushed by Andreas and Karla without seeming to notice them. He opened the gate and slammed it shut as he was leaving. Karla just got a glimpse of his angry face in the light of the courtyard.

"What's going on here?" Andreas whispered as they walked inside.

Rosa was sitting at the dining-room table. She smiled at them weakly. "I'm sorry you had to witness this."

"What happened?" Karla sat next to her.

"Well, I'm not exactly sure myself. A friend of Arturo's told him that he had seen Manuela and a young man come out of one of the cheap hotels in the middle of the day. There's only one reason why they would be there."

"Oh god," Karla said. "Do you know the man?"

"It's actually the son of a friend of ours, a decent kind of boy. I suspected she was seeing someone. I just didn't realize it had gone that far already." Rosa sighed. "She just seems awfully young for this."

"She is seventeen, Rosa. This isn't that young by today's standards," Karla said.

"Perhaps not, but I'm worried about her. You know, I was about the same age when I got pregnant with Manuela. You may not even know, but Manuela isn't Arturo's child. I had her before I met him."

"What? No, I didn't know," Karla said, stunned. "I guess that explains why she looks so much like you. She doesn't resemble Arturo at all. But who is Manuela's father?"

"Some young guy I was in love with many years ago. When he heard I was pregnant, he just up and left. One of those. Anyway, when I met Arturo, Manuela was four years old. When I first went out with him, I was afraid to tell him about her, thinking he would leave me, as well. Finally, I had to tell him, of course. I still remember that. I was so afraid. I was really in love with him and didn't want to lose him."

"What was his reaction?"

"It was a surprise." Rosa put her hand on Karla's arm. "He told me that he, too, had a child, who lived in Switzerland. He shrugged and said, '*Así es la vida.*' That's life. He accepted Manuela without hesitation." Rosa smiled. "He's a good man. I know he comes across as somewhat stern and hard sometimes, but he has a good heart." She took Karla's hand. "You probably want to go to bed, but if you don't mind, I'll go and talk to Manuela for a moment."

"Sure, go ahead. I'm not tired at all right now."

When they were alone, Karla said to Andreas: "What a shock. I had no idea Manuela wasn't Arturo's child. Just makes me realize how little I know about my family."

"I wonder where Arturo went." Andreas got up from the table. "He's probably sitting in some bar getting drunk."

"No, I don't think he is the type. He's probably in church praying for the soul of his wayward daughter," Karla said.

"Talking about drinking ... want a beer?" Andreas went into the kitchen and got a few bottles of Cusqueña.

"Good idea." Rosa pointed at the bottles when she came back. "I need something to calm my nerves."

Andreas poured her a glass. "How is Manuela?"

"She's still upset, but at least she is a little more forthcoming with what's been happening. She now realizes that she needs my help. She is afraid Arturo won't let her see her boyfriend anymore."

"Would he do this?" Karla took a sip of beer. It was cool and strong and tasted slightly bitter.

"I don't think so. He'll calm down. You know, Manuela and Arturo may not resemble each other physically, but they are very similar in many ways. That's one of the reasons they often have such a hard time with each other. They are both stubborn and irrational."

Manuela was sitting in bed looking at a magazine when Karla came into the room. She had stopped crying but still seemed upset. Karla sat next to her and gave her a hug. "How are you?"

"How should I be?" Manuela snapped at her.

Karla flinched at her sister's apparent coldness. "I'm sure things will turn out all right. Rosa seems to understand you, and I know Arturo will come around."

"How do you know?" Manuela gave Karla an angry look. "You seem to be the only one he cares about, and you're not even part of the family."

Karla felt as if she had been slapped.

"I'm sorry, I didn't mean it that way. What I meant is, you don't live here."

"You're right, Manuela." Karla got up from the bed. "I'm not really part of your immediate family, but Arturo is my father, as well, whether you like it or not." She realized that Manuela resented Karla's relationship with Arturo. *How absurd.* Karla pressed her hands against her forehead, feeling a headache coming on.

"I'm sorry, I didn't mean to hurt you." Manuela got out of bed and hugged Karla.

"It's all right. Let's go to bed and talk about it tomorrow." Karla waved her off. When she was in bed, she couldn't fall asleep. She kept thinking about Manuela's remark. Of all the members of the family, she had always felt closest to her. They had kept in touch over the years, sending each other postcards and talking on the phone occasionally. Now, she was surprised to find out that Manuela might not like her as much as she thought she did. After tossing and turning, unable to fall asleep, she got up again. She put on her sweatpants and sweatshirt and went outside, trying not to wake her sister.

Standing on the balcony above the courtyard, Karla stared into the dark. What hurt her most was the fact that, in a way, Manuela was right with what she had said. Karla wasn't really part of the family. She was Arturo's biological but, nevertheless, illegitimate daughter. She was lucky that he had acknowledged and accepted her.

Karla sighed. *I'm tired of being someone's illegitimate child, someone's half sister, someone's niece.*

There was a slight creaking sound. The door to Andreas's room opened, and he stepped outside. "What are you doing out here?"

"I couldn't sleep."

"Why? Nervous?" Andreas stood behind her, kissed her neck, and began to massage her shoulders.

"Wonderful. That's just what I need." As Karla relaxed, tears rose to her eyes, and she gave a soft sob.

"What's the matter?"

"I'm just confused." Karla suppressed the need to cry and told Andreas about the incident with Manuela. "I know Arturo loves me. I just wish I could love him back. Instead, I feel inhibited around him and resentful."

Andreas put his arms around her. "Let's go downstairs. There we can talk."

In the living room they sat on the couch. Karla wrapped a blanket around her; as usual, it was cool at night. The room still smelled a little bit of the roasted alpaca meat they had eaten for dinner.

Andreas touched Karla's cheek. "Perhaps you're trying too hard. I mean, trying to relate to him like to a normal father. He wasn't, or isn't, a normal father."

Karla nodded. "I know." She took a deep breath. "As a little girl, when my mother and grandmother were still alive, I didn't really miss not having a father nearby. On the contrary, I found this handsome man in the photo fascinating. I was proud when people exclaimed how cute I was, how much I looked like my father. He was like a prince in a fairy tale."

"And now, the fairy tale is over and you realize your father is a flawed human being, like the rest of us," Andreas said.

Karla nodded. "Yeah, and sometimes I resent it when he treats me like his daughter, when he falls into his 'concerned-father' role. And yet, at the same time, I want him to be like a father. I know, this doesn't make sense."

"It makes perfect sense. But you're too impatient."

"What do you mean?"

"Look, Arturo seems like a decent man, somewhat of a macho, perhaps, but that probably has to do with his culture, his background. But compared to the asshole I had as a father, your father is an angel. The problem is you can't force yourself to love him. Love develops over time, and he wasn't around when you could've developed a loving relationship."

"So what am I supposed to do? Accept the fact that I don't love my father, turn around and go back to Switzerland?" Karla was getting irritated. Andreas made perfect sense, but his logic didn't alleviate her pain.

"No. I don't mean that." Andreas paused. "Do you know why your parents didn't stay together? Do you know what happened back then?"

"No, not really. My mother never told me. I was too young to understand it anyway. My aunt didn't know much, either."

"Now you've a chance to find out. Whatever happened back then, your father is responsible for you being here. Ask him. Talk to him. You have a right to know."

"Yes, I know. I guess I'm afraid to discover the truth. I'm afraid to find out that my parents didn't love each other enough to stay together although they had a child. I'm afraid to find out that I'm the product of a one-night stand or that my father was too selfish to marry my mother." Karla's voice trembled.

"But that's the only way you'll ever find peace or, perhaps, be able to develop a healthy relationship to your father. And if it turns out that he was one of those young punks who didn't take responsibility for his actions, then he must have changed. He seems to really care for you now. Then you have to ask yourself if you're able to forgive him. And if you can't ... well, then that's that, but at least you know. I'm sorry, I'm not a psychologist." Andreas shook his head and shrugged. "I solved my problems with my father by completely cutting him out of my life. Probably not the best solution."

That's no solution at all. "You're right. I need to talk to him." Karla hugged Andreas. "Thanks. You helped me make a decision. I love you."

"I love you, too. And if this thing with your father doesn't work out, well, then we still have each other." Andreas pulled her close and kissed her. Karla pressed herself against him. "I want to be with you tonight. Let's go to my room. I'm sure Antonio is fast asleep."

They quietly went upstairs. It was dark and cool in the bedroom. Andreas led her to the bed. They undressed quickly and slipped under the cover. He made her turn on her stomach and began to massage her shoulders, working his way down her back and kneading her buttocks. She turned around and felt his breath on her face, his hair tickling her breasts. Karla closed her eyes and felt the last bit of tension dissipate, giving way to a pleasurable warmth.

Later that night, Karla listened to Andreas's regular breathing and the small smacking sounds coming from little Antonio's mouth. *He's probably dreaming of ice cream.* She smiled as she drifted off to sleep.

It was still dark when Andreas nudged her. "You better get back before they catch us. I'm not sure I'm up for dealing with another family crisis." He switched on the lamp next to the bed. They checked on little Antonio, who was deep asleep with only his coarse black hair sticking out from under the cover. Karla pulled on her shirt and sweatpants, kissed Andreas, and tiptoed toward the door.

"Good night, Juliet," he whispered as he lay back down.

When Karla stepped outside, Arturo was just walking across the patio, putting on his jacket. He was probably going to early Mass. When he looked up at her, she was sure he had seen her come out of Andreas's room. "*Hola,*" she said quietly, unsure what his reaction was going to be.

"*Buenos días.*" Arturo gave her a questioning look. "You're up early," he said and went on his way.

Karla stood outside for a while, inhaling the fresh air and watching as dawn began to spread. It had rained a little the evening before, the first time since their arrival. The cool air, the smells of the neighborhood, a mixture of damp grass and smoldering wood the neighbor had burnt in his yard, it all felt more and more like home. The sky on the horizon was tinged with purple, and a whitish glow lit up the mountains in the distance. In spite of the turmoil of the past night, she was overcome with a feeling of elation. *This landscape, these people, they are all part of my heritage. Nobody can take this from me.*

114

Chapter 17

"Antonio, stop playing with your food." Arturo gave the little boy a stern look. He had been unusually quiet all through breakfast. His normal scowl was intensified by a deep groove between his eyebrows.

Karla suspected that her father was still upset about the situation with Manuela and her boyfriend. Manuela was pale and looked dejected. Only Maria was her usual quiet and contented self. Rosa was friendly but seemed preoccupied. Andreas looked at Karla with a quick smile and raised his eyebrow, indicating that he, too, noticed the tension in the air, then focused his attention again at his plate of scrambled eggs. Karla took a sip of milk-coffee, which Elsa sweetened with vanilla and cinnamon. By now she had learned to enjoy its somewhat unusual taste.

Arturo glared at his son again. "Antonio, you don't seem to be hungry. Leave the table."

Antonio, all too happy to get away from his father's punishing looks, slid down from his chair and scampered out of the dining room. Karla watched, concerned, as Arturo finished his coffee and then looked around, tapping the tabletop with his finger.

Maria got up. "Papá, I have an early class."

Arturo nodded, then motioned with his head toward Manuela. "You can leave, as well."

Manuela gave her father a puzzled look. Karla, who had finished eating and felt increasingly uncomfortable around her father's foul mood, picked up her plate, excused herself, and started to follow Manuela.

"Karla, please stay here. I want to talk to you and Andreas." Arturo's voice was tense.

Karla sat again and looked at Andreas. *What now?*

Arturo pushed his coffee cup back and faced Karla. "I asked you and Andreas to sleep in separate rooms. I hope you respect my wish."

So this wasn't about Manuela but about her. Arturo had seen her come out of Andreas's room. Karla's first reaction was to make up some kind of excuse for her nightly visit, but the next minute she found her father's moral concern absurd. *How dare he treat me like a child?* She faced Arturo. "Papá, Andreas and I are adults. We are a couple. We're used to being together."

Arturo cleared his throat. "What you do in your own country is your own business. But here, under my roof, I expect you to adhere to our rules. Sleeping in the same room is not acceptable. You're not married yet."

Karla's irritation turned into anger. Her heart beat in her throat. "Not acceptable? You didn't seem to care about that when you slept with my mother, did you?"

There was an eerie silence in the room. Arturo's facial color deepened to a dark bronze. His usually full lips formed a thin line above his clenched chin. Karla felt Andreas's reassuring touch on her back.

"How dare you?" Arturo's voice sank to a whisper, then became loud again. "I'm your father. You owe me some respect."

"Respect? For what? Where have you been all these years? Where were you when I was a baby, a child? Now, you suddenly want to be my father and control me? Force your so-called morals on me?" Karla got up and crossed her arms in front of her chest. Her knees felt weak, but she couldn't hold back any longer. "You're a hypocrite."

Arturo leapt up from his chair and raised his arm. The next thing Karla knew was that Andreas stood between her and

Arturo. He held her with one hand and blocked Arturo with his other arm. "Don't you dare to hit her."

Karla gently touched Andreas's arm. "Andreas, please. It's all right." The fear of seeing a fight break out between Andreas and her father cooled her own anger.

The two men stared each other down. The color drained from Arturo's face. "You stay out of this. This is none of your business."

"It sure is. I won't let you hit my girlfriend."

"She's my daughter. You have no right to interfere. And I wasn't going to hit her."

"It sure looked that way," Andreas grumbled.

"Stop that nonsense." Rosa stepped between the two men. "Are you going to beat each other up like little boys, or can we deal with this in a civilized way?"

For a few seconds it was quiet in the room. The silence was interrupted by a soft voice. Someone was singing outside. It was Elsa. She often sang while doing housework. In spite of her age, she still had a beautiful voice, and she sang one of the traditional Andean songs. The melancholic tune stopped everybody in their tracks and melted the cold anger in the room.

Karla sat and burst into tears. Arturo slumped in his chair and bent his face into his hands. Andreas stepped back.

Rosa spoke in an emphatic tone: "You're wrong about your father, Karla. You two need to talk." Then she turned to Andreas. "I know things are different in your country and our customs may not make sense to you, but you live here now and we expect that you honor our rules. We asked you to sleep in different rooms because we have two young girls. If we let you stay together, that would signal to them that it's okay. Unfortunately, there is a double standard in this society. It may be all right for men to sleep around. However, there is a different code of ethics for young women. An unmarried girl who gets pregnant has a very tough time here. We don't want this to happen to our children."

Rosa gently touched Karla's arm. "And not all men are as loyal as your father is."

"We didn't mean to be disrespectful." Andreas's tone was calm again. "Karla was unhappy last night, and that's why I asked her to come into my room, to console her."

Arturo nodded, then looked at Karla. "I'd like to talk to my daughter alone. If I may still call her my daughter."

Karla had never seen Arturo so downcast. Her father wasn't a tall man, but he normally kept himself straight and exuded authority and control. Now, however, his shoulders slumped. He looked vulnerable. Karla started to feel sorry for him.

Rosa and Andreas got up. Andreas put his hand on Karla's shoulder. "I'll be in the next room if you need me."

After they left the room, Arturo faced Karla. "Karla. I don't know what your mother and your family told you, but I tried to be as good a father to you as was possible under the circumstances. You have to believe me."

"I'm sorry, but nobody ever told me what happened back then. All I know is, I grew up without a father and then I lost my mother, as well. You weren't around. I thought that ... perhaps, when my mother got pregnant, you didn't want to marry her."

"Did your mother tell you this?"

"No, she always spoke highly of you when I was little. But later I thought that, perhaps, she did that to protect me."

"Karla, I didn't even know Laura was pregnant. I only heard about it weeks after she had left. When she told me, I offered to marry her."

"You did?" Karla was stunned.

"Yes." Arturo nodded. "I wanted to do the right thing. I would've gone through with it if she had agreed. When she turned me down, I was sad ... sad and relieved." Arturo opened his hands, then pressed his palms together. "I was sad to know that you'd grow up away from me, that I wouldn't be part of your life. I lost my own father really early, so I know what it feels like to grow up without a father. I was also relieved, I have to admit. I had my first paid job before graduate school. I made very little money. Your mother wouldn't have been happy living here with what I was able to offer her. I thought that perhaps later, when I had a decent job, there would be a chance. But that was a pipe dream. We didn't have the kind of close connection that would've survived being away from each other for an extended period of time."

Arturo exhaled deeply. "Laura and I ... we were young, we were in love, but it wasn't the kind of love mature people feel for each other. We didn't think of the future. We were careless and irresponsible.

"I tried to stay in touch with you as much as possible. I know it wasn't enough. When your mother died, I wanted to bring you back to Peru with me. I discussed it with your aunt, but we decided it would be too traumatic for you to go and live in a totally foreign country with people you didn't know."

Karla nodded. "I'm sorry for accusing you. It was unfair. There is just so much I don't know about you and Mama. And as far as Andreas and I are concerned, I understand what you mean. If you want us to stay in separate rooms, we will. Don't worry."

Arturo sighed. "Perhaps I'm paranoid. I'm trying to shield my children from having to go through the same turmoil Rosa went through when she got pregnant. Or your mother and I, for that matter." He paused, then continued with a weak smile. "I'm afraid I'm going about it the wrong way."

Karla put her hand on his arm. "Papá, you and Rosa should talk to Manuela openly and get to know her boyfriend. Just telling her not to see him won't help."

Arturo nodded. "I'm not that naïve. I know they'll continue to see each other, unless I lock her up or put her in a convent, which

I'm not about to do. I'll have to talk to Rosa about it. She's a lot more levelheaded and reasonable about this than I am."

Karla was touched by the fact that her father confided in her and admitted his insecurities, so unlike his normal commanding behavior. "I'm sorry."

"It's okay. We should've talked a long time ago." He gave her a hug. Outside, they heard Elsa sing again, a *wayu*, a Peruvian love song in Quechua. It sounded a little off-key, but her voice brought out its tender message nevertheless.

Chapter 18

It was five thirty in the morning when Karla got up. It took all the energy she could muster to get out of bed, but she had decided to go to early Mass with Arturo. Ever since the confrontation the other morning, Karla had tried to spend time alone with her father, and he seemed to have the same need. The outburst and the subsequent talk had cleared the air and brought issues to the front they had never dealt with until then. Karla felt that participating in a ritual that was important to her father might give her the opportunity to get to know a side of him she wasn't familiar with.

Karla didn't consider herself religious. As her aunt had told her, she had been baptized in a Catholic church, mainly to please her mother's father, who had been Catholic. Her aunt hadn't belonged to any of the official churches, but she had let Karla take part in Catholic ceremonies as long as Karla had shown an interest, which hadn't been for very long.

Karla grabbed her jacket and went downstairs. Arturo was already waiting for her. They walked to the cathedral at the Plaza de Armas, which opened for worship at six o'clock in the morning. The church was close to Arturo's office, which enabled him to attend Mass on his way to work.

The city hadn't woken up yet, and Karla enjoyed the relative calm. It was a crisp, fresh morning after a night of light rain. The smells of fresh bread coming from the bakeries and detergent with which the cobblestone pavement in front of the stores was washed, mixed with an occasional whiff of urine, seemed more pronounced in the early morning than during the rest of the day. The rising sun colored the sky above the statue of *El Cristo* on the hill a soft purple.

With only few worshippers at this early hour, there was a hushed silence in the cathedral. Karla marveled at the ornate decorations and the huge bouquets of fresh flowers, so unlike the rather austere Catholic churches she was used to in Switzerland. She followed Arturo and went through the ritual of dipping her finger into holy water, bending her knee, and making the cross.

They kneeled next to each other on the wooden kneeler in front of the bench. When Karla's knees began to hurt, she sat. She discreetly observed her father, who was still kneeling and praying. Although she didn't share his religious fervor, she was touched by his devotion.

The ceremony consisted of a short sermon, in Spanish as well as in Quechua, interspersed with prayers, chanting and music, and the periodic ringing of a small bell. In the end, there was a short piece of Andean music with pan flutes. Karla listened to the soft tunes, which struck her as both beautiful and sad and brought tears to her eyes.

When Arturo gently nudged her, they got up and left the church. Arturo gave some money to a beggar woman outside. "Are you hungry?" he asked Karla.

"Not really, but I wouldn't mind some coffee or tea."

"Let's go over there." He pointed to a coffee shop across the street that served European-style espressos and cappuccinos.

They sat at one of the tables in an alcove on the second-floor balcony. It was a holiday, and by now, the city had come to life. The smell of exhaust fumes from the many old cars had intensified. The Plaza de Armas filled up with locals as well as tourists. Street vendors offered their wares to tourists. Little kids, always with one eye on the police, tried to sell postcards.

Karla watched the hustle and bustle for a while. She took a sip of coffee, then put her hand on her father's arm. "Papá, tell me about the time you were with my mother. I don't know anything about your relationship with her."

Arturo looked down at his hands. "It's been such a long time," he finally said in a low voice, as if talking to himself. Then he glanced at her. "Let's go to my office. It's closed today. We have more privacy there."

The tourist agency Arturo managed was in a side street off the plaza. They climbed a narrow staircase to the second floor. The business consisted of three small offices and a reception area. The walls were decorated with photos and maps of Machu Picchu as well as other sites in Peru. Arturo unlocked his office, a small room with a desk, a computer, a few bookshelves, a coffee table, a small sofa, and a couple of chairs.

While Arturo opened his desk and searched through the drawers, Karla looked out the window at a street lined with small stores and curio shops.

"Here they are." Arturo picked up an envelope, gave it to Karla, and sat on the sofa. "I kept the pictures."

Karla sat next to him and pulled out a bunch of photos. The first one showed a young couple sitting at the Plaza de Armas in Cusco. Karla recognized a much-younger version of Arturo next to a slender girl with long, reddish-blond hair. More photos followed. Arturo and Laura, her mother, in different places in Peru, smiling happily at Karla: Arturo on a stone slab at Machu Picchu, Arturo and Laura in the Sacred Valley of the Incas, Laura smiling from underneath a wide-brimmed sun hat next to a stand at the market in Pisac.

As Karla looked at the two young people in love, so happy together, she felt a great longing. Why was it that so little of their happiness, of their togetherness, had come down to her? She was the outcome of that time of love, and yet both of them had abandoned her. She tried to imagine a third person in the picture, a smiling little girl sitting between the man and the woman. At the thought of this, she covered her face with her hands and began to weep.

She felt her father's hand on her back. "What's the matter, Karla?"

Karla lifted her head. "I'm sorry, Papá. I missed out so much by not being able to be together with you and my mother. As a child, I always dreamt of having a normal family like the other children around me." Her voice broke. She searched her purse for Kleenex.

Arturo gave her his handkerchief. "I'm so sorry that it all turned out this way." He took her hand in his.

"I'm not trying to blame anybody," Karla said. "My aunt was a wonderful guardian. I couldn't have wished for a better person to take care of me. She really tried hard to be a mother. I owe her so much. But I often felt this great longing for something I couldn't even put my finger on. I was homesick for a past I didn't have." Karla suppressed a sob.

Arturo hugged her. "I know, Karla. It wasn't easy for me, either, knowing that I had a daughter so far away, whom I'd never get to know really well. We can't make up for lost time, but I'm happy you're here now and I hope you'll come back often."

Karla put her hand on Arturo's. "Tell me something happy about you and Mama, something I can keep as a memory of you both."

Arturo thought for a moment, then smiled. "I can still see Laura when we first met. I was working at a different tourist office at the time. It was actually my first real job after college, before going on to graduate school. One day she and her travel companion came in to book a few trips. She was a slender, beautiful girl with very long, reddish hair and dark blue eyes. You inherited her figure, although you got my eyes and hair." Arturo gently touched a strand of Karla's black hair.

"In some ways, she looked like the typical young European tourist I dealt with a lot. However, there was something different about her that caught my attention right away. She was a serious young woman. She asked me questions about certain places the everyday tourist wouldn't normally ask, questions I sometimes couldn't answer. I could tell she had studied Peruvian history before coming here and was eager to know more. Laura and her friend came back several times. I tried to think of a way to get together with her. I was attracted to her, and I felt that she liked me, too.

"Luck was on my side. One day the two of them invited me to dinner to thank me for the good deals I had given them. During that dinner I suggested we take an overnight trip together to the Sacred Valley and I would show them a few of the lesser-known places tourists normally didn't go to. They agreed right away, and I began to organize the trip. The night before we were set to go, her friend got sick. At first, Laura didn't know if she wanted to cancel the trip or if just the two of us should go. I prayed, of course, that she wouldn't cancel. I realized that this would be the perfect opportunity to be alone with her. I have to admit, I was kind of glad her friend got sick."

"That wasn't very nice of you." Karla jokingly shook her finger at him.

"I know, I know, but what can I say?" Arturo smiled. "Anyway, she decided she did want to go. I was, of course, very happy." He paused, then continued in a wistful tone. "It was during that trip that I really fell in love with her."

Arturo lowered his head, then gave Karla a quick glance. "You know, Karla, you may not have had a normal family, but you're not an unwanted child. The first time I saw a photo of you, I loved you." He smiled. "You were still tiny, but I could already tell you were going to be pretty like your mother. And you also looked like me. How could I have denied you?" He squeezed her hand. "And don't forget, your roots are in the Sacred Valley of the Incas. That should make you proud."

"It does. Thank you for sharing this with me." Karla hugged her father. As she looked into his eyes, she saw again the bronze circles surrounding his pupils. They were of a slightly lighter color than the centers of the pupils. She had the same marks in her eyes. They were a sign that united them.

"Why don't you keep the photos?" Arturo said.

"Not all of them, just a few." Karla picked out a few pictures and put them in her purse.

It was close to ten o'clock. Karla walked back to the Plaza de Armas and sat on the stone steps in front of the fountain, trying to recover from the emotional morning. She pulled the photos out of her purse and looked at them again. For the first time in all these years since her mother's death, she felt a deeper-than-usual connection to her parents. She had a story now she could cherish, that was based in reality and not merely in her imagination. When she looked up from the pictures, she saw Andreas walking toward her.

"Well, finally. We thought we had lost you guys for good." He sat next to her. "Where have you been?"

"First, we went to early Mass, and then—"

"You went to early Mass?" Andreas laughed out loud.

"Yes, believe it or not. I just wanted to be with my father."

Andreas looked at the photos in her hand. "Is that them?"

"Yes." Karla handed him the pictures.

"Wow, look how young Arturo looks. Your mother was very pretty. Not as pretty as you, though." Andreas gave the photos back to her. "So, how is it going with you and your old man?"

Karla gave a sigh, then nodded. "Today was the first time I felt he was my father, my true father."

"That's great." Andreas kissed her and smiled. "You do look happier." He brushed his hand through her hair. "By the way, you missed a few things while you were gone. Manuela's boyfriend came over. He seems like a nice guy. I guess they decided to do their homework together at Arturo's house.

"Rosa also said that it was all right for us to sleep in the same room. No need to keep up the pretense of virginity until marriage anymore, since your younger sister had already broken the taboo. Rosa was really funny the way she put it. However, there was a little unforeseen problem." Andreas sighed.

"Antonio?" Karla asked.

"Yeah. The moment he heard it, he started to cry so pitifully that I had to promise I'd continue to stay in his room and tell him good-night stories. I'm sorry, I probably blew it. But we can still switch after Antonio is asleep."

"Andreas, you're such a softy. It's all right. We have plenty of time to be together."

Chapter 19

"We'll make an early riser out of you yet." Andreas rubbed Karla's shoulder as they walked out onto the street.

Karla yawned. "I hate to get up early. For this trip, however, I don't mind. We'll get to see some of the most beautiful places in Peru aside from Machu Picchu."

They were waiting outside the gate for Arturo, who had gone to fill up the car. He had taken the day off from work to drive them through the Valle Sagrado, the Sacred Valley of the Incas.

When Arturo came back, he pulled out a map and placed it on the hood of his Honda. "We have to decide on a few places to visit. We won't be able to see everything in one day. What are you interested in?"

Karla put her arm around him. "Papá, take us to some of the places you visited with my mother."

Arturo looked at her pensively, then smiled. "All right. Let's go." He folded the map, and they got into the car. As they drove through Cusco, Karla wondered once again how her father managed to steer his car through the narrow streets in which drivers competed with one another to see how many traffic rules they could ignore without getting into trouble.

When they reached the outskirts of the city and drove through open countryside, she began to relax. The colors of the mountainous landscape, with its deep canyons of purple and orange rocks, where stretches of forest took turns with lush green fields and meadows, were striking at the end of the rainy season. Karla rolled down the window and inhaled the fragrance of eucalyptus trees and pines.

After about an hour's drive, they arrived at a hill overlooking the Urubamba River, or *Rio Wilcamayu*, Sacred River, as the river between Pisac and Ollantaytambo was also called. Arturo stopped the car at the side of the road where they had a good view of the city of Pisac.

They got out of the car. Arturo took Karla by the arm and pointed at the mountain above Pisac. "Laura had an interesting guidebook. It showed how some cities and towns were laid out in the shape of a sacred animal. The outline of early Cusco, for instance, resembled a puma. The book also showed how the Incas integrated their buildings, ceremonial platforms, agricultural

127

terraces, and other important places into the landscape so they adopted the forms of animals.

"The mountain over there is called Condor Mountain by some. See if you can make out the shape of the bird."

Karla and Andreas gazed at the mountain. "I think I see the head," Karla said. She pointed to the top of the mountain at a longish-shaped rock with a protrusion that looked like a beak. "But where is the rest?"

"Don't just focus on the natural parts," Arturo said. "Look at the terraces."

"Wings," Andreas exclaimed. "The terraces on the left and the right are the wings."

"Very good." Arturo smiled. "The condor is a huge bird and a scavenger, and according to some Andean beliefs, it was the guardian of the dead who carried the spirits of the departed to the other world. Interestingly enough, there are two cemeteries right next to the terraces. I didn't even know about that until Laura pointed it out to me."

"Oh my god," Karla whispered. "Do you realize how ominous this sounds? It was only five years later that she herself needed a guardian spirit of the dead."

Andreas put his arm around her. Nobody spoke for a while. They continued to gaze at the mountain. The meadow in front of them was filled with ornamental plants and sweet-smelling red, blue, and yellow flowers. On the hills along the agricultural terraces, Karla detected the ever-present potato and corn fields.

She took a deep breath. "No wonder they called this the Sacred Valley. This place is magical."

"Ready to move on?" Arturo held Karla's hand. "One of the next stops is Urubamba, where I introduced your mother to the sacred drink of *la Pachamama*, or Mother Earth, called *chicha*."

"What's that?" Karla asked.

"You'll see." Arturo gave a mysterious smile.

On the way to Urubamba, they stopped near the town of Calca. "I almost forgot something," Arturo said. "We stopped here, as well, your mother and I."

They got out of the car and climbed a short path up the hill. "Have you heard the myth of the two lovers who were turned into stone?"

"Yes," Karla said, excited. "I read it somewhere."

"Well, there they are."

The rocks Arturo pointed at did look like two people, and if you stretched your imagination somewhat, you could see the girl's long hair.

"How interesting." Karla turned to Arturo. "Do you know the story? I can't remember the details."

They sat on a rock in the meadow. "It basically goes like this," Arturo said. "A shepherd was herding the llamas that were to be sacrificed to the Capa Inca, the leader of the Incas. Two daughters of the Sun God, or Inti, were taking a walk across the meadow and came across the shepherd. It so happened that the older of the girls and the shepherd fell in love. However, it was impossible for the daughter of the highest being, the sun, to get married to a lowly shepherd. So the two lovers fled into the mountains, and for that they were turned into stone, as a punishment."

"How sad and how cruel," Karla said.

Arturo nodded. "Their love was doomed from the beginning. They didn't have a chance." He looked at Karla pensively, then sighed.

On the way to the car, Andreas put his arm around Karla and held her back. "I'd marry you, even if I was the Sun God and you a lowly shepherdess."

Karla gave him an impish look. "Wait a minute. You changed the story. I would be the daughter of the sun and you the lowly shepherd."

"Okay. So would you marry me anyway?"

"Not if we would be turned into stone. That would be terrible. We wouldn't be able to kiss or make love."

"True." Andreas squeezed her shoulder. "But in case we wouldn't be turned into stone. Would you marry me?"

Karla hesitated. "That's not fair. You put it in the conditional." She shook her head and walked to the car. Karla felt Andreas's way of trying to sound her out on how she felt about marriage was a little cowardly. At the same time, she was relieved not having to answer the question. *I love him, but marriage? Too early.*

In Urubamba, they had a late breakfast at one of the cafés owned by a friend of Arturo's. Urubamba was a fairly small town, so it didn't take them long to see it. Arturo showed them one of the markets where peasants and merchants sold everything from animals to potatoes to textiles to all kinds of tools.

This market wasn't geared toward tourists, but was a place where the locals sold and bought their stuff. It was a colorful sight. A wide variety of vegetables were spread out next to piles of yellow, red, and blue potatoes of all shapes and sizes. Karla's favorite corn, with its large kernels, simmered in huge pots. The smells of the animals, either in cages or roaming around freely, as well as those of the different foods and spices were overpowering at times.

Arturo stopped at one of the stands and pointed at a large pot filled with a pinkish liquid. He exchanged a few words in Quechua with the old, almost-toothless woman behind the table. She nodded and poured them three glasses of the drink.

"This is *chicha*. It's made of fermented corn. Be careful, it looks innocent, but it's quite potent." Arturo handed one to Karla. "Laura was such a serious girl, but after a glass of this, she was amused by everything she saw. I've never seen her giggle that much."

"You got my mother drunk?" Karla laughed. "How could you?"

"Not drunk, just a little tipsy. I didn't realize she had such a low tolerance for alcohol."

Andreas hollered. "Sounds just like the daughter."

Karla punched his arm. "Don't even go there."

After looking at the rest of the town, they continued along the road to Ollantaytambo and stopped in several places, looking at some smaller ruins Arturo knew about.

In Ollantaytambo, they drove through the lively city, where red-and-blue three-wheel motorcars were the perfect means of transportation for the narrow roads. They arrived at the Inca fortress and began to climb a steep stairway to the ruins above the agricultural terraces. When Karla reached the top, all out of breath, Arturo and Andreas were waiting for her.

"Look at this." Andreas pointed toward the mountain called Pinkuylluna.

High above the old town of Ollantaytambo was a huge rock in the shape of a human face, believed to be the profile of Tunupa, or Wiracocha, the legendary pilgrim preacher of knowledge. It was a work of art that integrated both the natural form of the rock and the man-made additions. The structure on top of Tunupa's head suggested his hat with four pointed corners, and the greenery at the bottom his beard.

They sat on the stones, relaxing and admiring the view of the town of Ollantaytambo and the surrounding mountains.

Karla pointed to the monument. "I'm fascinated by the way the Incas combined nature and art, how they used the natural setting and added just enough man-made elements to bring out the essence of what they wanted to display."

"True," Andreas said. "Besides, they were accomplished architects and stonemasons. The layouts and construction of their buildings are amazing." He turned to Arturo. "The way they fit huge, uneven boulders together without the use of mortar, like the walls at Sacsayhuaman, where you took me on the first day.

They must have had some ingenious rolling and assembly equipment to lift those big stones."

Arturo nodded. "Yes, and probably thousands of poor laborers who broke their backs and gave their lives to build those walls. A lot of what the Incas did is still a mystery to us. Remember, they didn't leave any written records, and what we know from the Spanish conquerors and chroniclers is extremely biased. This, of course, gave rise to a lot of conflicting ideas. The conquistadores vilified the Incas, and we modern Peruvians tend to glorify them.

"No doubt, the Spanish invaders were ignorant, crude, and extremely cruel. But the Incas weren't exactly angels, either. Many of their leaders were as power-hungry and vainglorious as our modern politicians are."

Arturo chuckled. "We glorify our ancestors, in part, because it bolsters our national pride. Peru is a poor country with many problems, and we long for a glorious past, a pre-Columbian civilization we feel is so vastly superior to our own troubled present. The problem is, we may glorify a past that, at least in part, is an illusion. Besides, the solution to Peru's problems doesn't lie in the past. It's not the conquistadores who are responsible for them, but our modern corrupt and inept leaders and the unwillingness of the powerful to deal with the extreme poverty in this country."

Karla looked at Arturo. The smile on his face had disappeared and was replaced by his normal scowl. She began understand the harsher side of her father. He lived in a country where making a living and taking care of a family was a constant battle unless you belonged to the few who had tons of money. There were almost no state-sponsored social programs for the less fortunate. You either survived or went under.

"In a way, I can understand that," Karla said wistfully. "I mean, longing for a past, even an imaginary one."

Arturo narrowed his eyes. "Yes, but you can't get trapped in the past, or you miss the present."

"Did you bring my mother here, as well?" Karla asked after a while.

Arturo nodded and his face softened. "Yes. I think we sat at the same place as we do right now." He was quiet and continued to gaze in the direction of the face of Tunupa.

Andreas squeezed Karla's hand and got up. "I'm going over there. I think that's a good spot to take pictures." He grabbed his camera and started to walk toward the other end of the terrace. Karla sensed he wanted to give her and Arturo some privacy.

Arturo looked after Andreas, then turned to Karla. "He is a nice man, and I can tell he loves you." He gave a quick smile. "And he's very protective of you. I was afraid he was going to hit me the other day."

"He wouldn't do that," Karla assured him. "I'm glad you aren't mad at him." She paused. "He does have a temper, though," she added with a sigh. "Tell me about the time you were here with my mother."

Arturo took Karla's hand in his. "It was foggy at first, just like this morning. We had to wait for a while to see Tunupa. Your mother was so excited when his face finally appeared. She had read all about him, and practically gave me a lecture. I listened somewhat impatiently. I was much more interested in her than in Tunupa."

Arturo laughed again quietly. The fine wrinkles around his eyes deepened. His usually tense face assumed a soft and dreamy expression, his voice trailed off, and he looked into the distance. He seemed to forget Karla's presence. Karla was moved by her father's sudden display of gentleness, a feature she hardly ever saw in him. As she inhaled, a soft sob escaped her. She felt his eyes on her.

"Does it make you sad when I talk about your mother?"

Karla shook her head. "No. I want you to talk about her. I have this need to know. I don't know if you understand this." She took a deep breath.

"Getting to know you, my parents, somehow helps me understand who I am. My whole life I've felt that I am missing an important part of my past. I didn't have any photo albums that I could look at and say, 'These are my parents, that's where we went on vacation, here we are at my graduation from primary school.' All I have are fading memories of my mother, a few pictures of her, and a couple of photos of you. Ever since coming here this time, I've tried to assemble a somewhat more complete picture of where I come from." Karla broke off, biting her lower lip.

Arturo hugged her. "I can't undo the past." His voice trembled a little. "All I can tell you is how much I love you and how much your being here means to me."

Karla nodded. "I'm so glad to be here. I'm finally starting to feel at home."

The sun was at its pinnacle, and the air was getting hot. Karla was beginning to feel sleepy. She leaned her head against Arturo's shoulder, and he put his arm around her. They sat next to each other without talking for a while. Karla sighed, then looked around. "I wonder where Andreas is."

"I saw him disappear behind that rock," Arturo said, pointing at a boulder at the end of one of the terraces.

"He's probably chasing after some stones. I keep losing him on this trip. When he sees something he is interested in, he forgets everything else," Karla said.

When they arrived at the end of the terrace, they spotted him. He was sitting down, writing or sketching something in his notebook.

Arturo stopped and held Karla back. He looked at her with a serious face. "We talk about the past a lot. I know it's important for you, for both of us. However, don't get stuck in the past." He motioned toward Andreas. "He's your future. He'll take care of you."

Karla looked at Arturo thoughtfully. His idea of a man taking care of a woman seemed outdated to her modern ideas about relationships. Arturo's words, however, resonated on a deeper level. They seemed fateful. Was Andreas her future? She remembered the dream she had had back in Switzerland, of the face of the Latin man turning into Andreas's face.

When Andreas saw them approach, he got up and put his notebook away. Karla went up to him, put her arms around him, and hugged him. "I love you," she whispered.

He smiled at her. His eyes were an intense green. "Love you, too." They kissed.

When they got ready to leave, Karla saw that her father was halfway down the hill, walking toward the car.

Tired from the day's activities, they drove back to Cusco without talking much. Arturo had to focus on the narrow, curvy road filled with potholes. The sun was setting, and Karla was moved once again by the transformation of the landscape. "Can we stop for a moment, please?"

Arturo parked the car, and they got out and looked on as twilight did its magic.

"Look at how the colors change," Karla said.

They watched as the vibrant greens of the fields darkened and the mountains turned from reddish brown to orange to vermilion to deep purple. The shadows lengthened and poured into the crevices along the folded rocks. Above the dark surface of a lake in the distance, the snow-covered mountains lit up once more before they, too, faded into the night. The sun left a band of intense crimson in the sky along the horizon, as if to remind the world that it will rise again.

Karla put her arm around Arturo. "Thanks so much for taking us on this trip. This is breathtaking. I'd like to come here and paint."

"She's having an artist's moment," Andreas explained, as Arturo smiled at Karla's enthusiasm. "I bet you don't even see all this anymore since you are so used to it."

Arturo nodded. "You're right. We just take it for granted."

Chapter 20

The last couple of weeks of Karla and Andreas's stay in Cusco passed quickly. The family went all out to make the remaining days as memorable as possible. Rosa and the girls took Karla to the markets in town to buy gifts to take home with them. When Arturo was at work and the girls were in school, Uncle Guillermo took Karla and Andreas to a couple of museums and other special places around town, most of the time with little Antonio in tow. He and Andreas had become inseparable. When Antonio got tired from walking—which happened after about five minutes into the outing—Andreas sat him on his shoulders, and the little boy proudly supervised the world from up high.

During the last week the women went shopping for the family party they had planned for the evening before Andreas and Karla's departure. It was going to be a big affair. Relatives and friends from surrounding towns and villages were invited. Rosa estimated there would be about fifty people, and Karla wondered how they would all fit into the house.

"We're going to eat outside in the courtyard," Rosa said. "We'll bring the tables out, and the kids can sit on blankets on the floor. It'll work out, you'll see." She sat at the table composing a list of things they had to buy.

Love of a Stonemason

They were going to have the traditional meal of guinea pig. Fortunately for Karla, the family didn't keep its own guinea pigs anymore, so at least she didn't have to witness them being slaughtered. On her last visit, she had watched Rosa and Elsa kill them. Although she realized that the procedure of quickly pulling their necks was no more painful than wringing the neck of a chicken, she didn't wish to witness it again.

The preparation for the party began at noon. Aside from the meat, they prepared different kinds of vegetables, rice, and a large variety of potato dishes. Karla, Manuela, Maria, and Elsa cleaned and chopped vegetables and washed potatoes until their hands hurt. Rosa dressed the meat and prepared the sauces to go with the different dishes.

In the late afternoon, the first guests arrived: Uncle Guillermo came with his wife and their little boy, Carlos; Arturo's uncles, aunts, and cousins; a few of Rosa's relatives who lived in Cusco; and lots of friends. The patio filled up fast. A few of the women were wearing their traditional colorful outfits of woven cloth, in all different shades of red mixed with green and blue. There was a lot of kissing, laughing, and backslapping. Since almost everybody brought a few kids, Antonio had a lot of playmates. Karla, who had met a few of the relatives during her stay ten years before, barely recognized them anymore. They had all either grown up or aged.

The eating, drinking, and celebrating lasted far into the night. When the last guests finally left, some of the small children were asleep, wrapped in blankets against the cool night. After everybody was gone, Rosa, Karla, and her sisters cleaned up, while Andreas and Arturo moved the furniture back inside. Afterward, Andreas picked up Antonio, who was asleep in a bundle of blankets, and carried him to bed.

Karla was moved by the care and patience he showed with the little boy. *He'd make a good father.* She wondered what it would be like to be married to him. She had thought about it ever since

Andreas had made the remark about marriage during their trip through the Valle Sagrado. Now, however, she thought about marriage for another reason. Her period was late, by more than the usual few days. It might be due to the change in climate and the traveling. She wasn't going to worry about it yet.

She went into the courtyard, where Arturo was putting the empty bottles into a trash bin. It was their last evening together, and she wanted to spend some quiet time with him. Arturo seemed to have the same thought. Karla got her jacket, and the two of them went for a short walk.

It was a clear night; the almost-full moon lit the surrounding landscape. During the week it had rained a little. Karla inhaled the moist air and realized, with a feeling of nostalgia, how much she had come to love this place.

Arturo put his arm around her. "We'll miss you, *mi hija*. Come back soon."

"I wish you could visit us once again," Karla said.

"It's difficult to get away. You know, the family and my business."

"I know, but you must have some vacation, as well. After all, you have a travel agency. You can stay with me, I have enough room."

"I'll think about it." Arturo put his arm around her. "If you and Andreas get married, I'll come over and attend the wedding. Unless, of course, you want to get married here."

Karla laughed. "I knew you'd bring it up again."

"I think he'd make a good husband. I probably sound like a broken record, but what's taking you guys so long to decide?"

"Papá, we haven't known each other that long, and we both are still getting our lives together. Andreas is working very hard to build up his business as a stonemason, so he'd be able to support a family." Karla figured that this would be a convincing enough argument for the traditional family man. "Besides, he hasn't asked me yet."

138

"He will. I can tell he loves you."

"Whatever happens, I promise I'll be back soon," Karla said. "The past few weeks have been one of the most important times in my life. They made me realize that I do have a family after all. Thanks for everything."

They hugged each other. When Arturo stepped back, his eyes were moist. "You are my daughter. We are your family, Karla. You'll always have a home here." He touched her cheek, then cleared his throat. "It's getting late. You need to get some rest before the trip back tomorrow."

Andreas and Karla were leaving in the morning for Lima, where they were going to spend a couple of days before returning to Switzerland. Karla dreaded the following day. The whole family would be at the airport in Cusco, and it would be an emotional farewell.

When she came into the bedroom, Manuela was already asleep. Karla bent down to kiss her lightly on the forehead. The girl stirred, opened her eyes, and looked at her sleepily. "Here you finally are." She yawned and checked her watch. "Two o'clock, already." She turned around and went back to sleep. Karla undressed and wrapped her blankets around her, trying to get warm.

When Rosa woke them the following morning, Karla felt as though she hadn't slept at all. She got up, splashed cold water on her face, and dressed, yawning constantly.

Downstairs, it smelled of coffee. Little Antonio was fussing because he was still tired and knew Andreas was going to leave. He held on to Andreas's pant leg and followed him everywhere.

"Come on, give Andreas some space," Rosa said. "He has to get ready."

"No." Antonio made a pouty face.

"It's all right, he doesn't bother me." Andreas picked the boy up. "Let's have some coffee."

Christa Polkinhorn

"No." Antonio hid his face on Andreas's chest and started to cry.

Karla, who had tried all morning to hold back her tears, began to cry, as well, and everybody else became teary-eyed.

"Come on, you guys, save this for the airport." Andreas tried to lighten up the mood, although his eyes glistened, as well. He put Antonio on his lap. "You know, I ran out of stories to tell you. I have to go back home to get some new ones."

A few minutes later, they heard Uncle Guillermo's booming voice. Karla was relieved, knowing he'd cheer everybody up. "Buenos días. Are we all ready for the big trip?" He kissed Karla. Fortunately, he had brought his little boy along. Antonio, happy to see his playmate, perked up again.

"We better leave, or they'll miss their plane." Arturo got up and went outside to start the car. They all piled into two cars, and arrived at the airport just in time to check in and proceed to the gate, which shortened the painful farewell somewhat. After a lot of hugging and kissing and promises to write and come back soon, Andreas and Karla paid the departure tax at the airport and went to their gate, waving back once more.

When they sat to wait for their plane, Karla leaned her head against Andreas's shoulder. "I am so glad this is over with. I hate good-byes. I'm so exhausted. I barely got any sleep last night."

"Same here," Andreas said, "but we better go. They just announced our flight."

Chapter 21

Karla looked out the window, savoring the last view of the tall mountain range of the Andes, where stark, brown fields took turns with patches of snow. In a way, she was relieved they were leaving. She was looking forward to being alone with Andreas once again, in their regular everyday life. It would take a while to digest all the impressions and emotions of the past several weeks.

"Are you sad?" Andreas put his arm around her.

"A little. Staying with my family has been such an emotional experience."

"I know."

"Andreas, you've been such a good sport putting up with everything. Here you traveled all the way to see Peruvian stone sculptures and ruins, and I dragged you into a Peruvian soap opera."

"Are you kidding? It was a wonderful trip for me, too. And as far as stone is concerned, I saw plenty of that. No, I don't regret anything. I really like your family, even the old patriarch, who turned out to be a nice guy after all. And besides, as my uncle always says: 'If you meet a girl, make sure you get to know her family. That way you find out what makes her tick.'"

"Great. I guess now you know why I'm crazy and overly emotional." Karla laughed. Then she sighed. "I wonder how Antonio is. He'll be lonely without you."

"I miss him, as well. He started to grow on me."

"You'd make a good father, Andreas."

"I don't know about that. Having to entertain a kid with a few stories in the evening and actually being responsible for him are two different things. I guess I could get used to it."

You may have to. Karla's period still hadn't started, and she was getting concerned. She decided to wait another few days before bringing it up, still hoping it was only delayed.

The flight attendant came by with snacks and beverages. Karla sipped her papaya juice, then leaned back in her seat, exhausted from lack of sleep. When she woke up again, the plane was descending toward Lima.

In Lima they took a cab to the same hotel in Miraflores they had stayed in before. As usual, the fog hung in big sheets over the city, but there were a few patches of blue sky visible.

After checking into their rooms, Karla let herself fall onto the bed. "I think I need to take a nap. I hope you don't mind. I'm still totally exhausted."

"That's fine with me. I'm pretty tired myself." Andreas lay down next to her. "After I put Antonio to bed, he woke up again and kept me awake half the night, wanting to hear more and more stories. I finally ran out of ideas."

"How come you know so many stories?"

Andreas yawned and stretched. "Uncle Alois was a great storyteller. That was actually our form of entertainment. We didn't have a TV until I was almost grown. So in the evenings and on Sunday afternoons, we usually played games or told stories. My uncle knows a lot of legends and myths from both the Ticino and the north. I think, though, quite a few of them he made up himself."

"I can just see him with his pipe and his *boccalino* of wine." Karla smiled. "My mother and grandmother, and later my aunt, told me stories, as well, mostly fairy tales. Those are actually my fondest memories of my childhood. I think none of the TV shows or the video games the kids play nowadays can come close to the art of storytelling as we experienced it. But perhaps we're just old-fashioned."

"No, you're right. I think something got lost. It wasn't just the stories. It was being together as a family, talking to each other rather than just sitting in front of a flickering screen.

"Anyway, it was interesting to see how Antonio reacted to the stories I told him. Most of them were probably foreign to him, although I tried to adapt them as much as possible to his culture. Remember the one about the Devil's Bridge?"

"Vaguely."

142

"There are many versions of the legend. In the one Uncle Alois told me, a farmer wanted to cross the river Reuss to visit his girlfriend. However, there was no bridge, and crossing the wild river was cumbersome and dangerous. So one day he called out: 'I wish the Devil would build a bridge here.' The Devil appeared and promised to build the bridge if he would get to keep the soul of the first living thing that crossed it. The farmer promised it, and the Devil built the bridge. After it was finished, the peasant sent an old goat across the bridge. The Devil, who, of course, expected a human being, was so upset at having been tricked that he tossed a huge boulder at the bridge, trying to destroy it. He missed, and the rock fell into the river, where supposedly it still is today.

"Anyway, I changed the story somewhat and made the Devil into a Spanish conquistador, the farmer into a campesino, and the river, of course, is the Urubamba. It goes something like this: A campesino wants to cross the Urubamba River to visit his *novia*. Unfortunately, there is no bridge. So he calls out: 'I wish the Devil would build a bridge.' At that moment, a conquistador on his horse appears. He tells the peasant he'd build him a bridge if he would let him have the first eighteen-year-old female who crosses the bridge to use as his slave. After the bridge was built, the campesino sent an eighteen-year-old female alpaca across. It was so old it could barely walk. The conquistador was furious. He got off his horse, picked up a huge stone, and tossed it at the bridge. While doing so, he slipped, fell into the river, and drowned. The campesino took back his alpaca and the conquistador's horse and lived happily ever after.

"Antonio loved this story. He wanted to hear it again and again. And you know the little guy is smart. Sometimes I changed something, forgetting what I had told him before. He noticed it right away and corrected me."

"You're so good with children. You'd really make a good father."

"You said that before, honey. Are you trying to tell me something?"

"No, no, it's just something I noticed." Karla yawned. "Let's sleep for a while." She snuggled up to him. Now would be the perfect time to tell him about her fear of being pregnant. However, she was simply too tired to deal with possibly another family drama.

The following morning they visited a few churches and an art museum in central Lima around the Plaza de Armas. Karla, however, wasn't as enthusiastic about looking at art as on their previous visit. She was preoccupied, trying to find a good opportunity to tell Andreas about her concerns. She would have to tell him now—her period was over ten days late.

Andreas noticed she was distracted. "You don't seem to be enjoying yourself. What's wrong?"

"I'm just a little tired from all the sights. Let's go back to El Parque del Amor and relax for a while." Karla felt that might be a good spot to give him the news.

They took a taxi back to Miraflores and walked, once more, along the coastline toward the park, then sat on the stone steps next to the sculpture. The morning mist and fog had disappeared, and the sun was out. Karla closed her eyes, letting the sun warm her face for a while, then sighed.

"What is it, Karla? Something is bothering you, I can tell," Andreas said. "Are you still sad about leaving?"

Karla took a deep breath. "I don't know how to tell you this. My period is late, more than the usual few days."

"Uh-oh," he simply said. Then after a moment: "How late?"

"Over ten days."

Another "Uh-oh." Then: "I thought an IUD was safe."

"It's supposed to be, at least ninety-seven to ninety-eight percent, or something like that. It has always worked so far. I don't want to worry you too much, it could just be the change in climate or the traveling."

"Hmm, you could also be among the two to three percent of the women who get pregnant anyway."

"I guess it's possible."

Andreas was quiet. Karla leaned her head against his shoulder, waiting for a reaction. Feeling his body shake, she thought for a split second that he was crying, then realized he was laughing. She looked at him, confused.

"I'm sorry. I know this is serious. But isn't this ironic? We complained and sneered about your family's seemingly outdated ideas about sleeping together, and now ... we're the ones in trouble." Andreas stopped laughing, then shook his head. "Shit. I'm going to be a father? We should've used those condoms after all." He stared out onto the ocean.

"I guess I could have an abortion," Karla said, her voice trembling.

"What? Are you crazy?" Andreas faced her. His expression was a mixture of shock and excitement. "No way are you going to have an abortion."

"But what are we going to do if I'm pregnant?"

"We're getting married, that's what. We're going to do this right. I don't want my child to grow up in a half-assed family like you and I did." Andreas spoke vehemently. He brushed through his tousled hair, then pressed his hands together and cracked his knuckles.

"I don't want to get married just because I'm pregnant." Karla put her hands on Andreas's to stop him from making the cracking sound she hated.

"That's not the only reason," Andreas protested. "We love each other, don't we? At least, I know I love you."

"I love you, too," Karla said. "I've been thinking about marriage lately, ever since you asked me in that roundabout way if I'd marry you if you were a shepherd. But you didn't really mean that, did you?"

"Yes, I did." Andreas gave her a quick glance. "I admit I was too chicken to ask you outright. I was afraid you might say no. But now I'm serious. Would you ... I mean, do you want to marry me?"

Karla smiled. "Yes." She sighed. "I just didn't want it to be that rushed. It would've been nice to be able to prepare for it. I mean, there's a lot to think about—how we would support a family, for instance."

"Well, we're not even sure you're actually pregnant. And if you are, things will work out somehow. I always have some kind of paid work. You'd work at home most of the time anyway, with or without a baby. We'll be fine."

"God, Andreas. I'm so relieved you take it that well." Karla hugged him. "You're wonderful. You make me feel safe. You're the rock in my life."

Andreas hugged her and laughed. "Unpolished rock." He kissed her. "Don't worry, I'll keep you safe."

They walked back to the hotel without talking much. Every once in a while Andreas cracked his knuckles again. Karla took his hand in hers. *He's worried.*

When Karla was lying in bed that night, she thought back to the past few weeks of their trip. It was the first time they had been together on a daily basis and had gotten to know each other more deeply.

In many ways, they were the opposite. She was quick-tempered, high-strung, and impatient. Aside from his occasional angry outbursts, Andreas was easy-going, slow-moving, and thoughtful. He could take forever admiring the shape and color of a rock, feeling its texture. Being with him, Karla was forced to slow down and appreciate the moment more. Occasionally, however, it got to be too much. If she hadn't constantly egged him on during their trip, they would have missed most of their bus and flight connections.

Andreas was voluptuous, a seeker of pleasure, a lover of the world of the senses, but he also had a spiritual leaning. He admired a religious painting in a church with the same enthusiasm as he savored the view of a sunset, the taste of a piece of roasted chicken, or the scent of her body when they made love. It was those qualities she found so attractive in him.

Karla smiled as she slowly drifted off to sleep. In the middle of the night, she woke up and felt the familiar pulling and pain in her abdomen. When she went to the bathroom, she noticed that her period had finally started. Although she was relieved, she also felt a little disappointed. She had almost gotten used to the thought of having a baby. She went back to bed and decided not wake Andreas. It would be early enough to tell him in the morning.

"What a pity," Andreas said the next morning. "I've already begun to think of names."

"You're disappointed?"

"Yes, a little, but to be honest, I'm also relieved. It does give us a little more time."

"What kind of names were you thinking of?" Karla yawned and stretched.

"Well, for a boy, something like Arturo, after your father, or Onyx, Opal, Jaspis, Serpiano, and for a girl, Jade or Kristal or Karla."

"Andreas, those are all names of stones, except for Arturo and Karla."

"Yeah, so what's wrong with that? Arturo, by the way, is the Italian or Spanish version of Arthur, which goes back to Celtic origins and means stone or bear. I looked that up somewhere."

Karla shook her head. "Honey, I'm not going to give my children stone names. Are you out of your mind? The other kids would make fun of them. Arturo is fine, but the rest, forget it."

"Okay, okay, let's forget about baby names for the time being." Andreas sat on the bed next to her, burying his hand in her long hair, stroking it gently. "What do you think Arturo and Rosa are going to say when we tell them we're engaged?"

"I know they'll be delighted," Karla said, "especially Arturo. He has made several remarks about it. However, they're not going to be satisfied until we are permanently bound to each other, preferably through a Catholic wedding."

"Uhhh, I don't know about taking it that far. Imagine, we'd have to go to confession."

"You're right. Forget it. We'd never make it out of the confession booth."

In the afternoon Andreas and Karla went shopping for a few last gifts in a large mall in central Lima, which specialized in indigenous handicraft. Whenever they passed a shop that sold baby clothes, they smiled at each other.

"We could get a few things, for the future," Andreas suggested, as he held up a colorful handwoven little girl's dress.

"I think it's a little early. We wouldn't even know if it was a girl or a boy," Karla objected.

"I guess you're right." Andreas put the dress back.

While Karla searched through a collection of CDs of Andean music, Andreas, who had been checking out a display of Peruvian stones, tapped her on the shoulder. "Listen. I saw something in a store farther back I want to look at again. Why don't I meet you at the coffee shop over there in, let's say, half an hour. Okay?"

Before Karla could say anything, Andreas was gone. "Great," she said to herself. "Here he goes again. No telling when he'll be back." She continued to browse, thinking that perhaps Andreas wanted to get her a gift. When he did show up after about half an hour, she was surprised that he was on time for once.

"Did you find what you wanted?" Karla asked.

"Nah." Andreas shook his head.

148

Karla was a little disappointed. *No gift, I guess.*

It was their last evening in Lima. After an early dinner, they went to El Parque del Amor since Andreas insisted on seeing *El Beso* one more time.

They were sitting on the steps behind the sculpture, watching the sun sink into the Pacific Ocean. The cumulus clouds along the horizon intensified the sunset glow. The colors of the sky ranged from yellow to a fiery orange. The ocean was a deep indigo blue, almost black, whereas the waves that broke on the beach lit up in white and bottle green.

Andreas cleared his throat. "Well, now that we aren't forced to get married ..." He stopped.

Karla looked at him, surprised. *Is he trying to back out?*

"Let's do this the right way." He bent his knee in front of her. "May I ask your hand in marriage, beautiful Daughter of the Sun? I'm only a lowly shepherd, but I sold a llama, so I can give you this." He pulled out a tiny box from his pocket and gave it to her.

"Andreas" was all Karla managed to say. She opened the box, which contained a ring, a silver band with a blue-and-green-sprinkled stone, a Peruvian opal. "How beautiful," she whispered.

"Try it on. I hope it fits. It's adjustable." Andreas was still kneeling.

Karla heard someone clapping and turned her head. An older couple nearby was watching the little ceremony with smiling faces. The man was applauding. "*Felicitaciones.*"

Karla embraced Andreas, then tried to pull him up. "Thank you so much. But please stop kneeling. I think we're the spectacle of the evening."

Andreas sat next to her and motioned at the sculpture. "What better way to honor Víctor Delfín." He kissed Karla, which evoked a further round of applause from the audience.

PART THREE

FISSURES

Chapter 22

After returning from Peru, Andreas moved into Karla's *rustico*. He was able to rent an additional small building, a former barn, adjacent to Karla's house, and converted it into his studio. It seemed like the perfect solution. They both lived together but had their separate working spaces.

At first, the new arrangements took some getting used to. They had to adjust to each other's living patterns and idiosyncrasies. Andreas tended to be messy, and soon the small house was cluttered with his shirts, pants, and shoes. Karla tried to be tolerant. One morning, however, still groggy from sleep, she stumbled over a hammer Andreas had left on the kitchen floor and shouted at him.

"I'm sorry." Andreas put the hammer on the kitchen table. Seeing the look on Karla's face, he lifted his hands in a gesture of submission. "Okay, okay. I get the point." He grabbed the tool and carried it outside.

After a few sips of espresso, Karla's mood improved. "Sorry I yelled at you," she greeted Andreas when he came back and gave her a cautious look. She hugged him.

He slid his hands under her blouse. "I know just the thing to get you into a better mood."

Aside from the initial problems Karla and Andreas experienced while learning to live together, the first few months after their trip to Peru were an exciting and intensely creative period for both of them. Andreas carved a series of stone plates and blocks that were inspired by the petroglyphs in the desert. Instead of the Peruvian indigenous symbols, he created patterns of European runes, which he cut into volcanic rock.

Karla's landscapes assumed a new boldness and increased vivacity. She had brought back a sketchbook filled with paintings and drawings and new inspirations for her art. On a personal level, the visit had been gratifying as well as unsettling. It had strengthened the bond between her and her father. Before the insightful talks with Arturo, she had always seen her mother as the victim, who had tried to raise a child by herself without the help of a husband. Now, she began to question her mother's actions.

"Why did she reject my father?" Karla asked. She was taking a break from painting and was watching Andreas carve letters onto a tombstone. "And why did she never take me to see him when I was little, so I could at least get to know him? How selfish."

"Perhaps she didn't have the money." Andreas looked up from his work. "Two tickets must have been expensive, and she couldn't very well let you travel alone."

"I'm sure her parents would've helped her. From what my aunt told me, my grandparents supported my mother financially and my father sent her money occasionally when he had some to spare."

"I don't know, Karla." Andreas sounded absentminded. He focused on his work again.

"Perhaps my mother was one of those women who felt that single motherhood was fine and children didn't need a father." Karla shook her head. "What's the use? She's dead. I can't ask her anymore."

Andreas picked up another chisel. "I'm sure your parents did the best they could at the time. You have to take them as they are." He went back to work.

Karla noticed the slight impatience in Andreas's voice. *Speak for yourself. You never even deal with your parents.* "I'm sorry, I won't bother you anymore." She got up.

Andreas put down his tools and faced her. "You're not bothering me. I just wish you could let it go. You finally feel better about your father. Don't start to doubt your mother now."

"Easy for you to say." Karla got up and walked back to her studio. She knew Andreas was trying to be helpful, but his down-to-earth advice irritated her. She needed someone to listen to her, not to tell her what to do and how to feel.

Chapter 23

It was spring, and the north wind had been blowing almost steadily for the past two weeks. The sky was a clear steel blue, and the sunlight harsh and blinding. At night, the wind howled around corners, rattling shutters. While Andreas seemed unperturbed by the noise, Karla lay awake half the night, tossed and turned, and fell asleep only in the early morning when the wind calmed down for a few hours. Lack of sleep and headaches began to affect her mood. She was irritable and depressed. Nothing seemed to help, neither Andreas's massages nor the painkillers she took occasionally.

Normally, once the wind calmed down again, her headaches disappeared and her mood improved. This time, however, Karla was faced with another problem. Her painting had stagnated. The creative enthusiasm after her trip to Peru was fading, and her experimenting with different media and styles hadn't led to anything she felt really good about. Her landscapes had become more vivid and expressive, but they were still basically the same landscapes she had painted for years.

Instead of the excitement she usually felt when starting a new painting, she stared at a fresh canvas with a blank mind. She filled it with large blobs of oil paints and was disgusted with the result.

One morning, she decided to continue the series of more experimental paintings she had begun before Peru. She tried her hand at collages, combining unusual objects with natural scenery. After a few unsuccessful attempts, she took a large brush and, in an attack of frustration, splashed paint all over the canvas. Tears of frustration filled her eyes. "This is all shit," she screamed. "It has no meaning."

Andreas, who had just come in from his workshop and washed his hands, looked at her, puzzled. He stood next to her and pointed at the canvas with the paint splashes. "This is interesting."

"Stop making fun of me," Karla yelled and burst into tears.

Andreas stared at her and shook his head. "I'm not making fun of you. There's a technique where painters throw paint at a canvas on purpose—"

"Yes, I know," Karla snapped. "That's not what I'm trying to do."

"Then what *are* you trying to do?"

"I don't know. That's the problem. I've been trying to paint something meaningful for weeks. It doesn't happen. I don't know what to do anymore." Karla suppressed a sob.

"Why don't you paint more of those landscapes? The ones you did after Peru are fabulous."

"I'm bored with landscapes. I want something new."

"Perhaps you're trying too hard. Just paint and forget about meaning for a while."

"That's what I've been doing for weeks now, and it doesn't get me anywhere. Fact is, I can't paint anymore." Karla tossed her brush into the bowl of paint thinner.

"Honey, this is nonsense. But with that kind of attitude, you're sabotaging yourself."

"Andreas, leave me alone. I don't need your moral advice."

"For Christ's sake, I'm just trying to be helpful."

"Well, you're not being helpful."

156

"Sorry." Andreas got up and left, closing the door with a bang.

Karla covered her face with her hands. *Why do I need to take it out on him?*

What made Karla's lack of inspiration even more glaring and difficult to deal with was the fact that Andreas's period of intense creativity continued. He worked almost nonstop, carving and cutting stone and designing metal sculptures. The sounds of activity and seemingly boundless energy coming from his workspace—the scraping of the chisel against stone, the clonking of metal, the grinding of the polishing machine—exacerbated her feelings of worthlessness.

Karla walked over to Andreas's studio. He was sitting at his desk sketching something. He gave her a quick glance, then continued to work. Karla embraced him and brushed a strand of hair out of his face. "I'm sorry. I don't mean to snap at you. I'm just going through a hard time."

Andreas pulled her down on his knees and hugged her. "I know. I wish there's something I could do. Don't be so discouraged. Every artist goes through rough times. It has happened to me, too."

"That's hard to believe, the way you're working these days." Karla pointed to one of Andreas's stone plates. "Beautiful." She felt a stab of jealousy.

Back in her studio, Karla looked at the messed-up painting, shook her head, and took it off the easel. While putting it into the storage room, she came across the painting with the dark, lonely woman figure she had never finished. She had almost forgotten about it. Now, she took it out, leaned it against the wall, and looked at it.

"That's exactly the way I feel. Lost and worthless." A profound sadness rose from deep within her. She sat on the sofa and began to cry. Painful sobs shook her body. *I'm so afraid. What if I can never paint again? This is the end. What else am I going to do? Please, dear God, help me.*

"What's the matter, for heaven's sake?" Andreas's shocked voice startled Karla. She hadn't heard him come in. He sat next to her.

She shook her head. "I just feel bad. Don't ask. Don't say anything. Just hold me." She leaned her head against his chest and poured her sorrow into him. He held her tight, rocking her gently.

Karla wiped the tears from her face. "I'm sorry. It's not your fault. Something is going on with my painting that I don't understand. Not being able to paint, not feeling good about my art, is terrible. It makes everything else I do meaningless. It sucks all the energy out of me. I don't know how to explain it." She sighed. "I don't know how to deal with it."

Andreas touched her face. "I know. I can relate to how you feel. I've had times when I felt that everything I carved was crap."

"So what did you do?"

"Nothing in particular." Andreas shrugged, then smiled. "One time, I took another sculpture class. It was a class for beginners to intermediate, a little too basic for me, but I wanted someone to tell me what to do, give me a task, just to be busy. That way I didn't feel so useless. Of course I always have my gravestones, but if I don't do anything more creative than that, I start to feel ... well, worthless, I guess."

"Yeah. I sure know what you mean. Perhaps that's what I need to do. Take another art class."

"Go for it. You can always learn something new." Andreas hugged her. He sounded excited and relieved.

He must think I'm a mental case. Karla forced a smile.

The following few weeks Andreas tried hard to help reignite Karla's creative spark and get her into a better state of mind again. He brought home art books and brochures about art classes. They went to galleries and museums. Karla enrolled in an art class in Lugano. After the class, Andreas picked her up and they went out to dinner or to the movies. Karla was touched by his loving concern and tried to be happy.

However, once she was home again and sat in front of her easel, all her fears and frustrations reemerged. She usually started the day searching for a picture in her sketchbook from Peru. She tried to revive the enthusiasm she had felt at the time she created the drawing. Sometimes a flash of inspiration lit up in her. She saw again the purple rocks, the deep-green eucalyptus trees, the crimson sky of a sunset. When she began to apply the paint on the fresh canvas, she hesitated. Soon, destructive thoughts invaded her mind. *This is going to be more of the same. I want to create something new. I can't. It's not happening. I'm finished. I'll never be a successful artist. I might as well give up.*

Halfway through the morning, Andreas found her sobbing or sitting listlessly in front of the easel, staring into space. No matter how hard she tried, she wasn't able to get past her creative block.

Then her nightmares began again. She woke up in the middle of the night in tears. Andreas tried to console her, but after a while her ups and downs during the day and the night terrors began to wear on him.

"Perhaps you should see someone, a psychologist," he suggested one day.

"You mean, I'm going crazy. Is that what you're trying to tell me?"

"No, of course not. But you're in pain. Nothing we do seems to make much difference. Perhaps you need professional help."

"Maybe you're right," Karla said, but without much conviction. She had no energy to undergo therapy again. The last time she had given up after a few weeks. Whenever the analyst tried to get her to dig deeper, the sessions became too painful.

Finally, Karla confided in Silvia. They were sitting in the small office of Silvia's art gallery. Karla had come to pick up a check for one of her landscape paintings. The sale was a flicker of light in her otherwise dark days. It reminded her of happier times, when she didn't worry about her creative growth.

Silvia gave her the same kind of advice as Andreas: "Don't worry. Just paint. You'll snap out of it."

"Oh, Silvia, I've heard this so often, and I keep telling myself the same thing, but it doesn't seem to work. I'm in a bad mood and depressed all the time, and I drive Andreas crazy. I know it has to do with my inability to paint."

"What about teaching?" Silvia asked. "I know of a family whose kids seem to be very artistic. There are two boys and a girl. Unfortunately, they can't afford regular art classes. It would be something new, and it may inspire you again."

"I don't know, Silvia. I've never taught before. I don't know if I'd be good at it."

"It wouldn't be a professional teaching job. I bet they'd be grateful for anything you showed them."

Karla hesitated and sighed. "I guess it could be fun." The truth was, she didn't have any energy left these days.

"You're in a rut. What else could we do?" Silvia propped her chin on her hand and looked at Karla pensively.

"I have an idea. I know an art teacher in Florence. He's originally from Paris, but he lives in Italy now. He teaches at one of the art academies there, and during the summer months he works privately with a small group of painters and sculptors, helping them with their work. As far as I know, he is excellent. I recommended a couple of artists to him, and they liked him a lot. He usually works with somewhat older and more experienced people, but there might be a good chance he'd accept you.

"I've known him for a long time. We went to art school together in Paris, and we were even dating for a while. Then he met this Italian woman, and that was the end of that. But we remained good friends. Would you be interested?"

"That sounds great." Karla felt a flicker of enthusiasm again. "I doubt, though, that Andreas would be able to take that much time off from work ... I'd have to go alone." She shrugged. "Perhaps, that's what we need. Being apart for a while. I've been an emotional wreck, and it has begun to seriously affect our relationship. And I love Florence."

"All right, I'll try to call him tonight. But don't get your hopes up yet. Perhaps the class for this summer is already full. You would have to pay for your own lodging. I think most of his students share a furnished apartment. It's usually cheaper than staying in a pension or a hotel."

On the way home, Karla's enthusiasm began to fade somewhat. What was Andreas going to say? It sounded like a great adventure, but what would such a separation do to their already tense relationship?

"I might have the opportunity to take part in a painting workshop in Florence this summer," Karla said to Andreas, who had just finished another sculpture and seemed to be in a good mood.

Andreas raised his eyebrow. "Huh?"

Karla told him of Silvia's suggestion, carefully gauging his reaction. Andreas finished drying his hands and dropped the towel on the kitchen chair.

"For how long?"

"I don't know yet, a few weeks. Perhaps, we could both go?"

"There's no way I can take several weeks off in the summer. Perhaps a week or so or a few days." Andreas brushed through his hair, then shook his head and peered at her.

He's going to blow up again. "Well, it was just a thought. Perhaps it would help me with my artwork. I don't even know yet if it's possible." Karla's heart sank. She sighed.

"Actually ..." Andreas cleared his throat. "I think it's not a bad idea. You definitely need a change. And I guess I could visit for a few days or so ..."

"You really think so?" Karla felt hopeful again. "You'd probably be glad to get rid of me for a while. I know I've been unbearable."

"Well, yes, you haven't been the easiest person to be around. I just want you to be a little happier again. And if a stay in Florence, the city of art, doesn't do it, then I'm at my wits' end."

Karla hugged him. "I'm sorry, I know."

The next day Silvia called her. "Good news. I got a hold of Jean Philippe, and he told me there was still room in the course. He's going to send you the application form. Fill it out and send it back right away so he can make a final decision."

A few days later, the envelope from Italy arrived. It contained a brochure with a brief description of the course, a photo of the teacher, his credentials, and a few pictures of the students at work in the studio. Karla spent the next day filling out the short form of questions about the applicant's background, experience, and education.

One of the questions read *What kind of project would you like to work on?* Karla tried to think of an answer. The problem was she didn't have a project. Finally, she just wrote *Anything you recommend. I've come to a dead end in my painting.* She picked out a few photos of her artwork and the announcement to her exhibition, and sent them off together with the application.

Then the waiting began. After about two weeks, Karla was overcome by doubts. She wondered if the whole thing had just been a pipe dream. She almost expected a rejection. She was probably too young, too inexperienced.

"Why always so negative?" Andreas asked when she mentioned her doubts. "I'm sure when he sees your prior work he'll take you. Besides, Silvia recommended you, that should count for something, as well."

The following morning Karla was woken by the sound of a shutter slamming against the wall. The wind had kicked up again, and she could feel the tension in her neck that preceded a headache. Andreas was already up. Karla turned around and tried to fall back to sleep. After another crashing sound, she got out of bed and went downstairs to fasten the shutter from the inside, but the wind kept yanking it out of her hand.

"Why can't you fix the darn thing so it won't always do this?" she snapped at Andreas, who came out of his studio and tried to secure the shutter with the latch. "How many times do we have to go through this before you finally do something?"

"Bad morning again?" Andreas asked, giving her a measuring look. "The latch is too old. The only thing I can do is take the whole shutter off."

"Then do it, please." Karla hated herself for the querulous tone that reminded her of an angry child.

"Yes, ma'am." Andreas yanked the shutter off its hinges.

Karla could tell he was irritated. "Thanks. I'm sorry. I didn't mean to snap at you."

Andreas mumbled something under his breath as he carried the shutter to the shed that sounded very much like "bitch." Karla knew she had gone too far.

What had started as a bad morning led to a worse rest of the day. The air was thick with tension. Andreas, who so far had always tried to be patient and withdraw rather than risk an open confrontation, was visibly angry. When he came back into the house, he glared at her.

"Next time something needs fixing, you can either ask me nicely or do it yourself. I am not your lackey, and I am sick of your stupid tantrums. And don't say you're sorry. You said that too many times, it doesn't mean anything anymore."

"Don't yell at me, please." Karla's eyes filled with tears.

"I've just about had it with your moods. I try to help you, but you reject any suggestions I give you. You refuse to get professional help. You sit around feeling sorry for yourself. You're angry all the time." Andreas banged his fist on the kitchen table.

Karla flinched. "I think you don't want to be helped. I think you actually enjoy feeling bad. Why don't you just grow up?"

"Are you crazy?" Karla's voice trembled. "What do you mean I enjoy feeling bad? Do you have any idea—"

"Yes. I do." Andreas, who had been on the point of leaving, turned around. He glared at her, his face pinched and angry. "I know what it means to feel bad. Do you really think you're the only one who's going through a hard time? How do you think I feel having to live with a basket case? I've had it. I'm moving out." He left and slammed the door.

"Andreas, please." Karla took a few steps toward the door, then turned around and let herself fall on the kitchen chair. She buried her head in her arms. Her whole body shook, but she couldn't cry. She had no tears left.

Andreas didn't come back the rest of the day. He spent the night on the couch in his studio.

In the morning Andreas and Karla managed to talk sensibly for a while. They both agreed that they had to do something or their relationship would end in disaster.

"I know it's my fault," Karla said, "and I wouldn't blame you if you didn't love me anymore."

"I still love you, but a few more of these arguments will kill the love that's left between us. We need to be apart, at least for a while. I went to talk to Lena. She is willing to rent me a couple of rooms upstairs at her place. It's very reasonable. I can still keep the studio here and help with the rent. That way, we aren't in each other's hair all the time."

"Andreas, what have I done to you, to our relationship?"

"It's not just you, we've done it to each other. We used to be so happy together when we lived apart. Sometimes I feel I'm stifling you. You used to be able to paint before I moved in."

"I don't think my inability to paint has anything to do with you living here."

"Well, I don't know what else to do, Karla."

Karla knew he was right. Relieved to get out from under the pressure of living in an increasingly impossible situation, she was also deeply sad. She had failed once again to have a relationship with a man, and this time with the one she had felt so sure about, the one she had loved more than any other man before. She doubted that they could go back to the old, carefree dating days. Something had changed between them. Wasn't this idea of a temporary separation just a Band-Aid that made their final breakup a little less painful?

I lost my art. I'm about to lose my boyfriend. What else is there to live for?

The following day a large envelope from Italy arrived. Karla opened it with trembling hands. She read the short letter of acceptance twice, wanting to make sure she hadn't misread it. Then it began to slowly sink in that she was going to Florence for the summer. Jean Philippe had suggested she stay about two months if possible. He had also included a list of other students who were looking for roommates. One of the names was highlighted in yellow, a woman by the name of Claudia. Karla tried to decipher the words scribbled next to her name, something like *She is about your age; you may want to contact her.*

Karla felt an upsurge of energy, as if she was waking up from a deep sleep. "Yes!" she shouted, and rushed outside to share the news with Andreas. He looked at her with distrust and caution when she came running toward him. *He is expecting another scene,* Karla thought with a pang. *Any show of emotion on my part these days seems to make him afraid.*

"I just wanted to show you this." She gave him the letter.

"See, I told you he'd accept you. I'm so happy for you." Andreas kissed her.

"You know, perhaps you don't have to move out now," Karla suggested. "I'll be gone for some time, and I'm sure afterwards things will be better."

"I don't know, Karla. I think I should keep my place at Lena's. For one thing, I'd feel strange living here alone, not knowing what the future will bring. I'd rather wait until you get back. Then we can make a decision together."

He doesn't trust me anymore. He doesn't trust my emotions, and I can't blame him.

She reread the letter of acceptance again and decided to call Claudia. Perhaps they would be able to share a place together. As she found out from the phone call, Claudia lived in the north of Italy and had worked with Jean Philippe before. She spoke very highly of him. Claudia had rented an apartment, as she had done during her former workshops. "We could share the place," she recommended. "It's small, but there are two beds, and we wouldn't be there most of the time anyway."

Karla agreed immediately. She liked the sound of Claudia's voice. At least she would have a friend in Florence. Now nothing seemed to stand in the way of a very exciting time for her.

On the day of the trip, Andreas took Karla to Lugano to send her off.

"I wish you'd come with me." Karla sighed. Their relationship had improved somewhat over the past few weeks. Karla's mood swings had disappeared, as she had been busy preparing for the trip. Although Andreas still seemed cautious around her, he, too, had become more affectionate again. Now Karla realized that they weren't going to see each other for quite some time.

"I'll try and take a few days off to visit you." Andreas kissed and hugged her. "Take care of yourself and have a wonderful time."

Karla's heart ached when she waved back at him as the train pulled out of the station. He looked forlorn, a tall, strong man with a boyish face and eyes that seemed to have lost their luster during the past few months.

PART FOUR

ALONG THE RIVER ARNO

Chapter 24

It was middle of the afternoon when the train arrived in Florence. Karla stepped out into the street and was overwhelmed not just by the splendor of the Renaissance buildings but by the exhaust fumes of the many cars and motorcycles swerving in and out of traffic lanes.

"*Attenzione,*" a young man on a motorbike yelled at her when she tried to cross the street. He pointed to an underpass that lead from the station to one of the piazzas on the other side. Karla nodded and smiled. "*Grazie.*" *I act like a dumb tourist.*

The apartment was a fifteen-minute walk from the train station and two short blocks from the Duomo, the famous cathedral with its dome and mosaic-covered marble walls. It was hot outside. The sun had developed its full strength and was bearing down on the cobblestone streets and piazzas. Fortunately, the high stone walls provided some shade and reprieve from the muggy heat. Karla took off her jacket and fanned her face with the street map of Florence. She found the apartment easily. It was located on the third floor of one of the ancient towers in a street called Via del Corso. There was no elevator, and Karla was short of breath after climbing the steep stairs to the top.

The doorbell gave a shrill tone, which seemed at odds with the venerable old building. There was the sound of quick footsteps; a young woman opened the door. "Welcome to Florence. Come in and sit down. It's really hot today. I just got home from the studio myself."

Claudia, a vivacious girl with chestnut hair and lively dark eyes, offered Karla a glass of cold lemonade, which she gratefully accepted. "Why don't you just relax for a while? I thought we'd go out for pizza later on, if that's all right with you. It's too hot to cook."

"That's fine with me," Karla said. "I still need to pick up my suitcase at the station."

"We'll do that after dinner. It should be a little cooler by then."

After finishing their drink, Claudia showed Karla the apartment. It was small but quaint, with orange-brown stone floors and plain rustic furniture. The living room faced the street, with its seemingly incessant noise of cars, people laughing and shouting, and screeching sounds of small motorbikes so popular in the narrow streets. Karla wondered whether she would get any sleep at all in this noisy city, which was so unlike the calm village she was used to.

Fortunately, the bedroom faced a quiet courtyard and led out onto a small terrace with a table, a few chairs, an assortment of plants, and a flowerpot filled with multicolored peonies and irises.

Karla stepped out on the balcony. "It's lovely."

"Yes, I fell in love with the terrace last time I stayed here. It's wonderful to relax out here after it cools down a little at night. We can have breakfast here, as well. So far I haven't managed to have breakfast at home, there never seems to be enough time. Going to bed late and not getting up early enough. So I usually end up grabbing a roll and an espresso on the way to the studio." Claudia gave a sparkling laugh. "Luckily, the workshop starts at ten and Jean Philippe is pretty loose about being on time. Everybody kind of comes and goes as they please. The studio is on the other side of the Arno. It takes about fifteen to twenty minutes to walk there." Claudia pointed in the direction of the river.

"You'll really like Jean Philippe. He's super. I've worked with him several times. I'm studying to become an art teacher, and he has given me a lot of good ideas about teaching."

The following morning Claudia and Karla left the apartment early enough so they would have time to take a detour and see some of the sights. They walked by the L-shaped Piazza della Signoria, one of the central plazas in Florence. On one side stood the fourteenth-century Palazzo Vecchio, a massive Romanesque fortress with a crenellated tower, which was now the town hall of Florence. Piazza della Signoria was like an open-air museum, with many statues and other works of art, such as the ornate *Fountain of Neptune.*

Karla stopped to admire Michelangelo's *David* in front of the palace.

"It's a copy," Claudia explained. "The original is in the gallery of the Accademia di Belle Arti. That's the academy Jean Philippe teaches at during the year."

They walked through the long, narrow courtyard between the two wings of the famous Uffizzi Gallery down to the river Arno, where they crossed Ponte Vecchio, a bridge lined with jewelry shops and tourist stores.

"I usually try to avoid Ponte Vecchio, since it's always mobbed by tourists and it's a slight detour, but today we have time. Besides, I have a weakness for the beautiful jewelry," Claudia admitted. "Of course I can't afford the prices, but I can dream about it."

The studio was on the second floor of what looked like a private residence in a square called Piazza di Cestello, near Ponte Vespucci, a few bridges west of Ponte Vecchio. It looked out on a large terrace with a wonderful view of the Arno. When Claudia and Karla arrived, some of the other students were already at work. There were a few painters, a man who worked with metal, and a woman who made wood carvings. The work area was fairly small, but each artist had his or her own space. The smell of paint and wood and the chipping, scratching, clonking, and swooshing sounds of the different tools gave the place a feeling of creative activity. The mood of concentrated intensity was interrupted once in a while by an exchange of words or laughter.

Karla noticed that these were serious artists focused on their work. She also realized that, aside from Claudia, she was by far the youngest student.

The teacher, whom Karla recognized from the brochure, greeted her and introduced her to the other artists, then asked her to join him in the small office next to the work area. As he shuffled through some papers, Karla was able to observe him more closely. He was probably in his early to mid fifties, of medium height, slim, with curly gray hair. He was dressed in jeans and a blue work shirt.

He measured her with gray, sparkling eyes. "So, you know Silvia."

"Yes." Karla remembered that this was the man who had left Silvia for "that Italian woman."

"How is she? I haven't seen her in a long time. We just talk on the phone once in a while."

"She is fine. She is very involved in her gallery."

"Oh, yes. She has a beautiful gallery. I saw it once a few years ago." Jean Philippe looked down at a piece of paper, and Karla noticed that he was reading her application. Then he faced her with a probing look. "And how are you?"

"I'm fine, I guess."

"It doesn't sound that way from your application. You mentioned here that you were stuck."

"Oh, that, yes, my painting. I've tried out a number of new styles and media, but nothing has come of it. I've painted in more or less the same style for years, and I want to change, but I don't know how."

"Hmm." Jean Philippe looked at the photos of her paintings. "You've done some nice work, and you had a solo exhibition at Silvia's gallery. How old did you say you were?"

"Twenty-four."

Jean Philippe gave an amused chuckle. "You're still a baby. You shouldn't worry about new styles. Style develops as you paint. Don't put all this pressure on yourself about creating something new." Jean Philippe put the papers away. "As far as you being stuck, that happens to a lot of artists. Don't worry about it. The best thing to do is forget about painting for a while. Have you done any drawings? Just simple pencil or charcoal drawings?"

"Some, yes, but not lately."

"Well, then that's what you should do for now. I'll set up some still lifes for a while, and then we'll go on to something else. I just want you to relax for the time being."

Chapter 25

The following few days Karla drew all kinds of objects Jean Philippe put in front of her: books, a hammer, other tools, a glove. At first, Karla enjoyed the process of drawing simple things. Jean Philippe more or less left her to herself. He came by occasionally, pointed out an interesting perspective or composition or made a slight correction. The rest of the time he talked to the other artists, discussing techniques and making suggestions. They all took breaks when they felt like it and sat outside on the terrace, smoking and talking. Karla usually went with Claudia. Sometimes Jean Philippe would join them, but he mainly talked to Claudia, whom he knew from before, and to some of the other students.

After a while, Karla began to get bored. She felt neglected and wondered what she was there for. The exciting workshop she had looked forward to seemed to turn into mere drudgery. All the other students were enjoying themselves. Jean Philippe continued to give her objects to draw. She normally drew them very quickly, then turned the page of her drawing pad and began to draw something else. Whenever Jean Philippe walked by her, she turned the page back and continued to draw what was in front of her. She knew she was being childish. She should just talk to him and voice her concern that she didn't feel she was learning anything useful.

At one point she got so absorbed in one of her other drawings that she didn't notice Jean Philippe standing next to her. He flipped through her drawing pad and looked at the drawings she had done on the side. It was only then that she realized that all her pictures were of Andreas.

"I suggest you stop drawing these kinds of things for the time being. You need to learn to observe closely what's in front of you and around you again. Don't draw from imagination. Your mind needs a rest, it's become attached to a single object in an unhealthy way." Jean Philippe went on and sat next to one of the other artists.

Karla felt humiliated. *Who does he think he is? Some kind of psychiatrist? He doesn't take me seriously.*

On Thursday of that week, Jean Philippe put an apple in front of her. "It's the fruit of knowledge and wisdom. Better make it nice." He was obviously referring to the apple of Adam and Eve in the Bible and meant it as a joke.

Karla, however, wasn't in a joking mood. Tears of anger rose to her eyes. She didn't even make an effort to draw the apple, but began to draw other motifs again. She drew frantically, one picture after the other, working herself into a frenzy. Jean Philippe walked by once in a while and watched her draw. She just continued without looking at him. He didn't say anything.

At the end of the session, Karla got up and left quickly without waiting for Claudia. She was thoroughly fed up and wanted to be alone. At home, she called Andreas and informed him that she was coming back.

"No, you're not." He sounded alarmed.

"Andreas, I'm not learning anything. This guy has me draw apples. That's not what I came here for. This is a waste of time."

"I don't care if he makes you draw shoelaces. You are not coming back, you are going to stick it out."

"What do you mean? You can't force me to stay."

"Of course I can't." Andreas sounded exasperated. "Why can't you be reasonable? You need to make the best of it. If you give up now, what are you going to do? Come back and moan and complain about not being able to paint? At least if you stay and give yourself a chance, you may gain some self-confidence again."

"How can you be so sure you know what you're talking about?"

"Karla, I don't want to argue. I'll just tell you one thing. If you come back now, that's the end of our relationship. I know exactly what's going to happen if you give up. You'll feel like a complete failure, and you'll take it out on me. And I'm sick and tired of your moods. I'm sick and tired of being your emotional garbage can. The last few months with you were hell for me. You acted like a bitch the whole time."

"How dare you talk to me like this." Karla's voice trembled. "Why don't you just go to hell."

She slammed the receiver down, then crumbled to the floor, hiding her face in her arms. Everything in her life was on the point of disintegrating. Her painting wasn't going anywhere. Her relationship with Andreas was coming to an end, or was already finished. She knew, of course, that he was right. She had made life miserable for him, for both of them.

After she calmed down a little, she wanted to call him and apologize for the last sentence she had thrown at him in anger. However, she only got his answering machine. He obviously didn't want to talk to her. She tried a few more times, then gave up. By then, she had a vicious headache. She decided to go for a walk along the Arno to clear her head.

It was early evening after a hot day. The sun was about to set. Karla stood on one of the bridges and admired the view of the beautiful old houses that lined the river. Colorful stained-glass windows, pointed arches, and flying buttresses and ornate spires at the top of the buildings gave some of the houses a gothic touch and formed a pleasant contrast to the rather heavy and strict medieval and Renaissance architecture. Sunrays bounced off one of the tin roofs, turning it into a shimmering square of light. *Such an exciting, wonderful city. Why can't I just be happy?*

Karla looked down at the water. She had noticed before that the current of the river seemed to change each day. Sometimes the Arno flowed slowly and smoothly. Today its water was a swirling yellow-brown mass rushing underneath the bridge. *It would be so easy to jump down and be carried away.* Although she had had fleeting thoughts of suicide in the past, she knew she could never go through with it.

"I wouldn't do it if I were you. It's cold and dirty down there." A young Italian man smiled at her.

Karla shook her head. "Don't worry, I don't intend to jump."

"Good decision. Wouldn't you rather have a cup of coffee or a glass of wine with me?" He gave her a big smile.

"No, grazie," she said, smiling back.

He walked on, checking out other young girls. Karla sighed and walked back to her apartment, stopping at a kiosk to buy a picture postcard. At home, she wrote a brief message on the card.

Dear Andreas,

I am sorry for what I said on the phone. I decided to stay and finish the course. You were right. Love, Karla

Karla hoped her roommate would come home in time for dinner. Easy-going Claudia would be good company for her tonight. While waiting for her, she took her drawing pad out of her bag and turned to a new page. She looked for an object in the room, and began with the first piece of furniture next to the door. After a while, she began to enjoy drawing simple, clean lines and then adding shadows, the way she had done years before during her first drawing lessons back home. She got so absorbed that she forgot the time. When Claudia opened the door, Karla looked up, surprised.

"Hello, how are you?" Claudia greeted her.

"I've been better, thanks." Karla closed her drawing pad.

"What's the matter? Why did you leave so fast?"

"I was upset. Jean Philippe is driving me crazy making me draw these dumb objects. I don't know what he is trying to do. I know I haven't done this in a while, and I'm sure there is still stuff to learn, but come on, drawing apples all day long? Give me a break."

Claudia laughed and put her arm around Karla. "Give him a chance, Karla. He doesn't always make sense at first, but he knows what he's doing. Trust me. It'll make sense eventually."

"Well, I hope so." Karla managed a weak smile. "I can't do anything else. I wanted to go home, but I got into a huge argument with my boyfriend, so that's not an option anymore. Anyway, let's go and eat. I'll treat you to a dessert."

Chapter 26

I'll draw whatever Jean Philippe puts in front of me, Karla decided. To her dismay, her teacher brought another apple. He came up to her, took a bite, and put the rest in front of her, keeping a straight face through the whole procedure. However, when she looked at him, appalled, she thought she detected a humorous glint in his eyes.

Karla stared at the half-eaten apple. She was on the point of getting angry again, but then something snapped in her and she had the overwhelming urge to laugh. She took the apple and ate the rest of it, then put the apple core in front of her and began to draw it. Claudia, who had been watching her, giggled. Another one of the artists guffawed, and soon everybody looked at her and laughed as she continued to draw the apple core. When Jean Philippe realized what was happening, he came back and stood in front of her. She stared down at her pad, shaking with suppressed laughter. When she looked up, he had a wide grin on his face.

"So you have a sense of humor after all. Good. Now you can draw whatever you want—except for me. I'm a taboo subject. Come to think of it, why don't we all go outside and do some drawing?" He went back to his office, got a bunch of drawing pads, and handed them out. "You can all profit from this seemingly simple exercise. Most of you are so obsessed with your projects that you forget what made you become artists in the first place. Drawing pictures like you used to do as kids. Relax and have fun."

The rest of the day everybody was drawing. Karla and Claudia drew each other. The others picked something outside. Jean Philippe lit a cigarette, went downstairs, and walked to an espresso bar nearby.

Karla looked at Claudia. "I understand less and less what's going on here, but I think I'm beginning to enjoy it."

"I told you so," Claudia said.

At the end of the class, when everybody was packing up, Jean Philippe took Karla by the arm. "Come on, you humorist, I'll buy you a drink and then we can talk. Claudia, you'll have to walk home by yourself today. I'm going to kidnap your friend for a couple of hours. Don't worry, I'll send her home safe and sound ... well, I don't know about sound." He squeezed Karla's arm a little. "Just kidding."

They went to the restaurant on the piazza downstairs and sat outside in the shade of the umbrellas. The restaurant wasn't open yet, but a short, stout man with curly brown hair came outside to greet them. He seemed to be the owner or manager.

"Ciao, Giorgio," Jean Philippe called to him. "I know we are early, but do you think we could have something to drink? We need to have some quiet time to talk before your excellent place gets mobbed by customers." He smiled at the man, obviously trying to sweet-talk him into letting them stay.

"Anything for you, *amico*." Giorgio slapped Jean Philippe on the back. "What would you like?"

"Bring us some red wine, please." Jean Philippe turned to Karla. "Is that all right with you, or would you rather have something else?"

"No, that's fine."

"We have some cold appetizers, as well." Giorgio handed them the menus. "Would you like some?"

"Sure, that's a good idea," Jean Philippe said. "And a bottle of mineral water. I don't want the young lady to get drunk."

"Of course not. I know you're a gentleman." Giorgio winked at Karla.

While waiting for the appetizers, Jean Philippe pulled out a packet of cigarettes, looked at it, then let it sit on the table. The smile had disappeared from his face. He didn't pay any attention to Karla, but was quietly watching the few tourists who walked by. Karla started to feel uneasy, wondering why he had invited her and what he was going to talk to her about. She felt guilty for having acted like a child during the week.

When Giorgio brought out a plate with appetizers—an assortment of crostini, thin slices of toasted bread topped with pâté—Jean Philippe woke up from his musing. He poured them both a glass of wine, then put the bottle down and faced Karla with a stern look.

"*Bene*. Now comes the serious part. You may not like what I am going to tell you, but I ask you to listen to me with a somewhat open mind. Okay?"

Karla nodded, and her heart began to beat faster. *What now?*

"When Silvia asked me to accept you into my course, I was a little hesitant, because you were quite young and inexperienced. I didn't know if you'd fit into the group or if I was able to teach you anything. Silvia, however, assured me that you were very mature for your age. So I figured, I'll get a young lady who is somewhat confused but is eager to learn. Based on that assumption, I accepted you.

"In the course of this past week, I realized that instead of the nice young woman Silvia promised—and I'll have to have a serious word with her about that—I get an emotionally disturbed, lazy, stuck-up, spoiled, and arrogant brat who thinks she is on the way to becoming a great painter."

Karla felt as if he had hit her. The blood shot into her face, and her eyes filled with tears. Jean Philippe stared her down coldly. "If you're trying to decide whether you want to cry or get angry, I'd prefer the second. I don't have any tissues with me."

"How dare you talk to me like this ... you ..." Karla suppressed an insult and got up.

Jean Philippe grabbed her hand and pulled her down again. "I don't care how angry you get or what you want to call me, but you're going to stay and listen to what I have to say. Otherwise, you don't need to come back tomorrow. You can go home. I'll even refund the money you paid for the course. In that case, however, you'd be throwing away a great chance to learn something quite wonderful, in spite of the unpleasant truth you're hearing right now." He smirked at her.

"You think that's funny?" Karla was still stunned by the unexpected rebuke.

"You know, you have beautiful eyes when you're angry. Like gleaming coals."

"Shut up."

"Sorry, I can't do this right now. I'll try to be a little less harsh. Here, have some more wine."

"I don't want any." Karla stared at her glass, then picked it up and took a sip.

"That's better. Look, I know you're unhappy, you're going through a hard time, but so do many other people. Not everything rotates around you.

"When I had you draw those objects, I wanted to give you a chance to become a beginner again, look at the world around you and draw without any preconceived notion of what you're supposed to draw. I wanted you to clear your mind, forget about yourself and whatever is bothering you right now. Simply move your pen or pencil across the page. Focus on a tiny bit of the so-called real world." He pointed at the glass in front of him and lifted a spoon. "Later on you can expand your vision. You've gotten lost in some corner of your imagination, perhaps having to do with that person you so obsessively draw again and again. Most of all, though, I wanted you to stop worrying about your inability to paint and come up with a new style. As I said before, a new style develops in time. You don't have to force it. All of a sudden, you watch yourself doing something different.

"So from now on you can choose what you want to draw, except for the young man. I think you should take a break from him. And I want you to stick with drawing for a while longer. We'll take up painting later. All right?"

"Okay." Karla was looking down at her hands. "Can I ask you something?"

"Sure, go ahead."

"When you put that half-eaten apple in front of me, were you serious about that?"

He chuckled. "No, of course not, that was a joke. I noticed how upset you got about the first apple, so I couldn't help having a little fun at your expense. I figured, it's better to get some kind of reaction out of you than have you sit there and wallow in self-pity and suppressed anger. I expected you to throw the apple back at me, or something like that. I was actually surprised how well you handled it. That made me think that perhaps there was hope, and if we had a talk, then we might come to an agreement."

"Yes, I guess so."

"Do you have the drawings you did of the young man with you?" Jean Philippe asked.

"Yes."

"Can I see them again?"

Karla searched through her bag, pulled out one of her drawing pads, and handed it to him. Jean Philippe leaned back in his chair and looked the drawings over, one after the other, very carefully. While watching him scrutinize the drawings, Karla remembered that some of them were quite intimate. She had drawn Andreas in different positions and situations. There were drawings of him in his studio sculpting, sitting on their granite bench outside, drinking coffee. Some of them portrayed him in the nude bending down to kiss her.

After Jean Philippe finished looking at the drawings, he gave the pad back to her. "Is he the source of your unhappiness?"

Karla was startled. "What do you mean?"

"Karla, a man you draw with such passion and obsession must be an object of either your love or your hate, or probably a little bit of both."

"Is it that obvious?"

"To me it is. But then, I have an eye for such things." He smiled.

"Yes. He is one of the reasons."

Jean Philippe lightly touched her hand. "Look. I can't help you with the problems you may have with your boyfriend, but I can try to help you with your artwork. However, you have to stop fighting me. You have to trust me a little. I'm not making any false promises. I can't predict if you're ever going to be a great or famous painter. You have talent, but talent alone isn't enough. You need hard work and perseverance ... and a lot of luck.

"I think one of the problems is that you had some success with your painting early in your life and that gave you a false sense of accomplishment. Come on, you've only spent a few years painting, and you're already desperate because things don't work out the way you want them to. That's why I called you lazy. Most artists have to work for decades before their stuff gets exhibited anywhere. You were lucky that you had the chance to show your work in Silvia's gallery. That's a wonderful thing, and you should be proud of it. However, let's put things into perspective. Silvia's gallery is a small gallery in a tiny country called Switzerland. It's not some famous art gallery in Paris, Rome, London, or New York."

He took another sip of wine. "Fame, however, shouldn't be your aim anyway. You didn't become an artist because you wanted to be famous. You became a painter because you loved the process of painting. Perhaps you liked to draw and paint as a kid. Perhaps you loved the smell of crayons, the touch of canvas and paper. Painting, after all, is a very sensuous experience. Whatever the reason, at least in the beginning, it wasn't the desire to achieve some kind of a goal, right?"

Karla nodded.

"If I can help you rekindle that flame which made you want to devote your time to this crazy thing called art in the first place, so that you are able to enjoy it again without constantly worrying about results, then you are on your way. The rest is up to destiny.

"One last thing and then I'll shut up, as you so elegantly put it. You have to get your emotions under control. My wife and I have raised two daughters, and I have no intention of babysitting a third one, so you better grow up fast.

"All right, that's the end of my pep talk. Now have some appetizers. They're tasty."

"I'm not very hungry," Karla said.

"Oh, come on, snap out of it. You need to eat, you're too thin." He put a few crostini on her plate and poured some more wine. Then he raised his glass.

"*Salute.* And by the way, the drawings you did of your boyfriend are excellent. I hope he deserves the attention."

"How was your date with Jean Philippe?" Claudia asked when Karla came home that evening.

"Date?" Karla exclaimed. "If that's a date, I'll never date again."

"Why? What happened?"

"He really let me have it. I felt like a schoolgirl being scolded. He called me all kinds of things. How did he put it? According to him, I'm lazy, arrogant, mentally disturbed—well, something like that."

"Oh my god. Jean Philippe called you that?" Claudia looked at her, stunned.

"Yes, your wonderful Jean Philippe." Karla sighed. "Well, to be honest, he was probably right with most of what he said. I've made a mess of things."

"I think he likes you. He really wants to help you."

"I don't know, Claudia. If he does like me, he shows it in a strange way. I have to admit, though, in spite of the fact that he made me furious today, I'm starting to like him, too. He has a strange sense of humor. Anyway, like or not like, I realize now I have to stick it out. If I go home, my boyfriend won't talk to me anymore. If I stay here and don't submit to Jean Philippe's obscure way of teaching, he'll throw me out. I guess I have my back against the wall."

Chapter 27

Jean Philippe kept his word and let Karla draw whatever she wanted. She began to fill one drawing pad after another with objects in the studio and in the neighborhood, things she remembered from back home, scenes from her trips to Peru. She drew pictures of her friends, of her aunt, of Arturo and his family. Jean Philippe began to pay more attention to her work. He often sat next to her and pointed out things in her drawings he liked or things he felt she could improve. He no longer treated her like a child, but as a serious student and a fellow artist.

One day Jean Philippe suggested they draw a picture together. She began to draw something and then handed him the pad, and he continued the drawing. They added strange and funny objects until they both burst out laughing. It reminded her of the game she used to play as a child with her friends. One would start to draw a picture, then fold the paper and turn it over so only the very bottom of the drawing showed. The next person continued the drawing without knowing what the first had drawn, folded the paper again, and handed it to the next child. The end product was usually a nonsensical funny picture.

Karla hadn't felt as energetic and happy in a long time. She enjoyed her work in the studio, and she particularly looked forward to being near Jean Philippe. He often asked her about the people she drew, and she told him a little bit about her life.

"Your father?" Jean Philippe asked as he commented on one of the drawings of Arturo.

Karla nodded.

"Draw him again, but this time exaggerate his features somewhat to bring out his character more. Is he an angry man?"

185

Christa Polkinhorn

"Not really. Well, sometimes. He is serious, but he is kind and has a good heart."

"That's what you have to show in your drawing. It's difficult to capture the inner being of a man, but you know how to do it." Jean Philippe touched Karla's arm and gave her an encouraging smile. The tender and affectionate look in his eyes tugged at her heart. She blushed and lowered her gaze, studying the charcoal smudges on her hands.

It was during that moment that her feelings for him began to change. More and more she saw him not just as a teacher but as a friend and, most of all, a desirable man. She had never been drawn to older men before, and when she realized that she was beginning to fall in love with him, she was shocked at her feelings. He was still attractive, with a trim body, curly gray hair, and lively eyes that could turn from serious to tender to humorous in a flash.

Sometimes, when Karla worked on the terrace, Jean Philippe stepped outside to smoke a cigarette. Afterward, he sat next to her to check out her drawing. Normally Karla didn't like the smell of tobacco on people, and she had never smoked herself. Now, the scent of cigarette smoke mixed with his after-shave excited her. *You can't let this happen,* her rational mind said. *You need to stop. He is more than twice your age, he is married, he has a family.* Her emotions, however, pulled her in the opposite direction. *I want to kiss him, I want to hug him. I want to sleep with him.*

But she loved Andreas, didn't she? Did she? Her feelings for him had been so conflicted, particularly since that ugly phone call. Aside from short notes of apologies, they hadn't spoken or written to each other since. She didn't know if they had a future together anymore. She still thought about him every day, but the more she began to focus on Jean Philippe, the more Andreas receded into the background. It wasn't a healthy situation, and she knew it. She was just at the beginning of a positive development in her artwork. The feelings she developed for her teacher could endanger that budding growth.

One day two women came to the studio. The older one was probably in her late forties, a lively, energetic brunette, tastefully dressed, who talked and laughed with one of the students. The younger one, a girl in her late teens, wearing tight jeans and a short top, picked up Jean Philippe's bag next to his chair and began to search through it. Karla, who watched them from the patio, realized that they must be his wife and daughter.

When Jean Philippe came back from getting a cup of espresso, the girl called "Ciao, Papa" and inundated him with a flood of words. He kissed them both and took his bag away from his daughter, shaking his head. They began to wrangle playfully, she trying to get a hold of his bag and he trying to prevent her from doing so. The mother watched them, laughing. Finally, Jean Philippe pulled out his wallet and gave the girl some money. "Grazie, Papa," she said. The three of them chatted for a while, then kissed good-bye, and the woman and the girl left.

The short, amusing family scene pulled Karla abruptly back to reality, making her feelings for Jean Philippe appear utterly ridiculous. He was a happily married man, who obviously loved his wife and daughter. In a way, she was relieved. She knew then what she had to do. She would fight any inappropriate feelings she had for him.

The following few days Karla was careful not to get too close to Jean Philippe. She stopped herself from thinking about him in the evenings and at night when he popped into her mind. She focused with great intensity on her artwork.

"I think you're ready to paint again," Jean Philippe told Karla one morning. "I can give you an easel and canvas. Get yourself some acrylic and oil paints at this store." He gave her a business card. "Tell them you're my student and they'll give you a discount."

Christa Polkinhorn

The first time Karla sat in front of an easel, she was scared. She stared at the canvas, unable to start. She had flashbacks to her studio at home, where she had sat that way, paralyzed, sometimes for hours.

"Are you afraid of the empty space?" Jean Philippe asked as he noticed her dilemma.

Karla nodded.

"Well, we can take care of that." He squeezed globs of acrylic paint onto the palette, took one of the brushes, and smeared the paint carelessly across the canvas.

"There. Now I got you started." He handed her the brush. "Just paint, it doesn't matter what it looks like. Don't paint anything realistic, though, nothing I can recognize. I just want you to play with form and color."

Karla found it difficult to paint in a purely abstract style. She wasn't used to it. Whenever she fell back into painting something that began to look realistic, Jean Philippe picked up a brush and painted over it. It was a game they played until evening. She ended up completing several paintings, none of which she felt was of any value, but it didn't seem to matter. She had overcome her fear and felt a great sense of relief.

The following day Jean Philippe put one of the canvases she had painted the day before back on the easel. Then he gave her a few tubes of plain white paint. "Cover it with white, and then you can start again." She painted over her pictures several times. Once in a while, Jean Philippe took one of the paintings and put it aside. After about five days of this, he brought out the last series of painted-over canvases and placed them in a row in front of her, then stood back.

"What do you think?" he asked.

"I don't know." Karla shrugged. She had been so busy painting that she hadn't even thought about the quality of her work.

"Pick the one you like best."

Karla hesitantly pointed to one. Jean Philippe set it aside, then chose another one himself and put them side by side. "All right. Tomorrow, you can work with the rest of the paintings. Add something to each one of them. It can be something realistic, anything you feel would fit what's already there, complement it or completely change it. Do you know what I mean?"

"Not really."

"Doesn't matter. Perhaps it'll make sense tomorrow when you try it."

Chapter 28

It was the end of the first month of Karla's stay in Florence. She still wondered about Jean Philippe's seemingly erratic teaching methods. Whenever she felt she was beginning to understand what he was doing, he changed his tactics, totally confusing her again. In the course of the past weeks, however, she had become more confident and courageous and had gained a new sense of presence in her work. She began to experiment with different techniques and content, mixing the new abstract style with more realistic depictions. Most importantly, however, she had stopped worrying about the artistic quality of her pictures. She was just happy being able to paint again.

The one problem that still faced her was her inability to get over her feelings for her teacher. Jean Philippe's wife and daughter hadn't been back, and the longer she was around him, the weaker her resistance became. The only thing that would have helped her was staying away from him, but that wasn't an option.

She thought of Andreas more often. If he were with her, if they were still together, she wouldn't constantly obsess about Jean Philippe. One evening she decided to call him. She longed to hear his voice, to know that he was still a reality in her life. When he answered the phone, she was startled and didn't know what to say at first. "Hello," she finally said. "It's Karla."

A slight hesitation at the other end. "Hello, what a surprise. How are you?"

"Great."

"How is the painting coming along?"

"Fine. I'm so glad I stayed. How are you doing?"

"Good. I'm pretty busy. I met this rich guy in Ascona who ordered sculptures for his villa."

"Oh? How interesting. You've got to tell me more about it. How is Lena?"

"Okay."

The conversation was friendly but awkward, and not at all what she had wished for. Where was the passion and warmth of their earlier times? "I miss you," she said, full of longing.

"So do I." A cool and polite answer.

"Well, I better go," she said. "It was great talking to you."

After she hung up the phone, she felt worse than before the call. She really needed him to express his love for her. If only he had said once "I love you" or "I really miss you," it would have helped her get her feelings straight.

The next morning she woke up with a headache. For the first time since the beginning of her stay, she felt depressed again. Jean Philippe suggested she spend the day drawing for a change. Although she wasn't really in the mood for anything, she knew she couldn't let depressive moods detract her from her artwork anymore. She sat outside on the terrace and tried to decide what to draw. She thought of her mother. Laura was the one person she hadn't drawn yet. She thought of the photos Arturo had given her and began to draw Laura as a young girl.

Whether it was the disappointing conversation with Andreas, her confused feelings for Jean Philippe, the realization of how much a talk with her mother would help her right then, or

190

everything combined, she felt an ache in her throat and an overwhelming urge to cry. She took deep breaths, trying to regain her composure. Jean Philippe stepped outside, lit a cigarette, and stood next to her, looking at her drawing. *Not now,* she begged inwardly, pressing her fist against her mouth, trying to suppress a sob.

"Are you all right?"

Karla nodded but continued to tremble from the effort to squelch the sobbing. She saw his cigarette drop to the floor and his foot stamp it out, and she felt him sit next to her. He put his arm around her. She pressed her face against his chest and cried. He held her close for a while, then gently pushed her back.

"I'm so sorry. I don't know what came over me. I haven't felt good all day," Karla said in between sobs.

"Who is this girl?" He pointed at Karla's half-finished drawing of Laura.

"My mother. She died a long time ago." Karla took a deep breath and stopped crying.

"Oh, I see." He pulled her toward him and hugged her.

No, you don't see. She smelled his after-shave, felt his hair on her cheek, and held on to him as though her life depended on it.

"You have to let me breathe," he said with a chuckle.

"I'm sorry." Karla pulled back, embarrassed. *Did he notice anything?* "I apologize. I got you all wet." She pointed to the stain on his shirt.

"Don't worry, it's an old work shirt."

"My mother died in a car accident when I was very young," Karla said. "I guess drawing her brought back memories. Normally, I don't get that emotional about it anymore. I'm sorry." *The real reason I cried is because I'm in love with you.*

"You don't need to apologize. You should take a break now." He went inside and came back out with Claudia. "Why don't you two go and have a cup of coffee?"

191

"What happened?" Claudia asked her as they walked to a cafeteria nearby.

Karla told Claudia about her mother's accident, giving the same explanation for her tears she had given Jean Philippe. *I'm sorry, Mama, you have to serve as an excuse for a lot these days,* she said silently.

In the evening, when she sat at home alone—Claudia had gone out to run a few errands—Karla thought over the events of the day. She didn't want to let her confused feelings ruin the opportunity she had to study with Jean Philippe for a few more weeks. She just had to control her emotions. She wouldn't call Andreas anymore. He was of no help to her now. No, she had to see this thing through by herself.

When Claudia invited her to go out to a discotheque, she agreed. That's what she needed to do. Keep busy during the day and go out in the evenings, enjoy the wonderful things Florence had to offer. And stop thinking about Jean Philippe.

Chapter 29

Karla started a new oil painting, which was different from anything she had done before. It showed the head of a woman in profile whose brain was filled with images of pain and sexuality—a hammer with blood dripping from it, a snake-like phallic form curled and ready to strike. The painting was a mixture of stylized and realistic depiction. The eyelids of the woman were stitched together with needles, and the wide-open mouth suggested screaming. Karla painted it in different shades of red, brown, and black, the colors of hell, as she imagined. The only light colors were at the top right corner of the canvas, a splash of yellow and purple, perhaps the suggestion of a sunrise announcing morning, a sign of hope.

The whole time she was working, Jean Philippe didn't make any comments or give her any suggestions. He just came by once in a while, looked at the painting, then left her alone again. Once, when he stood next to her and she looked up, he nodded: "Go on."

When she was finished, she sat back and studied the painting. She felt a moment of intense joy and elation, followed by embarrassment as she became aware of the explicit sexuality and psychological pain in the painting. Yet she knew it was the most powerful work she had ever done and the one she understood the least. It frightened her and made her feel vulnerable. While Jean Philippe looked at it for a long time, she felt more and more uncomfortable. A trickle of perspiration slid down her back.

"*Splendido*," he finally said. His admiration was unmistakable. "I think you've done it. Congratulations." He put his hands on her shoulders and began to massage them. She flinched at first, then gave in and relaxed, exhaling deeply. Tears of joy rose to her eyes. She wanted to turn around and hug and kiss him.

"You should submit this," Jean Philippe said. "There's a contest starting in about a month. I'll get the forms for you to fill out. This painting definitely has potential."

The following few weeks Karla felt a surge of creativity. The painting of the woman's head had opened the floodgate to her creative self. Images began to spill fast and furious onto the canvas. Most of the time she let the painting take on a life of its own. Not all of her pictures were successful. When something didn't turn out, she painted over it.

Jean Philippe left her pretty much to herself. The only time he interfered was when he caught her staring at a half-finished painting for too long. "Don't think, paint," he said, and when she was particularly stubborn, he would take her brush and slap a blob of paint on the canvas.

A few times they painted "acrylics comics," as he called them. They painted very quickly, adding to or modifying each other's work. He had the talent of changing things she painted into funny objects: fantasy animals, a string bean with a human face, a series of smiling and weeping grapes. These were the moments she cherished more than anything, just sitting close to him, having a good time. She had given up her resistance to her feelings for him. These were her last days in his class; she might as well enjoy them. After the workshop was finished, Claudia and she were going to Venice for a few days, and then she would return home.

One evening Karla was in the process of finishing a painting she had started when she noticed that she was the only student left. Jean Philippe sat near her on the patio, smoking. She looked at him. "Do you want to leave? I can finish tomorrow."

"No, go ahead and finish. I'm not in a rush."

After Karla was done, she cleaned her brushes and put her stuff away. Jean Philippe looked at the painting, then smiled. "Come on, sit down for a while." He extinguished his cigarette and motioned her to sit next to him. It was early evening in August, with the sun already quite low. It had rained a little in the afternoon. The sky was a lively display of white and dark clouds, and the colors of the evening sky — stripes of crimson and lemon yellow — were intensified by the smog. Karla inhaled the slightly moldy smell of wet leaves.

"So, how do you feel?" Jean Philippe asked. "About your painting, I mean."

"Good. Better than I've ever felt before. Thank you, you've done so much for me." Her voice trembled a little. He smiled at her, and the tenderness in his eyes made her feelings for him flare up again. She quickly looked away, sensing the heat rise to her cheeks.

"You should feel good about your progress," he said. "You've done marvelously, once you got over your—well, let's say, initial hesitation."

Karla laughed. "You mean, my arrogance, laziness, mental instability ... what else did you call it?"

Jean Philippe gave a quick smile. "Did I say all those things?"

"You sure did, and I guess most of them were true."

He lightly touched her arm and got up. "Well, I want to make up for being so nasty. Can I invite you to dinner after class tomorrow?"

Karla's heart skipped a beat. "Thanks, that would be nice."

"We can go to the same place, if that's all right with you."

"Sure, that's fine." She tried to sound casual.

In the evening Claudia asked her if she wanted to join her and a few of the other students the following day after class for a drink.

"I'm sorry," Karla said, "I already have plans for tomorrow evening ... with a friend of mine. Perhaps we can do something the day after tomorrow." *Why am I trying to hide the fact that I'm going out to dinner with Jean Philippe?*

Chapter 30

The following day a few of the students who had started the workshop earlier than Karla were getting ready to leave. They exchanged addresses and phone numbers and encouraged one another to stay in touch. There was a general farewell atmosphere. Nobody was in the mood for serious work anymore. Some left early, others hung around and talked to one another or to Jean Philippe. When the class was over, Claudia waved at Karla and took off with a small group of students.

After everybody had left, Jean Philippe was standing on the terrace, looking after them. Karla was beginning to feel melancholic. She thought back to the beginning of the class when she had felt out of place and unhappy. Now, the group had almost become a family to her.

"Are you happy the workshop will be over soon, or are you sad they're leaving?" she asked.

Jean Philippe was still standing in the same place, smoking a cigarette. He turned around and came over to her. "Well, a little bit of both, I guess." He extinguished his cigarette and sat on the low stone wall next to her. "I'm glad to have a couple of months to myself before fall classes at the accademia start again, but the people I work with during the summer are kind of special. They're usually older and more dedicated than the young kids I get during the year. The work with them is more intense, perhaps more personal. And yes, when they leave, it's always a little sad. But why do I say *they*? It's *you*, you are one of them."

"I don't know if I fit the category of students you're talking about."

"Of course you do. Well, after a little tweaking." He chuckled.

"I still don't understand what happened during the two months I was here. How you got me to overcome my fears and painter's block. Somehow it worked, like magic."

"Well, to be honest, Karla, most of the time I didn't know what I was doing. I was just kind of trying things out. But why don't we go the restaurant? It's a little early, but we can have a drink first."

Downstairs at the trattoria, they sat outside under the umbrellas again. It had been another hot Indian-summer day, and it was still warm in the evening. Giorgio came out and greeted them cordially. He slapped Jean Philippe on the back and said something to him very fast in a local dialect Karla didn't understand. He winked at her with a wide smile on his pudgy face. Jean Philippe shook his head and laughed. Giorgio told them that the kitchen would open in half an hour, but they could have some antipasti to start with.

"Okay, we'll have some and wine, as well," Jean Philippe said.

When the manager walked away, Jean Philippe smiled briefly. "He teased me about taking out young girls. He remembered you from last time."

"If that's true," Karla said, "he must have observed us during our heated discussion."

"Yeah, you're right. He probably thought we had a lovers' quarrel or something like that."

Karla felt her face flush, thinking of her secret longings. She looked down at her hands. *God, I make it so obvious. He must be able to read me like an open book by now.*

If Jean Philippe noticed anything, he didn't let on. He just touched her hand briefly. "What were we talking about before? Oh, yes, how I got you to loosen up. I guess, first of all, by totally confusing you, getting you upset, sad, angry." He snickered.

"I wanted to somehow get the feeling across to you that all this painting you were so obsessed with isn't all that important in the big scheme of things. What I mean is that the outcome, the result, is secondary to the process of painting or drawing or sculpting. Of course, we all want to create great works of art. However, if we start out with that thought in mind, then we very likely block ourselves and ruin the experience. There is a fine line between serious work and a certain playfulness, which both are necessary in the creative process."

Karla, feeling she had her normal facial color back, took a sip of wine.

"Anyway," Jean Philippe continued, "I wanted to get you into a playful mood and came up with some games, some sillier than others."

"Well, they obviously worked. I particularly enjoyed the paintings we did together."

"Yes, I liked those, too. A little bit like painting a communal mural—a silly one, of course."

"You know so much about teaching. I've asked myself off and on if I should start teaching, as well. Silvia told me of a family whose children wanted art lessons. I may work with them when I get back. I've just always been concerned that if you start teaching, you get so involved you don't have enough time for your own work."

"There is a danger in that if you teach full-time like I do," Jean Philippe said. "You just have to decide where you want to focus your energy. I don't think that doing a little teaching on the side is going to interfere with your painting, though. On the contrary, it may add a little balance to your life. Artists have a tendency to be very self-centered. I guess trying to make it in the competitive art world is one of the reasons. You have to develop a very strong ego to keep on going and not to get discouraged.

"However, having been around artists all my life, I've seen some pretty disgusting things. It's amazing how selfish, jealous, and petty we can be. Teaching is a good way to counter that narcissistic tendency. It forces you to step back from your own self for a while and share your talent with others. You should give it a try. And if you ever come to a point where you feel stuck again in your own work, you'd always be able to teach, and it may actually help you get unstuck. I don't think in your case there is a danger that you'd neglect your own work. You are too passionate about it."

Jean Philippe opened a package of cigarettes and pulled one out. He looked at it absentmindedly for a moment, and then put it back. "See, with me it was different. I realized early on in my career that I wasn't made for the competitive art world and I didn't have what it takes to really succeed in it. This insight probably saved me from a lot of misery and disappointment. So I went into teaching."

"But you're a great painter," Karla said. "I've seen some of your work in the gallery we visited."

"No, not great. I don't have as much talent as you do." Jean Philippe smiled and put his hand on hers. "Now, don't let that go to your head. As I said earlier, talent isn't everything. But no, I've had some success, and, of course, I enjoy painting more than anything.

"However, I've always loved teaching and working with young artists. By 'young,' I don't necessarily mean young in years. I've taught all kinds of older people who discovered that they loved drawing or painting or sculpting. That's what I feel passionate about. I enjoy watching them grow and change, and if some of them become successful, that's the icing on the cake."

"You know, that reminds me of Silvia," Karla said. "She also helps young people, and one of the main purposes of her gallery is to give unknown artists a chance to show their work."

"Yes, I know. I think that's one of the reasons we became friends. We both began to teach on the side while we were studying in Paris. That's how we met. I don't know if she told you that we were dating for a while."

"Oh, yes, she did." Karla laughed. "And then you left her for that Italian woman."

Jean Philippe chuckled. "Is that the way she put it? Well, I guess it's true. That's when I met Micaela." It was the first time he had mentioned his wife's name.

"But let's focus on the food now," Jean Philippe said, as the waiter brought the menus. "You haven't eaten anything yet." He pushed the plate of hors d'oeuvres toward her. "You sure are a skimpy eater. By the time you get back to your boyfriend, you'll be like a skeleton, and I'm sure he won't like that."

His mention of Andreas clouded Karla's mood. "I'm not sure I still have a boyfriend," she said quietly, looking down at the menu. She felt his eyes on her.

"So things haven't improved, I take it."

"No," she said, then added with a sigh, "Well, I don't know. We haven't really talked in weeks."

"Perhaps, when you get back, you'll see more clearly where you're at."

"Perhaps." She studied the menu absentmindedly.

"What are you in the mood for?" Jean Philippe asked after a while.

"I don't know."

"Well, since your mind is obviously not on food, I'll just recommend something that I know is good here and you tell me if you like it."

Karla nodded.

"So tell me, what is the problem with your boyfriend?" Jean Philippe asked after he had ordered. Then he put his hand on hers. "Sorry, you don't have to tell me, it's really none of my business."

"That's all right. It was my fault. It started out great. We got along really well, then we moved in together. At first, everything was fine. Then I began to have problems with painting, I got depressed, I had terrible mood swings, and, well, it started to affect our relationship."

"In other words, your drove the poor guy crazy."

"Something like that," Karla admitted.

"Oh boy, I can just see it. If you acted anything like you behaved in the first week of my course, then I can sympathize with him."

"It was much worse."

"Worse? He deserves a medal for not having killed you," Jean Philippe teased her. "But now that you feel a little better about your artwork, perhaps you can patch things up when you get back. And get yourself a shrink, while you're at it."

"Well, thanks for the vote of confidence," Karla said. "Actually, that's just what I decided to do."

"What? Seeing a shrink or patching things up?"

"Both, I guess."

"Oh, come on, I was joking about the shrink. You don't need a shrink. They just rob you blind, and most of them are messed up themselves."

"You don't seem to have a high opinion of analysts."

"No, not really. I tried them myself and didn't have much luck."

"You?" Karla asked.

"Yes, when I was younger, before I got married and had a real life."

"So being married helped you?"

"I guess it did. I got so busy teaching art and supporting a family that I didn't have time to go crazy."

"From what I saw, you have a really nice family."

He looked at her, surprised. "Oh, yes, I forgot. You saw my wife and my younger daughter. Yes, I have to admit, I'm very lucky. It'll happen to you, too, one day. Don't be in a rush. You're still so young. Enjoy yourself a little before buckling down and taking on all this responsibility. Anyway, here is the food."

The waiter served them and poured more wine.

"So let's stop talking about boyfriends and problems, and eat for a change." Jean Philippe assumed a commanding tone. "You're not getting up until you've eaten all of this." He pointed to Karla's plate.

"You're starting to sound like my father."

"I could be your father, as far as age goes."

They ate in silence. The food was excellent, and Karla, who had skipped lunch, realized that she was hungrier than she had thought at first. The fillet of sole cooked with spinach and butter and white wine was tender and juicy. It was served with a side dish of grilled eggplant, tomatoes, and green peppers. For dessert, the owner brought them a complimentary specialty of the restaurant, a three-chocolate soufflé with vanilla ice cream. Not even

Karla, who usually skipped dessert, could resist the creamy delicacy.

After dinner they remained seated for a while, talking, drinking espresso, and enjoying the warmth of the evening. When they got up to leave, Karla, who felt relaxed after the wine and the good meal, touched Jean Philippe's arm. "Let's go for a walk. I don't feel like going home yet. It's still so nice out."

They crossed the street and walked along the Arno toward the Amerigo Vespucci Bridge. It was quiet along this stretch on the south side of the river. There were fewer tourists than around the busier bridges, and most people were having dinner. The sun was already low in the sky, but it was still light.

"It's strange that there is almost no place along the Arno where you can walk right next to the water," Karla said, "except for the boating area next to Ponte Vecchio and that spot over there." She pointed west, past the Ponte Vespucci, to a path leading down to the river.

"That's true," Jean Philippe said. "Sometimes you see people walk their dogs or ride their bikes there."

"Let's check it out," Karla suggested. "It must be refreshing close to the water."

They walked down the path that led underneath the bridge. It was a peaceful spot. The noises of the city were dimmed by the sound of the river cascading over a few steps in the riverbed and creating a small waterfall. There was a pleasant breeze brushing through the tall grass and shrubs. They were standing quietly next to each other for a while, looking out onto the water.

"It's beautiful here. I wish I didn't have to leave." Karla sighed.

"You can always come back."

Karla turned to face him. His warm smile, which deepened the thin creases around his eyes; the slightly musky scent of the river; the closeness of his body—it all made the feelings she had tried to suppress over the past weeks erupt with renewed intensity. Before she knew what she was doing, she embraced him and began to kiss him. He stiffened for a moment, taken by surprise, then kissed her back. Karla pressed herself against him. That's what she had been waiting for all this time. She felt the quickening of his breath, his arousal. When he pushed her away, she almost fell.

He steadied her and looked at her, shocked. "Karla, for heaven's sake, what are we doing?"

"I'm sorry, I don't know what came over me," Karla murmured, embarrassed.

He exhaled deeply. "That's not what I had in mind when I invited you for dinner tonight."

Karla was close to tears. She covered her face with her hands.

Jean Philippe touched her arm. When she dared to face him again, she saw a mixture of kindness and confusion in his eyes. "How long have you been feeling this way about me?"

"For quite some time," Karla whispered. "Look, I'm really sorry. I think I should go home now."

"No, you can't leave now. Not like this. Let's go to the coffee shop near the studio. It's probably pretty empty at this time. Come on." Jean Philippe took her by the arm. They walked to the cafeteria in silence. He picked a table in a corner of the patio and ordered some coffee.

Karla stared at her hands, too embarrassed to face him. She felt his eyes on her, and finally looked up.

Jean Philippe lowered his gaze and sighed. "Karla, I don't know where to begin. You are a very attractive woman. Believe me, if nothing else existed but the two of us, I wouldn't hesitate one moment to do what I think you want me to do. Unfortunately, it's not that simple."

"I know, Jean Philippe. I know you're married and have a family. I shouldn't have approached you like this."

"Well, in a way I'm flattered, I guess. It's not every day that a beautiful young woman tries to seduce me." He smiled at her.

"Yes, I'm married and have a family and I love them very much, but I'm also thinking about you. You are my student. We have been working together to get you into a frame of mind, where you feel a little happier and good about yourself and your work. I don't want to endanger this by having sex with you. How would you feel afterwards? We can't have a normal relationship. And what about your boyfriend? You have trouble enough as it is. If we made love, it would confuse you even more. It's just not possible."

"I know. You're right."

"Listen, Karla. I want you to feel good about your stay here. I don't want you to go home feeling guilty and unhappy. I want you to think of me as your teacher, your mentor, your friend, not your lover."

Karla nodded. "I'm sorry about the way I behaved."

"Karla, I like you very much. Perhaps more than I should. You do mean a lot to me, and that's why I don't want to hurt you."

Karla listened to his words; they made perfect sense. She still wanted him.

"I think I better take you home now." Jean Philippe called the waiter and paid. They walked back to the studio. Karla, confused and ashamed, wanted to walk home to get away from him as quickly as possible. Jean Philippe, however, shook his head and motioned her to get into his car.

He drove her to her place and parked the car in the courtyard in the back, then turned off the ignition. He briefly touched her hand. "You don't have to feel ashamed for showing me your feelings. I don't want you to do anything silly, such as not coming back tomorrow. There is only about a week left in the course. You absolutely have to finish this workshop. We just have to be careful not to be alone together. I don't know how long I could resist your seductive charm." He gave her a quick hug. "Good night, my beautiful friend."

Karla got out of the car. He waved at her as he drove away. She climbed the three flights of stairs as if in trance. Up in her apartment she glanced at herself in the mirror. She didn't seem to know the woman who stared back at her. She sat in a chair next to the window and tried to come to terms with her feelings and what she had done. She had practically thrown herself at him. He had been nice not to make a big deal about it, but she still wondered what he really thought of her. However, he had kissed her back; she had felt his desire for her. She was confused, and she dreaded the thought of having to face him the following day.

Why is it that I always have to turn a good situation into a disaster? First Andreas, and now Jean Philippe.

There was the sound of the key turning; Claudia was coming back from her night out. "You're back already? How was your evening?"

"Great." Karla forced herself to sound cheerful. "How was yours?"

"We had a good time. Too bad you couldn't make it. I didn't know you had a friend in Florence."

"Well, it's actually a friend of Silvia's, of the woman who recommended this workshop to me," Karla explained. *I guess I'm not even lying about this. Jean Philippe is a friend of Silvia's.* She didn't feel like talking about the evening, so she pretended she had a headache and was tired. It was a little after eleven, and they both turned in for the night. It took Karla a long time to fall asleep. She thought of Andreas again. Jean Philippe was right. Her feelings for him were even more confused now.

Chapter 31

On the way to the studio the following morning, Karla and Claudia stopped at their usual espresso bar, having coffee and a roll for breakfast. Claudia was excited about their upcoming trip to Venice and talked in her normal lively fashion, babbling about all the things she wanted to do. Karla let her talk. She was grateful she didn't need to talk much. She had slept badly, and she felt awkward about meeting her teacher again.

Jean Philippe, however, behaved as if nothing unusual had happened. If anything, he treated her more kindly than before. After a while, she began to relax somewhat. However, the short moment of intimacy at the river had only intensified her feelings for him. She was caught in the clutches of a hopeless attraction, and felt vulnerable and raw inside.

Since it was the last week of the course, Karla didn't feel like starting anything new. She mainly sat on the terrace sketching. Occasionally, Jean Philippe stepped outside to join her. It was during those moments that she noticed the change in him. She felt him watching her. When she looked up and their eyes met, he'd smile, then look away. He would start a conversation, then stop and stare into space. She also noticed that he smoked more heavily. He was obviously preoccupied, and Karla felt it had to do with the incident down at the river.

She was careful not to betray her feelings for him anymore. She was relieved the course would be over soon. At the same time, she was sad, knowing it was probably the last time she'd be with him. In a few days Karla and Claudia were leaving for Venice, and on the weekend they would return home.

On the last day of the workshop, a few of the students went out after class again. They invited Jean Philippe to come along. He told them, however, that unfortunately he couldn't make it that evening.

"You're coming too, right?" Claudia asked Karla.

"I have to take care of something first, but I'll join you later. Where are you going?"

"To the usual place," Claudia said. It was a small restaurant and bar in the center of the city.

Karla wanted to stay back and have a few moments alone with Jean Philippe. She felt they needed to say something to each other, something that perhaps put a closure to her still-unresolved feelings. After the other students had left, she packed her painting materials. She had accumulated more than she had thought, and her bag was getting heavy. She put it outside on the patio and sat on the wall. Jean Philippe, who had been inside rearranging some of the equipment, came outside. He sat next to her.

"Aren't you going to have a drink with the others?"

"I'll probably join them later."

"You know, I just remembered. You need to complete the application form for the contest and sign it. When are you going to leave?" he asked.

"That's right." Karla, in her confusion, had forgotten all about the upcoming contest. "Claudia and I are going to Venice for a few days. We'll be back Friday. I'll be returning home that Sunday."

"All right. I have office hours at the accademia next Saturday. Do you think you could come then?

"Yes, of course."

They sat next to each other without speaking for a while. Karla watched the sun slip behind one the buildings, leaving a halo of light around it. She wanted to say something, to thank him and apologize again, but she couldn't get a word out.

"I'm going to miss you." The longing in his voice startled her. She looked at him. He took a draw from his cigarette, exhaling the smoke through his nose, then extinguished it and smiled at her.

"Well." He spoke in a normal tone again. "I hope you'll keep in touch after you leave, let me know how things are going with your painting."

"I certainly will. Thanks again for everything. ... And I'm sorry."

"Don't mention it." He gave her a hug, and she hoped she didn't cry. When he looked at her, she thought for a moment he was going to kiss her, but he didn't. He got up. "Is this all your stuff?" He pointed at her bulky bag lying on the ground and then lifted it. "That's too heavy for you to carry. Come on, I'll give you a ride home."

"Don't you have somewhere to go?"

"No. It's not important." Jean Philippe locked the studio. He made his way easily through the narrow streets, shaking his head once in a while when he had to stop for one of the many careless tourists who crossed the street without looking.

"So, you and Claudia are going to Venice." Jean Philippe parked the car in the courtyard at the back of her building. "Lucky you, you're going to have a great time." He got out and offered to help her carry her bag. She thanked him, remembering that the building had no elevator and her apartment was on the third floor.

Upstairs, Jean Philippe looked around. "This is a charming place."

"Yes, I was lucky to be able to share it with Claudia. It's small, but it has a great patio."

Jean Philippe stepped outside. "Beautiful." He came back in and smiled at her. "Well, I guess that's good-bye." He hugged her for a long time, then looked at her with great intensity. There was an awkward pause. "I know I shouldn't do this." He sighed and began to kiss her. She closed her eyes, and felt the last resistance fall away.

They kissed with the desperation of drowning people who struggled to keep their head above water in a turbulent river and finally let go, too tired to fight any longer. All of it had been leading to this moment: her feelings for him over the past weeks, the kiss down at the Arno, his desperate attempt not to give in, his absentminded behavior during the last week at the studio, his excuse for not going out for drinks with the other students, her ruse to stay back at the studio to be alone with him, his offer to help her carry her painting materials. It was as if the whole thing had been planned by some outside force, except the force was their own desire.

He pushed her down on the sofa and began to open her blouse.

"Not here," she said. "Claudia might come back."

He got up and sighed. "Karla, I've tried really hard not to get to this point."

"I know."

"Let's go somewhere else," he said.

"Wait a moment." Karla picked up a piece of paper and wrote a note to Claudia.

Sorry I couldn't meet you tonight. Something came up. I had a phone call from my friend. I'm going to stay with her tonight. See you tomorrow. Love, Karla

She put the note on Claudia's pillow. *This is the dumbest excuse I've come up with so far.* She followed Jean Philippe down the stairs. As they drove away, Karla asked him where they were going.

"To the studio, or rather to my apartment. I rent a place in the same building for the summer months when I teach my workshop. I only go home to Siena on weekends. It's too much driving otherwise."

"That's a beautiful city," Karla said.

"It is. We love it there."

"We"—his family. Karla sighed and looked out the window at the city buzzing by. The rest of the way they drove in silence. He parked the car next to the building adjacent to the studio. They walked up the stairs to the fourth floor. Jean Philippe lived in a studio apartment that consisted of a combined living room and bedroom, with a balcony, a kitchenette, and a bathroom. It was small, sparsely furnished, but had a beautiful view of the Arno.

"This is nice." Karla stepped out on a tiny balcony. The dark slick of water flowing by was barely visible now in the approaching night, except for the flickering reflections of city lights along the riverbanks.

"It's a simple place, but very convenient. And it's quiet, which is hard to find in Florence." Jean Philippe stepped behind her. He put his arms around her and kissed her neck and throat. "Karla," he whispered, holding her tight. "Well, here we are, getting ready to do exactly what we agreed we shouldn't do."

"Is this all my fault?" Karla asked.

"No, I'm equally responsible for it. I am the one who caved in during the last week, perhaps even earlier. One thing we have to agree on, though," Jean Philippe said as they stepped inside. "This is going to be the only night we can spend together. Anything beyond this might cause serious harm to my family as well as to both of us. You have to respect this and not try to convince me otherwise."

"I promise."

"And the other thing: we both have to deal with the consequences of what we do tonight on our own. Do you understand?"

"I understand."

"Do you really?" Jean Philippe gave her a probing look, which intensified the crease between his eyebrows. "I hope to god you do."

"Jean Philippe, if you have such scruples, perhaps we shouldn't do it." His obvious nervousness made her feel uneasy, as well.

"There is still time," he said. "We can back out now, and I can take you home."

They looked at each other for a while.

"I guess not." He sighed. "All right," he continued in a more cheerful tone, his face more relaxed, "would you like something to drink? I think I have just the thing for this. A friend of mine gave me a bottle of champagne the other day." He took out two glasses from the cupboard and opened the bottle. The cork popped and bounced off the ceiling.

Karla took a few sips. The bubbles from the champagne tickled her nose. She held the cool glass against her cheek. "It's warm in here."

"Yes. This August has been unusually hot." He opened the window on the side of the room opposite the balcony. The curtains bulged slightly in the evening breeze.

Karla got up and stood by the balcony door, looking out on the Arno again. Jean Philippe turned off the lights and stood next to her. She noticed that he had taken off his shirt. He was slim, with narrow shoulders, so unlike Andreas's broad chest.

Andreas, she thought for a split second, then pushed the memory of him to the back of her mind.

Jean Philippe helped her take off her top and kissed away a tiny pearl of sweat that was sliding down between her small breasts. He fiddled with the hooks of her bra. She had to help him open them. "Come on," he whispered. He led her to the bed. They undressed each other, letting the clothes drop to the floor. There was a sweet, pungent scent of overripe grapes coming from a bowl of fruit next to the bed. He pushed her gently onto the cool sheets. They kissed. His mouth tasted of champagne and tobacco. He circled the nipples of her breasts with his tongue, moving slowly down to her navel, kissing her belly. He reached for a

211

pillow and slid it under her hips, then gently parted her thighs. The curtains billowed in a sudden gust of wind.

Chapter 32

Karla woke to the sound of an electric shaver and someone coughing. When she opened her eyes, the morning sun poured through the window. At first she didn't know where she was; then it sank in. She sat up and looked around the room.

"So you're finally awake." Jean Philippe stepped out of the bathroom, drying his face with a towel. He was already half dressed. "How are you?" He sat on the bed and kissed her. His mouth tasted of peppermint.

"I was just thinking," Karla said. "How can something that feels so good be so wrong?"

"Is that the morning-after blues?" Jean Philippe scrutinized her.

Karla pulled her knees to her chest and sighed. "No, that's the problem. I don't feel bad. On the contrary, I feel a lot better than I should."

"That's the beginning of the corruption of the soul."

"Jean Philippe, you're so dramatic. You're beginning to sound like a priest. Are you Catholic?"

"Well, on paper, yes, but not really a practicing one. I converted to Catholicism when I got married. My wife and her family are Catholic. It was easier that way."

"Your wife ... now you're starting to make me feel guilty."

"Don't." Jean Philippe touched her cheek. "That's entirely my problem. You may have enough to deal with on your own later."

"Well, in spite of everything, it was a wonderful night," Karla said.

"That it was. You're a very sweet girl." Jean Philippe kissed her again, then checked his watch. "I almost forgot. I have a meeting in less than an hour. We better get moving." He brought a towel from the bathroom. "Here, if you want to take a shower."

In the bathroom Karla looked at herself in the mirror. *You just committed adultery,* she silently told the face that stared back at her. She sighed, then turned on the water in the shower.

Back in the living room, it smelled of coffee and cigarettes. Jean Philippe was standing by the balcony, smoking. He extinguished the half-smoked cigarette and pointed at the espresso pot. "Want some?"

"Yes, please. You have a funny way of smoking. Do you realize you always light a cigarette, take a few puffs, and then extinguish it?"

"I know," he admitted. "It's my silly way of trying to cut back, but obviously it's not working."

"You do smoke too much, you know."

Jean Philippe looked at her, amused. "Now, you start to sound like my wife. ... Sorry. I didn't mean to remind you." He took out a couple of cups and sugar from the kitchen cabinet and a bottle of milk from the refrigerator. "I'll go and get us some rolls at the bakery around the corner. I'll be right back. And I want you dressed by the time I get back."

"Yes, Papa," she teased him. He did remind her a little bit of Arturo.

Arturo. If Arturo knew. How would she ever explain this to him? He would be so disappointed in her, and so would probably a lot of other people. Silvia, for instance; she'd regret having recommended her to Jean Philippe. Lena? She might understand, but she certainly wouldn't approve. And Andreas? Too painful to think about.

Karla felt in some half-conscious part of herself an emptiness that she knew nobody would be able to fill, least of all the man with whom she had made love the night before. He would be gone, back with his family, and she would be with her friends, unable to confide in them. Her lighthearted mood of the morning slowly gave way to loneliness.

When Jean Philippe came back, Karla was standing by the balcony door, looking down at the river. He must have noticed her serious mood. He put his arm around her shoulder and gave her a probing look. "Are you having second thoughts?"

She sighed. "I was just thinking about all the people I know, the ones close to me, my father or even Silvia, and, of course, my boyfriend, and I just realized I couldn't tell any of them about us, about last night. Except perhaps for one person, none of them would understand, and certainly none of them would approve."

"Of course not," Jean Philippe said. "What do you expect? The same is true of me. My family would be shocked, my friends, as well. There may be a couple of male friends I could trust, who have gone through similar things, but that's about it.

"I know infidelity in relationships is very common, a lot of people do it, but it never goes over well. I've seen quite a few marriages and relationships ruined and people hurt because of the very thing we did last night. Which obviously didn't stop me from doing the same," he added with a bitter laugh. "So I no longer have the right to any kind of moral authority."

"You're being dramatic again," Karla said.

"Perhaps I should've gone into acting." He gave her a quick smile and pushed the paper bag toward her. "Here, have some rolls."

Karla realized she was hungry. After eating two of the rolls and drinking another cup of coffee, she sighed. "That was good."

"You know, that's the first time I've seen you eat with real appetite," Jean Philippe said.

Karla gave him a mischievous smile. "No wonder, after last night."

"You're funny." Then he checked his watch. *"Merde.* I just missed my meeting." He pulled her toward him. "Let's kiss good-bye here, before going outside."

"Why do you have to be so sweet?" He sighed as they finally stood apart, trying to catch their breath. He looked at his watch again. "Now, I really need to go." He touched her arm. "Don't forget to come by my office next Saturday to fill out the form ... and to say good-bye. Whatever your feelings are going to be about last night, I need to see you again. I need to know that you're all right."

"I promise. Please don't worry, I'll be okay."

"And have a wonderful time in Venice."

Karla took a deep breath as she watched him drive away. *Why is love so complicated?* She walked along the Arno and crossed the Santa Trinita Bridge. Now she had to come up with a plausible excuse for Claudia as to why she didn't come home last night. Karla stopped halfway across the bridge and looked down at the river as it slipped underneath it. It flowed rapidly and had a brownish, muddy color.

"Here you are, finally," Claudia exclaimed. "I was beginning to worry. When you didn't show up at the bar last night, I thought that perhaps you had gone somewhere with Jean Philippe. Then I found your note at home."

"I'm sorry. When I got home to drop off my stuff, I got a phone call from my friend. You know, the one I went to see the other day. She was in a really bad state of mind. She had just found out that her husband had a girlfriend and was going to leave her. As you can imagine, she was terribly upset. So I went over there to try to calm her down a little, and ended up spending the night." *Adultery again.*

"That's too bad," Claudia said.

Karla could feel Claudia's eyes on her as she put her stuff away. "Did you have a good time with the others? Too bad I didn't get to say good-bye."

"Yes, we missed you." Claudia's voice sounded hesitant. "Where does she live?"

"Who?"

"Your friend, of course."

"Oh ... nearby actually, at the Via Ricasoli." It was the first name that popped into her mind—the street of the academy. "Well, I better get going. I still need to do some shopping for tomorrow and then pack. When do we have to leave in the morning?" Karla grabbed her bag.

"The train leaves a little after ten thirty."

"That's not too early. What about tonight? Are you still up for going out?"

"I guess so." Claudia shrugged her shoulder. "Unless you get another phone call from your desperate friend."

"No, I don't think so. Her daughter is with her today." *How easily lies slip over my lips these days. What did he call it? Corruption of the soul.* "I have an idea. Let's go and have pizza somewhere and then check out the jazz club in Santa Croce we heard about."

Chapter 33

The trip from Florence to Venice took three hours. Karla and Claudia were tired, having been up later than planned the night before. They had met a few young Italians who had taken them to a couple of different nightclubs. The young men had been fun and entertaining but very insistent on extending their night out together.

Karla, who hadn't slept much the previous night, kept yawning and nodding off. At one point she noticed that Claudia was observing her.

"What are you looking at me that way for?" Karla yawned again.

Claudia smiled. "I was just thinking about you and Jean Philippe."

Karla felt a jolt in her stomach. "Why?"

"Remembering how you disliked him at first, the trouble you had with him, and how much you got to like him in the end."

She is trying to feel me out. "Yes, that's true. I have to admit, I was wrong about him. He's actually a very good teacher. In his quirky ways, he was able to help me get rid of my fear of painting."

"I think you like him more than just as a teacher. I think you are in love with him. And I think he has a crush on you, too."

"You're crazy." Karla felt the heat rise to her cheeks.

"Then why are you blushing?"

"Claudia, I admit, he is an attractive man. However, he is more than twice my age, he is married and has a family." *How many times have I repeated this to myself!* "And as far as he is concerned, I'm nothing more than his student. So you shouldn't spread rumors like this."

"I'm not spreading any rumors. I'm only telling you."

"Wipe the smirk off your face, Claudia. What makes you think Jean Philippe has a crush on me?"

"I was just observing the two of you together, the way you looked at each other. You know, woman's intuition."

"Well, your intuition is really off the mark. Look, he knew I was unhappy and he tried to help me. That's all."

"And you really were with your desperate friend last night?"

"Claudia, so far this has been teasing. But now, you're taking it too far. What are you implying? That I spent the night with Jean Philippe?"

"Well, did you?"

"No, I didn't. Claudia, you've been a good friend to me, but now you're making me angry."

"All right, I'm sorry. You know, things like this do happen. I wouldn't condemn you. I thought that perhaps you needed a friend to talk to."

"Well, that's very kind of you. However, there is nothing to talk about, so could we stop this conversation? Perhaps it's you who has a crush on Jean Philippe, the way you keep bringing him up."

"No. I really like Jean Philippe, and we have been good friends for many years, but no, I love Mauro too much." Claudia smiled dreamily.

Karla sighed. *I wish I could think in such an innocent, loving way about Andreas again.*

In Venice, Karla and Claudia walked to their pension in the center of town. They spent the following few days sightseeing, visiting the galleries and museums, admiring the Byzantine mosaics in the Cathedral of San Marco, riding through the canals on a water taxi. Most of the time, they simply walked through the city, stopped for coffee or to eat, and sat around relaxing.

Karla, who was there for the first time, was immediately taken by the charm of the city, in spite of the occasional sour reek from the canals, typical of the hot summer months. The only drawback was the hordes of tourists at this time of the year.

"I'd like to come here during the off-season, when there aren't that many people," she said. "It's tiring to have to stand in line everywhere just to look at a picture. But it is one of the most charming cities I've ever seen. I'd like to come back with Andreas. He'd love all the architecture and the art."

Ever since she had left Florence, and with it the turbulence surrounding her affair with Jean Philippe, Andreas had been on her mind. Seeing young couples walking along the canals or

218

riding the gondolas triggered memories of their happy times together when they first met, of their hikes and outings, of their adventures in Peru, and of the time when they first moved in together.

Why couldn't it be like that again? They still had a chance, even after everything that had happened. Would he forgive her if he knew? He didn't need to know. Jean Philippe was part of her time in Florence. She would leave him and everything that may hurt her relationship with Andreas behind, go back, and start fresh. It would be possible—it had to be possible. In the magical atmosphere of this romantic city, everything seemed possible.

Dear Andreas, she wrote on a postcard with a picture of one of the gondolas on the canal. *Venice is wonderful. The only sad thing is that you aren't here. I miss you. I'm coming home next Sunday. I'll call you to let you know when I get to Locarno. I can hardly wait to see you again. Love, Karla*

After looking at the art, Karla and Claudia went shopping for a few presents. Karla bought some T-shirts with pictures of Venice for Andreas and her friends. She wanted to get a little something for Jean Philippe, but didn't find anything suitable. She didn't know his tastes well enough. In the end, she decided against it. It made her realize how little she actually knew him. Perhaps once she was back home she'd have more time to think of something special to send him as a thank-you gift for helping her with her artwork. It would be less personal and more appropriate.

She almost wished she didn't have to see him again. Being away from him made her realize whom she really loved and what she wanted. She was afraid that being in his presence would reawaken her desire for him and confuse her again.

Chapter 34

The day after Karla and Claudia returned from Venice, Karla walked along the Via Ricasoli to the art school where Jean Philippe taught during the year. The Accademia di Belle Arti was in a beautiful old Romanesque building. Since the fall classes hadn't started yet, there was a quiet hush in the hallways, interrupted once in a while by the sound of an opening or closing door or by muffled voices in the distance.

Karla found Jean Philippe's office and knocked. He was sitting behind a desk littered with books and papers, in a fairly small and somewhat dingy-looking room, which seemed at odds with the regal appearance of the rest of the building.

"Karla," Jean Philippe greeted her. His eyes lit up. "How was Venice?"

"Great. Too many tourists at this time of the year, but what a wonderful city."

"It is, isn't it? We better enjoy it while it lasts, before it disappears into the sea."

"Is that really going to happen?" Karla asked.

"Eventually, unless the scientists find a solution to the rising water level, or rather, to the sinking land. Well, come on, sit down." He searched through a stack of papers on his desk. It was only now that Karla saw four of her paintings leaning against the wall: the one she was going to submit as well as three of the other ones she had done. They were all framed.

"You had my paintings framed?"

"Yes. They look better that way, don't they?"

"Yes, what a difference. But you have to let me know how much that cost."

"Don't worry. Those are just simple frames. Besides, I have connections, it didn't cost me very much." He gave her a quick smile. "All right, here's what we'll do. You're going to submit the one for the contest. If it gets nominated, it will be exhibited in a gallery chosen by the organizers. If it doesn't win anything, then I'll put it up in my gallery together with the other ones. I am the co-owner of one of the galleries around here. In any case, your paintings will get some exposure outside of your own country. We'll see if they sell."

"I don't know how to thank you." Karla was moved by his generosity, and her emotions began to stir again.

"Just keep on painting." He handed her some papers. "Here is the form you need to fill out. I'll be right back, in case you have questions."

He left the room, and Karla began to fill out the application. When she came to the title of the painting, she thought for a moment, then named it *Torment*. Jean Philippe came back and looked the form over briefly. "Good title," he said with a smile. "I guess that takes care of it. Should I need anything else from you, I'll let you know."

"Thanks for everything," Karla said.

"It's my pleasure, young lady." He looked at her tenderly. "What are you going to do now?"

"Nothing in particular. Tonight I'm going out with Claudia and her boyfriend, and tomorrow we're leaving." She felt a stab in her chest at the thought of her departure.

"Oh, I forgot to tell you," Jean Philippe said, "Claudia called me yesterday evening and invited me to go out to dinner with you tonight."

"She did? I hope you accepted."

"Yes, I did. I hesitated at first, thinking that the longer we wait to say good-bye the more difficult it'll be."

"I don't know, Jean Philippe. Saying good-bye when other people are around may be less painful than saying good-bye alone. It's strange, though." Karla wrinkled her brow. "She didn't tell me she was going to invite you. Oh, the scheming little witch ... I get it." She told Jean Philippe about the talk with Claudia in the train to Venice and Claudia's suspicions.

"Well, we better be careful how we act in front of her," Jean Philippe said. "It looks as if Claudia is very perceptive. Listen, we have a few hours. Have you been to the Boboli Gardens?"

"Yes, a couple of times."

"Let's go there. It'll be crowded on a Saturday, but at least we won't be alone and get tempted again, and it would give us some time to talk."

Karla nodded. She knew the minute she saw him again that her intention to close the chapter of Jean Philippe for good had been too idealistic.

As Jean Philippe had predicted, *Giardina di Boboli*, next to the Pitti Palace, was full of tourists who were relaxing in the gardens after visiting the palace and the museums. The beautiful grounds were spread out over a large area and, therefore, didn't feel as crowded as one would have expected, considering the large number of people who visited them day in and day out. Gravel paths lined with cypresses, willows, and chestnut trees led past sweet-scented flower beds and shrubs. Sculptures of mythical figures were tucked away in alcoves, peeking at the visitors from behind garden temples or rising out of the elaborate stone fountains.

After a visit to the *Grotto di Buontalenti*, they climbed the main stairs, past the *Neptune* fountain, toward the top of the hill. They found an unoccupied stone bench along one of the gravel terraces, from which they had a beautiful view of the city.

"I am going to miss this place." Karla sighed and hugged Jean Philippe.

He gave her a quick hug back, then pulled his arm away. "We have to be careful not to show our affection too openly. When I suggested coming here, I wasn't thinking about the fact that I know a lot of people in Florence. Some of them might be here right now, seeing me hug a gorgeous young woman." As if on cue, a man walked by and greeted him by name. Jean Philippe waved back. "See what I mean?"

"He gave me that look," Karla said, "as if he was checking me out."

"Yes, he's a friend of mine, and he'll be teasing me about you. So we better not hug or kiss in public."

Karla sighed. "I guess being the mistress of a married man is a tricky thing."

"Mistress!" Jean Philippe laughed out loud. "You're starting to sound as dramatic as I do. On a more serious note, though, how are you feeling? About us and about your boyfriend?"

Karla took a deep breath. "When I was away from you last week, I had time to think things over, and I realized that I still love Andreas a lot. I want to go home and try everything I can to save what's left of our relationship."

"I'm glad you've come to this decision. It makes me feel a little less guilty." Jean Philippe pulled out a cigarette and held it in his hand without lighting it. They both quietly watched the scenery. The skyline of Florence and the domes and spikes of the buildings were shrouded in a thin yellowish layer of haze.

"Jean Philippe, I've wanted to ask you this before," Karla said after a while. "Did you notice during the workshop that I was falling in love with you? Sometimes I felt I was so obvious about it."

"A few times I became a little suspicious, like the time you cried about your mother and almost hugged me to death. But you know, my feelings for you changed, as well. When I first met you, you were just a young, somewhat confused girl. Then, as your drawing and painting improved and you became more confident and happier, you changed. You exuded a radiance I hadn't noticed before. I began to think of you not just as a girl but as a beautiful and sexy woman. Not that I thought I'd ever go beyond what was appropriate, but I enjoyed being near you and talking to you. It was exciting. You made me feel young again." His eyes lit up with a smile. Then he became serious.

"My initial mistake was that I underestimated the intensity of my feelings. I felt I was in control and that there would be no danger I'd be losing my head. I also didn't take you seriously enough. I suspected you liked me more than you should, and instead of discouraging your feelings, I felt flattered and unconsciously—or perhaps not so unconsciously—encouraged them.

"When I invited you to dinner the second time, I thought of inviting Claudia, as well. Then I decided against it. I wanted to be alone with you. And down at the river when you kissed me, I was startled at first. Then realized it was exactly what I wanted myself.

"Everything I told you so rationally that evening was an attempt to convince myself as much as you. However, deep down I knew that I had already gone too far." Jean Philippe finally lit the cigarette he was holding, and blew the smoke through his nose, then glanced at her.

"Last week, when you were gone, I did some real soul-searching. I realized some unpleasant truths about myself. Not only am I much weaker than I thought I was but I'm not the ethical person I took myself for. I betrayed not only my wife but you as well."

"I think now you're being too hard on yourself." Karla lightly touched his arm. "I mean, I'm the one who took the first step."

"That's true, but that doesn't make my actions any less objectionable. You were a young woman in a vulnerable state of mind, and I took advantage of you. It didn't feel that way to me at the time. It wasn't anything conscious, but that doesn't make it right, does it?"

They were quiet, each occupied with their own thoughts.

"How long have you been married?" Karla asked.

"Almost thirty years."

"Did you ever sleep with anyone else before? I mean, after you were married. I'm sorry, perhaps that's too personal a question."

"That's okay," Jean Philippe said after a moment's silence. "One time I did, but that was long ago. My wife and I had problems, and we separated for a while. We both became involved with other people for a short time, but then we got back together. However, that was a different situation, and the woman wasn't my student."

"You still love your wife."

Jean Philippe looked at her. "Is this a question or a statement?"

"A statement. I know you love her. In fact, I can feel you slipping away from me."

"That's true. It has to happen to both of us, because we know very well we have no future together, at least not as lovers. But I hope we'll always be friends."

"Yes, I hope so, too," Karla said quietly. She realized, though, that it wouldn't be easy for her to think of Jean Philippe simply as a friend.

"You're right, I do love Micaela." Jean Philippe's voice interrupted her painful pondering.

"Is it possible to love more than one person—I mean, more than one woman or more than one man?" Karla asked after a slight hesitation.

Jean Philippe looked at her pensively, then gently touched her cheek. "I guess it must be possible. It happened to us, didn't it? I think the feelings we have for each other go beyond mere physical attraction. However, when it comes to the kind of love between a man and a woman, then at some point you have to make a decision. Otherwise, it gets too confusing. And you end up hurting and, eventually, losing them both."

"I guess so," Karla said hesitantly.

"Listen." Jean Philippe reached for another cigarette. He looked at it absentmindedly, then put it back into his shirt pocket. "I love you and I will always think of you fondly. However, we've only known each other for a very short time. The bond between Micaela and me goes back through thirty years of shared history. We've gone through a lot together, we have had ups and downs, we've watched our children grow, we've worried about them when they were sick and enjoyed their successes.

"Making love after thirty years may not be as exciting as it was when we were young, although we're still attracted to each other. Perhaps it's not the fireworks the two of us experienced a few nights ago, but it's ... what should I call it ... fulfilling, perhaps.

"When I wake up in the morning, I feel a quiet joy, knowing that after so many years I still love the woman next to me and that she still loves me. It's a precious gift I could've easily lost the other night." He quickly touched her arm. "I hope you understand what I'm trying to tell you. I'm not belittling the feelings the two of us have for each other, but there is a difference. Don't be sad, please."

"I'm not sad because of what you said." Karla sighed. "I'm sad because it reminds me of something that I experienced with Andreas. I know we don't have that kind of long-term relationship to fall back on. But you said 'fulfilling,' and that's the way I felt with Andreas when we made love. It was different from anything I experienced before I met him."

"And you don't think you can revive those feelings?" Jean Philippe asked.

"I don't know. I hope so, but I don't know how Andreas feels about me anymore."

"Karla, I really wish you could be happy with him again. Don't forget, though, you're still so young. If it's not Andreas, it'll be someone else."

"I guess so." Karla didn't feel convinced. She watched a group of young people walk by, laughing and talking animatedly.

"Promise me something, Karla. Let me know how things turn out with your boyfriend. And if I can help you with anything related to your painting, I certainly will."

Karla nodded and forced a smile. It all sounded so rational and right, but the words didn't penetrate to her heart. Her mind and her emotions were as out of sync as they had been when she first fell in love with this man sitting next to her.

In spite of the danger of being spotted by someone he knew, Jean Philippe hugged her and gave her a quick kiss, then got up from the bench. "I have some work to do before I meet with you guys tonight. Want me to give you a ride home?"

"No, thanks. I think I'll walk. It's my last day in Florence for a while. I have to say good-bye to the city."

They walked together to the exit of the gardens and then went their separate ways.

On the way to her apartment, Karla slowly regained her composure. *Yes, Jean Philippe is right, we have no future together and I better get used to it.* She stopped halfway across the Ponte Vecchio, which was mobbed by tourists from all over the world, laughing and talking and snapping pictures. Karla got a quick glimpse of the Arno through the throng of people. Its yellowish-brown water flowed sluggishly.

"You didn't tell me that you invited Jean Philippe for tonight," Karla said to Claudia when she got home.

Claudia and her boyfriend, Mauro, were sitting next to each other in the apartment, drinking coffee in the middle of suitcases, bags, and boxes. Mauro had arrived the evening before to pick up Claudia and take her home the following day.

"Oh, it was supposed to be a surprise." Claudia sounded a little disappointed. "How did you find out?"

"I went to see him at his office to fill out the application form for the contest next month."

"I thought it would be nice to treat him for dinner, to thank him for the workshop and everything, since he couldn't make it the other night ... the night you spent with ... your desperate friend."

"Little witch," Karla said, and went to her room to continue packing. She heard Claudia giggle.

In the evening Jean Philippe came to pick them up. He offered to drive them to a restaurant in Fiesole, a town perched on a hill above Florence. They parked the car at the main piazza and climbed a steep path up the hill. The restaurant La Reggia was situated just below the church San Francesco and its small monastery. From the terrace they had a view of Florence.

"Claudia, this is a wonderful place." Karla watched as the houses and roofs of the city faded into the night, while famous buildings, cathedrals, palaces, and the Duomo were brightly lit. "Being here makes it even more difficult to leave tomorrow."

"Well, I hope you all can come back. I am going to miss you," Jean Philippe said.

"We'll be back." Claudia turned to Karla. "You have to bring your boyfriend next time."

Was it an innocent suggestion or an indirect hint? Karla looked at Jean Philippe, who gave her a barely perceptible smile. "Yes, that would be great," Karla said in a matter-of-fact tone while checking out the large selection on the menu.

The evening was pleasant and much more lighthearted than Karla had expected. They talked about the workshop, about what they had learned. Claudia teased Karla and Jean Philippe about the incident with the half-eaten apple.

It was a little after eleven o'clock when they drove back to the apartment. Claudia and Mauro talked in a low voice in the backseat. Karla, who sat in front next to Jean Philippe, was quiet during the drive back. The thought of the upcoming farewell, which she had pushed away all evening, now surfaced. She may not see him again for many years, perhaps never again. It seemed so unreal.

After they got out of the car, Jean Philippe said good-bye to Mauro and Claudia. Claudia gave him a hug, then put her arm around Mauro and pulled him toward the door of the apartment tower, leaving Karla and Jean Philippe behind, obviously wanting to give them the chance to say good-bye alone. They both smiled at the touching gesture, then turned to face each other.

Karla pressed her lips together to stop them from trembling. Jean Philippe embraced her, and she held on to him, not wanting to let go. "I can't believe I won't see you again," she whispered, her voice failing her.

"Psst. You're just making it harder." He pulled back a little, but kept holding her hands. "Please don't cry." His voice sounded strained. "Let me know how you are." Then after a short pause: "I love you."

Karla nodded. Her throat tightened, and she was unable to speak. He gave her a quick kiss, then walked away. She barely saw him through the curtain of tears. She heard the car door open and close, the rubbing sound of the car engine. She waved in the direction of the noise, then turned and slowly climbed the stairs to the apartment, taking deep breaths to stop herself from crying. Inside, Claudia was getting ready for bed. "Are you all right?" she asked.

Karla nodded. "Thanks for inviting him tonight."

Claudia hugged her quietly, then joined Mauro in the bedroom. Karla spent the night on the living-room couch so Claudia could be with her boyfriend.

Sometime during the night, Karla woke up. She heard the muffled noises of lovemaking. She turned around and tried to fall back to sleep, thinking of Andreas and Jean Philippe.

PART FIVE

ON TREACHEROUS GROUND

Chapter 35

The train leaving Florence allowed a brief view of the top of the Duomo and the church Santa Maria Novella before it left behind the ancient splendor of Florence's palaces and cathedrals, its Michelangelo, Botticelli, Dante, and Medici, and passed by the less attractive sites—train tracks, gray walls smeared with graffiti, and modest dwellings of modern working-class Florentines.

The drab backside of Florence was in tune with Karla's mood. She felt melancholic, uneasy, and uprooted. Claudia and Mauro had given her a ride to the station before driving on to a beach town at the Riviera for a brief vacation to celebrate their reunion. Karla had been grateful for their company. After waking up in the middle of the night, she hadn't been able to fall back to sleep, feeling the acute pain of separation not just from Jean Philippe but from Florence in general and her intense life of the past two months. Thinking of Andreas didn't help much. In addition to the uncertainty about a common future, she now had to deal with feelings of guilt from having cheated on him. It wasn't that they had sworn loyalty to each other, but it was a betrayal nevertheless.

Watching the beautiful landscape with its lush meadows and the typical Tuscan stone farmhouses with their ocher and orange walls, in between the cities of Bologna and the towns of Modena and Parma, she felt her spirits revive. She was looking forward to painting again, and decided to give the children of Silvia's friend art lessons.

As the train approached the Swiss border, Karla tried to call Andreas on her cell phone but only got his answering machine. She realized that he may not even know she was coming back. It had been too optimistic of her to rely on her postcard from Venice arriving in time to let him know the date of her return. She decided not to leave a message, but to surprise him. Instead, she called Lena, who, fortunately, answered right away and promised to pick her up in Locarno.

Karla's home gave off the stale smell of a house that had been empty for a long time. She opened the windows to air out the rooms and let in the last few sunrays of the day. Andreas had taken good care of the place. Her plants were watered, and everything was in order. His studio, however, looked empty. A lot of his tools were gone, and Karla wondered about the absence of new sculptures and tombstones.

After dropping off her luggage, she went to Lena and Luigi's, who had invited her for dinner. Their house smelled of tomatoes and spices, and Karla realized she was hungry. She hadn't eaten anything except for a sandwich on the train. Luigi was in the process of stirring the sauce and cutting the vegetables for the salad. "Ciao, *bella*. Welcome home." He kissed her and handed her a glass of wine.

While Lena and the children were setting the table, Karla went to check Andreas's rooms upstairs. Standing in front of the door, she hesitated. She was nervous about meeting him again after all that had happened the past few months. She knocked and held her breath, but there was no answer. More relieved than disappointed, she left a note on his door and went downstairs. It would be easier to greet him at her place, in their familiar environment.

The children were unwrapping the presents Karla had brought them from her trip to Venice. After they tried on their new T-shirts, they all sat down to dinner. The good meal and the company of friends made Karla feel at home again.

At her house, she unpacked a few items, then sat in the living room with a cup of tea. It was only now, being by herself, that she realized how empty and lonely her place felt without Andreas living there. She missed him—at least, the Andreas she had known during their happy times together. At the same time, she was afraid to meet the man he may have become, the one with the angry or distant voice she remembered from her phone calls from Florence.

Please, dear God, she prayed silently, *give us another chance.*

She went to bed feeling sad, but fell asleep instantly, exhausted from her trip and the lack of sleep of the past few nights.

Karla woke to a beautiful early-fall day. The air was crisp and smelled of wet grass, a welcome change from the gasoline fumes of Florence. A thin layer of mist hovered over the dew-soaked fields, and in the south, thin yellowish lines were etched into the sky. She unpacked the rest of her stuff and arranged her painting materials in her studio. When she set up her easel, her mind flashed back to Jean Philippe. She wondered what he was doing at that moment. He was probably in Siena with his family, since his regular classes hadn't started yet. She smiled and gave her head a slight toss. Florence seemed far away.

She sat outside in the sun, sipping her coffee and enjoying the familiar landscape. The vineyards were full of ripening grapes that gave off a sweet aroma, and Lena's fields sparkled with the colors of late-blooming roses. After a good night's sleep, the future looked promising again. Karla decided to wait for a while before going shopping. Perhaps Andreas would come by, and she didn't want to miss him.

At ten o'clock she began to get impatient. There was still no word from him. He hadn't even called. He must have seen her note. Karla grabbed her bag and shopping list, hoping her car didn't have a dead battery. The car was covered with a thin layer of dust, but started right away.

Driving up the narrow road to her house on the way back from the store, she saw his car parked outside. The door to his studio was half open, and from the clunking of metal, it sounded as though he was moving stuff around. Karla carried her groceries inside and put them away, glancing once in a while through the window facing the studio. In the bathroom, she combed her hair and checked herself in the mirror. *Almost like a first date.*

He was just coming out of his studio when she stepped outside. He looked different. He seemed to have lost weight, and his hair had grown longer and was falling into his face. When he saw her, he stopped, hesitated, then gave her a quick smile.

"You changed," Karla said as she walked up to him. "Have you lost weight?"

"A little. What do you expect without your excellent cooking?" Andreas gave her a quick hug. "Lena told me you were back. I'm sorry I didn't pick you up. I had no idea you were coming. Why didn't you let me know?"

"I sent a postcard, but it obviously didn't make it in time."

"So, you're back." Andreas slid his hands into his pockets, shifted his weight from one foot to the other. "It's been so long. I have to get used to you again."

"I know. I'll get you some coffee." Karla, feeling equally awkward, turned around and went into the kitchen. After she came out with two cups of cappuccino, they sat on the stone bench in front of the house.

Andreas took a sip of coffee. "How was Florence?"

"Great. It did wonders for my painting."

"So your teacher wasn't that bad after all?"

"No, he wasn't. He had this odd way of teaching that drove me crazy at first, but it worked." It surprised Karla how easy it was for her to talk about Jean Philippe as a teacher. She told Andreas about the contest and the paintings Jean Philippe would exhibit in his gallery.

"I hope you took photos of them," Andreas said.

"I have a picture of the one for the contest, but not of the other ones. I didn't even think about it. Jean Philippe has a digital camera, though. I can ask him to send me photos."

"Jean Philippe? That doesn't sound Italian."

"He's originally from Paris, but he is married to an Italian and they live in Florence—well, actually in Siena. What have you been doing all this time?" Karla asked, wanting to change the subject.

"Mainly working. I met this rich guy in Ascona ... I think I told you about him. He ordered sculptures for his villa, and he knows quite a lot of people with money, so I've been quite busy. And then, of course, my regular work."

"Sounds like you got a real break. I noticed that your studio is half empty. Haven't you been working here?"

"Not in a while." He gave her a quick glance, then looked down at the coffee cup in his hand. "After you left, I really had a hard time working here. The place felt empty and lifeless without you. So one day I saw an ad in the paper of someone renting out a garage in Locarno. It seemed like a good temporary solution. It was easier to work in a totally new environment."

"I can understand that. Thanks, by the way, for taking care of the rustico and the car. I was so glad I didn't have a dead battery."

"Yes, I drove it occasionally."

They were both quiet. Sitting next to him again after all this time, Karla realized how much he still meant to her. She tried to find a way to reach him across the divide that had widened between them over the past few months, but she felt inhibited. "Andreas," she said, then stopped.

"Yes?"

She took a deep breath. "Are you going to work in your studio again, now that I'm back?"

He hesitated, cleared his throat, and took a sip of coffee. "I can try."

Karla put her arm around him. "Andreas, I want us to be together again. Can't we give each other another chance?"

Andreas kept staring at his coffee cup, turning it in his hand. "I'd like that, too, but I don't want to just move back in right away. I want us to be clear about what we have to do to make it work. I don't want to go through all this again."

"I'm willing to make some changes, since I'm the one who was responsible for our problems anyway," Karla said.

"It wasn't just you. It was my fault, too." Andreas hesitated, then went on. "Remember back in Peru, when you told me you felt safe with me and I promised to keep you safe? I felt flattered. I realized later on what a delusion that was. I can't keep you safe. I can't make you happy. You have to do it yourself, it has to come from inside. ... I don't know how to say it."

"I know what you mean, Andreas. It's true. I depended too much on you and didn't take responsibility for myself. I am really serious about making changes. I decided to see my analyst again."

Andreas hesitated. "We can try."

Karla bit her lower lip. "You don't seem to be glad I'm back."

"God, Karla, give me some time." Andreas touched her hand. "I'm still totally surprised you're back. We barely had any contact with each other for the past two months. And the few times we did talk weren't very pleasant. You can't expect me to behave as if everything was as it had always been. I have to come to terms with a few things first."

"I know. I'm sorry. I didn't mean to rush you."

Andreas put his cup down and embraced her, pulling her close. "I still love you. But sometimes love isn't enough to make things work." He looked at her with troubled eyes.

Karla put her arms around him. He kissed her. The scent of him, the taste of coffee in his mouth, the feeling of his hair on her face—it was like a gust of wind that made the fire still smoldering between them flare up again full force. They were kissing frantically.

"No." He pushed her away. "I don't want to start it this way."

"What's the matter?"

"I don't want to just jump into bed with you, as much as I want to." He shook his head and gave a quick chortle. "This doesn't make sense, I know. Look, you have to trust me with this. I just can't right now."

"Okay." She tried to read his face, but he turned away and got up.

"I have to go, Karla. I'll see you tomorrow." He went to lock his studio.

Karla was watching as the lime-green Fiat slowly made its way down the hill. She sighed and went inside. It would take time to rebuild the relationship and restore the trust between them. She was almost relieved to be alone again. His behavior had been odd; the way he had pushed her back when they kissed, as if they had done something forbidden. It was more than just feeling awkward after the long separation. It reminded her of the time she had kissed Jean Philippe during their walk.

A thought flashed through her mind. *Is there someone else?* She dismissed it instantly, but the suspicion lingered. Karla tried to think of any signs during their few phone conversations that would confirm her suspicion, but couldn't come up with anything concrete.

In the evening, Karla fixed a simple dinner of minestrone and salad and opened a bottle of red wine. She built a fire in the fireplace. Although lighting it made her feel melancholic—it had always been Andreas's job—she went ahead with it anyway. She had been able to enjoy the pleasures of a fire and a good meal before she met him, and she needed to do these things again. Depending on Andreas for her emotional well-being had been one of her biggest mistakes.

The sun was disappearing behind the hills. September was just around the corner, and the days were already getting a little shorter. Karla stepped outside to watch the light recede and the darkness slowly settle on the fields and mountains. The sky had reached a deep shade of indigo fading into black, which marked the transition from dusk to full night. Taking a deep breath, Karla felt content. It was good to be back.

Before going to bed, she made a list of things she wanted to accomplish in the following few months. She needed some sort of plan to stay focused and not get swept up again in a storm of emotions. Although she had plenty of ideas for her paintings and felt creative, she knew she could get stuck again.

First of all, she had to get a paid job. Her grant money and her savings had dwindled. She decided to talk to Silvia, who sometimes heard of temporary jobs in galleries or other businesses. In addition, she wanted to work with the children Silvia had recommended. Jean Philippe was right; it would help her not worry so much about her own creative success or failure.

The third decision—seeing a therapist again—was the one she had struggled most with. She had met a woman once, a Jungian analyst who, among other things, used painting as a method of healing. For this, however, she needed to save up money, but she wanted to at least contact her and set up an appointment. Otherwise she would just put it off again, as she had done so many times in the past.

Karla took a sip of merlot, enjoying its vigorous aroma and slightly woodsy taste as she read through her list. The tasks looked so easy, neatly written down on paper. Following through was another matter. This time, however, she would do it. It was the only way to keep afloat in the sea of constantly threatening emotional turbulences.

Chapter 36

"So how did you like Jean Philippe?" Silvia was sitting across from Karla in the small office in her gallery. The gallery was closed, and Silvia was taking care of her accounting. It smelled of oil paint and lacquer. Karla listened to the tapping of footsteps on the pavement outside as a group of tourists walked by. Laughter and a volley of foreign words slowly faded away.

"Oh, boy." Karla sighed. "That's a loaded question."

"Why?" Silvia laughed. "That sounds almost ominous."

"Well, at first we didn't get along at all. He almost threw me out of the class." Karla told her about her initial trouble and how well it all turned out. It made her feel good to be able to talk about Jean Philippe again, and to someone who knew him and, at one time, had been in love with him, as well. She didn't want to tell her what had happened between them, but she could at least admit liking him a lot.

Silvia caught on right away. "You look like a young girl in love."

"He is an attractive man and very charming, I have to admit."

"He must like you, too."

"Why do you say that?"

"Well, he called me yesterday, supposedly to just talk and find out how I was doing. Obviously, though, he was more interested in how you were. He asked if you had gotten home all right. Then he praised you and your painting. I could tell you made a deep impression on him."

Karla laughed. It warmed her heart to learn that he still cared about her. "I'm glad he said that, because after the first week he threatened to let you know what a rotten kid I was."

"Yes, Jean Philippe, he is quite the charmer," Silvia said with a dreamy voice.

Karla waved a hand in front of her face. "Come back to reality, Silvia."

"Oh yes." Silvia sighed. "So you're looking for a job? Well, I might just have the thing for you. How would you like to help run my gallery for a few weeks while I'm gone? Richard and I are going on an extended vacation next month. It's our thirtieth wedding anniversary."

"You've been married for thirty years?" Karla asked, surprised. "You guys don't look that old."

"Well, thank you." Silvia chuckled. "Here is the deal. I have a woman who'll come in twice a week, but I need someone for the remaining four days. Mondays we're closed. The other person I had lined up canceled on me. It wouldn't be anything difficult, just answering the phone and, if someone is interested, explain a little bit about the painting and the artist, something you're very familiar with. You'll get paid a regular salary, of course, and if you sell a painting, I'll give you the commission."

"Gee, that would be wonderful, if you trust me with something like this."

"Of course, you'd be perfect. Most of the time during the week it's quiet. It gets a little busier on weekends. During the slow times you can always do some painting in the adjacent room. In fact, that would be perfect—an artist at work, the best kind of advertisement for a gallery."

"Silvia, that's so much better than some kind of boring office job." Karla was excited.

"You know, it could lead to something in the future, if you like it. There is so much Richard and I would love to do together, and we're not getting any younger. If I had someone I could depend on who could fill in for me part-time, I could begin to cut back on my hours here."

This seems to be my lucky day. After leaving the gallery, Karla walked down the street, toward the lake. It was the middle of the afternoon. The steel-blue water of the Lago Maggiore shimmered in the sunshine, and the horizon was streaked with yellowish-white haze. Karla sat on the patio of a coffee shop and ordered a cappuccino. Waiting for her order, she looked around at the few guests more closely, and that's when she saw him.

Andreas was sitting at one of the tables at the other end of the rather large patio. He must not have seen her come in. Just as Karla was getting ready to get up and go over to him, a woman walked in from the street and sat next to him. Andreas looked up and smiled at her. She put her arm around his neck and kissed him. Karla's breath caught. It was a light kiss, but it was more than a sign of affection between casual friends.

At first Karla was so shocked that she simply stared at them. She barely noticed when the waiter put the coffee in front of her. Not wanting to attract their attention, she pushed her chair back a little behind a tall potted plant, where she could observe them unnoticed. They were too far away for Karla to understand what they were talking about.

Their gestures were animated. After the waiter brought the woman a cup of coffee, it was mainly Andreas who talked. The woman listened, taking a sip of coffee occasionally. Karla saw that she was quite a bit older than Andreas, probably in her thirties, and average looking, with light-brown hair reaching to her shoulders. She was wearing a simple but elegant outfit. All of this Karla took in while desperately trying to find an innocent explanation for the scene unfolding in front of her. At one point Andreas put his hand on the woman's cheek. She looked up at him, then lowered her head and supported it with her arm. Karla realized she was crying; her shoulders were trembling. Andreas gave the woman a hug, at which point Karla decided she had seen enough.

She took some money out of her purse and left it on the table. It was too much for the coffee, but she didn't want to call the waiter and attract their attention. All she wanted to do was get away and hide somewhere from the blunt and cruel truth. As she got up, Andreas looked over at her. Their eyes met for an instant, and she saw his shocked expression. She hurried to her car without looking back. Driving the car out of the parking lot, she almost hit a pedestrian. She took a deep breath and forced herself to focus on the road.

At home she sat on the couch. Too emotionally crushed to cry, she stared out the window. Now it all made sense: his odd behavior, the appearance of feeling guilty for something. That's what she had feared, and now it was true. *Why am I shocked?* she wondered. *After all, I did the same thing.*

However, in her case it was over; but to judge from the way he had treated the woman, he was still involved with her, and perhaps would be in the future. Had she lost him for good? This couldn't be true. She sat on the living-room couch without moving for a long time. Only once in her life had she felt so utterly lost.

She remembered when she heard from her aunt that her mother and grandmother had died. She had heard the words but didn't understand what they meant. For a long time Karla refused to believe they were dead. She held on to the illusion that one day the door would open and the two people she loved the most would come walking in again, just like after a long vacation. When she had finally been able to face the fact of their demise, she had felt cut off from her roots, insubstantial, as if she herself didn't exist anymore. It had taken her a long time to feel a more or less stable foundation upon which she could build her life. It was mainly through painting that she had slowly lost the fear of touching the world around her and letting the world touch her.

It was quiet in the room except for the grandfather clock ticking its normal indifferent beat. Someone knocked. She got up, as if in trance, and opened the door. It was Andreas.

"Can I come in?" he asked in a low voice, almost whispering.

She nodded and sat down again. He came in quietly and sat next to her. For a few moments a heavy, suffocating silence lingered between them. Andreas cleared his throat; his voice sounded labored. "I'm sorry, Karla, I didn't want you to find out this way."

She barely dared to breathe. "What does it mean, Andreas?"

"I'll try to explain it, but I want you to know that I broke up with her. I don't know if that still means anything to you."

"Was that the reason she was crying?"

"Yes," Andreas said. "Look, I'm sorry. I didn't want it to go that far. I've wanted to break it off, but I didn't have the courage, and then you came back and it got even more confusing, but at least I knew then that I still loved you. God, I guess I should start at the beginning. ..."

Karla began to sob. The tension of the past hours gave way to relief. *Thank god, I haven't lost him.* For the moment that thought eclipsed all the emotional turmoil she had experienced. "Who is that woman?"

"Her name is Annette." Andreas put his arm around her. "I'm sorry."

Karla sat up straight and brushed his arm away. "What's the story?"

"She's owner of the garage I rented as a studio. I ... Do you have anything to drink?"

"Want some wine?"

"Sure, perhaps it'll loosen my tongue."

Karla went into the kitchen and got two wineglasses and the bottle of merlot she had opened the night before. She poured them both a glass.

"Anyway," he continued after taking a sip, "after you left, I felt really lousy. I couldn't concentrate on my work, and I started falling behind. You know, you once told me that you felt I was the rock in your life. Well, that rock crumbled, and I had a hard time getting the pieces back together.

"I even went out drinking once with a few of my friends, which I hadn't done in years. I've always hated these getting-together-and-getting-drunk binges some of the other guys went on occasionally. One time, however, when I was really down, I joined them and actually managed to get totally tanked. I had such a hangover, I didn't get up the next day. Luigi finally came to check on me. I think Lena and he started to worry and invited me for dinner all the time, probably to keep an eye on me."

"God, Andreas, I've never seen you drunk."

"You haven't missed anything. It's not a pretty sight. Fortunately, I don't get aggressive like my father did. I just get really tired, and I have bloodshot eyes and a red—"

"Who cares? Tell me about the woman, for heaven's sake."

"I'm sorry. Anyway ..." Another sigh. "I saw this ad in the paper, and the woman who rented it out had just gotten divorced and lived by herself. She told me that later, of course—I mean, about the divorce."

"Stop rambling. I'm not interested in her divorce."

"Okay, okay. I'm trying. Anyway, after I moved my stuff into her garage, she once in a while came by to watch me work. So we got to talking. She told me about her divorce, and I told her a little bit about our problems—"

"You told her about our problems? How could you? You talked about me behind my back."

"Stop interrupting me, damn it, or I'll never get to the end." Andreas threw up his hands.

"Don't yell at me." Karla glared at him.

"I'm sorry, I don't mean to yell." Andreas lowered his voice. "But yes, it was great to be able to talk to someone. I didn't badmouth you, if that's what you mean. I was desperate, and here was someone who understood me and listened to me."

Unlike the crazy person I was. Karla sighed. "Go on."

"Anyway. Sometimes, she invited me for coffee and we sat in her yard. So, one day, one thing led to another, and so it happened. ..." Andreas looked down at his wineglass, turning it in his hands, then gave Karla a quick glance. He took a sip and put the glass down.

"At first it was just two unhappy people kind of trying to console each other. I never thought of it as a long-term thing. I liked her, but I wasn't in love with her." He picked up the glass, then put it down again without drinking. "After a few weeks, she hinted about getting together permanently. I told her that I didn't feel free enough to make such a decision ... that there was still you. She assured me she understood and she didn't want to rush me.

"Well, that's when I really blew it. I kind of took her word for it, but somehow I knew she just told me that not to lose me. And I myself wasn't ready yet to break it off. I lingered on, in part because ... I liked her ... and because it was convenient, I guess. Anyway, I was too much of a coward to tell her the truth." Andreas began to play with his hands, cracking his knuckles.

"Stop that, please." Karla put her hand on his.

Andreas took her hand and kissed it.

"Did you ... were you ever thinking of getting together with her ... for good?"

"A few times I thought about how it would be to have her as a steady girlfriend. She was nice, calm, and very mature in many ways. It was relaxing being with her."

"The opposite of what I was," Karla said.

"Just different ... and yes, a welcome calm after all the bullshit we had been through."

Andreas paused. He supported his head with his hands and rubbed his eyes. "But every time I came here to water your plants and take care of the house, I thought of you again. I remembered all the little things about you. The way you brushed your hair, the way you carefully arranged flowers. How you always burned yourself when cooking and had me kiss your finger ... all this silly stuff." He lifted his head.

"I just couldn't let go. You were in me ... somehow ... in my body and my heart, and I couldn't get rid of you." He was looking down at his hands again, holding on to his wineglass as though for protection. A strand of dark hair fell into his face.

Karla realized just how close she had come to losing him. How naïve and selfish it had been of her to think that only *she* could fall in love with someone else.

Andreas cleared his throat again. "What really makes me ashamed is the fact that I strung Annette along when I already knew she was in love with me and I couldn't return her feelings. When I finally did break it off, she was much more hurt than if I had done it earlier. What a mess." Andreas propped his head on his hands.

So that's how it is. He seems to be more concerned about how that woman feels than how I feel. Karla got up and walked to the window, and stared outside. She tried to come to terms with what she just heard. She was relieved, disappointed, and hurt at the same time. She was relieved that she hadn't lost Andreas for good, that he still loved her. However, she couldn't help feeling hurt when she realized how little time it seemed to have taken him to get involved with someone else. He had been sleeping with the woman for weeks, while she had tortured herself and fought her attraction to Jean Philippe.

I'm being unfair. It didn't take me long to fall in love with Jean Philippe. She sat again and took his hand in hers, preparing the ground for confessing her own trespass. "Andreas, we're all just human."

"I'm really grateful you're taking it so well." Andreas squeezed her hand. "You're a very generous person. I don't know if I could be that forgiving had it been the other way round."

Well, that settles the question about my confession. Now, Karla was relieved she hadn't told him anything. *What kind of a double standard is this? And I bet he isn't even aware of it. Jerk.*

"Who said I'm forgiving you? You carried on a relationship for weeks. You yelled at me on the phone. You never told me."

"I'm sorry. I was confused. It was a difficult time. But it also made me realize that I still loved you." Andreas cracked his knuckles again. "Please forgive me."

"I'll try."

They sat quietly without speaking for a while. Andreas picked up the sketchbook that was lying on the table and opened it. "Did you do these in Florence?"

Karla nodded. Andreas paged through the book. "These are great. I like the way you combine abstract elements with concrete objects."

"I have a few paintings I was able to bring with me. Want to see them?"

"Of course."

Andreas studied the pictures in his slow, careful way. "Wow. Look at the light." He pointed at two of the paintings. One was of a woman standing in a doorway. The sunlight from outside framed her like a halo. The almost angelic background formed a stark contrast to the expression on her face. She looked tortured and in pain. The other one was a scene from Florence. The buildings along the Arno were only adumbrated, and the scenery exploded in light and color.

Andreas looked up. His eyes shone, and his voice trembled with excitement. "This is a true breakthrough."

They sat next to each other, paging through the sketchbook and looking at the paintings and drawings. Andreas's enthusiasm and the look in his eyes stirred something deep within Karla. This was the man she had fallen in love with and whom she still loved. How could she ever forget?

"Are you really finished with that woman, what's her name?"

"Annette." Andreas sighed. "Yes. Definitely. I'm going to pick up the rest of my stuff in her garage."

"Andreas, you have some forgiving to do, as well. I was really ugly to you before I went to Florence. I didn't mean to be. No wonder you fell for someone else." She put her hand on his. "Do you think we have another chance?"

"I sure want to try." Andreas touched her cheek. His eyes had the tender expression she remembered from earlier times.

Karla hugged him. "I made an appointment with the analyst, and I told Silvia I'd teach the kids of her friend. I'm trying—" He closed her mouth with a kiss. His body exuded warmth and comfort. He gently caressed her breast through her T-shirt, giving her a questioning look. Karla pulled off her top.

They made love on the floor, surrounded by drawings and paintings. Through the open window, Karla heard birds twitter in the wisteria vine. Then the church bells began to ring in evening Mass, drowning out all other noises.

Later that night, Karla was still debating whether she should tell Andreas about Jean Philippe and just get it over with. He might get upset again. Jean Philippe, after all, was married, and Karla was well aware of Andreas's more traditional views on the subject. Perhaps later she would find an opportunity to tell him. Or perhaps Florence would just have to remain a secret between Jean Philippe and herself.

She knew it was a cop-out, a burden she wouldn't be able to carry for very long. She should be brave and make a clean breast of it, but Karla's heart was still too raw from the recent blows. Being close to Andreas again after all the turmoil, the pain, and the uncertainty was like waking up after a prolonged illness and feeling good for the first time again. She couldn't possibly let another cloud block the sun that had just begun to shine on the seeds of their new relationship.

Chapter 37

The chestnut trees had lost almost all their leaves, which covered the ground like a yellow-and-brown carpet sprinkled with red. The grapes in the vineyards were blue and plump, ready to be harvested and transformed into wine.

Karla was busy working at the gallery and giving drawing and painting lessons to the children of Silvia's friend. She was surprised how much the two boys and the girl enjoyed it and how creative they were. Particularly the oldest boy showed real talent, and Karla felt he would eventually need a professional teacher.

The rest of the time she devoted to her own work. To her amazement, her painting became more prolific with the limited time she had. She couldn't afford to sit in front of her easel daydreaming or worrying about the quality of a particular work. Being with other people and doing a variety of things inspired her and triggered ideas for her work. She always carried a small sketchbook with her, and after a few weeks, she had a whole collection of drawings she used as the basis for a new painting. She sometimes smiled, thinking how she initially had resisted drawing the "dumb objects" at Jean Philippe's workshop.

At the end of the month, Andreas moved in with her again. Since Karla now did some of her work away from home, as well, they sometimes saw each other only in the evening and for brief moments during the day, which made their time together more precious. Things seemed on an even keel. They decided to get married the following May.

Karla still thought of Jean Philippe once in a while. One day, sitting in the gallery, she was tempted to call him at his office, but then dropped the idea. It wouldn't be right to call him behind Andreas's back. Finally, Karla decided to write him a letter and send him the gift she had bought for him. It was a photo book with pictures of Locarno and the surrounding area. One of the photos was a shot of the street with Silvia's gallery on it. He would no doubt enjoy that picture.

One evening when she came home from work, Andreas told her that her painting teacher from Florence had called. Karla's heart skipped a beat. "Did he say what he wanted?"

"No. He only said to call him back, either tonight or to-morrow." Andreas gave her a slip of paper with Jean Philippe's office number and hours. Karla tried to keep her hand from shaking as she reached for it. "Why don't you call him now?" Andreas suggested. "You still got half an hour."

Karla would have preferred to call when Andreas wasn't around, but she couldn't think of an excuse to postpone the call. She punched the numbers with trembling fingers and waited, hoping Jean Philippe wouldn't answer and she'd have a reason to call the following day. The phone had barely rung twice when someone picked up and she heard his voice: "*Pronto.*"

Her heart was beating so fast she could barely speak. "Jean Philippe, this is Karla," she finally managed to say.

"Karla! How nice to hear your voice. How are you?"

"I'm fine. How are you?"

"Great, thanks. Listen, I have excellent news for you. Your painting won first prize."

"What did you say?" was the only thing she managed to get out. Then she realized he was talking about the contest. She had almost forgotten about it. "That's not true."

"Of course it's true. Do you think I'd lie to you about something like that?"

"I can't believe it. Are you sure?"

He laughed. "Karla, your modesty is endearing, but it's about time you felt a little more confident about your work. I told you you'd have a chance. Otherwise, I wouldn't have encouraged you to submit it. Of course, I couldn't have guessed that it would win first price. Aren't you happy?"

"Yes, of course. It's just overwhelming."

"You'll get something in the mail. They called me because there was something wrong with the address or the phone number you put down or they couldn't read it. Since my number was on the form as secondary contact, they called me about it. That's what you get for your lousy handwriting. I'm sure glad you paint better than you write."

"Jean Philippe, I'm still shocked."

"Well, snap out of it. Go out and celebrate. The only bad part about you winning is the fact that I won't get your painting in my gallery." After a brief pause: "By the way, was that Andreas who answered the phone?"

"Yes." Karla swallowed.

"So I take it you're back together?"

"Yes." She glanced at Andreas, who was going through a pile of mail in the living room.

"I can tell you can't talk, he's probably there. I'm happy to hear that things are going well. Are they?"

"Oh, yes, everything is fine." She took a deep breath. "I started teaching the children I told you about, and it's really fun. I'm also working in Silvia's gallery at the moment. She and her husband are on a vacation, celebrating their thirtieth wedding anniversary."

"Thirty years!" Jean Philippe laughed. "I didn't realize she was that old already."

"How are you doing with your classes?" Karla was beginning to feel more at ease and wished to prolong the conversation. She enjoyed the sound of his voice, his humor, and the slight Parisian accent.

"Not too bad. I miss my summer students, though. I think I'm just getting too old and impatient to deal with these young kids. By the way, I got a note from Claudia. She and Mauro are getting married."

"I know, I did, too," Karla said. "I am happy for them. They are such a nice couple."

"I agree. ... I hope to get a wedding announcement from you one of these days."

"I think you will."

"Wonderful. I wish you the best of luck."

"Thanks."

"Well, I better go. There's a student waiting for me. It's been great talking to you, and if one of your other paintings sells, I'll let you know."

"Thanks, Jean Philippe ... for everything."

"Ciao, cara. Stay in touch."

"Ciao," Karla whispered. She put the receiver on the table and sat down, staring at her hands. *I am still in love with him* was her first thought. *I won first prize,* her second.

"Once you wake up from your stupor, would you mind telling me what that was all about?" Andreas asked.

"Remember the contest I told you about? My painting won first prize."

"That's great. Congratulations. And because of that, you're crying?"

"I'm just overwhelmed." Karla smiled and brushed a tear from her cheek.

"We'll have to celebrate," Andreas said.

"Yes, we will." Karla began to feel excited as the reality of her success slowly sank in. "Let's wait until Silvia gets back, and then we'll have a party here and invite our friends and your family."

He bent down to kiss her, and she put her arms around him. Later that night, when they were lying next to each other, she thought about the question she had asked Jean Philippe: "Was it possible for a woman to love two men or for a man to love two women?"

"One day you'll have to make up your mind, or you risk losing them both," he had said.

I love Andreas, but I'm still in love with Jean Philippe. I made up my mind, but my heart seems to have room for both.

Chapter 38

The pale-blue sky, dappled with thin clouds the color of milk, promised another warm spring day. It was early March. Karla was sitting at the living-room table addressing the envelopes for the wedding announcements. She and Andreas were going to get married in May in the local Catholic church. Knowing how much Andreas's relatives and Karla's father would enjoy a religious wedding, they decided to go through with it. The church was small and personal, and they knew the priest who was going to marry them. Arturo promised to come. Karla was elated that her father would be able to give her away. She only regretted that Rosa and the children weren't able to attend the ceremony, but plane tickets for the whole family were beyond their reach.

The list of invited guests was short. Neither Karla nor Andreas were fond of huge parties, so only family members and the closest friends were invited. The church would be filled with villagers, for whom the ceremony was a welcome entertainment in this otherwise quiet town.

Karla was in the process of writing the last few invitations. She wrote Jean Philippe's office address on an envelope, having promised to send him an announcement. She had hardly thought about him in the past few months, having been busy with the preparations for the wedding. She still hadn't told Andreas about their fling in Florence. There never had been a good moment, and the longer she hid the truth, the harder it was to admit it. Florence seemed so far away. It was over; why bring it up again and possibly stir up a hornets' nest?

Thinking of Jean Philippe brought a smile to her face. She wrote a short note.

Dear Jean Philippe,

As promised, I am sending you our wedding announcement. The ceremony is going to be held in the local church. I am so glad my father will be able to attend. I still can't believe sometimes that Andreas and I are finally getting married, considering all the confusion we created in the past. I am very happy.

I hope you are doing well. I will always think of you as my very special friend and teacher, and of the wonderful time we spent together in Florence. Love, Karla

As she was getting ready to put the announcement and the note into the envelope, the phone rang. It was Lena. Her voice sounded strained.

"Karla, I need you to do me a big favor. I fell, and I may have strained or broken my ankle. The kids are still in school and Luigi is gone. I don't want to call the ambulance, but I can't really walk or drive. Would you mind giving me a ride to the doctor?"

"Of course, Lena. I'll be right there." Karla gathered the stack of wedding announcements and put them on the table in her studio, then grabbed the car keys and drove off.

Lena was sitting on a chair waiting for her. Her ankle had swollen so much she couldn't put on her shoe. Karla helped her into the car and drove her to the doctor.

"How did this happen?" Karla asked.

"Oh, I am so stupid. I was cleaning and climbed onto a chair to dust the top of the closet. When I tried to step down, I twisted my ankle and it just gave out."

"Lena, you work too hard."

"I know, I know, everybody says that."

"With a broken ankle, you may just be forced to take it easy for a while. I guess I shouldn't joke about it. Does it hurt much?"

"It's not too bad as long as I don't put any pressure on it."

"Well, here we are," Karla said. She parked in front of the doctor's office and helped Lena out of the car and into the clinic, supporting her. The waiting room was quite crowded, and since they didn't have an appointment and it wasn't an emergency, it took a while before Lena got taken care of. Fortunately, the ankle wasn't broken but only strained. After taking x-rays and securing an ankle brace, the doctor told her she would have to rest her foot and gave her some exercises to do after the pain subsided.

While waiting for Lena, Karla called Andreas to let him know what had happened. "I don't know yet when I'll be home. I may have to help Lena tonight."

"That's all right. Don't worry. Call me if you need help. Oh, by the way, where did you put the wedding announcements? I just thought of someone else I want to send one to."

"They're in my studio on the table," Karla answered, then froze, remembering the note she had written to Jean Philippe.

"Okay, see you later." Andreas hung up the phone.

Karla pushed a button on her cell phone, then tried to remember. *Did I seal Jean Philippe's envelope already? I don't think so. The note I wrote was quite personal, but it didn't say anything suspicious. Or did it? I hope he doesn't get the wrong idea ... or the right idea.*

When Karla got home, Andreas was in the kitchen eating a slice of pizza. "Have some." He pushed the pizza box toward her. "I thought we probably wouldn't have time to cook tonight. Sorry, I didn't wait for you. I didn't know when you'd be back. How is Lena?"

"She'll be all right. Fortunately, her ankle is just strained and not broken. I'll go and check on her tomorrow."

He seemed to act normal, Karla thought. He probably didn't even see the note. She went into her studio. She could see that the wedding announcements had been shuffled through. Jean Philippe's envelope was on top, and the note and announcement were lying next to it. She stuffed the note and announcement into the envelope, sealed it, and put it into the middle of the stack of mail.

After eating a slice of pizza, Karla went into the living room with a cup of espresso. Andreas sat next to her. "I noticed you're sending your art teacher a wedding announcement. You're not thinking of inviting him, are you? At least, you didn't mention anything."

There it was; the question she had dreaded all afternoon. If she were innocent, she could have given a simple answer, such as *I just thought it would be nice to send him one, to let him know I'm getting married* and be done with it. Instead, Karla felt the heat rising to her face before she even uttered a word.

"I read the note," Andreas said. "It was just lying there. I know you admire him, but the tone in that note made me wonder what you really feel for him. That, and the fact that you blush whenever you talk about him. You're sure there is nothing more than friendship?" He took her face between his hands and forced her to look him in the eyes, as he sometimes did when he suspected she was trying to hide something from him. Normally, he would beam at her when she squirmed and finally told him the truth. Then he'd say: "Honey, you're the world's worst liar, and I love you for it."

This time, however, it wouldn't be that easy. She had to tell him now or keep it a secret for the rest of her life. "Andreas, I wish you wouldn't ask. You may not like the answer."

"I'm afraid I won't." His voice was calm but guarded. "But don't you think I have a right to know?"

"Yes, you do, and I should've told you a long time ago, but I was too afraid and ashamed, and there never seemed to be the

258

right moment." She took a deep breath. "We spent the night together, at the very end of my stay. It only happened once. I'm sorry."

For a moment it was completely still in the room. Karla didn't dare to face him.

"God, Karla, and you're telling me this now?" Andreas sounded stunned. "I suspected all along that there was a little more than just friendly feelings. I figured you had a little crush on him. I didn't realize it went that far." He got up, walked over to the window, and looked outside for quite a long time. Karla barely dared to breathe. He turned around, facing her. "Why didn't you tell me? I told you about Annette."

"I'm sorry, Andreas. Believe me, I wanted to tell you right then, but you made this remark that you didn't think you could be as forgiving as I was, and then I lost my courage." She swallowed.

"God, that's a lot to digest. I mean, I know, it happened to me, too, but ... you kept this hidden all this time. You looked me in the face and ... The guy is married. He has a family. You could've hurt a lot of people."

"I know. It wasn't as if we did it lightheartedly. We both tried to fight it."

"Then how did you end up sleeping with him? Did he come on to you? He sounds like a real creep to me, yet you keep referring to him as this wonderful person. I don't get it."

"That's not the way it was. It wasn't he who seduced me," Karla blurted out, then bit her lip. She was afraid to tell him that she had taken the first step, but if she didn't, he would blame Jean Philippe for everything, and she couldn't accept that.

"What do you mean by that?" Andreas's voice rose in pitch.

Karla told him the truth, about her kissing Jean Philippe during their walk, about the talk they had had, about how they had tried to stay away from each other, and about how they had finally given in.

Christa Polkinhorn

"Jesus Christ!" Andreas slammed his fist on the table. A vase fell and shattered on the floor.

Karla recoiled. "Look, Andreas, neither of us behaved in a very mature way. Can't we just accept it and forgive each other? Please don't be so angry."

"Don't be angry? Is that what you said?" he screamed. "My wife-to-be throws herself at a married man like a ... a bitch in heat, and I shouldn't get angry? Thanks. That's asking for a lot."

Karla felt his words like a slap in the face. She didn't know what to say. When she finally spoke, her voice sounded foreign to her. "Andreas, that was a really cruel thing to say. I understand that you're upset. I hoped you'd be a little more compassionate. I just want you to ask yourself one thing. Are you sure this couldn't have happened to you? Are you sure you wouldn't have slept with Annette if she had been married?"

"The point is, she wasn't married," Andreas shouted.

"No, I don't think that's the point," Karla said. "Look, if you truly believe you could never be tempted like that and be too weak to resist, then ... I'm not the woman you should marry and you are not the man for me. You'd be a saint, and I'd always feel inferior to you.

"I really don't think you have the right to make me feel cheap, in spite of what I did. What Jean Philippe and I had together was more than mere lust."

"Oh, yeah?" Andreas glared at her, his eyes blazing and his face scrunched.

"Yes." Karla got up. "There were true feelings involved. He gave me something I sorely needed at the time. He cared for me and helped me. Is that so different from what happened between you and Annette? You talk about me hurting a family. Well, you hurt Annette. I saw her cry. So perhaps you aren't as noble as you want me to believe. You sleep with another woman for weeks, behaving as if you loved her. You don't need to be so self-

260

righteous." Karla trembled from the exertion of trying to defend herself.

"I'm really sorry, Andreas, sorry for what I did. But it happened and I can't make it undone. I can only ask for your forgiveness, and if that's not enough, then I don't know what else to do. If you want to cancel the wedding, I'll pay for all the expenses we already incurred."

Karla pulled off her ring and put it on the table. She went outside and sat on the low granite wall. Her head was spinning, her mouth parched, and she felt drained of all emotion. *I may have lost him again, and this time for good.*

After a while, she heard Andreas come outside. He sat next to her. "Do you still love him?" His voice was tense.

Karla thought about it for a while. She wanted to be honest. "I still care for him, but not in the same way I care for you. You are the one I love. I've loved you ever since I met you, and all the stupid things I did over the past few months couldn't change that."

They sat quietly, looking out into the night. There was a faint scent of smoke from the neighbor's house.

"I don't know what to say, Karla. I need time to think this through. I'm all confused. I don't know who you are anymore." Andreas sounded sad, discouraged, and in pain, and it hurt her to see him like this.

"That's okay," she murmured. "If you don't want to be with me tonight, I can sleep on the couch."

"Don't be ridiculous. I just need to be by myself for a while."

Although Karla was exhausted after the evening's turmoil, she couldn't fall asleep. She heard the clock strike each hour. Just after one o'clock in the morning, there was the familiar squeaking of the stairs. Andreas sat on the bed next to her. "Are you asleep?" he whispered.

"No." Karla hardly dared to breathe, afraid of the decision he may have made.

261

She felt his hand searching for her face in the dark. He bent down to kiss her forehead, then took her hand and slipped the ring back on her finger. "I'm sorry about the ugly remark I made."

Karla sat up and hugged him. She was trembling as the tension of the past hours gave way to relief. "Can you forgive me?"

"Yes." Then, after a pause: "You were right with some of the things you said. Perhaps it could've happened to me, too. Falling in love with a married woman." He sighed. "And it's true, I didn't love Annette. I knew she was falling in love with me, and I waited too long to tell her the truth." He got undressed and lay down next to her. "Honey?" he asked, reaching for her hand.

"Yes?"

"Do you have anything else to confess before we get married?"

"No, and you?"

"No."

They lay quietly next to each other. Karla heard a bird sing. It sounded like a mockingbird trying to attract a mate. *Dear God,* she prayed silently, *let this be the last disaster before we get married.* A brief gust of wind shook the trees in the yard. The rustling of leaves eventually soothed her to sleep.

In the morning Karla was sitting outside on the stone bench in front of the house, trying to wake up. In spite of the little sleep they had gotten the night before, Andreas had been up early and was already in his workshop. She heard the familiar chipping sound of the chisel. Karla put her coffee cup on the ground and leaned her head against the wall of the house.

She woke up, startled, when she felt Andreas kissing her. He sat next to her and took a few sips of her coffee.

"God, I'm so tired." Karla yawned loudly. "I think I'm getting too old for all this emotional upheaval. Do you realize, Andreas, we're not even married yet and we've already broken up or almost broken up about three times? What's wrong with us?"

"I don't know, Karla, why do we make it so difficult?" Andreas squeezed her thigh. "Well," he added, a tiny smile on his face, "if you kept your pants on when you're around other men, we could've avoided last night's disaster."

"Well, what about your pants? I bet you anything they came off a lot more often during those two months than mine did."

"All right. Touché," Andreas said.

Karla hugged him. She brushed through his hair, which was sprinkled with white stone dust. "I'm so happy you are not mad at me anymore. Tell me, was it really the fact that he is married that got you so upset, or just the fact that I slept with someone else?"

"I think both," Andreas admitted. "I do believe in something called the sanctity of marriage. It may sound somewhat antiquated." He paused and looked down at his hands.

Karla hugged him. "Andreas, if you're still worried about Jean Philippe, I can only tell you, no matter what happened in Florence, I love you, and it's you I'd like to spend my life with, not Jean Philippe or anyone else."

"Not even if he wasn't married?" Andreas asked.

"Not even then." And this time Karla meant it.

"I guess we should leave it at that." Andreas gave her a quick kiss. "Can we put this whole drama behind us and finally get married? You know, you're just too damn attractive to be on the loose. You are a danger to mankind."

"Oh, and you think by marrying me you can protect your fellow men?"

"Yes, I'll keep you pregnant and barefoot in the kitchen."

Karla slapped his leg.

"Don't forget to mail the announcements, including the one to him. After all, he needs to know who is in charge now." He pinched her breast, then got up quickly, avoiding another slap, and walked back to his studio.

"Just the male chauvinist I suspected you of being all along," she called after him.

Chapter 39

Dear Karla,

Yes, we finally did it. It's the first real vacation for Luigi and me in—I don't even remember how many years. I have to get used to doing nothing, meaning eating, drinking, swimming in the Mediterranean. The water is at least 25 degrees, almost like a bathtub. Everything is wonderful.

I had to let you know, though, how much we enjoyed the wedding. I was particularly happy to finally meet your father. I am so glad he could be with you during this important moment in your life. It was a real joy to feel the strong bond that has developed between the two of you and to see him so proud of you. Your mother would have been happy to witness this.

I loved the fact that you decided to have the wedding in our small church. You looked beautiful in your dress, and I barely recognized Andreas in his elegant suit (and with combed hair!). I could tell he felt uncomfortable all dressed up, and I had to laugh when he ripped off his tie the minute the photographer was done—to the dismay of his aunt, who made him put it on again.

I am ashamed to say it, but I already miss the kids, my friends, my work, my rose fields. I'm just a country-woman, not used to a life of leisure! Have a wonderful beginning of your married life. See you soon. Luigi says hello.

Love, Lena

Love of a Stonemason

Karla smiled as she put the letter on the pile of mail next to her. She was sitting outside, gazing at the mountains in the distance, which were surrounded by small swaths of early-summer haze. It was the middle of June, three weeks after the wedding. Karla and Andreas had spent a few days relaxing and pampering themselves at Casa Berno, a luxury hotel in the hills above Ascona, all paid for by Silvia and Richard. It had been their wedding gift. There were still cards and letters arriving from well-wishers. One of them was from Claudia and Mauro, who had gotten married half a year before.

Karla had also received an envelope with the return address of Jean Philippe's gallery in Florence. Inside were a check for €3,000 and a note from Jean Philippe congratulating them on their wedding and on the sale of one of Karla's paintings. She noticed from the receipt that he had given her the full sales amount without deducting the commission the gallery normally gets. When she told Andreas, he sneered. "That's the least this French adulterer can do for us. ... Well, congratulations." He picked up Lena's letter and read it, then put it back on the pile. "About Jean Philippe ..."

"What about him?" Karla asked with a sigh, expecting another criticism.

"I know you'll be in touch with him about your paintings. I have no problem with that. However, I hope you at least have the decency not to carry on an extended personal correspondence behind my back."

"No, I'm not." Karla felt a surge of irritation. "I don't intend to correspond with him beyond what's necessary, and you're welcome to read our mail if you need reassurance."

"I don't want to read your mail. I trust you."

"No, you don't trust me, and I'm getting sick and tired of your suspicions. I haven't mentioned Annette once since you told me about her, and yet you keep bringing up Jean Philippe, usually in the most unflattering terms. I never once insulted

265

Annette. On the contrary, I felt bad for her and for what she had to go through. You still think kindly of her, don't you?"

"Yes, but that doesn't mean—"

"So why can't you accept the fact that I still like Jean Philippe and consider him my friend?"

"Because I know damn well that your feelings for him go deeper than friendship."

"No, they don't, not anymore. I told you that before, and I'm telling you now, and if you don't believe me, then that's your problem. You are jealous, and your jealousy is beginning to get on my nerves. I'm going to write to Jean Philippe to let him know that we can't correspond except if it has to do with business. Are you satisfied now?"

"You don't have to be so uppity about it."

"God, Andreas, why can't you let it go?"

"Sorry," Andreas mumbled, then got up and walked back to his studio.

"Men," Karla muttered under her breath, and slapped Jean Philippe's envelope down on the pile of mail. She picked up another letter, checking out the name of the sender. *Well, there are exceptions.* She smiled as she ripped open the envelope.

Querida Karla,

Thank you for your letter and the lovely photo album of the wedding. It gives me the opportunity to share some of the moments with Rosa and the kids. They all send you their love.

I don't have words to tell you how much I loved being with you and Andreas and your friends and family during this important time in your life. I also enjoyed seeing a little more of your beautiful country. I hope that in the future Rosa and the children will have a chance to visit you, as well.

Here, everything is more or less the same. Manuela and Pedro seem to be a steady pair. They are even talking about getting married. (I think seeing how beautiful you looked in your wedding dress made quite an impression on your sister!) I wish they would wait awhile before making such an important decision. She is still so young, but I guess parents always believe their children are too young to be on their own. Fortunately, Manuela does well at the university and promised she'd finish all her studies before getting married. She also received a scholarship, which is a big break for our finances.

Maria just got accepted into a new private high school, and Antonio started primary school. Private schools are expensive. Since Papá is paying, they better do their homework!

Antonio is absolutely crazy about the tapes with the stories Andreas recorded for him. He listens to them every night before going to sleep. That was a great idea. Thanks a lot, Andreas.

That's all the news I have for right now. I hope to see you soon. Say hello to Andreas, and have a wonderful time together.

Always thinking of you with love.

Un abrazo, Papá

"Come here," Karla called in a curt tone when she saw Andreas walk toward the house. "Something for you." Karla pointed at Arturo's letter without looking at him.

When Andreas tried to kiss her, she turned her head away. She wasn't in a forgiving mood yet. "I'm still mad at you. I hate it when you distrust me. We're married now, and I know damn well what that means. So you don't have to treat me like a child."

Andreas put his arm around her. "I apologized. Are you going to punish me the whole day?"

"Yes." She pushed him away. As usual, though, she couldn't stay angry at him for very long. She shuffled through the mail, trying to suppress a smile.

Dear Jean Philippe,

Thank you very much for your card and the check. I noticed that you didn't subtract your commission. That's not what we agreed on; you already paid for the frames and never charged me for them. That's very generous of you, and I gratefully accept your gift.

The wedding was very beautiful and emotional. I was so happy my father was able to attend. I was, of course, a sobbing mess during the ceremony and could barely get the words "I do" out. I think my father was close to tears, as well. Fortunately, Andreas saved the moment by dropping my ring when he was supposed to put it on my finger. It rolled down the few steps next to the altar, and he had to run after it. Of course, the whole congregation laughed, including the priest, who said that he hoped that wasn't a bad omen.

Now, I have to confess something, and I hope you won't be mad at me. I ended up telling Andreas about us. I was too naïve to believe that, by leaving Florence, I could just put everything behind me and not worry about it anymore. I should have known better. Andreas has a way of detecting things I try to hide from him, and so it all came out. It was painful, but I'm glad I told him. I didn't want to start our marriage with a lie. He was pretty upset, mainly about the fact that I got involved with a married man. (He himself was involved with someone else and told me about it. She was single, and for him that was a big difference.)

I would have loved to keep in touch with you, but that's not possible, because I would betray Andreas's trust. I'll still let you know important things having to do with my artwork, and I hope one day we can all step past this and see each other again.

I want you to know that, even if you don't hear much from me, I still think of you as my friend. I hope you understand.

Love always, Karla

Dear Karla,

Thank you very much for your letter. No, I am not mad at you for having told Andreas. I somehow suspected it would happen. I am just grateful it didn't cause the breakup of your relationship. That would have really made me sad. I can understand very well that your husband doesn't think highly of me.

I don't think our friendship depends on how often we communicate, and you are absolutely right we shouldn't keep corresponding on a personal level. That wouldn't be fair to either your husband or my wife. Perhaps one day I'll be as courageous as you are and confess, as well.

Love of a Stonemason

I wish you all the best in your married life, and I know you will do well with your artwork. I will always think of you with love.

Jean Philippe

Email to Claudia:

Listen to this: The painting which won first prize sold for 5000 Euro! I still can't believe that anybody would pay that much for it. (I know, I know. I should be more confident about my work, Jean Philippe used to say.) I have no idea who bought it, but it must be hanging in someone's home in Florence or somewhere else in Italy. I hope you newlyweds are doing well. Andreas and I just came back from our honeymoon. Say hello to Mauro.

Love, Karla

PART SIX

THE ABYSS

Chapter 40

What did I eat last night? Karla wondered as she woke up sick to her stomach. From the kitchen downstairs came the clatter of dishes and Andreas's off-key humming of a popular song. Karla sank back onto the pillow and sighed. The next minute she was leaning over the toilet bowl, throwing up. Back in bed, she took deep breaths, trying to calm her upset stomach.

"Good morning. You're going to be late." Andreas's loud, cheerful voice ripped Karla out of her slumber. She moaned, remembering that it was her day to work at Silvia's gallery.

"I'm not feeling well. Something must have been wrong with dinner last night."

Karla and Andreas had eaten out at a trattoria in Locarno before going to see *Psycho* by Hitchcock, one of Andreas's favorite directors.

"That's strange," Andreas said. "We had the same thing, and I feel fine." He touched her forehead. "You feel a little warm. Perhaps you're coming down with something. There's a summer flu going around. Lena's children have it. Why don't you stay in bed and rest. I'll bring you some tea. Want me to call Silvia and cancel?"

"Yes, please. Thanks." Karla closed her eyes and dozed off. By the time Andreas came back with a cup of chamomile tea, her stomach seemed to have settled. She took a couple of sips and made a face. She hated chamomile tea. "It smells like piss."

Andreas chortled. "I know what you mean, but it'll make you feel better."

An hour later, Karla felt well enough to get up. She turned on the espresso machine and searched the refrigerator for something edible that wouldn't upset her stomach again.

"Feeling better?" Andreas came in from watering the plants.

"Yes. I think it was false alarm."

"Well, take it easy today. It's going to be another scorcher." Andreas wiped the sweat from his forehead. "And the Maggia is mobbed by *tedeschi*."

It had been an unusually hot and dry July, and since it was vacation time, Andreas and Karla's small village was inundated with tourists from the German part of Switzerland who camped along the Maggia River and went for hikes in the nearby mountains.

When Karla stepped outside, the air quivered, and the colors of the flowers and blooming bushes and the smells seemed particularly vivid this morning. Normally Karla enjoyed the fragrance of summer, but today the sweet scent of Lena's roses made her feel queasy again. She sat to relax on the granite bench underneath the chestnut tree, the only cool and comfortable spot outside.

"What are you doing here?" Silvia asked when Karla showed up at the gallery. Silvia was in the process of putting up a few paintings. "Andreas said you were ill."

"I'm feeling better. It must have been one of those mini-bugs. I don't know. I still feel a little queasy, and somehow I seem to be very sensitive to smells today. Have you doused yourself in patchouli this morning?" Karla sniffed and wrinkled her nose.

Silvia laughed. "Not more than usual." She peered at Karla. "Hmm. That's interesting."

"What?" Karla looked at her, surprised.

"Well, young lady. When did you have your last period?"

Karla stared at her. "Why? Oh no."

"Think about it. Sick in the morning for no obvious reason. Acute sense of smell. Ring a bell?"

"Jesus. You may be right. I didn't even think about it."

"Well, let's not jump to conclusions. See how you feel to-morrow."

In the evening of the next day, Karla applied the finishing strokes to a painting. It was still hot, but the front of blue-black clouds in the northern sky announced a possible thunderstorm. Karla put her brush away, yawned, and stretched. Andreas stepped behind her and began to massage her shoulders. His experienced hands applied just the right pressure. Karla closed her eyes, feeling the stiffness dissolve.

"Andreas, I think I'm pregnant."

"What? Already?"

"Well, I was sick in the morning twice. I don't have the flu. What else could it be?"

"But you just had your IUD removed."

"You're obviously a very potent man." She chuckled.

"Of course." He hit his chest with his fists in a Tarzan-like fashion. "Well, in this case you can't have any of this." He removed the glasses of spritzer—white wine mixed with lemonade.

"Wait, wait. I'm not sure yet. Besides, I don't think a tiny bit of diluted white wine at dinnertime will do any harm." Karla got up and reached for the glass.

"No way." Andreas picked it up. "Pregnant. No alcohol. I'll get us some lemonade."

"Dictator," she called after him, and looked longingly at the cold, frosted glass with the whitish-yellow liquid. It looked so inviting on this hot day.

The doctor confirmed Karla's suspicion. When she phoned Arturo to tell him that, instead of a wedding party, he might have to prepare a christening, he was exuberant. The joyful news of his first grandchild outweighed the disappointment of having to wait for their visit longer than expected.

Of all people, it was Andreas who was most excited about the news. He overwhelmed Karla with attention, hovering over her like a mother hen, until she couldn't stand it anymore. "Andreas, I'm not ill. Stop fussing."

The first few months of Karla's pregnancy were one of the happiest times in their relationship. Except for a couple of weeks in the beginning when she was troubled by the typical morning sickness, she felt amazingly good, both physically and emotionally. She experienced a period of unusual calm and serenity that surprised them both. The granite bench under the chestnut tree became a kind of meditation place for her, where she would sit and gaze at the fields of blooming wild flowers, vineyards, and mountains in the distance. She began a journal of letters to her unborn child, interspersed with drawings. Nothing seemed to be able to upset her these days, not even the pesky north wind, which occasionally blew for a few days during the summer months. And then, within a few seconds, everything changed.

It was a clear day in early fall. In the morning puffs of mist hovered over the fields. The sky was pale blue with splashes of cream white on the horizon. Karla was in her third month of pregnancy. Andreas and she were on the way to visit Silvia and Richard, who had invited them for lunch. They lived in a small village above the city of Ascona.

As they were driving up the windy road toward Ronco, Karla switched on the radio and turned the dial. Having found the news station, she looked up again. They had just passed a narrow curve when a black shadow—a car on the wrong side of the road—came shooting toward them. Andreas had just enough time to yank the steering wheel to the left and avoid a frontal collision. The last things Karla registered were the powerful jolt, the tightening of the seat belt, the thunderous noise of crushed metal, the broken glass, and the stench of gasoline. She closed her eyes, and all sound faded.

Out of the eerie silence came the thumping of a heartbeat. Karla opened her eyes again and watched the scene unfolding before her. She was a little girl, strapped into her booster, staring at the two mangled, bloody bodies spread across the dashboard, trapped between crushed metal. There was broken glass all over. A piece had fallen onto her small hand, which gripped the bar of her seat. Blood began to trickle down her legs, staining her pants and shoes. Flames leapt into the air, leaving a suffocating stench of burning rubber. She screamed at the top of her lungs.

An excruciating pain in her abdomen pulled Karla out of the past. It wasn't a little girl but she herself who screamed. Blood was soaking through her pants. Someone was holding her; then a terrified voice: "Get an ambulance. My wife is pregnant." Screaming sirens. Somebody lifted her out of the car, just as the world went dark around her.

When Karla opened her eyes, the glare of white light blinded her. She closed them again. There was a faint smell of burnt rubber and gasoline, but no noise. It was very still. *It's like being dead. It's good to be dead, all quiet and no feelings.* Some force in her, however, urged her toward life. She opened her eyes again. There were people in white around her, a woman and man in white coats.

"Mrs. Bocelli," a voice said. "Can you hear me?"

Karla looked at the man in white bending over her. He was young, with light-brown hair and brown eyes. "I'm Dr. Russo. How are you feeling?"

"All right," Karla heard herself say. "No, not all right. It hurts." She put her hands on her abdomen.

"The nurse will give you something for that." The man in white sat on the chair next to the bed. He took her hand in his. "Do you remember what happened?"

"An accident," Karla said hesitantly, desperately trying to penetrate the fog she was floating in and out of. Fear overwhelmed her. "Andreas." She tried to sit up. The pain forced her down again. "Where is Andreas?"

"He's all right. Don't worry. He'll be with you right away. Don't strain yourself."

"There was a little girl," Karla said. "But no, that was me. I don't know ..."

"You had a shock. That's why everything is a blur right now." He was still holding her hand.

"The baby," Karla whispered. "I lost the baby, didn't I?"

"I'm sorry. Yes, you had a miscarriage."

Karla began to weep, and each sob tore into her like a knife and made her wail with pain. She felt someone push back the sleeve of her nightgown, then registered a slight burn in her arm. "This will lessen the pain and help you sleep," a voice said.

"Andreas," Karla whispered.

"I'll get him right now."

It was the last thing she heard before she sank into darkness again.

It seemed that whenever Karla opened her eyes another face was in front of her. There were people she recognized—Andreas and his relatives, Silvia, Lena—and the faces of unknown men and women. Finally, she woke up more fully and looked toward the light coming from the window.

"Karla." She felt a hand touching her arm and turned her head. She tried to say his name but couldn't utter a sound. Her throat was a tight knot. She barely recognized him. He looked haggard and pale, his hair disheveled. He hugged her carefully. "Are you still in pain?"

She shook her head. "The baby." She began to sob.

"I know. I'm so sorry." His voice cracked.

They were both crying and hugging each other. After a while, Andreas sat back and blew his nose. "God, Karla. At least you're not injured. I was so scared when I saw the blood."

"Andreas. I saw it again."

"What do you mean?"

"The accident when I was little. It was all there in front of me. I saw my mother and grandmother lying there. It was so clear. I know now, my mother wasn't calling me for help. It was horrible, the way they looked ... but somehow ... I don't feel guilty anymore."

Andreas hugged her. "I wish I could say the same for me."

"Why?" Karla asked.

Andreas sighed. "I keep going over the accident again and again, asking myself why I couldn't have turned the steering wheel a little more and perhaps avoided the crash altogether."

"Andreas, that's ridiculous. It wasn't your fault," a male voice said. "I've told you this a hundred times. Even the police assured him, he was one hundred percent innocent, but try to get this into his head."

Another voice: "You have to give him time."

Karla turned her head. Lena and Luigi were standing at the door, next to Silvia and Richard. They came over, and Lena bent down to kiss her. "How are you, Karla?"

Karla tried to smile. "I could be better, but I guess it could be worse, too."

"That's right. Andreas did the only thing he could do, and he saved your life. If he hadn't reacted so fast, you would have had a frontal collision and you'd be both dead, as well," Richard said.

"Who is dead? What exactly happened?" Karla asked. "I just remember the car ... and the blow ... and then everything was a mess."

"After the car hit ours, it veered off the road and tumbled into the gorge," Andreas said. "Both passengers are dead. It was a

mother and her son. The little boy was only four years old."
Andreas covered his face with his hands.

"It's not your fault." Karla reached for his hand. "The woman
drove on the wrong side of the road. Why?"

"They're in the process of checking it out. I guess they're
going to do an autopsy to find out if she had been intoxicated or
on drugs," Richard explained. "Fortunately, there are several
witnesses. There were cars following you, so there was never a
question about what really happened."

"How long have I been here?" Karla asked Andreas.

"Just since this morning."

"It seems forever to me. I want to go home."

"Tomorrow you can go home," the man who just came into
the room said. Karla recognized him as the doctor. "I'd like to
keep you for the night to make sure there are no complications.
Besides, I don't think your husband is in any state of mind to take
care of you right now. How are you feeling?" He turned to
Andreas.

Andreas lifted a shoulder.

"Here are some pills. Take them before going to bed, so you
get some rest and stop torturing yourself." His voice sounded
stern, but he gave Andreas a friendly pat on the back. "There is
someone from the police waiting for you in the hallway. They just
need a signature from you."

"I've never seen him so desperate. I don't want him to be
alone at home," Karla said after Andreas left the room.

"Don't worry." Luigi gently touched her arm. "He isn't going
home, he is either staying with us or his family."

"Don't worry too much about Andreas," Lena said. "We'll
make sure he is all right. You need to take care of yourself now."

Silvia sat on the bed next to Karla. "I know it'll take time to
get over the loss of your baby. You shouldn't try to gloss over it. I
had three miscarriages myself, and I know how much it hurts, not
just physically but emotionally."

"Silvia, I didn't know that. You never told me. That's terrible."

"It happened a long time ago. That's when Richard and I decided we couldn't have children."

The door opened, and an elderly stout nurse came in carrying a tray with dishes. "Dinnertime," she said in an energetic, cheerful voice.

"I don't think I can eat." Karla shook her head.

"Oh yes, sweetheart, you can." The nurse smiled. "You need to get your strength back." She put the tray on the small table next to the bed, then pressed a button and brought the bed into a more upright position. "Here you go." She handed Karla the napkin.

At that moment Andreas came back in. The nurse scrutinized him sharply. "Are you the husband?" she asked.

"Yes." Andreas gave a nod.

"Then come here, sit down, and make sure your wife eats," the nurse said in an authoritarian tone.

Andreas gave a crooked smile that looked more like suppressed crying. "Yes, ma'am."

Chapter 41

"All the tests came out normal, so you're fine." Dr. Russo looked down at a folder with Karla's health history, then removed his reading glasses and glanced at her.

Karla and Andreas were sitting in the doctor's office for a last consultation before Karla was discharged from the hospital. "Nothing should prevent you from having another baby soon. I recommend waiting about six to eight weeks before getting pregnant again. And try to take it very easy the first three months. That's when most early miscarriages happen. Get regular checkups. Talk to your doctor if something unusual happens. But don't panic. Okay?

"I also have some news for you." The doctor turned to Andreas. "We got the autopsy report from the driver of the other car. The woman was pumped full of drugs. If anybody is to blame for that accident, it's her. She not only killed her son but endangered your lives, as well. So there is no reason for you to feel guilty."

Andreas sighed. "I still feel I was involved in something that caused the death of two people. One of them was a little kid. I can't just dismiss this."

"I understand. But it wasn't your fault. You did everything right and saved your wife's life. You both could've been killed or badly injured. All in all, you were very lucky."

"I know," Andreas said in a low voice.

"I'm not trying to make light of your feelings." Dr. Russo spoke with empathy. "Everybody would have a hard time digesting what happened to you. Don't be ashamed to ask for help to deal with it. I can recommend someone."

Andreas nodded and gave the doctor a weak smile. "Thanks. I think I'll be okay."

The following weeks Andreas and Karla tried to reestablish some kind of normalcy in their lives. The first days back at home were the hardest for Karla. Every time she looked at the baby things they had already bought—a bed, a stroller, a few toys—she felt a stab in her chest. She cried a lot these days; tears seem to lodge in her eyes, ready to flow at the slightest provocation. The miscarriage added another death to her young life and reawakened the pain of her many losses.

"I'm trying to be grateful that we weren't injured, that I didn't lose you, as well," she said to Andreas when he found her sitting in tears next to a pile of toys. "But it's so hard."

Andreas sat next to her and hugged her. "I know" was all he was able to say before choking up, too. He picked up a teddy bear he had brought home the day before the accident. "Perhaps we should put the stuff away for the time being. So it doesn't always remind us ..."

"No." Karla shook her head. "We'll have another baby soon, won't we?"

Andreas nodded and squeezed Karla's hand. "I'm in my studio if you need me."

Karla watched him leave the room. His normally tall figure seemed to have shrunk. He slumped forward, as if he were carrying a ton of rocks on his back. *He looks so miserable. I've only been thinking about my own pain.*

"Andreas," Karla called after him. "I made an appointment with my analyst. Why don't you come along? She's really good. She's helped me a lot in the past."

Andreas gave a shrug. "Perhaps later. Why don't you go first? I think I'll be all right. I just need time."

The analyst Karla had been seeing off and on since returning from Florence had helped her deal with the feelings of loss and fear of abandonment left over from her childhood trauma. Now that Karla remembered the earlier car accident, she was able to mourn not just the death of her unborn child but of her mother, as well, without the feelings of guilt that had haunted her all her life.

Vivianne was a slim, soft-spoken French woman in her sixties whose accent reminded Karla a little bit of Jean Philippe. Aside from the talks they had during the sessions, Vivianne encouraged Karla to paint. "Put down what you feel, but don't think of the pictures as art. Don't worry about quality."

It was difficult for Karla to paint without trying to create art. Vivianne shook her head as she studied Karla's first attempts. "Is that how you feel? You got to be kidding. You're trying to paint a beautiful infant? All that's left of your baby is a swatch of bloody tissue in some garbage can. Try again."

Karla felt as though the air had been knocked out of her by the harsh remark from this otherwise kind woman. Her feelings turned from disbelief to rage. She grabbed the brush, dunked it in red, and tossed the paint onto canvas, splashing some of it on the analyst's blouse and face. "I'm so sorry." Karla's anger deflated; she dropped the brush and burst into tears.

"Good," Vivianne said, wiping the smears of paint off her face. "We're getting somewhere."

While Karla moved step by step beyond the accident, Andreas had a much harder time dealing with it. He appeared subdued, listless, and unfocused. Karla watched him anxiously as he sat around, sometimes staring into space for a long time. The familiar sounds of activity in his studio were followed by long periods of silence. His work habits deteriorated. Before the accident, he occasionally procrastinated and had to put in extra hours to finish a project on time. Now, he sometimes outright forgot about a project.

What also worried Karla was his apparent lack of sexual energy. In the beginning she wasn't in the mood herself. After a few weeks, however, she reminded him that, according to the doctor, they could try to have another baby. Although he acknowledged it with a nod, he didn't seem eager to follow through. He was no longer the pleasure-loving, sensuous man she had known him to be. Andreas had lost his joie de vivre.

One evening after dinner—Andreas had hardly eaten anything and seemed more lethargic than ever—Karla sat next to him. "Why are you hiding your grief from me?"

"What do you mean?" Andreas sat at the table hunched over, stirring his coffee listlessly.

"You know exactly what I mean." Karla gently brushed a strand of hair out of his face. "You have been acting like the living dead for the past few weeks. This can't go on. Why don't you tell me what's wrong with you?"

"I don't want to bother you with my feelings. You've enough of your own to deal with."

"That's ridiculous. Don't you realize we are in this together? Andreas, don't shut me out." Karla put her arms around him.

"God, Karla. He was only four years old. He wasn't even as old as little Antonio. He never had a chance." His voice faltered; his eyes filled with flickering lights. He lowered his head onto his arms and wept.

Karla let him cry, gently stroking his hair and heaving back. His sobbing seemed to go on forever, and Karla began to worry that he was having an outright nervous breakdown. Finally, he lifted his head and took a deep breath. "I'm sorry. I don't know what came over me. I felt I was slipping into an abyss."

Karla got up to get a washrag, and soaked it in cold water. He put it on his face, which was swollen from crying. "I'm totally exhausted. I'm sorry, Karla, I'm turning into a wimp."

"No, you're not. That's what you should've done weeks ago, instead of lugging your sorrow around with you and hiding it from me."

The following morning during breakfast, Karla noticed, relieved, that Andreas looked less miserable. The dullness of his skin had given way to a more lively hue. "How are you feeling?" she asked, handing him a roll.

Andreas shrugged. "A little better. I feel I'm slowly waking up from a nightmare."

"Andreas, you need help. I want you to see someone."

"Not necessary. I'm getting over it by myself."

"Why are you so stubborn?"

"I don't need a shrink."

"What are you afraid of? That the analyst uncovers your past? Perhaps that's what you need."

"Karla, stop it." Andreas slapped his hand on the table. His face was flushed, and he glowered at her.

Fine. I like you better angry. At least you seem alive. "I'm not going to stop until I have my husband back, the one who communicated with me, the one who loved sex."

"Fuck, Karla, give me some time."

"Time? It's been weeks. Yes, fucking would be great."

They stared at each other. Finally, Andreas lowered his gaze. "I'm sorry." He took a deep breath. "Things will change, I promise. There's something I need to do, something I've been avoiding. Not just grieving and talking to you. I admit, I should've done that, too. I'm going to meet the father of the child who was killed in the accident."

"What? I don't think that's a good idea. You'd be meeting a grief-stricken man who has just lost his wife and son. How can he be objective? He may blame you and make you feel even worse."

"I just have to do it. I got his name, and I already called him. He agreed to see me. The way he sounded, he doesn't blame me. I need to know who he is and tell him what happened. He has a right to hear it from me, not just from the police or other authorities."

Andreas took the car key from the hook on the wall. "If I were in his place, I'd be grateful if the person who witnessed my wife's and child's last moments would share that with me. I know it wasn't my fault. I still feel I have a certain responsibility toward him. Perhaps it was just a coincidence that I drove around the curve right at the moment her car was there. But it was me, not somebody else."

"Then I'll come with you." Karla got up. "After all, I was involved in the accident, too."

"Karla, I need to do this on my own. It may not make sense to you, but—"

"You're shutting me out again." Karla was close to tears.

"I'm not shutting you out. I just have a different way of dealing with things than you do. Can't you understand this?" Andreas tried to hug her. "I really need you to understand."

286

Karla shrugged his hand off. "Go."

"Don't be angry. Please." Andreas took Karla's face into his hands.

"Go. If that's what you need to do."

"He behaves as if this were his problem alone. He refuses to get help. He goes on his own to see the father of the boy who was killed. He shuts me out of his pain. This is supposed to be the man I'm married to?" Karla paced Lena's kitchen, then sat next to her. Lena was in the process of peeling potatoes. Karla grabbed a peeling knife and started to help, then put the knife down again. "It just makes me furious."

"I understand." Lena patted Karla's hand, then continued her work. "You know, men just have a different way of dealing with their emotions. Or not dealing with them. Whatever you want to call it. Believe me, I couldn't get my husband to ask for help. No way. Do you think he confides in me when he has a problem? No, he tells me after the fact. Men are such machos, they don't need help, specially not from a woman. At least, that's what they think."

"But normally Andreas isn't that way. He's very open about his feelings—at least, he's been so far. Except when it comes to his relationship with his father ... and his mother. I think that's what he's afraid of. That the analyst would start to dig into his past."

"Well, Karla, you have to let him deal with this on his own. You know, we women always think we can fix our husbands, make them see things our way. Forget it. Doesn't work. They're stubborn as mules."

In the evening Karla watched anxiously as Andreas came walking toward the house. He seemed all right, with no outward signs of distress. It was only now that Karla noticed how much weight he had lost over the past few weeks. His jeans hung loose, and he kept pulling them up. "Boy, what a day." He exhaled deeply. "Don't worry. I'm not breaking down again."

Karla was relieved that Andreas seemed to be in a better mood. "So, how did it go?"

He nodded. "Good. I'm glad I went." He gave her a cautious look. "I'm sorry. I made a mistake. You should've come with me. He asked about you. He said how sorry he was, about the miscarriage."

"Oh, yeah?" Karla glared at him and slapped the packet of spaghetti on the table. "Well, thanks for relating this to me. Although, I'm just a minor figure in this drama."

"Karla, don't be that way. I didn't mean to shut you out. I was just afraid. I didn't know how he was going to react ... how I was going to react. And I worried how it might affect you. I mean, it was out of consideration for you—"

"Andreas, I don't need this kind of consideration. I'm not a child. I'm your wife, which you seem to have forgotten. I thought that means we share things, particularly such important things. You don't need to treat me like an imbecile. So far I've dealt with this whole disaster in a more mature way than you have."

"You're right. I'm sorry." Andreas stepped behind her and wrapped his arms around her. "Friends again?"

"Only if you promise to treat me like an equal from now on and stop babying me. I can take care of myself."

"I will." He kissed her.

Karla dropped the spaghetti into boiling water and handed Andreas a hunk of parmesan cheese. "Here, make yourself useful and grate the cheese."

"This smells wonderful." Andreas picked a piece of ham from a frying pan.

Karla was happy to see that his appetite was back. He lit a fire in the fireplace. It was the end of October, and the evenings were getting cool. The smell of burning wood, garlic, and ham and the sounds of the pine logs popping and hissing gave their place a feeling of renewed life.

"He was a great guy, and he thanked me for coming to see him. His ex-wife had had a host of mental problems, was in and out of institutions, and had attempted suicide several times. He had custody of the children. Whenever the mother felt good enough, the kids would spend a few days with her."

"So they had more than one child?" Karla pushed the plate of pasta in his direction. Andreas helped himself to another portion.

"Yes, a little girl who was sick and stayed home. Can you imagine if she had been in the car, as well? I don't even want to think about it. He suspects that she tried to commit suicide again and take the boy with her."

"My god. You think she could've driven on the wrong side of the road on purpose because she wanted to drive the car off the cliff? How terrible." Karla put her hand on Andreas's arm. "You know, in hindsight, we've been very lucky. Losing a four-year-old child must be so much worse than having a miscarriage. I don't think I could ever get over something like that."

Andreas looked at her thoughtfully. "Perhaps this having-children business isn't such a good idea after all."

"Not having kids because we're afraid something might happen to them? That's absurd." Karla shook her head. "Didn't we have a similar conversation once before?"

Andreas smiled. "Yeah, I remember, when you were afraid of getting involved with me."

PART SEVEN

LAURA AND TONIO

Chapter 42

It had rained off and on the past week, and the last layer of muddy snow was gone overnight. The fields and meadows had the dull brown hues of late winter, but the sun was able to coax nature into displaying the first vibrant greens.

The morning after a day of sunshine, Karla found a patch of yellow daffodils and blue crocuses along the stone wall on the patio, with their faces turned toward the sun. The air smelled of moss and wet leaves. Karla turned around when she heard the crunching of gravel behind her.

Andreas sat next to her on the granite bench. "Spring, finally." He stretched and gave a groan of pleasure. "New life everywhere." He snapped off a leaf from the wisteria vine and sniffed it.

Karla chuckled. "Funny you'd say that."

"Why?" He looked at her, puzzled, then his green eyes widened. "No."

Karla nodded. "I'm pregnant again."

"Oh god."

"Aren't you happy?"

"Um ... yes. Are you sure?"

"Yeah. I felt sick again the other morning, so I went to see the doctor yesterday."

"You didn't tell me. I thought that was just your regular checkup."

"I didn't want to tell you before I was certain."

"Aha. And who is withholding important information now? I thought we agreed to share this kind of stuff." Andreas glared at her. "Remember?"

"I wasn't holding anything back. I just wanted to surprise you with the happy news." Karla felt herself flushing.

"You're such a bad liar."

"All right. So I didn't want to worry you."

"Aha."

Karla studied his face. "Well, it's good news, isn't it?"

"Of course it is." Andreas wrapped his arms around her. "I just wish we were past the first three months."

"We'll be fine." Karla tried to convince herself.

Andreas gently rubbed her belly. "Stay in there, little one, until it's time." He put his ear against Karla's abdomen. Karla heard her stomach growl.

"She said 'okay.'" Andreas grinned.

"How do you know it's a she?"

"Just guessing." Andreas looked at her with a serious face. "I want you to quit the gallery for a while."

"What? Why?"

"Because you need to take it easy the first three months. You need to rest. You can't lift anything. You can't do any heavy work. You should just stay home and lie down a lot."

Here he goes again. "Am I allowed to breathe?" Karla asked, miffed.

Andreas rolled his eyes. "Don't fight me. You want us to have a baby, don't you?"

"Of course I do. But I'm not the baby. I'm going to be as careful as possible, but I still want to lead a halfway normal life."

The first few months of Karla's second pregnancy were a challenge. No matter how hard Karla tried to look forward to having a baby, she wasn't able to recapture her former calm and serenity. Andreas's constantly hovering over her didn't make things any easier.

"What do you think you're doing?" he yelled at Karla when he caught her carrying a full garbage bag to the dumpster.

"It's not heavy," Karla protested.

Andreas glared at her and yanked the bag out of her hands. Karla swallowed the rising tears. "I'm not in prison, and you're not my warden. Leave me alone."

"I just don't want another disaster to happen."

"It's so difficult not to be able to do anything. It makes me feel useless and nervous." Karla began to cry.

Andreas hugged her. "I'm sorry. I didn't mean to yell at you. I'm nervous, too. One more month, then we should be over the most critical time."

Karla had given in to Andreas's wishes and quit the job at the gallery. Instead, she took over Silvia's simple accounting. It was a boring job, but it was something she could do at home and it gave her the feeling of still being somewhat involved. She insisted, however, on continuing the children's drawing and painting lessons. "They relax me. I don't think of my pregnancy all the time," she told Andreas.

The rest of the time Karla did her own work and tried to take frequent naps. Lena, Maria, and Emilia helped with household chores and entertained Karla when Andreas was gone. Emilia, who was a good seamstress, made bed skirts for the baby's crib and knitted all kinds of cute clothes and blankets. Looking forward to her first grandchild, she was more lively and outgoing than Karla had ever seen her.

"Probably wants to make up for doing a lousy job with her son," Andreas grunted one evening after his family had left.

"Don't be so hard on her. I really enjoy her company," Karla said. "It helps, you know." *More than your constant fussing.*

"I know." Andreas shrugged. "At least the baby will have a good grandma."

Cutting back on her work at the gallery and other jobs around the house gave Karla more time for painting. However, she didn't feel as creative as she had during her first pregnancy. She didn't write in her journal and didn't paint anything related to the baby.

295

"I don't want to tempt the Fates," she said. "If I paint an infant, the dark forces may become alerted to her or his presence."

"I didn't know you were superstitious," Andreas said.

"I didn't know, either, until now."

The first trimester passed without problems, and after a visit to the doctor, who told them that everything looked fine, Karla and Andreas breathed a sigh of relief.

"Can I move around again?" Karla asked with a side-glance at Andreas.

"Of course." Dr. Rovsing, a thin, wiry, middle-aged Danish woman with soft blue eyes, who always had a calming influence on Karla, nodded. "I wouldn't take up martial arts or marathons right now. Otherwise, regular moderate exercise is good. Do things you enjoy. Remember, when the mother is happy, the baby is happy." The doctor gave Karla a sunny smile. "You know the things to avoid: caffeine, alcohol, smoking."

The doctor's encouraging words seemed to have a calming influence on Andreas. He was still the overly concerned husband, but at least he stopped watching Karla like a hawk and concentrated on his work more.

Karla, who felt more relaxed, as well, went back to painting with renewed vigor. Now, she included sketches of babies in her pictures. They were always somewhat concealed. A toddler with curly dark hair sat under a tree with his back to the observer. In a cityscape a little girl looked out the window from behind a curtain, and in another painting a boy was on top of a tree, peeking through the leaves.

"I think the Fates have accepted the child, but I don't want to provoke them," she said to Andreas, who loved to discover hidden infants in Karla's paintings.

It was the twentieth week of Karla's pregnancy, and Andreas and Karla were in Dr. Rovsing's office waiting for their first ultrasound. Karla was nervous, having slept little the night before. She had been plagued by dreams of distorted, strange-looking fetuses. She hadn't had a nightmare since the car accident, so the reoccurrence of frightening dreams felt like a bad omen to her.

"Everything is going to be all right." Andreas squeezed her hand as she gave another sigh. The waiting room was full of expectant couples and mothers with infants or little kids who played or fought over toys. Women gave each other probing looks, trying to gauge the progress of their pregnancies.

In Dr. Rovsing's office, Karla was asked to lie down on the table, and got her belly greased and hooked up to a low-humming machine. Andreas held her hand, and the two stared at the monitor, where, pixel by pixel, an image of new life began to appear. Karla gasped.

"There it is," Andreas whispered.

"There *she* is." Dr. Rovsing gave one of her pearly laughs. "It's a girl, and she's big. Must take after the daddy."

"A girl. I knew it." Andreas's voice trembled.

The tears in Karla's eyes blurred the image. She blinked.

"She's smiling." Dr. Rovsing pointed at a spot on the monitor. The baby moved her tiny hands, as if she wanted to greet them.

"Ouch." Karla held her belly. "She kicked again."

"She's a trooper." Dr. Rovsing nodded.

Chapter 43

On a warm afternoon in early October, Karla dunked her brush into a glass of turpentine. She had just finished painting a fall landscape with Lena's tall and narrow stone house, the beige walls, her garden with a few late-blooming roses, the wooden rabbit hutch, and the trees with their red, orange, and yellow leaves. A thin layer of haze grazed the mountains in the background. The painting was a present for Lena's fiftieth birthday.

Karla lowered her heavy body on a chair and rested her hands on her swollen abdomen. She was big by now. Her narrow frame made her protruding belly seem even larger. Her face had softened, and her cheeks had filled out a little. The baby was due in one week, but the way the little one kept kicking, Karla was convinced she wouldn't wait that long.

"Ouch," she said, as another punch made her bend over. "Okay, I get it." Karla picked up the brush again and, with an impish smile curling her lips, she painted a little girl peeping from behind the rabbit hutch. She took the canvas carefully from the easel, holding it by the stretcher frame in the back. It wasn't dry yet, but she wanted to give it to Lena that day.

When she stepped outside, she inhaled the sweet smell of the neighbor's grapes. October, the month of wine, was a good month for a birth, Karla felt. Lena as well as Karla's aunt were born in October, and so little Laura would have good company.

"I'm going to take the painting to Lena's," she told Andreas, who was in the process of polishing a small piece of pink tourmaline, the birth stone of October, which he wanted to hang above the baby's crib.

"Let me carry it," Andreas said.

"No, it's not heavy, and I need to move. The baby is pressing on my spine." Karla leaned the painting against the wall, pressed her hands against her lower back, and sighed. "I'll be glad when this is over with. She's getting so heavy."

Andreas grabbed Karla's hand and lowered her onto his knees. He kissed her belly and gently rubbed her back. "I know. Only another week or so."

"All right. I'll waddle down the street." Karla put her hand on Andreas's shoulder and groaned.

Andreas pushed her up. "Be careful, though."

Karla picked up the canvas and maneuvered her body slowly down the short path to Lena's. *I feel like a beached whale.* She had never seen a beached whale, but imagined it to be a huge shapeless mound of flesh. She stopped a few times and gazed at the red and yellow trees, inhaling the scent of the last of Lena's roses. The season would be over soon.

The first contraction hit when Karla entered Lena's kitchen. She had just enough time to drop the painting on its backside and grab the edge of the kitchen table. She toppled over and let out a groan of pain. "Crap," she moaned, her eyes watering. "That hurts."

Lena, who was arranging a few roses in a vase, rushed over and helped her sit. "Relax. Breathe deeply. It'll go away." She looked at the clock. "See how far apart they are."

After the pain subsided, Karla relaxed somewhat. "I don't need to go to the hospital yet, do I? Gee, we learned all this in the birthing class, but the real thing is a little different."

"No, this is going to take a while, probably hours considering it's your first one. That's why we have to time them." Lena picked up the painting.

"I'm sorry I dropped it. It's your birthday present. I'll frame it later, but I wanted to show it to you on your birthday."

"This is great. Thanks a lot." Lena held the painting up. "How beautiful." She carried it into the living room and leaned it against the wall. "Luigi will help me put it up. You want to lie down for a while?"

"No, I'd rather go home and let Andreas know. Perhaps we should call the doctor. I'm nervous, Lena."

"Oh, I understand. I remember my first one as if it was yesterday. Luigi was frantic. He dropped my suitcase as we rushed out of the house, spilling my nightgown and cosmetics all over the place." Lena chuckled. "Come on. I'll come with you. Walking a little will help."

299

Lena put her arm around Karla, and the two women walked
up the hill, stopping frequently. Karla instinctively kept touching
her belly. Andreas came out of his studio. His eyes widened as he
saw Lena supporting Karla. "What happened?"

"Everything is fine. The contractions started."

Lena's cheerful voice, however, did little to calm Andreas. He
blanched. "Holy cow. Already? It's not even due yet."

"Well, babies don't always adhere to our schedule," Lena
said.

"We better go to the hospital. I'll get your overnight bag."

"Hold your horses. Haven't you learned anything at Lamaze?
You're as bad as Luigi. She's not ready yet. You have to time the
contractions."

As if on cue, Karla moaned, her hands clenched over her
belly. Andreas held her. Sweat trickled down her face, but this
time she remembered her breathing exercise. "I better get used to
this. Does it get much worse?"

"A little," Lena said absentmindedly. She looked at her
watch. "Twenty minutes. That's normal for the first ones. I'd call
the doctor to inform her, but this could take hours, even until
tomorrow. Why don't you take a warm bath? That really helps to
relax you and the baby. I'll come back a little later to check on
you. Call me if you need help."

Andreas hugged Karla carefully. "Everything will be fine."
He tried to sound reassuring, but his voice had a tinge of alarm.

"A bath would be great," Karla said.

"I'll draw you one." Karla undressed while Andreas ran the
bathwater and poured in some of her favorite lavender oil. He
helped her into the tub. She groaned as she lowered herself into
the water, then leaned her head against the plastic pillow Andreas
put behind her back and relaxed, enjoying the soothing warmth
of the bath.

"I'll put your overnight bag in the car. That way we don't
forget it ... in case we need to rush. I'll call the doctor to let her

know." Karla had to smile at Andreas's attempt to hide his anxiety by keeping busy.

Later that evening, after eating a little of the soup Lena brought, Karla went to lie down and tried to get some sleep. Exhausted from the pain, she dozed off in between contractions, which became closer together and stronger. Every once in a while Karla gave a groan of pain, which sounded almost inhuman and shocked Andreas, who sat up in bed and held her, massaged her a little, then sank back down on the pillow.

In the middle of the night, Karla woke up feeling wet, thinking for a second that she had wet the bed, then realized that her water had broken. She shook Andreas, who shot up and jumped out of bed, hitting his leg on the chest of drawers. "What's the matter?"

"I'm leaking. The water broke. It's time to go."

"Right." Andreas rubbed his shin and searched for his pants, stumbling over his shoes. He finally managed to pull on his jeans.

"You might want to turn on the light." In spite of the pain and the excitement, Karla had to laugh. Andreas looked like a wild man, his hair sticking out and his eyes wide with fear. "Calm down, I need you to be calm now, please," she begged him.

"Right," he repeated. Then, as if waking up from a stupor, he helped Karla stand and pull on her sweatshirt. "Should we call Lena?"

"She said to call her. She wants to come with us."

"I'd rather just leave," Andreas said, grabbing his shirt. "I don't want to get to the hospital too late. I don't think I'd make a good midwife."

"All right, let's go—oh, here is Lena."

Lena, in her sweat suit, combing her disheveled hair with her fingers, rushed toward them. "I woke up and saw the light," she explained.

"You must be psychic." Andreas smiled at her and gave a sigh of relief. He hugged her. "I'm glad you're here. We're a little nervous."

"You just focus on your driving and get us to the hospital safe. I'll take care of Karla." Lena helped Karla into the back of the car and sat next to her. "Remember to breathe." She rubbed Karla's back as another contraction overcame her, tearing at her insides. Karla shrieked and tears streamed down her face.

"Don't speed." Lena patted Andreas's shoulder as he gunned the engine and jerked the car into gear. "Believe me, we've plenty of time."

At the hospital, Andreas helped Lena and Karla out of the car, and the three of them lumbered into the foyer. A skinny, tired-looking male receptionist glanced at them, bored, and pushed a form in Andreas's direction. "Fill this out, please."

Andreas narrowed his eyes and stared at the man. "We've already registered. The doctor has all the information."

"Still need to fill this out."

Karla clutched her belly and gave another yelp of pain. Lena supported her. The receptionist eyed them curiously, then waved at a bench on the wall. "You can sit down over there."

Karla glanced at Andreas, whose facial color darkened. He stepped behind the receptionist's desk, grabbed the man by the collar, and yelled. "Listen, punk, my wife is in extreme pain, and you make a big deal about a stupid form. Now, you either call a doctor or a nurse, or you're going to wake up tomorrow with a broken nose."

The receptionist's face paled. "All right, all right. Let go." He stumbled back and reached for the phone as Andreas released him with a push.

"Andreas, please, calm down," Karla begged.

Lena shrugged. "That's one way of getting results."

An elderly nurse came rushing to the front desk. She eyed Andreas suspiciously. "Any problems?"

"No, we took care of it." Andreas shot the receptionist a threatening look.

The young man, who still looked shocked, nodded his head. The nurse took Karla by the arm and led them all to a room. She helped Karla get undressed and gave her a hospital gown while Lena put her things away. The nurse had Karla lie down on the bed and checked her cervix. "Excellent. Five centimeters. You're doing well."

"Thanks," Karla murmured, then squirmed and screamed. The nurse and Andreas helped her to a sitting position. "Breathe. That's a good girl." The nurse took Karla's vital signs and scribbled something on a piece of paper. "Now, just try to relax. The doctor will be with you shortly."

"I'm scared." Karla held Andreas's arm. "Why did we get ourselves into this in the first place?"

"Ahem." Andreas scratched his head. "I think it has something to do with taking home a little girl once this is all over with. We can put her into the crib I made for her. We can dress her in the cute outfits we got ... and ... play with her. She may bring some joy to our lives ... have I forgotten anything?"

Karla smiled. "Something to do with love?"

"Oh, yes, gee, I almost forgot the most important thing." Andreas kissed Karla just as she clutched her belly again and let out another yell.

Dr. Rovsing opened the door and marched into the room. Her energetic gait and thick white-blond hair reminded Karla of a Viking warrior. "How are we all doing?" she thundered and walked up to Karla. "Not too good, I see."

"It hurts like hell." Karla wiped a few tears from her face and tried to smile.

"I know, I know. I've two of them at home." She studied the sheet of paper the nurse put into her hands, then examined Karla and wrinkled her forehead.

"What's wrong?" Karla sounded alarmed.

"Nothing to worry about. Your baby's heartbeat is a little fast. She's afraid. She knows you're afraid."

"I can't help it. The contractions are killing me."

"Nobody is going to get killed here. Your little one is quite big and you're very slim, so, yes, it hurts. I suggest we administer a light epidural. This will relax you and the baby. Is that all right with you?"

Karla and Andreas both nodded enthusiastically. The doctor and Lena smiled.

Dr. Rovsing turned to Andreas. "And how are you? I heard you had a little problem at the front desk." Her eyes had a humorous glint.

Andreas gave a sheepish smile. "Perhaps I overreacted."

All at once the room got busy. A tall, burly anesthesiologist with curly blond hair came in and told Karla to lie on her side. "Ready for some fun?" He searched her lower back with his hand. Karla felt a slight burning sensation. Machines started to hum and lights blinked. "There we go. Great, you're already smiling." Karla gave a deep sigh and felt some of the tension dissipate.

Dr. Rovsing studied the monitor and nodded her head. "Nice and relaxed. That's good. You already picked a name?"

"Laura," Andreas said.

"Laura Anna, after my mother and my aunt," Karla explained.

"Beautiful name. All right, Laura, relax." The doctor examined Karla. "There we go. Heartbeat normal. Wonderful. I'll see you in a while." Dr. Rovsing patted Karla's hip and marched out of the room.

The nurse pointed to the string for the alarm hanging over the bed. "Call me if you need anything. This is going to take a while. You can watch TV. There's a channel with nice music." She handed Andreas the remote control.

"Well, since this is obviously going to take a few hours, I'll rush home and make sure the kids get up and go to school," Lena said. "Can I take your car?"

"Sure, no problem." Andreas handed her the keys.

"I'll be back soon." Lena patted Karla's cheek.

"How are you feeling?" Andreas sat on the bed, trying not to interfere with the machinery and tubes.

"Better," Karla sighed. "I can still feel the contractions, but they don't hurt as much. I feel like I'm on drugs."

"Well, you are." Andreas laughed. "I wouldn't mind having a little of what they gave you. I could use some relaxing."

"I'm fine, Andreas, you can relax." Karla squeezed his hand. "Some music would be nice."

Andreas switched on the TV and searched for one of the music channels. He stretched out on the bed next to Karla and started to massage her belly gently. The contractions faded in and out, muted now, and Karla was able to relax during them more while she listened to the soothing meditation music, feeling Andreas's body next to hers. She perceived the world as though from inside a bubble, which shielded her from the worst pain and the harsher noises. She vaguely noticed people come into the room and leave again. Occasionally, someone touched her, brushed her hair out of her face.

Karla was able to doze in between contractions. When she opened her eyes again, the light in the room seemed brighter. A golden glow surrounded the monitor. Karla felt a presence in the room other than Andreas's. She thought she saw the hazy outline of a woman, a smiling woman. "Mama." Karla exhaled.

"Honey?" She felt Andreas's hand on her shoulder.

Karla smiled and closed her eyes again. "It's going to be fine," she whispered.

The door opened. Dr. Rovsing stepped into the room, followed by the anesthesiologist. "How's everything?"

"Good." Karla nodded. "I think I'm ready for more."

"Great. We'll decrease the cocktail a little. All right?"

The contractions followed each other faster now and the pain increased, but Karla wasn't afraid anymore. The pain was intense but bearable. Each contraction pushed their little girl closer to home.

"We're ready," Dr. Rovsing said to the nurse. Karla was shaved and washed. She noticed that everybody, including Andreas, was wearing surgical masks and gear. The contractions came fast and furious, like powerful waves crashing on the beach and rolling out again.

A voice—the doctor's or the nurse's? "Here's the head. Perfect."

Karla reached down and felt something wet and slick. Andreas's eyes, looking down on her, swam in tears. Then everything seemed to happen at once. Karla pushed again and felt as though her insides were spilling out.

"Ah," somebody exclaimed. Then a determined scream, followed by loud crying.

"A big, healthy girl," the doctor said.

The baby was washed and cleaned, wrapped in a soft pink towel, and laid on Karla's now-limp belly. At first, Karla barely saw her daughter through her tears. She blinked and looked at the red, wrinkled face; the dark, slick hair; the long, dark eyelashes over the closed eyes. Karla hugged the little bundle and inhaled its sweet baby smell. "Welcome, Laura. Grandma says hello."

Laura turned her head toward Karla's breast, her mouth searching for a nipple. "She's already hungry," the doctor said.

Karla nursed her daughter, who caught on right away.

"She's sucking like a pro." Andreas gently brushed his hand over Laura's cheeks. He touched her hand. She grabbed his finger and held it. "She's perfect. Just like her mother."

Karla smiled and yawned. "Boy, am I exhausted."

"No wonder." Andreas kissed Karla. "What did you mean by 'Grandma says hello'?"

"I don't know. I suddenly felt my mother was here. As if she was watching over us."

Chapter 44

Karla woke up, surprised at how light it was in the room. She had fallen asleep again after the last nursing. Andreas was sitting on the bed, bare-chested and dressed in jeans. He held Laura and grinned. "She's trying to eat."

Laura, with eyes still closed, was rubbing her mouth against his chest, groping for a breast. Then she turned her head, making smacking sounds and blowing little bubbles of spit. Her face turned red and she opened her mouth wide, letting out one of her powerful screams. Karla turned and moved her still-sore body into the right position, and Andreas put the baby on the pillow next to her. Laura latched on to Karla's breast and stopped crying, giving little grunts of pleasure instead.

"Ouch," Karla said. "She bit me."

"She doesn't have any teeth yet." Andreas touched Laura's hand. She grabbed his finger.

"No, but strong gums." Karla kissed the dark fuzz on Laura's head.

"Strong hands, too," Andreas said, moving his finger while Laura kept holding on to it.

Karla and Andreas had been home with the baby for a couple of weeks and were trying to adjust to being parents. Andreas seemed to take to his new role with an ease that surprised Karla. She had always imagined a man would initially feel a little awkward with a tiny baby. That wasn't the case with Andreas. He changed her diapers, washed and dressed her as though he had raised a whole bunch of kids. Cooing and murmuring endearing names, he carried his freshly bathed and impeccably dressed daughter into the living room, her face and the fuzz on her head shiny with baby oil. He was still his normal messy self, though, and left a pile of smelly diapers and dirty clothes on the changing table. Karla cleaned up after him but didn't complain, not wanting to dampen his enthusiasm.

When Laura fussed without being hungry, it was often Andreas who held her and was able to rock her to sleep. He carried her around or lay on his back with the baby propped on his chest. His heartbeat and his dark, throaty voice seemed to have a calming effect on her.

It was a busy time at the O'Reillys. Relatives and friends dropped by, bringing presents and flowers. Emilia, Maria, and Lena helped with laundry and gave the new parents the usual advice and instructions.

"Weak fennel tea helps against cramps," Lena claimed.

But Laura wanted none of it. She spit and screamed when Karla tried to bottle-feed her an infusion of tea during a night when Andreas and Karla took turns carrying a whining baby around. Fortunately for her exhausted parents, Laura got over her colicky time pretty fast, but she kept them busy in other ways. She was a lively child, a strapping little thing who tried to lift her head during the first few weeks. She refused to sleep through the night for a long time, and without Andreas's help, Karla would have despaired.

Andreas was in love with his daughter, and she was clearly a daddy's girl. As soon as she was able to hold up her head on her own, he took her everywhere in her cloth seat strapped to his body. He was the proudest father in the whole village.

"You're getting us all into trouble." Luigi pointed an accusing finger at Andreas. Karla and Andreas had brought Laura for a visit.

"Why? What's the matter?" Andreas asked, bouncing little Laura on his arm.

"The guys at the inn call you 'Mama Andreas' and 'henpecked.'"

"Huh?" Andreas raised an eyebrow.

"Your friends are a bunch of chauvinist pigs." Lena threw a towel at Luigi, who caught it and chuckled.

"I think the wives are giving the guys a hard time. They swoon over you. 'Andreas is such a strong man and so kind, and look how he takes care of the baby. Andreas does this, Andreas does that. Why don't *you* help a little more at home?'" Luigi was trying to imitate a woman's high-pitched voice. Lena punched his arm.

Andreas grunted and laughed. "Okay. Next time I join you guys for a drink, I'll bring Laura along. We'll see what those machos have to say to that."

Chapter 45

Karla listened to the drumming of rain on the stone roof. Every once in a while a gust of wind splashed water against the windowpane. She had built a fire in the fireplace. The living room was warm and cozy with the smell and occasional popping sound of burning wood.

Eight-month-old Laura was lying on a thick padded blanket on the living-room floor. She had just been fed and changed, and was deep asleep, her head turned toward Karla, her face flushed, her chest rising and falling gently. Karla was making a drawing of her.

The last couple of weeks Karla hadn't painted or drawn much. Laura had been taking up all of her time, having been sick and cranky. Andreas was gone a lot, planting tombstones at different cemeteries, and Lena, who usually helped out, was busy preparing her roses for the upcoming market.

As always, when Karla neglected her artwork, she felt dissatisfied, almost bereft, as if something inside her was dying. The love and joy she felt taking care of her child stilled her creative hunger somewhat, but after a while her longing for the touch of paper and canvas and the smell of paint became too strong to be ignored.

Karla chose a warm ocher paper. She began by sketching a rough outline of Laura with a white pencil, the rounding of her head, the neck, the ribcage and belly to the point where it bulged over the narrow diaper, the slightly curved legs, the tiny feet. She drew the outline of Laura's left arm, the soft rounding of her upper arm, the protruding elbow, the lower arm angled toward the face. She continued with the right arm, which was stretched out sideways with a slight curve upward. She drew the curled fingers.

Karla picked different orange, pink, and red pastels and blocked in the larger areas. Warm reds and oranges on the cheeks and forehead, the inside of the arms and legs, and whitish tones to bring out the highlights on the shoulders, on the backs of the arms and the jaw line, on the right side of the nose. She then continued to fill in the smaller areas of the face and the body with blues and lavenders as well as pinks.

Finally, Karla painted the shadows along the arms and legs in dark blues and greens, the larger one along Laura's side where body and face touched the blanket, another one where the full, round belly met the diaper. With the shadows and highlights, the flat form on the paper came to life, jumped off the page, and was transformed into its three-dimensional shape.

Karla sat up straight and studied the drawing. She made some minor adjustments, then took a deep breath and leaned back. There she was—Laura, and at the same time not Laura. It was a new being made of paper and pastels, one that might survive both mother and child.

But now, the other Laura, the child of flesh and blood, was here, stirring, stretching, rubbing her nose with her tiny fist, opening her eyes. Laura looked up at Karla, yawned, made a face, then smiled.

Karla put the drawing pad aside, kneeled down, and picked Laura up, holding her warm, soft body. She kissed her cheek and inhaled the sweet smell of baby powder.

Chapter 46

It was snowing when Karla and Andreas walked through the old town of Locarno on their way to Silvia's gallery. Andreas carried Laura on his arm. She was wrapped in a red coat and matching hat and gloves, and squealed with delight as she tried to catch the thick snowflakes falling from the sky.

They were on their way to a charity function in support of a school for underprivileged children in Peru. Karla and Andreas had been contributing to the school for several years, but it had been Silvia's idea to have an art exhibition of Karla's paintings and Andreas's sculptures. The proceeds from the sale of the paintings and sculptures would go to support art programs at the school. Silvia and her husband had done quite a bit of advertising, and they hoped for a fairly large crowd.

By the time Karla and Andreas arrived at the gallery, the snow had begun to settle. It was early December, and the Christmas decorations gave the street of Silvia's gallery a festive atmosphere.

"Lights," Laura screamed, pointing at the Christmas tree in front of the gallery. Her face was flushed from the cold, and her large green eyes sparkled.

"Yes, lights," Karla said, and brushed a strand of dark wavy hair that had escaped Laura's cap out of her face.

At the gallery, Silvia and Richard welcomed them. Richard picked up Laura and bounced her on his arm. "What a pretty girl." He smiled at Laura, who seemed totally unimpressed by his compliment. She struggled to get free, and as soon as Richard put her down, she headed for the table with the drinks and snacks. Andreas rushed after her.

"How is it going?" Karla asked, looking around at the visitors who scanned the paintings and sculptures.

"Excellent. Three of your paintings and a few of Andreas's sculptures are already reserved. I guess the holiday season brings out people's generosity."

"Great," Karla said. She took a deep breath and surreptitiously touched her abdomen.

"Everything okay?" Andreas, holding Laura by the hand, gave her a probing look.

Karla nodded, then got ready to walk after her child, who slipped out of Andreas's grasp and made a beeline toward the other end of the gallery.

Andreas held Karla back. "Don't worry. I'll keep an eye on her. Why don't you entertain the guests?" He followed Laura around.

Karla quickly brushed her hand over her belly again. Silvia gave her a quizzical look. "Is there something you want to tell me?"

"Well, yeah. I'm pregnant again, two months."

"Congratulations. Boy, you'll be busy with two of them. Let's hope the second one is a little less ... well, shall we say ... a little less lively."

Karla chuckled. "That's an understatement. Laura is a very active child." The two women watched as Andreas followed Laura, who was meandering through the room, stumbling into people, falling down, getting up, and taking off again. Andreas finally picked her up and put her on his shoulders. She wiggled back and forth and laughed out loud.

"She resembles Andreas more and more," Silvia said. "The same dazzling green eyes and wild hair, and almost the same physique."

Karla sighed. "If she didn't resemble Andreas so much, I'd say they gave us the wrong baby at the hospital. I don't see myself in her at all. She's such a tomboy."

"Perhaps the next one will be a nice, quiet Latin-looking girl."

"I don't know about quiet. My Peruvian family is pretty loud, too. ... Oh no, not again," Karla said. She turned around.

At the other end of the gallery, little Laura was throwing a tantrum. She was lying on the floor, kicking and screaming. Everyone turned to watch the scene. Andreas picked her up and put her on her feet, talking calmly to her. The next minute she was on the floor again. Andreas scooped her up in his arms and carried her toward the door. He grabbed her coat and glanced at Karla. "I'll take her outside. A little cold air will do her good."

"Do you want me to take her?" Karla walked him to the door.

"No, it's all right. Perhaps I can put her up for sale, as a Christmas gift." He gave a husky laugh, opened the door, and carried screaming Laura outside.

"I doubt he'll find a buyer." Karla sighed. She looked around. Some of the visitors chuckled and gave her sympathetic glances.

"It's her newest way of tyrannizing us," Karla said to Silvia. "When something doesn't go her way, she goes ballistic."

Silvia patted her shoulder. "The next one will be an angel."

"You think so? I think we deserve a break." Karla smiled. "Actually, most of the time she's all right. She's a little on the wild side, but in general a happy child. The doctor told us that all kids go through periods like this."

"Well, that means there's hope," Silvia said. "But let's look how your artwork is doing." She put her arm around Karla, and the two of them walked around the room. Karla had put up the group of paintings she had done during her pregnancy with Laura, which depicted the semi-hidden infants. She had set the prices low enough so that they were affordable for people with modest incomes, and she figured those fairy-tale-like pictures might appeal to parents who wanted to hang them in their children's bedrooms. The goal was to sell as many as possible.

Another series of paintings consisted of new landscapes. "These are absolutely magnificent. I adore them." Silvia's face shone with enthusiasm.

"Thanks," Karla said.

"You really found your style. From far away these pictures give the impression of conventional landscapes, but up close the images break down into lush blobs of paint and patches of raw canvas. They're bold and vivid. I was so impressed that I wrote a critique of your pictures for one of the art journals."

"Thank you. That's great." Karla's face flushed. Silvia was generally not one to gush over a painting, so her praise meant something.

"You deserve it, you've worked hard. And by the way, I'm impressed with Andreas's work, as well. What I love most about him is that he never stops experimenting."

Karla nodded. "He got a real break, too. He's invited to take part in an exhibition in Germany next spring." She pointed at one of Andreas's sculptures. "I love the way you set them up."

Andreas had used the most colorful stones he was able to get, and carved them into small, elegant shapes. Silvia had arranged the sculptures in such a way that they complemented the paintings. The color of each sculpture matched a dominant color in a painting. It looked as if painting and sculpture were a pair, and one person had bought both the painting and the matching sculpture.

"Oh, by the way, Jean Philippe says hello," Silvia said.

Karla felt a small jolt in her stomach, which had nothing to do with her pregnancy. "Jesus, that's a name from the past. How is he? I haven't heard from him in ages, not since the last of my paintings in his gallery sold."

"He's fine. I told him about our charity drive, and he made a generous contribution. He also wants a few of your paintings for his gallery. I sent him photos of your newest work, and he was really excited. He said he was very proud to have been a teacher of such an accomplished artist."

Karla felt the heat rise to her face. She knew she was blushing.

Silvia laughed out loud. "What did you do to this man to make him swoon over you like this? Or what did he do to you? ... Well, here is your darling child again."

The door opened, and Andreas came in carrying Laura, who was deep asleep, her head resting on Andreas's shoulder. "So how did we do?"

"Great. We sold quite a bit. I'll give you the final amount once I add it all up," Silvia said.

"Why was she throwing a tantrum?" Karla asked as they were walking toward the car.

"She wanted to drink wine." Andreas chuckled.

"Come on, what are you talking about?"

"Yes. She pointed at a glass of red wine, probably thinking it was her favorite juice. I told her she wouldn't like it. I wanted to give her some apple juice, but, of course, it wasn't red. So she started to scream."

Karla shook her head. "What is it with this child?"

"The thing with the wine reminded me of something."

"Of what?" Karla fastened the belt on Laura's car seat.

315

Andreas didn't say anything for a while. He started the car and drove it carefully through the streets. It had snowed quite heavily for a few hours, and the roads were slick.

"My father. He was the only one in my family I can remember who had a problem with anger. I hope Laura didn't inherit his rage."

Karla gently touched his arm. "Don't worry. She'll outgrow it."

Andreas gave her a quick smile, then focused on the road again. "I know."

"Want to talk about your father?"

"No."

"Then why did you bring him up?"

"I don't know. Just a thought."

"Perhaps it would help us understand Laura better."

"I doubt it." Andreas cleared his throat. "Anyway, I think we were very lucky today. This should give us a nice sum for the school."

"You're avoiding the topic."

"Karla, please. I can't focus on the road and talk about my father. You want me to drive us into a ditch?"

"All right, never mind."

Chapter 47

"He's so tiny. I'd be afraid to hold him for fear of squeezing too hard." Uncle Alois bent over the three-month-old baby, who was asleep, lying in a basket under the pergola of Alois and Maria's house. He gently touched Tonio's hand. The little boy opened his small fist, uncurling his fingers, then clenched it again. He stirred as a sunray slipped through the grape leaves on the trellis and pricked his face. Karla moved his basket a little more into the shade.

"He's sturdier than he looks. But yes, he's quite a bit smaller than Laura was when she was born. Only a little over seven pounds, whereas Laura weighed almost nine. I didn't mind at all. His delivery was so much easier. We barely made it to the hospital in time."

Karla looked in the direction of Monte Sosto, where a few puffy cumulus clouds hugged the mountain. Otherwise, the sky was a deep blue except for a thin stretch of haze on the horizon, as if someone had taken a brush and painted a few strokes of ecru to add some texture to the evenly blue sky.

Alois continued to watch Tonio with a smile on his face, which deepened the creases around his eyes. He turned to Karla. "What made you choose three names? Tonio Arturo Alois, that's quite a mouthful."

"Andreas insisted on giving him the short form of my brother's name since he looks exactly like Antonio in one of his baby pictures. Then, of course, we named him after my father, and I wanted to give him a name from Andreas's side of the family. Obviously his father's name is a no-no, and you, after all, were his true father. So we gave him yours as the third name. In Peru a lot of people have several names, from both their mother's and father's sides."

"Well, I'm honored." Alois chuckled. "He does seem to take after you more than Laura. His skin is darker, too. Must be the Latin element."

"Tell us about Peru," Aunt Maria said as she and Emilia stepped outside to set the granite table for Sunday lunch. She was referring to Karla and Andreas's recent trip to Peru. They had taken the children to see Arturo and his family for the first time. It had been over four years since the wedding, where Karla had last seen her father, and seven years since their last trip to Peru. They didn't travel all the way to Cusco because the high altitude might have been too strenuous for little Tonio. Instead, the family met at Arturo's relatives in a town near Lima.

"It was great to see everybody again," Karla said. "Arturo was the perfect grandfather. He and Rosa and the whole family spoiled the kids rotten. I think my father tried to compensate for the fact that he wasn't around when I was little."

"What about the other members of your family?" Emilia asked.

"Doing well. They all have changed so much. Manuela and Pedro are married and have a little baby girl, and Maria is engaged. Little Antonio isn't so little anymore. He probably changed the most. He is a typical teenage boy, a little on the gangly side, but he's going to be very handsome. Laura fell in love with him. She followed him everywhere, being a little pest, but he was real patient with her. The best part about it was that she acted like a girl for once. She wanted to wear a dress, believe it or not, probably to impress Antonio. We've never seen her so well-behaved."

Maria laughed. "I don't think I've ever seen her in a dress."

"Yeah, and you probably won't for a while. Her good behavior lasted only until we came back. She's being her usual street urchin again. Yesterday she came home with a torn T-shirt. She got into a fight with a boy bigger than her."

Alois laughed. "I think God made a small mistake when he assigned gender. He probably meant for Laura to be the boy and Tonio the girl, and somehow got the whole thing mixed up."

"I think you're right." Karla turned to Emilia. "If Tonio had been a girl, we would have named the baby Emilia Maria," Karla said. "Perhaps the next child will be a girl again, if we decide to have a third one."

"There you go. Have a few more. We wouldn't mind having some young blood in our aging family. Since Alois and I couldn't have children and Emilia here refused to find another husband ..." Maria gave Emilia a friendly pat on the shoulder. "And with

Andreas all grown up and getting old, we're looking forward to having a bunch of grandchildren."

"What do you mean, getting old?" Andreas stood in the doorway, holding Laura by the hand. Andreas had taken her to see the baby lambs at the farm next door.

Tonio, waking up from the noises, stirred, rubbed his face with his fist, and tried to open his eyes. He gave a quick peek, then closed them again and started to fuss.

Alois chuckled. "Don't like what you see? The big world is still a little scary for you, huh? I understand."

"I think he's just hungry." Karla lifted Tonio out of his basket, opened her blouse, and got ready to feed him.

"Let me hold him," Laura demanded in a loud, angry voice, running toward her mother, who held out her arm to stop her from throwing herself at Tonio.

"Hush, Laura. You scare him when you're that loud." Tonio let go of Karla's nipple and grimaced, as if he was going to cry. Karla quickly settled him at her breast again. Laura's eyes darkened with disappointment. She turned around, grabbed Andreas's hand, and gave her mother an accusing look.

She's jealous, Karla thought. "Come here, sweetie. You can hold his hand while he eats. But gently." She took Laura's hand and held it over Tonio's fist. Laura touched his hand, then kissed him on the cheek. Tonio gave a little grunt and continued to suck. "See, he likes that." Karla patted Laura's face.

"Can I burp him?" Laura's eyes sparkled again.

"Yes. But you have to be gentle. All right?"

Laura nodded, then turned around and clasped Andreas's knees. He lifted her up and put her on his lap.

"Sibling rivalry?" Maria winked at Karla.

Karla nodded. "She's having a hard time, particularly when she sees Andreas holding him."

"She'll get used to it," Andreas said and hugged Laura. "You know you're still Papa's favorite girl, right?"

Christa Polkinhorn

Laura nodded and pressed her face against his chest.

At home that evening, after Laura was finally in bed—having weaseled several good-night stories out of Andreas—and Tonio had been fed and was asleep, Karla and Andreas tried to decide how to accommodate their growing family in their fairly cramped living quarters. They were sitting outside, enjoying the fresh breeze after a hot day. The sun slipped behind the mountains, erasing the last glimmers of light in the sky and coloring it in increasingly darker hues. It was one of Karla's favorite times of the day.

She took a sip of *gazosa*, sparkling lemonade from the Ticino. "I could store my canvases somewhere else, and then we could convert that room into a bedroom for Laura, and Tonio could eventually have Laura's room. We could start by making the room into a playroom for her. She would have her own special private space with all her toys. I bet she'd like that."

Andreas put his arm around her and pulled her close. "Talking about private space, I sure could use some of that. It was bad enough not having sex for weeks, for obvious reasons. And now, we have a little chaperone who jumps into bed with us whenever we want a little privacy."

"I know. She claims to be afraid of the dark, but I think she's just confused and fearful with all the changes around here. And jealous of Tonio." Karla kissed Andreas, who slid his hand under her shirt, gently stroking her breasts.

"We could make love out here," Karla whispered. "It's still warm, and nobody would see us in the dark."

Andreas gave her a mischievous smile. "No, but they could hear you scream."

"I'll be quiet. We used to do this once in a while in summer, on that patch of grass, next to the wisteria vine, remember?"

"Hmm. I sure do." Andreas kissed her.

Karla opened the zipper of his pants, then stripped off her top.

"We need a blanket," he moaned.

Karla pulled the towel from the hammock hanging between the chestnut trees and spread it on the patch of grass.

Andreas struggled out of his jeans. "I feel like a teenager."

"That's the point." Karla slid off her underwear. "We need a little spice again."

"Spice? I'm on fire." Andreas kissed her, then lapped her skin with his tongue, tasting the folds of her body. Karla felt his breath, which had a light smell of lemon soda, in her face. He moved on top of her, then hesitated. "Are you still hurting?"

Karla shook her head. "No. I'm fine."

He slid into her slowly. She gave a muffled cry, feeling a slight pain that was washed away by waves of lust as they moved in strong, steady strokes.

Afterward, Andreas rested his head on her chest. She moved him aside a little, her full breasts tender to his touch.

"Sorry," he murmured. He stretched out next to her, holding her hand.

Slick with sweat, Karla enjoyed the cool evening breeze. She caught the sweet scent of wisteria. Andreas turned toward her and rested his palm on her abdomen. A sense of wonder and gratitude filled her—wonder at the immensity of the sky above with its glittering stars, and gratitude for the company of the man beside her.

"I love you. I think I told you that before." His voice was dark.

Karla touched his face. "I never get tired of hearing it. I love you, too."

Around them crickets were chirping loudly, and from down the river came the croaking of frogs.

Karla pushed up a little, supporting herself on her elbows. "I think I heard something."

"We would hear them cry, the windows are open," Andreas said.

"I better check on them." Karla got up.

They collected whatever pieces of clothes they could find in the dark and went inside. Karla checked on Tonio, who was sound asleep, making slight cooing noises. As soon as the lights were out and they were settled next to each other, they heard the tapping of naked feet.

"Mama."

Andreas turned on the lamp next to the bed. Laura stood in the doorway, her cheeks flushed and her eyes full of sleep, hugging her plush bunny to her chest.

"What's the matter, honey?" Andreas sat up.

Instead of an answer, Laura rushed to the bed, pulled herself up, climbed over Andreas, and plopped herself down in the middle. She snuggled up to Karla, then to Andreas, as if to convince herself that both were there. She closed her eyes and fell asleep, her bunny clutched under her arm.

Andreas and Karla smiled at each other.

"I guess this means we'll have to make love outside from now on." Andreas brushed a lock of hair out of Laura's face and kissed her forehead.

The following morning Karla was cleaning out the room next to her studio. She hauled the paintings outside, where Andreas picked them up and carried them to the storage area of his workspace. Tonio was asleep in his crib in the living room. Laura sat on the floor, a finger in her mouth. After Tonio was born, Laura had reverted to sucking her thumb, an unconscious wish, perhaps, to be the baby again and get all her parents' attention. She was watching the goings-on with eager eyes. Karla had told her that she was going to have her own special playroom right next to her mother's studio.

"Hmm. The unfinished Bocelli." Andreas pointed to the picture with the dark, lonely woman.

"I don't know what to do with it. I don't like it the way it is. I've wanted to paint over it several times, but for some reason, I've put it off." Karla shrugged. "Just put it with the others. Perhaps one day I'll finish it."

Chapter 48

Karla walked to the car, balancing Tonio on her hip and carrying the usual assortment of bags she took with her when she went on an errand with her son: shopping bag, diaper bag, baby-bottle bag. *I'm the ultimate bag lady,* she thought and snickered as she dropped them into the trunk of her car.

"One day we won't need all this junk anymore, huh?" She smiled at Tonio, who was wearing short yellow pants and a matching top. With his sun hat, tiny sunglasses, and tanned skin, he looked like an advertisement for a day at the beach.

It was a sultry day in August. Karla scanned the sky in the north, where the familiar pattern before a thunderstorm began to show. The closest clouds, still benign and white, were churning. Behind them, however, dark gray ones were forming, and the spaces between the clouds were filled with an ominous-looking purple-black color. "I hope we make it back before it hits," Karla muttered to herself.

Andreas and five-year-old Laura were sitting in front of Andreas's workspace. Andreas was carving a piece of soft, reddish alabaster, and Laura, who sat next to him, was kneading a large hunk of Play-Doh. Karla watched the two for a while. The picture in front of her was a painting in the making: father and daughter working and playing together. Andreas, in black shorts and green undershirt, his longish hair tied into ponytail, looked up once in a while from his work to smile at Laura, who was happily babbling away, telling her father some kind of a story. She was a child version of Andreas: dark ponytail, shorts, and a similar shirt. Even her sturdy figure resembled her father's.

It was a picture of perfect unity. Laura was happiest when she was with Andreas. He let her join him when he worked outside, away from the machines and the stone dust. She had her own small workbench and collection of stones, in all different shades and colors, with which she built imaginary landscapes.

Karla almost hesitated to interrupt them. They both turned when she came closer. Two pairs of green eyes looked at her. Andreas got up and smiled.

"I'm going to run some errands," Karla said. "I should be back in a couple of hours."

"Wouldn't it be easier if you left him with me?" Andreas tickled Tonio under his chin, making him squeal.

"Yes, but you wouldn't get any work done."

"I'm not that busy. I can watch them both. You want to stay with Papa?" Andreas lifted Tonio out of Karla's arms and bounced him on his arm.

"No," Laura piped. "He can't stay."

Karla and Andreas gave each other knowing glances. Laura was very territorial when it came to her father's workspace.

"Why not?" Andreas asked.

Laura glared at Tonio, then hit her piece of clay. "It's too dangerous."

"Why dangerous?" Andreas asked.

"Because ... he'll get into things," Laura said in a whining tone.

Andreas winked at Karla, a humorous glint in his eyes. "Not if you help me watch him," he said to Laura.

Laura shook her head. "No." She pressed her lips together, and clenched her chin.

"Perhaps I should just take him." Karla felt guilty for ruining the perfect mood of the place.

Andreas shook his head. "No. She has to learn." He turned to Laura, put his hand under her chin, and forced her to look at him. His face was serious now. "Laura, he is your little brother, and he's going to stay with us. You can either accept it and be nice, or you can go to your room. Your choice."

"But he can't use my tools." Laura punched her piece of clay in defeat.

"He won't use your tools. I'll give him something else to play with."

"But—"

"No buts. End of discussion."

Tears formed in the corners of Laura's eyes. Karla bent down to kiss her, but Laura turned her head away. "I'll be back soon. I'll bring you guys some ice cream." Karla kissed Tonio and patted Laura's head.

"No need to feel guilty," Andreas said, hugging her. "We can't have a little tyrant control our lives." He gave Laura a stern look.

Laura bent her head and pushed out her lower lip. A tear was sliding down her cheek.

Karla sighed as she walked to her car. She felt sorry for her daughter, who had such a hard time accepting the fact that she had to share her parents' love and attention with her younger brother. Laura was in the throes of troubling emotions she didn't understand. One minute she loved Tonio, and the next moment she hated him.

When Andreas and Karla had first brought him home, Laura had been excited and had wanted to take care of him. Karla had let her help as much as possible, so she wouldn't feel excluded. But Laura, being the tomboy she was and feeling little spurts of jealousy even then, was often too rough with him. When Tonio cried and Karla reprimanded her, she usually fled into Andreas's arms. She spent as much time with her father in his studio as possible. There she had all his love and attention to herself. When Tonio started to intrude into her sanctuary, she fought to protect her territory with every means possible.

She'll get over it, Karla tried to convince herself. She glanced at the sky in the north. The ominous-looking storm clouds seemed to have receded. A pleasant breeze dispersed the muggy air. It looked like the storm was kept at bay for the moment.

Karla drove the narrow road to Locarno. She took her time, enjoying the beauty of the landscape she loved so much. Lush trees in all shades of greens, yellows, and browns bordered the river—willows, birches, oaks, ashes, and ever-present chestnut trees. Stopped at a red light, Karla watched the turbulent water of the river, its deeper parts almost black, topped by white foam where the water tumbled over the rocks. The shallower stretches along the bank, with the water flowing more slowly, lit up in a light green with patches of blue and gray. Sunrays burst through the leaves, and long beams of gold landed on the river surface at different angles, creating an irregular pattern of shimmering lights.

I've never quite managed to paint the rapid change of shadows and light on moving water, Karla mused. A honking car from behind woke her from her daydreaming. The light had turned green. She lifted her hand in an apologetic gesture and drove on. As the valley opened at its lower end, the mountains looked purplish against the hazy sky.

Karla savored the few hours of leisure, which were rare these days. Both she and Andreas had a full schedule with the children, their artwork, and the constant struggle to make a living. Fortunately, Andreas's relatives and Lena helped out with babysitting, so Karla and Andreas could go out together once in a while in the evening. But a few hours' freedom during the day was a luxury.

After shopping for art supplies, Karla dropped by Silvia's gallery for a chat and a cup of cappuccino. They discussed which of Karla's paintings to send to an art gallery in Germany. Silvia's article and review of Karla's paintings in the art magazine a few years back had had results. Several galleries in Germany, Italy, and the French part of Switzerland had asked to display her work.

Back at home, Karla parked the car behind the house and went to check on Andreas and the kids. They were still outside the workshop. Laura and Tonio were standing next to each other, and Andreas was sitting a few feet away, carving some letters onto a tombstone.

So they can play nicely together, after all, Karla thought, relieved. When she came closer, however, her breath caught.

Laura had built an elaborate structure of stones and pebbles on a board. Tonio wanted to touch it, but Laura pushed him away. During the shuffle Tonio knocked over the board and the stones fell to the ground. At first Laura stared at the mess on the floor, and then at Tonio. The look in her eyes changed from amazement to boiling hatred. She picked up a hammer and raised it, getting ready to strike Tonio.

"Laura! No!" Karla rushed toward her.

Andreas wheeled around on his chair, yanked the hammer out of Laura's hand just in time, and stared at her, shocked, the blood draining from his face. "Are you out of your mind?" he yelled. "Don't you ever do this again." He jumped up and glared at Laura, his face ashen.

Laura flinched and stared at the threatening figure her father had become. Karla instinctively raised a hand, as if trying to ward off danger, but it was too late. Andreas hit Laura. He only struck her once on her bottom, but the blow sent her stumbling forward until her legs buckled and she fell to her knees. She stayed kneeling on the floor for a few seconds, stunned by what had happened. Then she scrambled to her feet and looked at Andreas, terrified. Her eyes glittered like cracked ice. She pressed her lips together, trying to hold back the tears, then ran down the road toward Lena's house. It was only then that she gave way to her emotion, crying loudly and pitifully.

Tonio, upset because of the commotion, began to cry, as well. Karla picked him up, but her knees trembled so badly from the shock she had to sit. It wasn't only the fear of what Laura could've done to Tonio that scared her, but Andreas's reaction to it. She could understand him losing his temper, but the expression of pure rage on his face, a kind of rage she'd never seen in him before, frightened her.

Andreas slumped down on the chair and covered his face with his hands. "Damn. I hit her. Damn. Damn."

"Andreas, she almost killed Tonio." Karla's voice trembled. "This can't go on. We have to do something. This isn't simple sibling rivalry anymore. She is outright dangerous."

"I hit her, Karla. I hit her. The one thing I swore I'd never do. Hitting my child." His voice sounded muffled. He lowered his hands and got up. "I have to get her."

He started down the hill. Karla picked up Tonio, kissed him, and followed Andreas. When she caught up with him, she put Tonio down and grabbed Andreas's arm, trying to hold him back. "Andreas, let's wait for a minute. You're too upset right now."

He gave her a quick glance but walked on. His tortured eyes didn't seem to register her presence.

"Andreas." Karla tried again to hold him back. "You need to calm down. You're feeling guilty, and you're going to react the wrong way. Laura needs to know that what she did is wrong."

"Guilty? I feel a lot worse than guilty. I feel like a monster." He yanked his arm out of Karla's grasp and walked on.

"Darn it." Karla picked up Tonio again and ran after Andreas. She placed herself in front of him. "Will you please stop and listen to me?"

"What?" Andreas glared at her.

"Look, Andreas. You were shocked. You lost your temper. You spanked her once. You're blowing your reaction out of proportion. We need to be calm so we can deal with this the right way." Karla hoisted Tonio onto her hip.

Andreas sighed and brushed a tangle of hair out of his face. "I'm trying to calm down. Laura is afraid of me now. I need to reassure her first, and then we can talk." He lifted Tonio out of her arm. "He's getting heavy, isn't he?"

Karla nodded and put her arm around Andreas's waist. They continued to walk down the street.

Lena was waiting for them outside. "What happened?"

"Where is Laura?" Andreas asked.

"She's inside with Christina. She's calmed down a little."

Andreas went inside. Lena gave Karla a quick hug. "What happened? Laura was crying her eyes out, saying that her papa hit her."

Karla nodded and told Lena what happened. Andreas came outside, holding Laura by the hand. She had stopped crying, but she gave Andreas wary glances.

"Can I stay with Lena?" Laura asked with a thin voice. Karla had never seen her act so subdued around Andreas.

Andreas's eyes registered pain, but his voice was firm. "No, not now. We need to talk first." He picked Laura up and slowly walked up the hill.

Karla looked after him, then turned to Lena. "He's more upset about hitting Laura than about the fact that she almost killed Tonio."

Lena nodded. "I can understand that. He's so uptight about any kind of harshness toward his children. Probably because of what he went through as a child himself."

"I know. Well, I'll talk to you later. I have to feed Tonio. We haven't even had lunch yet, and it's almost two o'clock."

"Why don't you leave him here?" Lena suggested. "We just finished lunch ourselves. I'll fix him something. That way you can concentrate on getting Laura straightened out ... or Andreas, for that matter. I think he needs it even more." She smiled and patted Karla's back.

"That's probably a good idea. Thanks, Lena. I'll pick him up later for his nap." Karla watched as Tonio chewed on a slice of salami Lena gave him. He seemed to have forgotten all the uproar he created.

Karla walked up the hill, wondering what she would find at home. When she reached their yard, she saw Andreas lift Laura onto the granite table. Karla sat on the stone wall nearby, wanting to give them some time to themselves.

Andreas took Laura's hands in his. "Do you know why I got so angry at you before?" Laura looked down at her knees. "Look at me when I am talking to you." Andreas held her chin and forced her to face him. Laura's eyes filled with tears, and her lips trembled.

"Do you know what would have happened if you had hit your brother with that hammer? You could have hurt him very badly, or even killed him. He may never have gotten well again. Then you and everybody else would have been terribly unhappy. These are very dangerous tools, and I can't let you work with them anymore if you are going to hit your brother."

"But he ruined my stone garden." Laura wailed and started to cry again. Her little body was heaving with sobs.

Andreas hugged her and gently patted her back. "I know, Laura, but he's still so little. He didn't do it on purpose. He just wanted to play. When you were his age, you broke things, too, and didn't mean it. I know it's difficult having a little brother, but don't you think you'd be sad if he wasn't here anymore?"

Laura, still sobbing, nodded her head.

"Look, we have to be patient with him. He'll learn one day. I can't always watch out for him, so you have to help me with it. Okay?" Andreas pulled out his handkerchief and brushed away her tears. "This afternoon I'll help you rebuild your stone garden, and we'll put it up high enough so Tonio won't be able to reach it.

"And Laura." Andreas took her face between his hands. "I'm very sorry I hit you. I lost my temper. I shouldn't have done that. I promise it won't happen again. Will you forgive me?"

"Yes." Laura gave a last little sob. She put her arms around him.

After lunch Laura looked so tired that Karla suggested she take a nap. Andreas went to lie down with her. Karla cleaned up the kitchen and went to pick up Tonio. Tonio, however, was asleep on Lena's sofa in the living room.

"He conked out right after lunch," Lena said. "Let's go outside."

They went to sit at the table in the garden, underneath the trellis of grapevines. Karla took a deep breath, enjoying the calm and the scent of the many flowers in Lena's garden—lilacs, roses, lavender—mixed with the earthier smell of soil in the freshly dug-up vegetable garden.

"So how is our little troublemaker?" Lena asked.

"Asleep. Both of them." Karla gave a wistful smile. "Oh, Lena, little did I know how difficult raising children can be."

"You two have done very well so far. You can't expect smooth sailing all the time."

"I know. Now, however, we do have a problem. I'm afraid Laura's jealousy is really endangering us all. What would you do, Lena?"

Lena hesitated, then put her hand on Karla's arm. "I think you may expect too much of Laura right now. Yes, she does need to get over her jealousy eventually, but perhaps she just isn't ready for it yet. Try to see things from her five-year-old point of view. She is in love with her father. In her mind, Tonio is the evil intruder who takes Andreas away from her. It's not so different from any other love relationship. Look how irrational, and even violent, adults can get when they feel slighted in love or cheated. And then we expect little kids to somehow act more mature than we do."

"I guess you're right. I've never looked at it that way. So what should we do?"

"First of all, Laura needs to get her confidence back and know that she is still number one with Andreas, at least for now. I'd keep Tonio out of his studio for a while. Take him with you when you go away or let me watch him. That way Laura can have her father to herself again once in a while. I bet you once she feels secure again, she'll be more loving toward her brother. It's worth a try."

Karla nodded. "Perhaps we've been too demanding. Thanks for your help. What would I do without you?" She hugged Lena. "But I better get back. Let me know when Tonio wakes up."

Karla walked up the path to their house. It was only now, in the full sun, that she noticed the heat and humidity. The air felt stagnant, and a trickle of sweat ran down her back between the shoulder blades. Inside the stone house, it was pleasantly cool and quiet. Karla tiptoed to Laura's bedroom. Both Andreas and Laura were asleep. They presented such a peaceful picture that the ugly scene Karla had witnessed a few hours ago seemed like a bad dream. She felt like capturing the serenity of the moment. She went to get her drawing pad and a few charcoal pens, then sat on a chair and began to make a rough draft, leaving the details for later.

Andreas was lying on his back, one arm around Laura, the other one stretched out above his head, exposing the tuft of hair in his armpit. Laura was curled up against his side, her head on his chest. A strand of her dark, wavy hair fell into her face. Her hand was draped over her father's shoulder, her fingers opening and closing.

Andreas had taken off his undershirt, and his broad, suntanned chest rose and fell with his breath. He hadn't shaved in the morning, and Karla wondered if he meant to grow a beard. She smiled as she drew his long legs. One of his legs was bent at the knee, exposing a strong, muscular calf. The other leg was stretched out and reached past the end of the short bed. Karla was just about finished drawing one of his large, calloused feet when Andreas gave a loud snore, which woke him up. He opened his eyes and looked around, surprised, then slowly and carefully moved Laura off his chest and put her head on the pillow. Laura opened her eyes halfway, then closed them and turned over, falling back to sleep.

Andreas gave Karla a startled look, then smiled when he saw her drawing pad. Karla added a few more lines, then lowered her pen. "Just in time, I can finish the rest later."

"You were spying on us." Andreas sat up, slid his legs off the bed, propped his elbows on his knees, and brushed through his hair. "Boy, I sure conked out." He sighed, then stretched and yawned.

Karla got up. "I'll make us some coffee."

"Good idea. I feel all groggy."

Karla turned on the espresso machine in the kitchen, and then poured two cups of coffee. She carried them outside to the stone bench under the chestnut tree. Andreas came out and sat next to her. He reached for his cup and took a few sips, then sighed. He still looked tired. Karla noticed the dark shadows under his eyes. She touched his hand. He put the cup on the bench and embraced her.

"Do you realize we tend to sit on this stone bench whenever there is a crisis of some sort?" Karla asked.

Andreas nodded and gave a weak smile. "Yeah, something like the Wailing Wall in Jerusalem. I guess we could call it the Wailing Bench." He chuckled, then became serious again. "What are we going to do about Laura?"

Karla told him about the talk she had had with Lena. "We should try it. Lena offered to watch Tonio while I'm at the gallery, and I can take him with me when I give painting lessons. He'd probably enjoy drawing with the kids. You know how much he loves to scribble and play with paints."

Unlike Laura, who was more interested in sculpting clay and knocking on stone, Tonio loved to draw and paint. He particularly liked finger paints. His bedroom walls showed examples of his artistic endeavors. There were smears of crayons and paints all over.

Karla observed Andreas from the side. She knew he was still troubled about the morning's incident. "There is another question we should ask ourselves."

"What's that?" Andreas took another sip of coffee.

"What to do about you?"

"What do you mean?" He gave her a quick, defensive glance.

"You scared me this morning when you hit Laura. Not so much the fact that you hit her—any parent would probably have done that at that moment. It's ... you were so angry. I've never seen you that way. For a moment, I didn't recognize you anymore. It scared me."

"I know." Andreas's voice sounded hollow. "I scared myself. I've known all along it would show itself one day. That terrible anger which dominated my father's life. It's come right down to us. I felt it in myself today, and I saw it in Laura's eyes when she lifted that hammer."

"I don't know, Andreas, if it's that simple. You are not your father, and neither is Laura. You're not an alcoholic. You're normally not an angry person. You have a temper and blow up sometimes, but you're more softhearted than any man I've ever known. Perhaps you inherited some of your father's tendencies. If you learned to deal with your feelings for your father—"

Andreas cut her off with a sneer. "You're beginning to sound like a shrink."

"Look, Andreas, you told me once many years ago not to ask you about your father. I've respected your wish all this time.

Now, however, it's beginning to affect our lives and the life of our family. Don't you think I've a right to know what really happened back then?"

"Okay. But please let me recover from today's upheaval before I get into another one." Andreas got up abruptly and grabbed Karla's cup. "Want some more coffee?"

"Yes, thanks." Karla watched him go inside. *I guess that's how far I got with him today. At least it's a first step.*

PART EIGHT

AN UNEXPECTED REUNION

Chapter 49

Karla had just finished painting and was cleaning her hands with turpentine when she heard the noise of a car engine. She checked her watch. *Andreas can't be back yet.*

"Alois, what a surprise. Come in. I was just about to make coffee. Would you like some?"

"Sure, I could go for a cup." Alois gave her a hug. "Is your lord and master home?"

Karla laughed. "If you mean Andreas, he's out right now. He took the kids for a ride to the store, but he should be back soon." She put two cups of cappuccino and a plate with slices of chocolate cake on the table. "Homemade. Every once in a while I play housewife for my lord and master. You're welcome to a piece."

"Oh, Karla, I shouldn't." Alois patted his potbelly. "I need to lose weight. Well, perhaps a little piece." He took a slice and bit into it. "Excellent. I hope your lord and master appreciates your services. Actually, I'm not in a joking mood at all." He put the half-eaten piece of cake back on his plate.

"Is something wrong?" Karla asked.

"You can say that. And Andreas will hit the ceiling when he finds out. I'm actually glad he isn't here, so I can tell you first."

"What happened?

Alois took sip of coffee and then sighed. "Andreas's father is here."

"What did you say?"

"Yep, he's staying with us."

Karla stared at him, stunned. "That's not possible," she whispered. "What is Andreas going to say?"

"That's what I'm worried about, too."

"How did this happen? Why is he here? What does he want? Oh, Alois, I just mentioned his father to him the other day." Karla told Alois about the incident of Laura threatening Tonio and the talk they had had later.

"Well, it looks like now he is forced to deal with it one way or the other," Alois said. "Sounds almost like fate caught up with him. But to answer your questions, Robert has actually been in touch with Emilia off and on over the past few years. She never told Andreas, for obvious reasons. You know, in spite of the fact that Robert was a real bastard back then and a very unhappy man, he did have his good sides. When he was sober, he was a nice guy, even loving. Of course, Andreas doesn't remember any of that. His whole relationship with his father was overshadowed by the beatings he got from him.

"A few years after Robert returned to the United States, he must have gotten himself straightened out somewhat. He started to make regular child-support payments, although Emilia never claimed any. She kept the money in an account for Andreas but never told him about it, because she was afraid he wouldn't accept it. She figured she'd give it to you guys once you were married, but so far there has never been a good moment. Anyway, that's not the important issue right now."

"But why is he here?" Karla asked.

"Well, he wrote to us a while back, telling us that he was ill, that he had had a heart attack and kidney problems, obviously from all the boozing he did years ago. He said his only wish was to see Andreas once again and ask for his forgiveness."

"After all these years?" Karla shook her head. "Why didn't he ever contact him before?"

"Robert claimed he wrote to him several times but never got an answer back. That was, of course, long before you guys met. So, after we got his letter, Emilia called him and told him that Andreas probably wouldn't want to see him. He said he understood, but he'd like to try anyway. If we could put him up for a few weeks. What could I say? I couldn't very well refuse a sick and dying man such a wish. He got here about a week ago. He has been resting. It took him a while to get over the long journey and the jet lag. He's fairly weak and has aged. I was afraid the whole time that Andreas would drop by unexpectedly before I could prepare him." Alois took a deep breath.

"I was wondering why we hadn't heard from you."

"Well, in a way I feel like a traitor to Andreas, having done all this behind his back, but I didn't have much of a choice."

"How does Emilia feel? It must have been a shock for her, as well."

"Yes, it was quite emotional. You know, my sister never stopped caring for him. It's really tragic. I wish she had gotten married again, or at least met another man, but she never did."

"Did he ever get married again?"

"No, I don't think so. Perhaps he still loves her, as well. When you see them together now, they act just like a normal couple."

"God, how sad," Karla said. "They wasted their whole lives when they could've loved each other."

"Yes, if it hadn't been for that damn alcohol, although that wasn't the only reason. He was a troubled man. I think the cause for his heavy drinking lies far back in his past."

"Andreas is here." Karla's heartbeat picked up speed. She realized she was afraid of his reaction. Now, he wouldn't have a chance to take baby steps toward dealing with his father. This was the real thing. "Alois, don't tell him right away. I'm going to get rid of the kids first. I don't want them to witness this. There's been enough upheaval here lately. I'll ask Lena if she can take the children for a few hours."

Karla called Lena and explained what had happened. Lena told her she would pick up Laura and Tonio on her way to the rose field and offered to keep them overnight. Karla stuffed the children's pajamas, toothbrushes, and a few toys into a bag and carried it outside.

Laura jumped out of the car and yipped with excitement when she heard she was going to spend the night at Lena's. There was always a lot of entertainment at her house, with the four children and all the animals. They got to stay up a little later than at home and watch videos on a large-screen TV.

"What's the occasion?" Andreas asked as he helped Laura climb into Lena's pickup truck and lifted Tonio in after her.

"Just for fun," Lena explained. "Luigi brought home a couple of movies for the kids."

Andreas looked on as Lena's old truck scuttled down the hill, then turned to greet his uncle. "Hey, old man. Where have you been hiding? I called you a few times, but nobody answered."

Alois cleared his throat. "Well, we were in Zurich a few days ago to pick someone up at the airport." He gave Karla a quick glance.

"Really? Who?" Andreas asked, surprised, as they went inside. He brushed a tangle of hair out of his face and kissed Karla. "Any cake left?"

"Yes, I cut some for Alois." Karla pointed at the plate on the table. Andreas sat down and bit into a slice.

"So who did you pick up at the airport? And why are you two acting so funny?"

"Why don't you enjoy your cake first?" Karla put a cup of coffee next to his plate.

Andreas put the slice of cake back on the plate and looked at them. "What's going on here? Anything happened to Maria? Or to Mother?"

"No, they're fine." Alois cleared his throat again. "Since you're already sitting down, I might as well tell you now." Alois took a deep breath while Karla held hers. "Your father is here."

There was a prolonged silence. Andreas's face showed no signs of emotion. It was as though he hadn't understood what his uncle had just sprung on him. He stared at him with unbelieving eyes. "What the hell are you talking about?"

"Just as I said. Your father is here. He got here a few days ago. He's staying with us right now."

Karla put her hand on Andreas's, as if to protect him from the blow. He pulled his arm away and continued to stare at Alois, who looked down at his hands. "Alois, if this is a joke, it's a bad one." Andreas's voice almost gave out.

"No, it's not a joke. I wish it was." Alois proceeded to tell Andreas what he had told Karla before, that his father was ill and had come here to see his son and apologize for what he had done to him years before.

After Alois stopped talking, there was a moment of silence. Then Andreas banged his fist on the table so hard that the plate with the half-eaten cake slipped off the edge and fell to the floor. Karla and Alois both flinched. "Are you insane?" Andreas screamed.

"Andreas, please calm down. It's not Alois's fault." Karla reached for his arm again, but he pushed her away.

"What do you mean, it's not his fault?" he yelled. "He lets the jerk stay at his house."

"Andreas, please try to understand," Alois begged. "I couldn't possibly turn him away. Your father is a totally different man now. He straightened himself out, and his only wish is to see you and ask for your forgiveness. He came here all the way from the United States just for this reason. Please give him a chance."

"Well, you can tell him to take his sorry ass right back to where he came from. There is no way I'm going to see that prick." Andreas got up from his chair so abruptly that he knocked it over, and let out a flood of obscenities, which shocked Karla, who had never heard him use that kind of language before. The more Karla and Alois tried to calm him down, the angrier he got. Finally, he grabbed his jacket and yelled at Karla: "Don't wait with dinner for me. In fact, don't wait for me at all."

"Andreas, please, it's not my fault." Karla was close to tears.

"Now, wait a minute." Alois got up and pointed his finger at Andreas. "Don't you dare to take it out on Karla. If you want to hurt someone, take it out on me." His voice assumed a stern, threatening tone Karla had never heard from him before. The two men stared each other down. Finally, Andreas lowered his gaze.

Alois sat down again and continued to talk more gently. "I just ask you to think this thing over when you're a little calmer. If you don't want to see him, you don't have to. He came here fully prepared that you would reject him. However, this is an opportunity not just for him but for you, as well, to deal with a very painful chapter of your past and perhaps put it behind you for good. At least think about it."

"Do you know what you're asking me to do? Do you have any idea?" Andreas's face was pale, and his voice trembled. He tossed his jacket onto a chair and sat again.

"Yes, Andreas, I do. I was the one who watched over you when you had your nightmares. I know how hurt you were. I didn't ask him to come here, but I also know that people can change for the better, and he has changed. Nobody can force you to forgive him for what he did to you. I'd only be sad if you had to carry your hatred of him to the end of your life. Perhaps this is a chance for you to let go." Alois got up. He gently touched Andreas's shoulder and then left the kitchen. Karla accompanied him to the car. "I'm sorry, Karla."

"We'll be all right." Karla tried to smile. "I apologize for Andreas's behavior. He isn't himself right now."

"I know." Alois gave her a hug.

When Karla came back into the kitchen, Andreas was sitting at the table, staring at his hands. "How long have you known about this?" he asked her in an icy voice.

"I didn't know anything. I only found out today. Do you really think I would've hidden this from you?"

"How do I know?" Andreas grumbled. "I don't know who to believe anymore."

"Andreas, your anger makes you unfair and cruel." Karla picked up the plate with the piece of cake Andreas had knocked on the floor.

"I'm sorry." Andreas got up and helped her clean up. "I don't mean to take it out on you. I just don't know what to do with my feelings right now. It's such a shock." He sat down, with his elbows on the table and his head in his hands. Karla, who thought he was going to cry, sat next to him and hugged him. Andreas hugged her back, then got up. "I'm going for a walk. I need to clear my head, or it's going to explode."

"Let me come with you. It's been a shock for me, too."

"Fine, if you can bear being around an angry and foulmouthed companion."

"It couldn't be worse than what came out of your mouth a few minutes ago. Where did you pick up all those juicy expressions?" Karla asked.

"I don't know myself." A weak smiled flashed across Andreas's face.

They walked the path up the hill in silence until they came to a small park with a children's playground. They sat on a bench from which they had a view of the town. Karla gazed at the small vineyards, neatly divided by low granite walls, the forest with its birches and ashes, and the mountains in the background. *How is it possible that a man living more than six thousand kilometers away is able to disturb the peace and serenity of this beautiful place?*

"How dare he come here and upset our lives," Andreas said, echoing Karla's feelings.

Karla put her hand on his and hoped he would finally be able to talk.

"I think my whole childhood I was afraid of him. I used to wait in bed when he was out late and I suspected he was on one of his drinking binges. I was afraid to fall asleep. Finally, I fell asleep in spite of myself." Andreas gave a painful groan and brushed through his untidy hair.

"I woke up in the middle of the night. I heard them arguing. My mother cried, and my father beat and insulted her. ... I put my pillow over my ears, trying to drown out the noises. I was paralyzed." Andreas's voice faltered.

Karla touched his cheek. He looked at her with so much pain in his eyes that it made her heart stutter. He took her hand in his and cleared his throat.

"Whenever he was totally tanked, he would just go to bed and sleep it off. But when he was still half aware, that's when all his anger came out. Sometimes he stumbled into my room. I never will forget the way he looked: disheveled hair hanging into his face, the bloodshot eyes. His breath reeked of alcohol. He asked me to fix him something to eat, since 'your no-good bitch of a mother refused to do it,' as he put it.

"I was about seven at the time and didn't know how to prepare dinner. I got up and tried to get him something out of the refrigerator. Being so frightened, I usually ended up dropping something, and that got him started. It seemed that he had just been waiting for the moment he could take off his belt or grab anything nearby and start hitting me. My mother came rushing into the kitchen and tried to stop him, but he just belted her, as well, until he was too tired to lift his arm. Then he stumbled into his bedroom.

"My mother took me to my room and lay down next to me. We were both trembling. As a result of all this, I began to wet my bed again. My schoolwork deteriorated. My grades dropped." Andreas propped his elbows on his knees and covered his face with his hands. "How can you do something like that to a little kid?" His voice broke.

Karla put her arm around him. He suppressed the urge to cry and went on. "Eventually, my teacher noticed the bruises on my body and asked me about them. The strange thing was, I was too ashamed to admit the truth. So I just mumbled something about falling down somewhere. I actually felt guilty, thinking I was bad and it was somehow my fault that my father acted that way. My teacher got suspicious and came to my home one day to talk to my mother. She lied, as well, telling him that I had gotten into a fight with another boy. Since our stories didn't match, the teacher began to put two and two together. Somehow, he got ahold of my aunt and uncle and informed them of his suspicions."

"How come your aunt and uncle didn't notice anything before?"

"Well, they didn't live nearby. We lived up north, and we didn't have much contact with them. My aunt and uncle never approved of my mother's marriage to my father. My father and Uncle Alois didn't exactly get along, as Alois told me much later.

"Anyway, once Uncle Alois heard about the possible abuse, he appeared one day, unannounced, and confronted my father. He, of course, lied about it and told Alois to get the hell out of his home. My mother and I were in the living room with them. Alois then asked my mother, who denied everything, as well.

"I remember that day so well. It was at this moment that it hit me. I knew then that I couldn't depend on my mother anymore. Uncle Alois turned to me. He didn't ask me anything, just lifted my shirt and opened my pants. It went so fast that my father couldn't stop him. By chance, he had just beaten me again a couple of days before, and I still had welts all over my back."

Andreas took a deep breath. "It was probably the only time I was grateful for my punishment. Now, there was no way anybody could deny the truth. I'll never forget my uncle's face when he saw my body. You know how good-natured he normally is. He turned pale and looked at me, shocked. Then he faced my father, and if you think my language was bad today, you should've heard him scream and swear."

Karla shook her head. "I've never heard Alois cuss."

"Well, he did then, believe me. He told my father that I was coming with him right then, and if he tried to stop him, he would take him to court and have him thrown out of the country.

"Now, mind you. My father was about twice as strong as Uncle Alois and could've easily knocked him down. Something in my uncle's demeanor must have scared him, though. Then Alois turned to my mother, who was crying by then, and yelled at her, as well. He told her she was always welcome to stay with them if she ever got rid of her mishap of a husband, or something like that. Then he pulled me along and we left. ... That was probably the happiest day of my childhood." Andreas sighed.

"What about your mother?"

"After I went to live with my aunt and uncle, my father was subdued enough that he stopped drinking for a while and didn't beat her anymore. He even came by one day to see me. He apologized and promised he'd never lay hands on me again if I came back with him. However, by then I had lost all trust in him. My uncle took me aside and asked me if I wanted to go back. I told him no. I still remember my father's disappointed face. He actually had tears in his eyes.

"Of course, his good intentions didn't last. He began to drink again. One day my mother came to our house with a black eye and bruises on her face. She stayed with us off and on, but always moved back again, until she finally had the courage to stay and file for divorce.

"That's the story of my childhood." Andreas exhaled deeply. "It took me quite some time to feel like a halfway normal kid again. They took me to a psychiatrist. But it was really my aunt and uncle and Father Chiesa who helped me recover somewhat and get my confidence back. Father Chiesa is the priest in my aunt and uncle's parish."

Karla put her arm around Andreas. "I asked you this question once before, and you got angry at me. Don't you have any pleasant memories of your father at all?"

"I don't know, Karla. I'm sure there were some good times. I was about six when he began to drink heavily. He wasn't always drunk, and when he was in a sober period, we did do fun things together as a family. However, there was always that fear that he would turn on me again. I didn't trust him anymore. His anger and violence destroyed everything that at one time may have been good in our lives.

"I think the worst thing you can do to children is destroy their feelings of security. Once a child doesn't trust you anymore, you've lost it. The worst moment as a father was when I hit Laura the other day and I saw fear in her eyes. She was afraid of me." Andreas sighed.

"Yes, but she has overcome that," Karla assured him. "I know Laura is secure when it comes to your love for her. I think somehow she understood that you both weren't your true selves at that moment."

"Yes, but imagine I did that on a regular basis. God, Karla, I remember my early childhood as one continuous saga of fear and pain, and now I should confront this devil and accept his apologies. I don't think I can do it." His voice was husky, and he looked at Karla with pain-filled eyes.

"Andreas, you don't have to. You have to do what's right for you, not what's right for your father or anybody else." They sat quietly for a while, watching the disk of the June sun slide down behind the hills. Karla took Andreas's hand. "I'm so sorry you have to deal with this. Whatever you decide to do, I love you." She kissed him. His eyes glittered with unwept tears.

That night Andreas woke up sobbing from a dream he couldn't remember. Karla held him until he fell back to sleep. In the morning he seemed subdued and less angry. He didn't mention his father again, and Karla didn't bring up the topic, either, wanting to give him time to make his own decision.

The next couple of days, Andreas seemed distracted and preoccupied. He was unusually quiet and stared into space a lot.

He reminded Karla of the time after the car accident they were involved in years ago, when she had her miscarriage. The children noticed the change in him, as well.

"You're not listening to me, Papa," Laura whined and stamped her foot when he wasn't responding to the story she told him.

"I'm sorry, honey, I was thinking about something. What were you saying?" Andreas hugged her and forced a smile.

Chapter 50

It was a bright, sunny, and breezy day. *Nordfoehn*, Karla thought as she woke up, feeling the familiar numb pain radiating from her neck up the back of her head. She sat up and turned her head left and right to release the tension.

The door opened, and Andreas walked in with a cup in his hand. "How is the headache? I thought this might help." He put the cup of black coffee on the nightstand and began to massage her shoulders for a while.

"Ah, that feels great." Karla moaned as some of the tension dissolved. "It's going to be all right. Thanks for the coffee." She was surprised that Andreas even remembered her reaction to the dry northern wind, considering how absentminded he had been the last couple of days.

"Andreas," she called after him as he got up and was about to leave the room. He turned around. He seemed a little more relaxed. His shoulders and arms weren't stiff-looking, as they had been, but there was still that troubled expression in his eyes. "Have you come to any conclusion … about your father?"

Andreas sighed, and his shoulders slumped. "I still don't know what to do. It's eating me alive. I don't want to see the jerk, but not seeing him doesn't seem like an option, either. I'd probably feel like a coward for the rest of my life."

"Andreas, putting it off won't help. Just get it over with. You might be surprised. You'll probably feel so much better afterwards."

"After what? After I kill the guy?"

"Come on. You wouldn't do that." Karla got up. "You won't have to go through this alone. You have a family. We'll be here with you."

Andreas shook his head. "I don't think so. If I'm going to see him, I want to meet him alone. I don't want any witnesses. I'll make up my mind today. I'll be in my studio." He marched out of the room.

"No, you're not going to do this alone. Not this time," Karla muttered to herself.

After showering and dressing, she went to pick up the children, who had spent the night at Lena's. Luigi opened the door and gave her a hug. "So how is the situation with the prodigal father?"

Karla shrugged. "He may agree to see his father. Of course, being the macho he is, he wants to confront his enemy on his own. That's not going to happen, though. I'm going to be there. I don't want to have to visit him in jail after he manhandles, or possibly kills, his dad."

"Right you are. Brave woman." Luigi laughed. "I don't think it'll come to that, though. And if you need help, we'll be here."

"Thanks. It'll work out ... somehow." Karla sighed, then turned to Lena. "And thanks for having the kids again last night. It gives me a little more quiet time with Andreas. He needs all the moral support he can get. I just hope he can let go of his anger. Ever since Alois gave him the news, he's been short-tempered with all of us, even the kids. And he's normally very patient with them. Perhaps he did inherit some of his father's tendencies."

"Perhaps," Lena said. "But he's also Emilia's son, and you know how kind and gentle she is. Besides, he is also his own person, and he can't keep blaming his father for his own anger. That's just a cop-out."

Karla nodded. "You're right, but we better get going or Laura will be late for kindergarten."

After dropping Laura off at the town's small nursery school, which was just around the corner, behind the church, Karla and Tonio walked up the hill to their home. As they crossed the patio, a car pulled up and parked in their driveway.

"Alois?" Karla asked.

"Grandma," Tonio called, excited, and rushed toward the car.

When Karla realized that there were four people in the car, one of them an older man with snow-white hair, her heart lurched. "Oh my god," she whispered.

Alois got out of the car, and after giving Tonio a quick hug, he looked at Karla with an apologetic half smile. "Sorry about that. I know we shouldn't drop in on you like this. But we were in the neighborhood, and Robert insisted on coming by. We haven't heard from you, and he didn't want to wait any longer. I tried everything to stop him, but ..."

Karla didn't listen to the rest of Alois's explanation. She looked toward Andreas's studio at the other end of the patio. The noise of the polishing machine told her that he probably hadn't heard them yet. She watched with trepidation as Maria, Emilia, and the man got out of the car. Even if Karla hadn't been informed of his arrival, she would have recognized him right away.

Andreas's father looked old and fragile, but the resemblance to his son was unmistakable. He was tall, and although he hunched over slightly and his shoulders slumped, Karla could tell he had been a strong, muscular man once. He still had a full head of unruly hair, much like his son's, though it was white. All this

Karla took in while throwing furtive glances toward Andreas's studio, waiting for him to step out, waiting for a possible disaster.

"Robert, this is Karla, Andreas's wife." Emilia held Robert's arm and supported him.

Robert stretched out his hand and smiled at Karla. "I've seen photos of you, but you're even more beautiful than in the pictures." He spoke with an accent, but almost flawlessly, enunciating each word carefully.

Karla was startled that he had the presence of mind to give her a compliment. When she shook his hand, she noticed that his arm was trembling slightly. Karla looked at his face more closely and marveled once again how familiar it seemed. His face was creased and lined, far beyond his age—he couldn't be much past sixty—but his features were an older version of Andreas's. He had the same color eyes, verdigris green, but that's where the similarity stopped.

It wasn't just that Robert's eyes had lost the luster of youth; there was something like lingering pain in them. Although he smiled, the smile didn't reach his eyes.

Karla's eyes flicked to the studio again, but the machine was still running. "I'm ... pleased to meet you."

Robert nodded and gave her another smile, then his face clouded over. "I don't know how this visit will end, but I want you to know how much I appreciate being able to see you and your family." He smiled at Tonio, who was holding on to Karla and eyeing the strange man suspiciously.

"This is your grandpa." Emilia bent down and hugged Tonio.

"Grandpa?" Tonio asked in a serious voice, still measuring Robert, then shook his head. "Not Grandpa Arturo."

"No, Tonio, this is your other grandpa. This is Papa's daddy," Karla explained.

"I'm so happy to meet you," Robert said, gently touching Tonio's cheek.

Tonio looked at him for a while, wrinkling his brow, then his face turned into a wide smile. "Grandpa."

The word *Grandpa* had a magical meaning for Tonio. Grandpa was someone like Arturo, who, together with Rosa, had visited the family half a year before. As usual, they had spoiled the children with presents and attention. *Grandpa* ranked right up there with *Mama* and *Papa*.

At once, Karla became aware that the noise of the machine in the workshop had stopped. She watched anxiously as Andreas stepped outside. He stopped in his tracks and stared at them with incredulous eyes.

Robert, still smiling at Tonio, must have felt the changing mood in the people around him. He turned and looked in Andreas's direction. He blanched, and the hand that gently stroked Tonio's hair began to tremble more. "Andreas." It was a mere whisper.

Karla exhaled, realizing she had held her breath, and began to walk in Andreas's direction, hoping to be able to prevent ... what? She didn't know what was going to happen. Andreas stood there, motionless, like one of his stone sculptures.

Tonio saw Andreas and scampered toward him with a bright smile on his face. He stopped halfway and turned back, pointing at Robert. "Grandpa," he screeched, then continued to run toward his father, his arm still pointing back. "Grandpa?" He stumbled just before reaching Andreas, who caught him and lifted him up, pressing him to his chest.

Andreas stared at his father, the shock in his eyes giving way to anger—or was it agony? Karla couldn't tell, but the expression in his eyes worried her. She stood next to him and touched his arm. "Andreas?"

He pushed her arm away, then lowered Tonio to the ground. "Take him away," he said in a low, harsh voice.

"Andreas, please."

"I said, take Tonio away. I don't want him to witness this."

"Andreas, please, give your dad a chance."

He whipped around and glared at her with furious eyes. "You stay out of this. Take Tonio and leave us alone."

Karla flinched under his look, then felt the heat of anger rise in her. "Don't use that tone with me."

Andreas faltered. "I just don't want Tonio to be around ... him."

"Him? Why him? Who is the bully here now? I know you and your father have issues, but we're still civilized people." Karla gave a toss of her head. "They're family, and right now they're our guests."

"Papa? Mad?" Tonio piped anxiously.

"It's all right, Tonio." Karla hugged him. *And we're not going anywhere. You're the perfect peace ambassador.*

"Papa. Grandpa." Tonio looked at Andreas hesitantly, trying to make sense of his father's hostile mood. He pointed at the group of people on the other side of the patio, who stood huddled together, as if they were a flock of sheep facing an angry wolf.

"Yes, Tonio. This is Grandpa," Karla confirmed.

"Andreas." Robert's voice was husky. He walked slowly, with a slight limp. Without the support of Emilia, he looked even more fragile.

"Grandpa is here. Look." Tonio grabbed Andreas's hand and shook it.

Andreas glanced at his son and gave a quick nod. "Yes, I see," he said in a curt voice, then added more gently: "Why don't you go and talk to Grandma?"

Tonio shook his head. Karla kissed him. "Tell them to sit down and wait. I'll be with them right away, okay?" Tonio looked at his parents, puzzled, then walked over to his relatives, glancing back a few times.

As soon as Tonio had left, Andreas crossed his arms in front of his chest and stared at his father coldly.

Robert faced him, his eyes full of sorrow. "Andreas. I know how difficult this is for you. I understand that you hate me. I've done terrible things to you ... and to Emilia." His voice broke, but he forced himself to go on. "I'd give my life if I could undo my past. I don't expect you to forgive me. I just wanted to see you, to tell you ... how very sorry I am." He suppressed a sob. He was trembling now.

Andreas continued to stare at his father, his lips pressed together, his chin square and aggressive. Then he turned around and walked back into his studio. Robert tried to follow him, but Karla took his arm.

"Give him time. Why don't you sit at the table under the chestnut tree? It's shady and more comfortable there."

Robert nodded and followed her. He sat down and reached into his pocket, pulling out a small bottle of pills, and poured some into his trembling palm.

"Wait," Karla said. "I'll get you some water. Or would you like something else? Tea? Coffee?"

"No, water would be great. Thanks." Robert gave her a grateful look.

Karla went inside and brought out a pitcher of water and a few bottles of lemonade. She poured Robert a glass of water, then went to the studio.

Andreas stood by the window, his back to her, looking outside. Karla walked up to him and hesitantly touched his arm, afraid he might push her away again. He turned around, and to her surprise, she saw tears in his eyes. She hugged him. "Honey, it's going to be all right."

Andreas wiped his hand across his eyes. "I guess I'll go and talk to the jerk," he muttered.

"Please, Andreas, he's an old and sick—"

"Yeah, yeah. I got it." He shrugged. "And you don't have to hover over us. I'm not going to kill him. Do you think we could have a few private moments? Or do I have to be watched like a criminal on parole?"

"Of course not. I—"

But Andreas was already outside. He walked over to the table with a swagger and sat opposite his father. "What do you think you're doing? What do you want? Forgiveness? That's asking for a little much, isn't it? Considering you ruined my childhood." His voice, which started out in a loud and belligerent tone, broke.

Robert started to talk, then began to cough. He reached for the water with a trembling hand, spilling a little.

"You okay?" Andreas squinted his eyes and gave him a probing look.

"Yes. I'm fine."

Karla walked over to Alois, who was sitting on the low stone wall bordering the patio, waiting.

He winked at her. "No bloodshed yet, huh?"

"Thank God." Karla sat next to Alois.

"And you think you can just come here and say a few words of apology and that settles it. You bastard." Andreas's loud, angry voice made Karla flinch. Andreas got up and kicked at a stone.

Karla held her breath and watched anxiously as he sat again and stared at his father. Robert talked in a subdued voice, and Andreas lowered his head. Karla felt Alois's arm around her. His shirt smelled slightly of pipe tobacco. Somehow, it had a soothing effect on her. Karla realized how emotionally drained she felt. She leaned her head against his shoulder. "What turmoil."

"I know. Well, they're talking and shouting. At least they're beginning to communicate. I was beginning to doubt it would come to this."

He took a deep breath, then gave a light chuckle. "Emilia and Maria took Tonio for a walk and an ice cream. He told them that Grandpa always buys him ice cream. He must be thinking of your father."

Karla smiled. "Wasn't he great, the way he welcomed his grandfather? I couldn't believe how fast he took to him. You know how shy he normally is."

"Yeah, I was surprised, too. Perfect timing. Andreas couldn't get too much out of hand with his kid around." Alois wrinkled his forehead. "You know, he's always had a temper problem. He's mellowed quite a bit, but when he was younger, I worried sometimes he'd take after his father. Fortunately, he never had a problem with alcohol. And ever since he met you, I could feel a real change in him. You and the children have been able to soften his rough edges, if you know what I mean. Kind of bring out his gentler, loving side."

"Thanks, Alois. But I think he owes you a lot more. He told me many times that, without you and Maria, he may have gone down the drain. He really feels you're his true parents."

"We tried our best, and we do love him like our own son. However, I've always believed that one day he would have to come to terms with his parents, perhaps understand them a little better. Emilia has really suffered under his coldness. She isn't a bad person. She was a confused young woman and she made a lot of mistakes, but she loved Andreas. And Robert ... he's done a lot of damage, but I believe that, deep underneath that anger and violence, there's a good core. He's really trying to make amends, and I hope ..." Alois sighed.

"Well, they're still talking. I guess that's a good sign. I haven't heard any insults from Andreas in a while." Karla looked over at the two men sitting at the table. Andreas's posture had lost its rigidity. He sat slightly hunched over. With one hand he held a bottle of lemonade, turning it around absentmindedly. He looked down at the table, supporting his head with the other arm, nodding once in a while. He seemed to listen to his father, who sat there talking, his hands folded in front of him, eyes lowered, as well.

The two men talked for about fifteen minutes, more quietly now. When they got up, Robert held on to the table for support. He walked in his unsteady stride toward Karla and Alois. Andreas watched him briefly, then walked back to his studio and disappeared inside.

"Well, Robert, you look like you need a rest." Alois stood and held Robert's arm.

At the same time, Maria and Emilia came back with Tonio, who licked off the last of his ice-cream cone, then wiped his hands on his yellow T-shirt. Maria tried to stop him, but it was too late. She gave Karla an apologetic look.

Karla smiled back. "If that's the only bad thing which came out of this afternoon, I think we've done pretty well."

Robert turned to her and took her hand. "I hope we'll see each other real soon. Thank you so much for your help." He looked exhausted. The eyes in his pale face were half closed, but his handshake was firm.

Emilia took his arm. "Everything all right?"

Robert gave a shrug. "I hope so."

Chapter 51

"That's not fair. Tonio got to see our new grandpa and I didn't." Laura stamped her foot. She stood in front of her parents, her fists propped on her sides, what Andreas called her "warrior's stance."

Andreas and Karla were sitting outside, trying to relax after the tumultuous day with the unexpected visitors. After Andreas's family had left, Karla had picked up Laura at kindergarten. Her class had been on a short field trip, and so Laura had missed the drama of the day.

"And you never told me you had a father, too." She peered at Andreas with reproachful eyes, her chin jutting out aggressively.

"Everybody has a father," Karla said. "But Papa's father lived far away."

Laura, however, was quick to notice her mother's faulty logic. "Grandpa Arturo lives far away, too, and we still got to see him."

"All right, stop whining. You'll get to meet him soon. Can we have some peace now?" Andreas grabbed Laura and sat her on his lap. "Tell me about your outing."

The attempt at distraction failed. Laura wiggled out of his arms and slid down. "How come Grandpa doesn't live with Grandma Emilia?"

Andreas sighed and rolled his eyes.

"That's a long story," Karla said. "They didn't get along when they were young. They were fighting a lot, and then they separated. So Grandpa Robert moved back to America."

"Why didn't they get along?" Laura asked.

"I don't know exactly why. Sometimes grown-ups fight, too, just like children. You fight with your friends and Tonio once in a while, don't you?"

Laura was quiet, thinking things over. "When you and Papa fight, is Papa moving to America, too?"

"No, of course not." Karla brushed Laura's hair out of her face. "Papa and Mama don't fight much. Only when married people fight a lot and for a long time do they sometimes get separated. Papa and Mama love each other, so don't worry."

"Come here." Andreas hugged Laura, then took her face between his hands. "I'll never move anywhere without you and Tonio and Mama. I couldn't live without you."

Reassured enough, Laura slipped out of her father's grasp. "So when are we going to see Grandpa?"

"I think it's time for you to go to bed. Tonio is already asleep."

"I'm not tired." Laura kicked a pebble.

"But I am," Andreas said. "We can all turn in a little earlier for once. Won't do us any harm." He yawned.

Karla noticed how tired he looked. It made her realize how worn-out she was, as well. All the emotional turmoil had taken its toll.

"So when are we going to see him?" Laura kicked at another pebble.

"Soon. And now, no more questions. I want you to put on your pajamas. Right now." Andreas's voice was impatient.

"Are you going to tell me a good-night story?"

"Not tonight. I'm very tired."

"But—"

"Laura!" There were dangerous lights in Andreas's eyes.

Laura flipped her black, wavy hair and marched toward the house.

Karla put her hand on Andreas's shoulder. "How are you feeling?"

Andreas shrugged, but didn't say anything.

"Was it as bad as you thought it would be?"

"What do you want me to feel?" He sounded exasperated.

Andreas's irritation puzzled Karla. He had been quiet and somewhat withdrawn after his relatives had left. They hadn't had a chance to talk, having been busy with the children and getting dinner on the table. "I don't know. I would expect you to have some feelings or thoughts about it. I mean, this was a huge thing for you."

"I wish you'd all stop forcing me to feel a certain way—you and my relatives." He slapped the tabletop with his hand.

"What do you mean?" Karla looked at him, stunned. "I'm not trying to make you feel a certain way."

"You all want me to forgive my father, to behave as if nothing had happened, to become one happy family again. Well, it's not going to happen. At least not the way you want it to happen. I'll deal with it my own way."

361

"Nobody said anything different. Of course you have to deal with it your own way."

"Then why the whole setup with him coming here? Forcing me into a confrontation?"

"Setup? What are you talking about?"

He stared at her with narrow eyes. "You're trying to tell me you didn't know about them coming here? I told you this morning I was going to make a decision today whether I want to see him or not. And the next thing I know, here he is with his whole entourage."

"If you really think I arranged this, then you're so wrong. I can't believe it. All the years we've been married and you don't seem to know the first thing about me. I was as surprised as you were when they showed up."

"Well, then I'm sorry." Andreas sounded a little more subdued.

"Oh? And you think that makes it right? You accuse me of things I didn't do. You have been acting like a jerk for the past weeks. You yell at me. You yell at the kids. You're angry with everybody. You think you can dump on everybody, just because you're going through a difficult time."

Karla didn't want to cry, but anger always launched her tears. "I tried to help you. Don't you think this is difficult for me, too? But I'm tired of it. From now on, you can deal with your family on your own. I've had it." Karla walked away, sobbing.

Andreas followed her and tried to hold her back. "Karla, please."

She shook him off. "Leave me alone. Don't even think of coming after me."

Halfway down the street to Lena's, Karla stopped. She glanced back; Andreas didn't seem to be following her. She continued to walk toward the center of the village. The streets were empty at this time. At the local inn, a few men were sitting outside, drinking beer or wine, talking and laughing. Otherwise, it was quiet.

Karla opened the door to the small Catholic church at the center of town. There was no service, and the church was empty and dimly lit. It smelled of incense. Candles flickered next to the altar and lit up parts of the few paintings. Karla sat on one of the wooden benches, trying to steady her breath.

She felt betrayed. She had tried so hard to help Andreas, to support him, only to have him accuse her of subterfuge. Instead of sharing his feelings with her, he pushed her away. She was tired of being the target of his irrational anger. Tears rose to her eyes again.

The side door behind the altar opened, and a darkly clad figure stepped into the church. It wasn't their regular priest. He picked up a few prayer books lying on the benches in front and walked toward the back of the church. Now, she recognized him; it was Father Chiesa, the priest of Alois and Maria's parish. He was the one who had helped Andreas after his uncle had rescued him from his abusive father. Karla had met him a few times when they visited their relatives in Olivone.

He smiled as he walked by her, then stopped with a look of recognition. Karla surreptitiously dabbed the corners of her eyes. "Father Chiesa. What are you doing here?"

"Karla?" His face opened into a wide smile. Father Chiesa was in his sixties, a short, stocky man with curly dark hair and warm brown eyes. "I'm filling in for Father Santori, who is absent for a few weeks." Then he added with a mischievous chuckle: "If you and your husband came to the service once in a while, you'd know that."

Karla gave a sheepish smile. She and Andreas weren't regular churchgoers. They attended the major celebrations occasionally.

"I'm surprised to see you here at this time," Father Chiesa continued.

"I needed a quiet place to recover. Andreas and I ... we had a fight. ..." It was out before she could stop herself. Karla felt embarrassed. She hardly knew the man, but there was something about him that invited her in. His open face and kind eyes made her want to confide in him. "I'm sorry, I don't know why I said that."

"Don't feel bad. I've known Andreas for a long time, and I know he isn't always easy to be around. May I?" He pointed at the bench.

"Of course." Karla moved over a little, and the priest sat next to her.

"So Andreas is giving you a hard time?" Father Chiesa talked in a hushed voice. "And I don't mean to intrude, if it's too personal," he added quickly.

"No. It's all right. You know the story about his father. Andreas told me that you took care of him when he came to live with his aunt and uncle."

"Yes, that's true. It was a rough time for him," Father Chiesa said.

"Well, his father showed up the other day after more than twenty years, wanting to ask for his forgiveness. It totally upset our lives." Karla found herself telling Father Chiesa the whole story, from the time Uncle Alois gave them the news to the first meeting between father and son.

The priest listened and nodded his head off and on. When Karla finished talking, he remained silent for a while, then faced her. "I've always said miracles do happen." He chuckled, but quickly checked himself. "I don't mean to sound flippant. I know this is a difficult time for Andreas as well as for his father. But it's also a great opportunity for both of them to grow as human beings. God couldn't have sent them a more challenging and helpful test. I have no doubt that Andreas is up to the task. Just the fact that he was able to sit with the torturer his father used to be and talk, this is already quite an achievement."

Father Chiesa looked at Karla with a wistful smile. "And you're in the middle of it all, aren't you?"

"Yes. He controls himself when he's around his father, and then yells at me ... or his uncle," Karla said sadly.

Father Chiesa gently touched her hand. "We do this often, don't we? Hurt those who are closest to us, when in reality we're angry at someone else."

"I just wanted to help him." Karla's voice trembled.

"You want to make things right for him, and sometimes it doesn't work. Everybody has to work out his or her own destiny. We can support those we love, be there for them, pray for them, but in the end, we can't do it for them. And it's very difficult for us, because we don't want them to suffer."

"Andreas has always been afraid he inherited his father's tendencies, his rage. I think if he could realize that his father is no longer the angry person he used to be, if he could even forgive his father, he ... he no longer has any reason to be so angry himself," Karla said.

"Yes, and that's crux of the matter, isn't it?" Father Chiesa winked at her. "Then he wouldn't have an excuse anymore for his own violent temper, would he? He'd have to realize that his anger is all his own. And then the real soul work begins. ... I know all about that."

"You?" Karla looked at him, surprised. The gentle priest didn't seem to have one angry bone in him.

"Oh, yes. One of the reasons I understand Andreas so well is because as a young man I had similar tendencies. I was a very troubled and angry person, for reasons I don't even want to get into. I joined the church as an escape, thinking that becoming a priest would somehow do away with those feelings of anger and hate. Little did I know ..." Father Chiesa sighed. "But I learned. And so will Andreas."

The priest gave Karla a probing look. "I just hope that, in the meantime, he doesn't make you suffer. He isn't abusive, is he? If he is, you have to do something about it. Don't make the same mistake his mother made."

Karla shook her head. "Oh, no. Andreas has a temper, but most of the time he is gentle and loving. He's never been physical. No, I don't want to give the wrong impression."

"Good." Father Chiesa smiled, relieved. "And you love him." It was more a statement than a question.

"Yes, very much."

"Things will work out. I'm sure of that."

He sounded so convinced that Karla's last misgivings faded and she felt at peace, almost joyous. She looked up at the stained-glass window, where the last light of the evening lit up the colors, the red, blue, green, and yellow of a saint. "Yes. I think so, too. But I better go. He probably thinks I ran away."

They both got up and walked along the main aisle to the entrance of the church, past an old woman who was kneeling on the prayer bench, turning her rosary. Outside, twilight trickled through the trees, leaving silver dapples on the churchyard. Karla inhaled the smell of the summer evening, the faint scent of hay and of smoldering barbecue fires from the campground by the Maggia River. She turned to the priest. "Thanks for listening to me and for your advice. I feel much better. ... And we'll see you in church one of these days."

Father Chiesa smiled. "Don't come out of guilt but come when your heart is in it. There're many ways to worship, and not all of them are in church." He slightly touched her arm. "I wish you all the best, and give Andreas my regards and tell him—but wait until he is calm—tell him it's been a while since I had him in Confession. I think he might have a few things to tell me." The priest gave a chortle, then walked away, his long, black habit rippling around his stout body. Before he turned the corner, he lifted his arm and waved.

Back at their house, it was quiet. Andreas and the children were inside. Karla walked across the patio and tripped over

Love of a Stonemason

Laura's bicycle, which lay abandoned in the driveway. *She's as messy as her father.* Karla shook her head and picked up the bike, leaning it against the wall. She didn't want to complain; she came back to make peace.

Inside, she heard muffled voices. Tonio was asleep in the children's bedroom. Laura was lying in Andreas and Karla's bed, and Andreas was sitting next to her. Laura obviously had been able to manipulate her father into telling her a story after all.

Karla stood at the door, listening quietly. Laura was trying to stay awake. Her eyelids fluttered, trying to close, but she kept yanking them open again.

"And then there was a loud bang, and the ugly frog turned into a beautiful prince. He said to the princess: 'Many years ago, a bad witch cursed me and I was turned into a frog. Now, because you helped me and because you love me, the spell is broken.' And the princess and the prince got married and rode in a golden carriage drawn by white horses to the castle, where they lived happily ever after." Andreas glanced at Laura, who finally had succumbed to sleep. He bent down to kiss her, then sat up and leaned his head against the headboard.

Seeing him so tired and vulnerable, Karla was flooded by love and pity. She stepped into the room. He looked at her, surprised and cautious. She sat on the bed and wrapped her arms around him, leaning her head against his chest. He hugged her, and they sat quietly next to each other.

"Sorry," Andreas murmured.

"Me, too," Karla said. "For pushing you too much."

"Let me put her to bed." Andreas picked up Laura, who was deep asleep, and carried her into the children's bedroom.

Karla went outside and sat at the granite table. The mountains were slowly slipping into dusk. The sky, flushed with streaks of crimson and orange, faded into the black-blue of night. It smelled of dry grass and honeysuckle. Peals of laughter erupted from the neighbor's yard, where children were still playing hide-

and-seek. Karla heard the squeaking of the door. Andreas stepped outside and sat next to her.

"How beautiful." Karla pointed at the sky in the south.

"Yes," he whispered. Then after a while: "Where have you been?"

"In church."

"In church?"

"Yeah. I needed a quiet place to calm down."

"I'm really sorry. I acted like an ass. I don't know why I do it, take it out on you—you of all people."

"Father Chiesa said that we hurt those who are closest to us, when in reality we're angry at someone else."

"You met Father Chiesa?"

Karla smiled. "Yes." She told him about their talk.

"Jesus. He must think I'm such a jerk." Andreas groaned.

"No, he doesn't. He understands you. He said ..." Karla faced Andreas. "But before I tell you, I have to make sure you're in a calm mood." She gave him an impish smile.

"Why?"

"Well, are you in a calm mood?"

"Yes. As calm as it gets, under the circumstances. What did he say?" Andreas looked at her, alarmed.

"He expects you in Confession."

"Ouch." Andreas groaned again and put his head on his arms. "I haven't been to Confession in years, decades," he mumbled. "That's why I try to avoid him as much as possible. I thought I was beyond this ridiculous Catholic guilt trip, but around Father Chiesa I still feel like the young kid who messed up."

"He really cares for you, Andreas. Perhaps it might help you. Confessing, I mean."

"Perhaps. One of these days. I might as well wait until this thing with my father is over. Then I can unload everything at once." He paused. "About my father ..."

"Yes?"

"We didn't really talk much, just kind of sounding each other out. But he did say he'd really love to see my work and your paintings. So I thought ... perhaps we could have him over, and I can show him the studio and the few paintings of yours we have here. That way Laura could meet him and stop hounding us about her 'new grandpa.'" Andreas sneered. "Some grandpa."

"Why don't we have them all over for dinner on Sunday?" Karla suggested. She felt excited about Andreas's willingness to meet with his father again. "Perhaps we can drive him around and show him your other sculptures, and if he wants to, we can take him to the gallery—"

"Whoa, whoa. Hold your horses." Andreas lifted his hands. "You're at it again. Peacemaker." Andreas shook his head but smiled. "Let's take this slowly. I'm not ready for a big family reunion yet. Just a short visit, please?"

"Okay. And you're sure you want me around when he comes?"

"Of course I want you around. I need you to be here. I don't trust myself around my father. I promise I won't yell at you again." He hugged her. "But no dinner. Just coffee."

"Coffee and dessert." Karla brushed her lips over the small scar above his cheekbone and gave him a swift kiss.

Andreas sighed in defeat. "All right, then. Coffee and dessert."

It struck Karla that Andreas hadn't referred to his father once in his usual offensive language.

Chapter 52

Karla opened the refrigerator to check on the consistency of the chocolate mousse she had prepared the evening before. "Perfect," she murmured, gently tapping the surface. Outside, Laura and Tonio were each licking one of the hand-mixer accessories Karla had used to whip the heavy cream for the topping. In between licks the children were discussing the upcoming visit of their mystery grandfather.

Tonio, proud of having met him before, for once being better informed than his older, bossy sister, made up stories, trying to impress Laura. "He is very, very tall." Tonio lifted his hand up high. "And he has long, wild hair. And he said he'll bring me lots of presents."

"Tonio." Karla shook her finger at him. "Don't lie. He didn't say anything about presents."

Laura wrinkled her forehead. "I wonder if he'll bring us something."

"All right, you two. Listen carefully. I don't want you to say anything to him about presents. That's not polite. Grandpa Robert traveled a long distance. And he had to pay lots of money for a plane ticket so he could visit us. That's like a present."

"Some present." Andreas, stepping out of his studio, grunted. He ruffled Tonio's hair. "All right, mind Mama. No asking for presents."

The family arrived a few minutes later. Emilia got out of the car, waved at them, then helped Robert out. Alois opened the trunk and pulled out two large, nicely wrapped packages and gave them to Robert and Maria to carry.

"Grandpa brought me presents. See. I told you. I told you." Tonio jumped up and down, then scampered toward the guests.

"That isn't my kid. I'll deny any connection," Andreas grumbled. "Tonio, come back here."

But Tonio wasn't listening. He made a beeline toward Robert, his face gleaming with joy. However, he hadn't reckoned his sister.

Laura marched after him. She grabbed him by the shoulder. "Now, Tonio. This is very rude. Mama and Papa told us not to say anything about presents. Shame on you."

The guests burst out laughing, while Karla and Andreas looked at each other, shaking their heads. Tonio, having lost his burst of enthusiasm, slinked back to Karla and buried his face in her lap. Feeling embarrassed, he started to cry. Karla patted his head. "It's okay, Tonio."

Robert and Emilia walked up to them. Robert gently held Tonio by the arm and turned him around. "Don't feel bad. You're right. I did bring you a present, and one for your sister, as well."

"Can we open them?" Laura asked, having forgotten her role as taskmaster.

"Not right now," Andreas said. "First, I want you to thank Grandpa. I'm going to show him the studio and the house. We'll have coffee and dessert later, and then you can open the gifts."

Laura made a face but didn't protest. She went up to Robert. "Thanks, Grandpa. And don't feel bad about Tonio. He's just a crybaby."

"I'm not, either." Tonio wiped the tears from his face and went up to Robert. He took his hand and glared at his sister.

Robert patted his back. "I know you're not." He turned to Karla. "He looks so much like you. He's going to be a real lady's man one day." Then he looked at Laura and gently mussed up her hair. "Now, here's a true O'Reilly. Don't you think so?" He put his hand on Emilia's shoulder.

"She sure is, in looks and a little bit in character, too."

"Don't say that, Mother," Andreas protested. "Wonderful, that's all we need, another O'Reilly in the family."

"Well, you know, not all O'Reillys are bad people," his father said. "That reminds me. Your uncle Francis sends his regards. That's my older brother. You don't know him, of course, and he only knows you from your baby pictures."

"You have baby pictures of me?" Andreas stared at him.

"I sure do. In fact, that's all I had of you." A shadow flashed over his face. There was an awkward silence, and Karla prayed Andreas wouldn't make some kind of snide remark.

However, as usual, jovial Uncle Alois saved the moment. "No confessionals today. Save that for later." He gently slapped Robert on the back, then turned to Andreas. "Why don't you show your dad around? We'll try to entertain Laura and Tonio in the meantime."

While Andreas showed his father his workspace and some of his sculptures, Karla was able to observe Robert more closely. He was more relaxed and energetic than during his first visit. He walked with a firmer step, and his gestures were livelier. He spoke with his hands a lot, just like his son.

Robert seemed to know quite a lot about the different types of stones and their characteristics. "You use a lot of granite," he remarked. "That is one of the harder stones to work with."

"Yes, I love the challenge," Andreas said. "Granite is very resistant to environmental influences. Most of my larger sculptures are outside, so granite is ideal. It's also the stone of the area. Granite and Peccia marble. Marble is softer, and I use it sometimes when I want to do more detailed carving. But, yeah, granite and gneiss are my favorites. Besides, granite doesn't bruise easily. It's almost indestructible."

"I hear you." Robert pointed at some of Andreas's granite mandalas. "These are beautiful." He bent down to look at the carvings more carefully. "You must have used a flat-blade chisel."

Andreas looked at his father, surprised. "How come you know so much about sculpting?"

Robert took a deep breath. "I don't know that much, but I started an apprenticeship as a stonemason myself."

"What?" Andreas stared at him. "I didn't know that. Did you finish it?"

"No. ... I joined the Navy ... and afterwards things kind of changed." There was a moment of silence. "When I was young, I still believed in something ... unfortunately in the wrong thing, as it turned out." Robert waved his hand in front of his face, as if to chase away a troubling thought. Andreas and Karla kept waiting for an explanation, but none followed.

Robert faced Andreas. He cleared his throat. "This is a real treat, seeing your work. I'm very proud of you, of what you've become and what you've achieved ... in spite of me and my treatment of you." The last few words were a mere whisper.

Andreas's eyes narrowed. "You can thank Maria and Alois for this."

Robert nodded. "I know. And Emilia."

Andreas shrugged and made no comment.

"Andreas, what happened back then was entirely my fault. Don't blame your mother."

"I'm afraid you have to leave that up to me." Andreas spoke with a cold edge to his voice.

Karla was worried he might revert back to his hostile behavior. However, he caught himself. "Well, let's go inside, and we'll show you a few of Karla's paintings. A lot of her work is in a gallery in Locarno, though. If you want to, we can take you there one of these days."

Robert gave Karla a warm smile. "I saw one of your paintings at Alois's place. Beautiful and very interesting work. I'd love to see more."

After a short tour of the house, Robert stood in front of one of Karla's paintings. It was one of the acrylics she had done in

Florence, of the woman standing in a doorway. Her figure was flooded by sunlight coming in through the open door. Robert had been enthusiastic about Karla's colorful oil paintings, but it was this painting he came back to several times. He studied it carefully.

"You almost miss it," he said after a while, in a quiet voice. "At first sight, this painting is peaceful, almost angelic. But look at the shadows on her face. They make her look ... sad, almost despondent. There's a lot of pain here."

Karla was surprised at how quickly he had noticed it. She had painted it during the time she had been tormented by her attraction to Jean Philippe and her confused feelings for Andreas. The painting wasn't as explicitly tortured as the one she had submitted for the contest, but there was a more subdued sadness about it.

It was also one of Andreas's favorite paintings, although he had never told her why. "There is something about it that intrigues me. The way the light radiates around the woman, the face ... I don't know. I just like it," he said.

It was his father, a man who had not only inflicted pain on others but seemed to have experienced a lot of pain himself, who was able to put it into words.

How interesting, Karla thought. Andreas was a sensitive person with intense feelings. But there were emotions he shied away from—deep sadness being one of them. *My anger often turns into sadness. Andreas seems to get angry when he doesn't want to feel sad.*

Karla was still looking at the painting when she heard voices outside. "Mama, can we have dessert now and open the presents, finally?" Laura stood in the doorway, her face flushed from running around, hair untidy as usual, her green eyes flashing.

Karla went up to her and hugged her tightly. *What will be your destiny? My happy, angry, impatient child.* "Yes, honey, we can have dessert now."

They all sat at the granite table outside. It was a warm, sunny late afternoon in July. The weather had been scorching hot for the past two weeks, and Karla was relieved that it had cooled down somewhat. Under the chestnut trees, it was pleasant.

As usual, Alois and Maria were chatting and laughing. Robert and Emilia sat quietly next to each other, eating and smiling once in a while. Andreas, sipping his espresso, observed his parents with caution but without hostility. Laura and Tonio were gobbling down their dessert, fidgeting, and flicking their eyes at the two packages propped against the low stone wall.

"This is the best chocolate mousse I've ever had," Robert said.

"I agree." Alois was on his second helping.

"Yes, Karla isn't just a great artist. She's also an excellent cook." Emilia touched Karla's arm. "She and Maria could open a gourmet restaurant."

"You're too kind, Emilia. But Maria definitely gets first prize for cooking," Karla said.

Laura, having finished her dessert, slid down from the chair and went over to Andreas. She hugged him and whispered something into his ear.

Andreas gave her a quick smile and nodded. "You can open your gifts now."

"Yippee." Laura rushed toward the packages.

Tonio tossed his spoon on the table, scrambled down from the bench, and bolted after his sister.

Laura turned around. "Which one is mine?"

Alois laughed out loud. "You have to guess. If you guess right, you can keep it. If you guess wrong, it goes back to the store."

"Alois, you're so cruel." Emilia slapped his arm.

"Really, Alois." Maria shook her head. "The large square one is yours, and the big fat one is Tonio's."

Andreas got up and grabbed the packages. "Come on, I'll help you open them."

Karla laughed. "Andreas, I think your dad brought these gifts for the children, not for you."

"Just helping so they don't break whatever is inside."

Karla was relieved to see him in a more lighthearted mood. The children tore into the packages, with Andreas helping to loosen the wrapping paper.

Laura unpacked a large colorful kite with long tassels, and Tonio got a bright red fire truck with a remote control that had lots of knobs and buttons, which produced all kinds of sounds.

"Look how beautiful." Andreas helped Laura untangle the tassels. It was a large bird with multicolored wings. Andreas turned it around and admired it from all sides. "I think I used to have one of these."

"Yes, you did. We used to fly it down by the lake ... what was it called?" Robert turned to Emilia.

She nodded. "Lago Maggiore. I remember. You were about five then."

Andreas stared at them. "You're right. I totally forgot about this ... Jesus." He shook his head, as if waking from a dream.

"Can we fly it, Papa?" Laura asked.

Andreas held the kite up in the air, then shook his head. "I'm afraid the breeze isn't strong enough right now, and there isn't enough room here."

Laura looked disappointed. Andreas kissed her. "Tell you what. We'll take it down to Lago Maggiore tomorrow. There's a lot more space and wind there. It'll be much more fun."

Chapter 53

After the first few family gatherings, Andreas began to spend time alone with his father. He took him on trips around the area. Since Robert's health did not allow for any extended hikes, they went for short walks along Lake Maggiore or in the Blenio Valley. This gave them the chance to talk about issues they couldn't discuss in front of the family and the children, and from what Andreas told Karla, there were moments of intense emotions between them.

"I'm always afraid I'm causing him another heart attack when we talk about the past. But we have to do it. I want him to know what he did to me. How I felt about him. It's painful for both of us. I also want to know what drove him to do what he did." Andreas sighed.

It was early evening after a hot day. It hadn't rained in weeks, and the grass was yellow and brown, burned by the scorching sun. Rangers were deployed to watch out for wildfires. The soil in the gardens was caked and cracked. Lettuce and green, leafy vegetables wilted and had to be picked every day to be edible. Some of the flowers withered and drooped. Only the chestnuts and grapes didn't mind the dry heat. On the contrary, the extended time of sunny days promised an excellent harvest.

Karla and Andreas were taking a leisurely walk along the Maggia River. The children were with Andreas's family, so they had some time to themselves.

"The problem is, whenever I lose my temper and shout at him, he always remains calm and apologetic," Andreas continued. "The only emotion he shows me is intense sadness. I don't know what happened to that anger I remember so well.

Sometimes I wish he'd get angry again, so I'd recognize him for who he was. I'm the only one who seems to get angry. It drives me nuts."

"Well, this is your chance to get it all out," Karla said. "Your father certainly didn't expect to have a nice little vacation and reunion with his long-lost family. He came in order to settle with his past, and now you have a chance to do the same."

"Yeah, I guess so." Andreas stopped and looked down at the river. Karla stood next to him, feeling the cool air rising from the turbulent water fan her face. It was a welcome reprieve from the scorching sun. Birch leaves trembled in the light breeze. There was a faint smell of moss and a hint of peppermint.

"Let's sit down for a while." Andreas pointed to a rock at the side of the path. They settled on a smooth slab of stone. Andreas put his arm around Karla. They watched quietly as the late afternoon gave way to evening and the colors faded, turning into light and shadows. The loud shrieks of a mockingbird interrupted the peaceful mood.

"What did your father say about hitting you and your mother?"

"That was the most incredible moment of our talks." Andreas sighed, then proceeded to tell Karla what had happened between him and his father during the boat ride to the Brissago Islands on Lago Maggiore.

They left early on a foggy morning. Not too many tourists were on the boat yet. After drinking a quick cup of coffee inside the cabin, Andreas and Robert stood at the railing of the small ferry, watching the wooded mountains on the Italian side of the lake slowly emerge from the mist. The first sunrays peeked through the clouds.

It was a peaceful morning, but Andreas felt unsettled. He had slept badly the past night, having woken up from a nightmare. He had forgotten most of the dream, but he knew it had to do with his childhood and his father. He turned to face the now-mild-mannered old man next to him.

"To this day I can't understand what went through your mind when you slugged my mother and beat me to a pulp." Andreas felt the anger, which had given way to more subdued feelings toward his father over the past few days, flare up again.

As usual when they talked about Robert's abuse of his son, Robert looked at Andreas with eyes full of remorse. "I don't remember hitting you or Emilia when I was drunk."

"What?" Andreas felt as though he had been punched in the stomach.

Robert shook his head. "I know you won't believe me, but I swear to you, I don't remember."

Andreas knew that he was on the point of losing it. He could have hit his father, felled him with one punch, killed him even, and wouldn't have felt any remorse. He held on to the railing, his knuckles turning white. "You damn liar."

The couple of people on the deck of the boat turned around and looked at him, shocked, as he screamed. Andreas turned to his father and grabbed him by the shoulder. Looking into the tortured eyes and feeling the thin bones in his grip—he could've broken them easily, snapped them like a dry branch—he let go. He felt sick to his stomach. He propped his elbows on the railing and put his face in his hands. "Jesus."

It was quiet for a while, then a suppressed sob rose next to Andreas. Robert wiped his eyes. "Andreas, I've tortured myself for the past thirty years about this. I know you hate me. But believe me, I probably hate myself even more. I'll never get over the fact that I mistreated the two people in my life I've loved the most. This knowledge I'll carry to my grave."

Andreas strained to get hold of his emotions. He exhaled deeply. "Then tell me what happened." He looked around the boat. A man and a woman had retreated to the other end of the ferry and kept giving him furtive glances. One of the crew members stepped outside and eyed him suspiciously. "It seems like I'm the bad guy here," Andreas sneered.

"Can we sit down?" Robert's voice sounded weak.

Andreas motioned to a wooden bench along the cabin wall. They sat and looked out onto the lake.

"I'm not lying to you," his father continued. "I know, of course, I hit you. I saw the bruises afterwards, Emilia's black eye. But I can't remember having done it. The last thing I remember after I forced myself into a drunken stupor was a flash of red light in front of my eyes. I didn't know how I got home. I have bits and pieces of memories, but most of it is just one huge blank." Robert suppressed another sob.

"The next morning I woke up with the awful realization that I had done it again. I didn't dare to face you or your mother, and I usually just left. I didn't have a job then, couldn't hold one down. So, after I recovered somewhat, I couldn't stand the pain and went right back to drinking. It was a vicious circle.

"After the divorce and after I got back to the United States, there were many times I was close to killing myself. The only thing that kept me alive was the desire to straighten out enough so I'd be able to tell you how much I regret what I had done."

"So what could I say?" Andreas said to Karla. "I even believe him, I don't think he's a liar. I mean, I know that you can forget things when you're drunk." His voice sounded husky. "It's just so hard to come to terms with the fact that the man who was supposed to love and protect me and instead caused all this pain and terror in me, that this man can't remember having done it. How can I make him realize what it felt like? I have no target for my anger. Every once in a while I wonder if this is just a bad dream or if I made it all up."

"No, of course not." Karla hugged him. "It's real, Andreas. It was terrible what your father did. But I think his remorse is real, too."

"I guess so." Andreas brushed his hand across his eyes.

They were quiet again. The sun had set in the meantime. The shadows of tree trunks lengthened across the river.

"It's interesting, though," Andreas continued more calmly. "You can't fully trust your memory. From what he and my mother and my aunt and uncle tell me, only half a year passed between the time he started drinking heavily and beating us and the time I went to stay with my aunt and uncle. It started after he had lost his job and couldn't find another one. He had had problems with alcohol before, but he had always been functional up to that point. To me it seemed as if the heavy drinking and the beatings had been going on for several years.

"In fact, until recently this is all I was able to remember of my childhood at home. It's only now, being with him, that I start having flashbacks to better moments, like the time he brought me that kite."

"That I can understand very well," Karla said. "A child has a different sense of time than an adult. Half a year of misery and fear can easily seem like several years and drown out everything else."

Chapter 54

"Why did you never tell me that Father was in Vietnam?" Andreas asked his mother. He was sitting with Karla and Emilia on a bench near the lake watching Robert, Alois, and the children fly the kite.

The breeze along the lake lifted the kite effortlessly into the air. Laura laughed out loud as she watched the red, green, and blue bird ride the wind and flap its multicolored wings, jerking occasionally when caught by a gust. Robert had tied the end of the string around her waist so she wouldn't let go by mistake, and helped her steer the kite. Tonio was running after them, and Laura let him hold the string once in a while.

"How did you find out?" Emilia asked Andreas.

"He mentioned being in the service the other day, and so he told me. He didn't elaborate on it, but I could tell it must have been an awful time. Why did you never say anything?"

Emilia took Andreas's hand in hers, and he let her hold it. Only a few weeks before, he probably would've pulled it back. Karla had noticed that Andreas treated his mother with more warmth.

"Andreas, whenever I started to talk about your father, you got so angry that I was afraid you'd hit me."

"I'm sorry, Mom. I guess you're right."

It was the first time Karla heard him use the short form *Mom* instead of the more formal *Mother*.

"Perhaps I would've been able to understand him a little better had I known." Andreas sighed. "Then again, who knows?"

"That war destroyed so many souls," Emilia said in a bitter tone. "Robert was eventually captured and became a POW. Of course, that all happened before we met. He never wanted to talk about it, but his brother, your uncle Francis, once told me that he was tortured."

"Damn," Andreas muttered. "I don't seem to know anything about him."

"Robert told me that he had tried to contact you several times. Didn't you get his letters?" Emilia asked.

"Yeah, I did. I threw them into the trash without reading them. I was just too angry at him. Seeing his name on the envelope made me furious." Andreas got up from the bench and kicked a small stone out of the way, then joined his father and the children.

Karla and Emilia smiled at each other. "His attitude toward his dad is changing, slowly but surely," Karla said. She took her drawing pad and a charcoal pen out of her purse and made a quick sketch of the two men.

The following day Karla was converting the sketch into a painting. She planned to give it to Robert to take home with him, and chose a format and size he would be able to put into his suitcase.

The picture depicted Robert and Andreas standing next to each other, watching the kite fly, their heads tilted back, their white and black hair blowing in the wind. The colorful bird in the sky seemed to her like a sign of a positive outcome of the reunion between father and son.

A couple of days ago, Karla had found Andreas outside watching the sun set behind the trees. When she sat next to him, she noticed his red-rimmed eyes. He looked as if he had been crying.

"When I see him play with Laura and Tonio ... it makes me sad," Andreas tried to explain.

"Why sad?" Karla took his hand.

"That I was never able to experience him as a loving father. We missed all the good times we could've had together had he not been the violent alcoholic he was."

Karla hugged him. "I'm so sorry. I think I know how you feel. We're not supposed to have abusive parents or lose them so early, but it happens."

Andreas took a deep breath. "No use crying over spilt milk. At least the kids get to enjoy him as a grandfather for a while, even if I wasn't able to have him as a father."

"He still is your father, Andreas. You can't change the past. But you do have an opportunity to develop a new relationship with him. It was a lesson I had to learn with my own father."

Andreas nodded. "I guess so. It's just ... the man I see now is nothing like the father I knew. I don't seem to be able to connect the two."

Chapter 55

Andreas was on his way to Olivone to pick up his parents. Karla and Andreas decided to take the children swimming down at the Maggia, since it was such a hot day. Laura and Tonio wanted Grandpa and Grandma along and had been begging all morning until Andreas agreed to invite them.

Karla was halfway through the painting of Robert and Andreas when she heard the car. She put the painting away; she wanted to surprise Robert with it.

Down at the river, the summer heat was bearable. Karla had prepared a picnic basket with sandwiches and lemonade. She was sitting next to Emilia on towels in the shade of the beeches, oaks, and hazels on a small patch of sand surrounded by boulders, which lined the shores of the river.

The children were playing ball with Robert and Andreas in one of the shallow pools formed by water trapped by the rocks. These small ponds were ideal bathing spots for children or adults who didn't feel comfortable in the deeper and more turbulent water of the mountain river. Tonio was wearing a bright-red life vest, but Laura, who already knew how to swim, didn't want to wear one anymore.

Karla always felt a little uneasy with her children in the river. She squinted her eyes against the glare from the water surface and watched them. Although the Maggia wasn't as turbulent and dangerous as some of the rivers in the neighboring valleys, there were still occasional accidents and people had drowned in the past.

"I guess they'll be okay with the two men there," she said to Emilia. She was just about to call to Laura not to get too close to the deep part when Robert threw the ball a little too far. It bounced off a rock and fell into the actual river. Laura rushed after the ball, trying to catch it before it was swept away by the current.

"No, Laura, let it go," Andreas called. But it was too late.

Then everything seemed to happen at once. Laura slipped, fell, and knocked her head on one of the boulders. She went under, then reemerged, then went under again. The next time she reemerged, she was out in the deep being carried away by the current.

"Laura!" Karla rushed into the water and screamed. "Andreas, get her." She slipped on a smooth stone and fell.

Robert plunged headfirst into the river and followed her with a powerful crawl. Andreas lunged after him. Laura resurfaced again, close to the rapids. Karla's heart lurched, and she felt she was going faint. She noticed the coppery taste of blood in her mouth. She had bitten her lower lip.

Robert got hold of Laura just in time, before she was hurled over the rapids. He held her in a lifesaver's grip. Struggling against the current, he swam at an angle until he reached the shore somewhat farther down the river, where Andreas caught up with him. Andreas heaved her onto firm ground, then grabbed his father's hand and pulled him up the bank.

"It's all right, Karla, she's safe." Karla felt Emilia's arm around her.

Hearing Laura cry and knowing that she was safe, Karla gave way to her own emotions and began to tremble and sob. Emilia led her to the shore, pulling little Tonio behind her, who was crying, as well.

"Everything is fine," Emilia said, hugging them both.

Karla ran toward Andreas, who carried Laura in his arms. She threw her arms around them. Laura wasn't screaming anymore. She had a bump on her forehead and scratches on her arms and legs from scraping against stones.

"I think she'll be all right," Andreas said, hugging and kissing Laura.

Karla turned to Robert, who slowly followed behind. She hugged him. "Thank you so much for saving her."

"It was my fault. I shouldn't have thrown the ball so far," Robert said, his voice trembling. He looked pale and exhausted, and put his hand on Emilia's shoulder for support.

Andreas turned around and said in a sharp voice: "No, Dad, this wasn't your fault. This was entirely my fault. I should've never let her be in the water without her life vest. You saved her. I would've never made it in time to catch her before she went down the rapids."

"Still, if I hadn't—"

"Dad, please. You may be responsible for a lot of bad stuff, but not for this. You saved her. She could've been hurt really badly." Andreas's voice broke. He gently lowered Laura to the ground and let Karla take her. He sat on a stone and covered his face with his hands. "I don't even want to think about what could've happened," he murmured.

"He's right, Robert." Karla wrapped her arms around Laura. "We know this river. We should've been more careful."

"All right. Everybody calm down. Thank God, we're all safe," Emilia said. She was still holding Tonio, who had stopped crying.

"You got a bump." He pointed at Laura.

"We better take her to the doctor. What if she has a concussion?" Karla gently touched Laura's face. "Are you feeling sick, honey?"

Laura shook her head. "But it hurts." She touched the bruise on her forehead and winced.

Andreas kissed her. "Yes, we should have the doctor look at her."

"He can check Robert out, as well. I don't like the looks of him. He strained himself too much." Emilia put her hand on Robert's shoulder.

Robert's face was ashen, and he kept touching his chest. "Oh, no. I'll be fine. I just need my medicine." He waved Emilia off.

"I think Mom's right," Andreas said. "Better safe than sorry."

"Stop worrying about me. I'm fine."

"No, you're not fine," Emilia said, getting up. "Let's go."

"Emilia, please, don't fuss." Robert gave her an imploring look.

"Robert Brendan O'Reilly, would you just once in your life ..." Emilia shook him gently by the shoulder. "Just once, listen and take my advice. Just once. Is that asking for too much?" She spoke in an exasperated voice, which was out of character with her normal timid demeanor.

Robert looked at her, surprised, then gave a quick chuckle. "All right, Milly, have it your way."

"We better go, before they close the clinic." Andreas turned to his father. "Where did you learn to swim like that?"

"I was a Navy SEAL."

"Navy SEAL? What's that?"

"It's a special force in the U.S. Navy. Perhaps one good thing did come out of that. I became a good swimmer," he said quietly.

Then Andreas did something that stunned both Karla and Emilia. He went up to his father and hugged him. "Thanks, Dad. That's a huge good thing."

Robert looked at him, surprised. Tears rose to his eyes.

As it turned out, Laura wasn't seriously hurt. The doctor cleaned her scrapes, gave her a soothing balm and a mild medicine against the pain, and told her she looked like a brave warrior with her bruises.

Robert, on the other hand, didn't get away that easily. He received a stronger medicine for his heart and the strict order to rest for the next few days.

"We'll see about that," the old man mumbled under his breath as they left.

"Dad, are you always that stubborn?" Andreas asked him on the way out.

Robert gave a quick smile. "I guess I haven't lost that yet."

Chapter 56

In early August Robert returned home, and to the surprise of everyone, Emilia decided to accompany him and stay with him for some time.

"I've always wanted to go back to the United States one day. I lived there for a year, in Maine, working as an au pair, and I loved it. That was long before I met Robert," she told Karla.

It was an emotional farewell at the airport. Having finally found each other, Andreas and his father didn't know when or if they would see each other again. Robert's heart had given him more trouble. The excitement and emotional upheaval of reuniting with his son and former wife as well as the exertion in the river had weakened him.

When it was time to go through customs, Andreas hugged his mother, wishing her a wonderful time. Then he turned to Robert. "Well, Dad, I never thought I'd say this ... but I'm glad you came."

"Thank you so much for everything." Robert's voice quivered. The two men hugged each other.

"Come and visit us. October is the most beautiful month in Vermont," Robert said. "I told you I'd pay for the tickets and—"

"Dad, we talked about this. There's no way you're going to pay for our tickets. Perhaps we'll get a good deal. We'll see."

When Robert said good-bye to Karla, she saw tears in his eyes. And when Tonio began to cry because Grandma and Grandpa were leaving, Robert's lips trembled. He reached for his handkerchief and blew his nose. Emilia took him by the arm, and the two of them went through customs, waving back once more.

The following few weeks, picture postcards began to arrive from different places in the United States and Canada. Emilia and Robert were obviously having the time of their lives. They seemed to travel everywhere. There were pictures of Vermont; of different seaports in Connecticut and Maine; of Boston, New York City, and Washington, D.C.

More postcards followed, and Laura and Tonio collected them and showed them off to their friends in school and kinder-garten. One day, Karla received an email on her computer from Emilia.

"Gee, your mother is getting hip." Karla chuckled as she and Andreas perused one of the messages with photos attached, looking at one of Emilia and Robert in front of the Niagara Falls.

"But look at this one," Andreas exclaimed. It showed a picture of a pet cemetery in California, with a note underneath the picture: *Good business for you, Andreas.* "Americans must be nuts. The tombstones for their animals are more elaborate than the ones we have for humans."

A letter that arrived a few days later included a piece of news that shocked them at first. Robert and Emilia had gotten married again, in Las Vegas of all places.

"Nothing surprises me anymore." Andreas shook his head. "Well, why not? What do they have to lose at this point? I just wonder where they're going to live. Does that mean my mother will move to Vermont? In that case, we'd have to visit her. Look at these photos. Gorgeous landscape." Andreas showed Karla one of the pictures, a Vermont forest in fall with its striking red maple leaves.

Karla, Andreas, and the children were at their relatives' place in Olivone, relaxing on the pergola after another one of Maria's filling Sunday meals. It was a sunny and somewhat nippy day in early September. Patches of thin white mist hovered around Monte Sosto. It smelled of autumn—of chrysanthemums and wood-stove fires.

"Well, you better make your reservations soon," Uncle Alois said. He smoked his after-lunch pipe and entertained Laura and Tonio by blowing smoke ringlets into the air.

"That's a nice dream," Andreas said. "But we really don't have the money for four tickets, and I'm not going without the kids."

Uncle Alois coughed and cleared his throat. "Well, I might as well tell you now. You have more money than you think." He told Andreas about the account with the child-support payments Robert had made over the years. "Don't yell at me, it's not my fault." Uncle Alois lifted his hands as he faced Andreas, who narrowed his eyes and stared at him.

"I'm not yelling at you. Why did you never tell me?" Andreas said.

Alois gave a grunt. "You really can't imagine why? What would your reaction have been if I had told you anything about your father, let alone that he gave you money? I wasn't ready to sign my death sentence."

"Oh, c'mon, Alois, I'm not that bad, am I?" Andreas said.

Maria, Karla, and Alois laughed out loud.

"Geez, guys. Thanks for the support. All right, so I lose my temper once in a while."

Karla hugged him. "You've improved a lot."

"Well, anyway. I can't accept that money. That's my mother's or yours. You paid for all my expenses, my schooling and everything."

"No, not for everything. We did use some of that money for your education," Alois said, "but there's enough left to cover any expenses you and your family would have, and more."

Andreas shook his head. "No. I'm not going to touch that money. If you don't want it, we'll keep it for Laura and Tonio, right?" He turned to Karla.

Karla nodded. "Yes, that might be a nice down payment for their education."

"Well, in that case, I have something else for you." Alois got up, opened a drawer, and took out a thick envelope. He handed it to Andreas. "Now, before you blow your top. I'm just the go-between. Your father gave this to me for you."

Andreas gave Alois an accusing look. "Wheeling and dealing behind my back again, huh?" He opened the envelope and took out a bunch of papers. After looking at them, he slapped them on the table. "Don't I have any say in this family at all anymore? I told him not to do this."

"What is it?" Karla reached for the papers.

"Gift certificates for airline tickets, for the whole family," Andreas grumbled. "I'm going to ..." He glanced at the children and stopped himself.

"Oh my god, that's ... wonderful," Karla exclaimed. She looked at Andreas, waiting for his outburst.

He merely sighed. "I give up."

A week later Karla and Andreas received a phone call from Emilia with troubling news. Robert had had another heart attack. Fortunately, he was out of intensive care, but according to the doctor, he was seriously ill. The prognosis was bad. It could be a matter of days, weeks, perhaps months. At this point, nobody knew for sure.

When Karla and Andreas called Robert at the hospital, he sounded very weak but upbeat. "Don't listen to those doom-sayers," he said to Karla. "I've been here before, I'll get out again. You know, 'Bad weeds grow tall.'" He laughed, then coughed and tried to catch his breath.

Karla gave the receiver to Andreas. The two men talked for a while. "Take care of yourself, Dad. ... Yes, we got the gift certificates. ... Yes, we'll do it. I should be yelling at you, but, well, thanks. ... Yes, promise."

After he put down the phone and the children were outside, Andreas turned to Karla and shook his head. "I'm afraid he's not going to make it."

Chapter 57

The family's travel plans remained an unfulfilled dream. As Andreas had feared, Robert died a few days later with Emilia by his side. The children took it hard, not just because they were disappointed that the eagerly awaited trip to America they had been bragging about to their playmates wouldn't come true, but because for the first time in their lives, a family member had died.

Death wasn't an unfamiliar concept to them. After all, their father made gravestones for the "dead people," as Laura called them, and she felt confident that those who had the privilege to rest underneath those beautifully carved rocks were content. However, the thought that their grandfather, who had played with them just a few weeks ago, was gone forever disturbed them. They had known him only a short time, but they had bonded with him and they felt he belonged to them.

Karla and Andreas tried to be as honest about the subject as they felt was appropriate for the children's age. Neither of them believed in the rigid Christian interpretation of death, re-surrection, last judgment, heaven, and hell. Religion, much like mythology, was an attempt to explain and deal with the un-fathomable and unknowable. As far as the existence of a god was concerned, they considered themselves somewhere between believers and agnostics, or as Andreas put it: "When I feel happy, the question of the existence of God doesn't trouble me much. I feel grateful to be alive, and if God should exist, then I thank him or her. When I read and hear about the atrocities and the pain and suffering in the world, then the whole existence appears to me like chaos without a benevolent being. However, when I'm really desperate, then I pray with my whole heart to that being who I'm not sure exists. Ridiculous, isn't it?"

Karla, who had experienced loss at an early age, remembered that the idea of her mother and grandmother being in heaven and God taking care of them had been a source of great comfort to her, and she felt it would help her children, as well. She was thinking about that when she and Andreas sat outside during one of the last warm evenings in September. The children had gone to bed, but after a while, the door opened and Laura came outside in her nightgown. She climbed on Andreas's lap and put her head against his chest.

"You can't sleep, honey?" he asked her.

Laura shook her head. "Papa, is Grandpa going to heaven now?" she asked after a while.

Andreas and Karla looked at each other. Andreas raised an eyebrow. "Hmm. We might have to bribe Saint Peter to let him in," he whispered to Karla.

"Huh?" Laura looked at him, puzzled.

"Nothing, sweetie. Of course Grandpa is going to heaven."

Laura was quiet for a while, then slipped down and came over to Karla. "Then, he'll meet Grandma Laura?"

Karla looked at her, surprised, and hugged her. "You remember who Grandma Laura is?"

"Yes." Laura nodded. "She's your mama and I was named after her, and she's in heaven, too," she said proudly, then added: "Too bad I never got to meet her."

"I know." Karla, moved by her daughter's innocent beliefs, felt tears rise to her eyes.

Laura crawled up on Karla's lap, and Karla held her, waiting for the next question. Instead, she heard a soft snore. Laura had fallen asleep. Andreas picked her up and carried her inside.

Karla watched as the last shimmer of light faded into the night. It was getting cool, and she went inside. Andreas was lighting a fire in the fireplace. Karla sat next to him.

"He went fast," he said quietly.

"Yes, too bad you didn't get to see him anymore."

"Yeah. Well, I'm grateful we were able to have a few good moments together." Andreas took a deep breath. "I feel sorry for my mother. I wish she could've enjoyed him a little longer."

"But how do *you* feel about him now?"

"Sometimes I think I should've read the letters he sent me. Perhaps I wouldn't have waited that long to make peace with him."

"So you've forgiven him?" Karla asked.

Andreas didn't say anything for a while. He watched the fire. Light and shadows danced across his face. "When I think about the man I spent time with this summer, I don't feel resentful anymore. I even got to like him. When I think about him, as he was back then, I'm more sad than angry. ... I don't know if you can call this forgiveness."

"I think you can." Karla gently touched the small scar under his eye. It was wet. She put her arm around him.

Andreas kept staring into the fire, then covered his face with his hands and sobbed. "I don't even know why I'm crying."

"Sure you do. You just lost your father a second time."

The flames leapt up, the wood popped and hissed. Finally, the flames settled around the chestnut logs and emitted a steady glow.

Chapter 58

"What are you looking for?" Karla asked when she found Andreas on his knees searching through a drawer in the living-room dresser.

"My old catechism," Andreas said. He sorted through the papers, then shook his head. "No idea where I put the darn thing."

"What do you need it for? Where does this sudden religious fervor come from?"

Andreas got up and began to peruse the bookshelf. "Well, I ran into Father Chiesa the other day and told him I wanted to go to Confession, finally. He suggested I see him after Mass on Sunday in his place. We could talk, and I could make a personal confession. He said that since I haven't been in Confession for decades, my list of sins would most likely be so long that I would take up too much time in the confessional." Andreas chortled. "Of course, I know what Father Chiesa's 'personal talks' usually turn into. There's something about him that makes you want to spill your guts."

"I know what you mean," Karla said. "That's what happened to me when I met him in church that one time when your father was here. I ended up telling him the whole family story."

"Yes, he knows his business well. Somehow, you can't resist his trusting eyes. Anyway, we'll be at Uncle Alois's on Sunday, so I thought that would be a good time. But I wanted to prepare a little. I don't even know the Ten Commandments anymore, or which ones are considered mortal or venial sins."

"Oh, Andreas. Forget all that. Just think of the things you've done or felt or said that you feel bad about. Tell him what bothers you. I don't think Father Chiesa will expect you to go down the list like a little boy. He doesn't strike me as a stickler."

Andreas nodded. "True. Well, here it is." He held up a small blue book, which was on the verge of falling apart.

"That looks like it has been used a lot," Karla said. "I didn't realize you had been such an avid student of religion. Mine looks almost new."

Andreas laughed. "Are you kidding? We boys used to throw it at each other on the way home from Sunday school."

Karla shook her head. "You're a lost cause."

"Perhaps we could all go to Mass at the same time," Andreas suggested. "Wouldn't do the kids any harm, either. Teach the little heathens some morals."

"Good idea," Karla said. She felt that, in spite of Andreas's glib remarks, he was probably more serious about finding comfort in church, or at least with Father Chiesa, than he let on. Besides, Karla liked Father Chiesa. The few sermons she had attended had been unusual and interesting.

Sunday started out as a gloomy day. Thick clouds hid the tops of the mountains, and it began to drizzle as Karla, Andreas, and the children left for church. The air smelled damp and musty.

It had been a chaotic preparation for church at the house. Andreas, who wasn't used to dressing up, stood in front of his closet muttering under his breath. He pulled out pants and shirts, hung them back in, and finally asked Karla for help. Laura, who hated wearing nice clothes almost as much as her father, threw one of her tantrums because she didn't want to wear a dress. Tonio insisted on bringing along the fire truck he had received from Grandpa.

"All right, everybody," Karla yelled, finally losing her temper. She glowered at the children. "If you're not ready in five minutes in the clothes I put out for you and without toys, I'll make you go to Confession and church every week from now on. You obviously need it."

Finally, they were all in the car, ready to leave. Karla glanced at the sky in the east, where a few patches of blue pointed to a possible improvement of the weather. The children were in the backseat, and Andreas started the car.

"This is going to be so boring," Laura complained, stabbing the front seat with her foot.

Karla turned around and glared at her furiously. "You want to stay home alone, without lunch and dessert?"

Laura shook her head.

"Then I don't want to hear another peep out of you. I've just about had it." Karla yanked at her seat belt and snapped it into the buckle.

It was quiet in the car for a while. All of a sudden, Andreas chortled. "We violated the Ten Commandments and committed a few deadly sins, and this all in one morning. Use God's name in vain, not honoring your parents, wrath and anger, including threatening your children with church service and bribing them with lunch and dessert."

Karla rolled her eyes and exhaled. "Family."

Andreas touched her arm. "What would you do without us?"

"Paint all day," Karla grumbled.

That was one of the reasons she was irritable that morning. She had neglected her painting, having been consumed with the upheavals of the past few weeks. It was time to get back to it again. She had an exhibition coming up in the French part of Switzerland, and she needed to prepare.

They arrived early at the small church in the Blenio Valley, where Aunt Maria and Uncle Alois lived. Outside, the portly Father Chiesa, in his robe and holding a prayer book, was waiting for the parishioners. His face lit up when he saw the family.

"What an unexpected honor." He patted Andreas's arm, shook hands with Karla, then bent down and smiled at Laura and Tonio. "You're all ready for Confession?"

Tonio held on to Karla with both hands, and Laura shook her head vehemently and gave Karla an imploring look.

"No quite ready yet, huh?" Father Chiesa chuckled and gently mussed Tonio's hair.

"Not ... yet." Karla gave the kids a stern look.

"Only Papa," Laura piped.

"I see. That's good. Papa sets the example." Father Chiesa winked at Andreas. "I'll see you at my place after the service." He tapped Andreas's chest with his finger. "Don't forget, you can't take Holy Communion today."

Andreas nodded. "I wasn't planning to."

"Good. See you later." Father Chiesa walked toward the entrance of the church, shaking hands with a few of the parishioners.

Andreas put his arm around Karla. "They serve cheap wine at Holy Communion anyway," he whispered.

"You're impossible." Karla shook her head.

The sermon Father Chiesa gave dealt with the topic of hate and forgiveness. Andreas and Karla glanced at each other, surprised. Karla wondered if the priest had had some kind of foreknowledge that Andreas was going to show up for Mass, or if it was a mere coincidence, or if Father Chiesa made up the sermon on the fly, which was possible.

Father Chiesa was known as an excellent and passionate orator, and his talks were unusual, not necessarily strict Catholic doctrine, and often punctuated with humorous details. As Andreas had told Karla, his unorthodox ways occasionally got him into trouble with the church elders.

After Mass, Karla and the children walked the short path to their relatives for Sunday lunch. While waiting for Andreas,

Uncle Alois poured the adults a drink. The children went next door, where they had a few playmates.

"Well, Andreas finally made it," Uncle Alois said. "I wonder how many Our Fathers he will have to pray. Quite a few, I take it, considering how long it's been since this pagan went to church."

"Knowing Father Chiesa, he may very likely give Andreas an unusual task to atone for his sins," Karla said.

She was right. When Andreas showed up an hour later and she asked him jokingly if he now had to climb a mountain on his knees, he gave a quick smile.

"No, nothing like that. Father Chiesa asked me to carve a gravestone for my father. He'll see to it that I can put it up in the local cemetery of his parish, even though my father had lived and passed away elsewhere. Since my parents were married again and my mother lives here, he thinks he can arrange it."

"That's a great idea," Maria exclaimed. "I'm sure Emilia would love it. It gives her something to remember him by."

"When is she coming back?" Karla asked Alois.

"After the memorial service. She's staying with Robert's relatives right now."

"She must be pretty shaken up," Karla said.

"I'm sure it's hard for her. But she seems to be pretty level-headed about it."

"How sad," Karla said. "They were finally happy together, and they had so little time."

"Perhaps that's what made it more precious." Maria hugged Andreas. "You're so quiet today. Feeling better after your talk with Father Chiesa?"

Andreas nodded. A quick smile flashed across his face. Karla noticed, however, that his eyelids looked slightly puffy, as if he had been crying. His talk with the priest must have been emotional. Karla noted that Andreas had cried more often during the past couple of months than in all the years she had known him.

399

Chapter 59

The following weeks Karla and her family settled into their regular routine again. The children went back to school. Laura was in first grade now, and Tonio had started kindergarten. They still talked about Grandpa Robert and the fascinating time with him, but their new school environment and their friends filled their days, and in time the memory of their short-term grandfather faded.

Andreas began to carve the tombstone for his father. It became an intense experience for him, painful and uplifting at the same time, as he told Karla.

"Each letter of his name I carve into the stone feels like an affirmation of my father. It's like I'm chipping away at whatever negative feelings I may still have and putting them to rest. Father Chiesa talked about grace, and somehow carving a stone for the man I used to hate so much feels like an act of grace."

Karla nodded. "I understand."

"Thank you for putting up with me ... and all the family drama. I haven't made it easy for you." Andreas sighed.

"It's all right," Karla said. "The fact that you and your father made peace has helped us all. Sometimes I feel as if a dark cloud has lifted."

"Yes, you're right. I should've done this a long time ago. I've used my father for years as a convenient scapegoat for all my own hang-ups."

Karla put her arm around him. "I'm proud of you." She noticed the fine lines around his eyes. His face had lost its boyish softness. His features seemed sharper, and the expression in his eyes more pensive and serious. *We're getting older.*

A breeze kicked up. "Fall again." Karla took a deep breath. "Where has the year gone?"

They were sitting on their usual granite bench in the yard, taking a break from work and enjoying the warm afternoon sun. It was late September, and the breeze carried the musty smell of dew-soaked grass. The horse-chestnut trees in their yard were beginning to shed their leaves. The chestnut shells, which had split open, offered their brown, shiny seeds to the outside world. The day before, Laura and Tonio had gathered chestnuts, and Karla had helped them create figurines of animals and people. They had drilled small holes into the chestnuts and fastened them together with matchsticks. It was an autumn ritual Karla remembered from her own childhood.

Autumn brought a stillness with it, a slowing down of life. The farmers had brought in the summer harvest and were waiting for the grapes to fully ripen. The campers along the Maggia River had left, and the children were back in school. Karla enjoyed this more reflective time after the hustle and bustle of summer.

It was a time of renewed creativity for both Karla and Andreas. While Andreas was busy carving his father's gravestone and catching up with his other work, Karla focused on her painting again. In the past, not painting for an extended period of time had made her feel anxious, empty, and depressed. Now, the muse still poked and pushed her, made her feel impatient and irritable. But she was better able to strike a balance between her artwork and her family. It was all right to focus on other parts of her life.

What she had endured with Andreas—the fights, the anger, the sorrow as well as the love and passion—had brought them closer. The "flesh-and-blood" life with her husband and her family was as important as the colors, the shapes, and the light and shadows on her canvas. In fact, one wouldn't be possible without the other. They complemented each other and fed from each other. Each time Karla went through a crisis or transformation in her life, it showed up in one form or another on the canvas. It was often unconscious at first. Sometimes she noticed it only when someone else pointed it out to her, and at other times it came to her in a flash of intuition.

Once she picked up her regular painting routine, however, she realized how much she had missed it. She enjoyed the physical sensation of stretching the canvas, pulling the brush through the paints, and the smell of turpentine and lacquer.

Karla stood back and squinted her eyes, trying to decide which paintings she was going to show in the upcoming exhibition in the French part of Switzerland. Andreas came in, and the two of them studied her newer work. This time, the pictures were of a coherent style—landscapes and cityscapes combined representational and abstract features. The unifying elements were the contrast between light and shadow and the luminosity, which made the paintings truly her own.

"You paint a lot more human figures than you used to," Andreas remarked. "And the mood in some of your paintings is more unsettling, darker." He pointed to a picture of a female figure standing in water up to her waist. Her head was tilted, and her long, dark hair reached down to the water. Her eyes were closed, and a light twist in her mouth gave her a pained expression.

Karla nodded thoughtfully. "It's kind of ironic. I am more content and happier than I've ever been in my life, yet my pictures have become more somber." Karla shook her head. "In the past, when I was depressed and afraid a lot, I used to paint these large, colorful oil landscapes, and sometimes I think it was a way to 'paint over' my darker feelings. I tried to push them away, and now ..."

"And now?" Andreas asked.

"I'm not sure, but the darkness doesn't scare me as much anymore. I know I'll get out of it again." Karla sighed. "And when I do, when the darkness lifts, somehow everything seems brighter. ..." She shrugged. "It's difficult to explain."

"I know what you're trying to say." Andreas nodded.

Karla narrowed her eyes and glanced at one of her pictures. "Jean Philippe once told me that the better you're able to paint shades and shadows, the more luminous the light appears. It's a little bit like life, isn't it?

"When you're able to deal with a dark phase in your life and emerge from it and you see light again, you're more joyful, perhaps more humble. Then, of course, you forget again, and you go about your business, whining and complaining, fighting unnecessary fights, until a real tragedy hits again. And then it starts all over. ... So I keep on painting, and perhaps one day I'll know enough to strike the right balance between shadows and light, and not just in my pictures."

Andreas sighed. "I think that's something we'll be struggling with all our lives." He put his arm around her. "You know, your paintings are almost scary because they are so powerful."

It was the most important compliment Karla had ever received from anyone.

PART NINE

A BELATED APOLOGY

Chapter 60

Karla's exhibition took place in Montreux, a city at the Lake of Geneva. Andreas and Karla traveled on the small, clunky train from Locarno along the Centovalli—the valley named after its "hundred" side valleys—through the mountains, across the Italian border via Domodossola to the French part of Switzerland. It was a scenic ride past breathtaking canyons with crashing waterfalls and across precarious bridges and viaducts. Small villages with their typical stone houses, their *grotti*—small rustic inns—and vineyards hugged the mountains. As they crossed the border into Italy, they left the manicured hedges that divided the vineyards on the Swiss side and passed by the somewhat rickety family farms of the Italian north. From Domodossola, another train took them through the Simplon Tunnel and then along the lake to the city of Montreux.

"We should bring the children next time," Andreas said as they passed the Château de Chillon, the old castle with its dungeons and ghost lore, which had inspired such writers as Lord Byron and Henry James.

"It's nice to have a vacation with just the two of us, but yes, I already miss them." Karla sighed. "They'd love the castle."

They arrived in Montreux in the early afternoon and checked into their hotel. It was one of the older hotels built at the beginning of the twentieth century, with an atmosphere of traditional elegance and Art Nouveau architecture typical of that era. After freshening up, they got ready for the opening. The exhibition at the gallery in the center of town, near the lake, was devoted to three different artists. Aside from Karla, there was a sculptor from France and another painter from Germany.

When they arrived at the gallery, the exhibition was in full swing, and there were quite a few people there. Karla greeted the French sculptor, whom she had met at one of the art festivals Andreas had been part of. After answering a few of the regular questions from a reporter for the local paper, Karla and Andreas looked at the paintings and sculptures, exchanged a few words with the owner of the gallery and the French woman, and nibbled at the appetizers.

Karla was grateful for any exposure her artwork got and was always excited when she received an offer from a gallery to show her paintings. The first few openings had made her nervous. She had watched anxiously as some people rushed through the exhibition, sipped their wine, chatted, and left with hardly a glance at the pictures. After a while, she got used to the fact that only a small number of attendees were truly interested in art.

"Have you ever noticed that these occasions have little to do with art and a lot more with socializing and packing in the goodies?" Karla motioned with her eyes at a young man who scooped up a handful of salted nuts and tossed them into his mouth.

Andreas nodded and chuckled. "Yes, and yet they're important. Think of all the connections you've made and the work you've received."

Karla cast her eyes around the gallery. She noticed an older couple at the other end. She only saw them from behind, but they caught her attention because the man looked familiar to her. He was holding the woman in a gentle embrace, with one arm around her waist. With the other arm, he pointed at a couple of the paintings, seemingly commenting on them. He turned his head, so Karla saw his profile, and smiled at the woman. Karla's breath caught. She waited for him to turn around. As he did, she froze.

It was him. He had aged. His hair was almost all white, with streaks of gray, and he seemed to be even thinner than she remembered him. She recognized his wife standing next to him. She was somewhat older, as well, but compared to him, she still looked young.

"Andreas." Karla's voice trembled, and she held on to his arm.

He looked at her, surprised. "What's the matter? Why are you so pale?"

Karla took a deep breath and whispered, "Jean Philippe is here."

"What? Where?"

"Over there, next to one of my paintings. But don't stare. His wife is with him."

"That old guy over there?"

"They've seen us. They're coming over. Please, Andreas, don't say anything wrong. His wife probably doesn't know anything about ... you know, that time in Florence." Karla finally put down her wineglass for fear of spilling it.

"Calm down." Andreas chuckled. "Don't worry, I'll behave like a true gentleman to the man who screwed my wife."

"Andreas, please. We weren't even married yet."

"Karla." Jean Philippe extended his arms as he walked toward her. "How wonderful to see you again, and your masterful work." He took her hand in his. "May I introduce my wife, Micaela, to you?"

"I'm pleased to finally meet you." Micaela smiled at Karla and shook hands with her.

"This is Andreas, my husband." Karla tried to regain her composure. Her mouth felt dry. She didn't dare to look at the two men's faces when they shook hands.

"It's very rewarding for Jean Philippe to see one of his former students doing so well," Micaela said.

"Thank you." Karla felt the blood rush to her face.

"From what I heard, my wife had an excellent teacher in Florence." Andreas looked at Jean Philippe with a barely perceptible grin. Karla secretly pinched his arm, worried he would make an inappropriate remark. Jean Philippe acknowledged the ambiguous compliment with a quick smile.

"I'm so surprised to see you here." Karla tried to steer the conversation in a different direction. "I sure didn't expect this."

"Well, it was a somewhat last-minute decision," Jean Philippe explained. "We are on our way to France for a short vacation to visit my family and friends. It's kind of a reunion." He and his wife gave each other a quick glance, and Karla thought she detected a flash of sadness on their faces. "So we decided to drive to Paris by way of Switzerland and visit some of our old friends. We saw Silvia and her husband two days ago, and she told us of your exhibition in Montreux. And here we are. I haven't seen any of your newer paintings yet, and so this is a perfect opportunity. I am very impressed."

"I'm really glad you could make it. This is a wonderful surprise." Karla, realizing that she was still clutching Andreas's arm, let go and tried to steady her breath.

"Unfortunately, we arrived rather late. I think they're just about to wrap things up." Jean Philippe looked around.

The owner started to pick up empty glasses and abandoned paper plates. "Take your time," he said with a friendly smile. "I'll be here for a while, and we're open tomorrow, as well, and the paintings will be up for several months."

"Good," Jean Philippe said. "We'll be here in the morning. That way we have a chance to look at the paintings more closely without a lot of people around." He took Micaela's hand in his and looked at Karla. "Are you still going to be here tomorrow?"

"Yes. We're staying at a hotel nearby. I have to come here, as well, to talk to Luc. He's the owner," Karla explained.

"Great." Jean Philippe smiled. "Perhaps we'll see each other then." He looked at Andreas.

"I won't be able to make it, but Karla will be here." Andreas squeezed Karla's hand. "I'm sure you've a lot of catching up to do, not having seen each other for so long."

Karla glanced at Andreas, but to her relief, there was no trace of sarcasm on his face. "The gallery opens at nine, so I'll probably be here around nine or nine thirty," she said.

"Wonderful. Well, let's look around a little more before they throw us out." Jean Philippe put his arm around Micaela, and they walked over to the section with Karla's paintings. Karla flicked her eyes at Andreas. It was only now that his face stretched into a wide, mischievous grin. "Please behave yourself," Karla whispered imploringly.

They joined Jean Philippe and Micaela and walked around the gallery, looking at pictures. Having recovered a little from the shock of running into her former teacher and lover, Karla was able to observe him more closely.

Jean Philippe looked ill, as if he was recovering from the flu. In spite of that, Karla still detected some of the features in him that made her fall in love so many years before: his warm smile and the sometimes-humorous glint in his sparkling gray eyes. He noticed that she was looking at him, and when their eyes met, she felt her heart skip a beat. It was still there, the tenderness and even some of the attraction that had brought them together that one summer night.

It so happened that Karla found herself standing next to Micaela in front of one of the sculptures of the French artist Karla particularly liked. She felt inhibited around the woman, whom she had betrayed. They were exchanging a few comments about the sculpture, and Micaela treated her in such a friendly way that Karla began to relax. She couldn't possibly know about Jean Philippe and Karla's fling in Florence. Karla glanced across the room to where Andreas and Jean Philippe were looking at the paintings and talking. At one point she saw, to her surprise, that they were shaking hands. *I wonder what that's all about.*

It was getting dark when Karla and Andreas walked the short distance back to their hotel. The city lights along the shoreline reflected off the surface of the lake, and the brightly lit Château de Chillon cast beams of yellow and orange onto the water. A thin strip of lavender grazed the horizon, and the last shimmer of daylight shone through an opening in the clouds.

Karla, usually acutely aware of the colors in her surroundings, barely noticed the changes in the light. "What a shock," she said.

"It sure was. Your old flame … and with his wife." Andreas chortled.

"Thanks for being a good sport. I was so embarrassed."

"Well, as Father Chiesa would say, 'Our old sins have a way of eventually catching up with us,'" Andreas said.

"Tell me about it." Karla sighed. "Are you sure you don't mind if I see him tomorrow? Why don't you just come along?"

"You really think I'm afraid you'd run off with that old geezer?"

"Don't be ridiculous. Besides, his wife will be there," Karla said.

"Hmm. I bet you anything she won't. He wants to see you alone. He sure seemed relieved when I told him I wasn't going to be able to make it."

"That's nonsense, Andreas. It's not that way between us anymore. This isn't a get-together between lovers. We're just friends."

"Oh, yeah?" Andreas raised his eyebrow. "Come on, Karla, be honest. You turned white and almost fainted when you saw him. The way you clutched my arm, I'm sure I'll have bruises tomorrow. That wasn't just the shock of seeing him again, and he certainly didn't hide the fact how much he still likes you."

"I'm not denying that I still like him, but as a teacher and a friend."

"Aha?"

"Stop it, Andreas. You're being silly." Karla shook her head. "He looked ill. He was always slim, but I was shocked how much weight he lost."

"Probably screwing too many young girls." Andreas leered at her.

Karla was getting irritated. She stopped and stared at Andreas. "Jean Philippe isn't that way. You're really being unfair."

"You're sure very protective of him."

"I don't like it when you make lewd remarks about a person I care for and you don't even know him." Karla sensed she was being coerced into admitting feelings for her teacher she thought she no longer had but which, as she realized now, were still there. And it irked her that Andreas kept poking at emotions she would rather not confront.

"So you admit you still love him." Andreas flashed a mocking smile.

"I didn't say 'love.' Stop twisting my words. I care for Jean Philippe, but I love *you*, although right now I don't know why. You're really starting to piss me off. I'm going upstairs."

They had reached the hotel, and Karla was heading for the elevator. Andreas, however, caught up with her and grabbed her by the arm. "You're not going anywhere. We're going to have a drink in the bar and talk this thing over sensibly and in earnest. You're pissed off because I told you the truth and you don't want to admit it."

"Ouch, you're hurting me." Karla tried to pull her arm away.

"Good, you deserve it." Andreas eased his grip somewhat and led her to the bar, which was almost empty. He picked a booth in the back. Karla sat down with a sigh, wondering why their first vacation alone together was heading toward a crisis.

After the waiter brought two glasses of wine, Andreas took a sip, then put the glass down and peered at Karla. "Why can't you just be honest? I've known all along that there's a man out there who has always meant a great deal to you. I've accepted it. So, please, stop trying to assure me that you love me more than you love Jean Philippe. I assume that's the case and that he is no longer a threat to our relationship. Otherwise, we wouldn't still be together, would we? And I certainly wouldn't encourage you to see him tomorrow. I don't need to be placated like a child whenever the topic of Jean Philippe comes up and you start feeling guilty because you still love him. I'm not stupid."

Karla looked at her hands and felt a tear sliding down her cheek. Andreas didn't say anything but handed her a Kleenex. "I'm sorry," she said and dabbed at her eyes.

"Karla." Andreas touched her hand. "Where's the woman who helped me get my feelings about my father straight, who always encouraged me to be honest? And you were right. That's why I want *you* to be honest about *your* feelings, not just to me but to yourself. Don't you see? It's important. I'm not angry at you because you also have feelings for someone else. I'm not that possessive. But if you keep denying it, then I start to wonder how deep these feelings really are and if we've lived a lie all these years. ... I couldn't imagine it."

"No, of course not. What I feel for Jean Philippe pales in comparison to what I feel for you. And yes, I admit, my heart fluttered when I saw him today. But a flutter isn't a steady heartbeat." Karla paused. "Back in Florence, Jean Philippe and I talked about love, and he tried to explain to me what he felt for his wife. He said, and I can't remember his exact words, but he said the most wonderful thing about being in a long-term relationship was waking up in the morning next to the person you've known for so long and realizing that after all these years you still love her."

"And yet he slept with you and cheated on his wife," Andreas said.

"Yes, and that was wrong. But I brought it up for another reason," Karla continued. "I feel that way about us. We've been together for a long time and we have something very special, and I'm not going to ruin it. And if you're really worried, then I don't need to see him tomorrow."

"No. You should see him. Because I know you want to. If you don't, you'll just regret it later. You've unfinished business with him. If I stand in the way, it'll just backfire." Andreas took a deep breath. "I just have to trust that this is the right thing to do."

"You don't have to worry, Andreas, I—"

Andreas waved her off. "But you should know something, and I'm telling you this not to make you feel bad but to warn you. You may think his wife doesn't know about your affair. Well, I have to burst your bubble. Micaela does know."

"What? That can't be. How do you know?"

"When we were at the gallery looking at pictures, Jean Philippe came up to me and apologized for what happened in Florence."

"Is that when you shook hands?" Karla remembered the short scene she had witnessed.

"Yes. Anyway, I told him that it was a thing of the past, that it wasn't important anymore. And if he wanted to apologize, he should apologize to his wife."

"What did he say?" Karla feared the worst.

"He said that he had already done that."

"Oh no." Karla leaned her head into her hands, almost knocking over her wineglass. Andreas caught it just in time. "Relax. Look, she's obviously a very generous person. Perhaps they had marriage problems back then, perhaps she was having an affair, too. What do we know? But she doesn't seem to be angry at you anymore. Otherwise, they wouldn't have come to your opening and she wouldn't have been so friendly."

Karla shook her head. "Still. What am I going to do now when I see her tomorrow? If I don't say anything to her, she'll think I'm a hypocrite. Great. Well, serves me right, I guess."

"If I'm right about Jean Philippe, she won't show up tomorrow. And if she does, perhaps you'll have a moment alone with her. Just be honest and apologize. She'll probably smile at you and say something similar to what I told Jean Philippe."

"You're right." Karla sighed. "I feel like an idiot, but I guess that's all I can do now."

"Talking about former lovers," Andreas continued after a pause. "I ran into Annette the other day."

"You're kidding? When?"

"Oh, about a couple of weeks ago. I saw her in a store in Bellinzona. She remarried and seems to be very happy."

"Why didn't you tell me?"

"I simply forgot until now. I wasn't trying to hide anything. See, unlike your involvement with Jean Philippe, my affair with Annette was never based on any kind of deep feelings on my part. I'm not proud of that. In retrospect, I have to admit that I probably acted more reprehensibly than you did. At least you were in love with the man you slept with. For me, Annette was merely a nice person, someone to fill in for you. Basically, I took advantage of her feelings for me and used her. So you're not the only one who made a bad decision once.

"Anyway, why don't you finish your wine so we can go to bed? You need your beauty sleep so you're fresh for tomorrow's encounter with ... well, let's just leave it at that." Andreas gave a quick smile. "Stop worrying. It'll be all right."

In spite of Andreas's attempt to reassure her, Karla had a difficult time falling asleep. Andreas had made her aware that she had been at the point of reverting back to that immature young girl she once was and which was obviously still part of her adult psyche. He was right. She had bullied him into accepting and dealing with his own unresolved feelings. It was about time she did the same.

Tossing and turning, Karla faded in and out of a fitful slumber, interrupted by strange dreams she couldn't remember the following morning.

Chapter 61

Karla stood in front of the mirror, brushing her hair and putting on lipstick. "What are you going to do while I'm at the gallery? And don't pretend you're going to pick up another woman. I won't believe you."

"I didn't have any such thoughts, but now that you mention it ... I did see some pretty girls yesterday. And since you're about to meet your lover—"

"Stop it. I told you, you could come along if you're worried."

"I'm not worried. Besides, I don't think he can get it up anymore."

"Andreas, you know, you can be really vulgar sometimes." Karla glared at him.

Andreas chortled and began to whistle the old song *"Voulez-vous coucher avec moi, çe soir."*

Karla grabbed a pillow and tossed it at him. Andreas caught it and gave his loud, throaty laugh. Karla suspected that his boisterous behavior was, in part, an attempt to cover up his true feelings: he was concerned. She went up to him. "I don't need to do this."

Andreas rolled his eyes. "Go, for heaven's sake. You're going to be late." He grabbed her purse, put it into her hands, and pushed her toward the door.

Karla turned around and hugged him. "I'll be back soon."

Andreas gave her a quick kiss, then stepped out on the balcony. Karla took the elevator to the ground floor.

It was still dewy at nine in the morning. The sun struggled to pierce the thin layer of mist and didn't give off much warmth yet. Karla buttoned up her jacket. The sunrays bounced off the gray-green lake, leaving glittering diamonds on its surface. On the other side of the lake, dark-green pinewoods were interspersed with patches of lighter green and the yellow of birch leaves which were beginning to turn.

The gallery had just opened. As Karla approached, she saw Jean Philippe through the shop window. She entered and flicked her eyes around. Aside from him and the owner, the gallery was empty. *Well, Andreas, I guess you won the bet.* Karla was relieved, not just because it saved her from a possibly embarrassing situation with Micaela but because she wanted to be alone with Jean Philippe. It had been so long since she had seen him, and her heart and mind were full of things she wanted to share with him.

Jean Philippe stood in front of her paintings, examining them, one hand on the small of the back, the index finger of the other hand touching his chin, seemingly deep in thought.

Luc came over, winked at her, and motioned with his head in the direction of Jean Philippe. "Your friend bought three of your paintings," he whispered.

Jean Philippe turned around and approached Karla with a wide smile. They embraced each other, and with her arms around him, she felt how thin he had become. "You've lost weight."

Jean Philippe's face became serious, then he flashed a smile again. "And you've filled out a little, thank God."

"You mean to say, I gained weight. I had two children," Karla said.

"No, it's very becoming. You used to be so thin, I was always afraid I'd break you in two." He put his arm around her and led her to her paintings.

"I can't tell you how impressed I am. You've grown so much as a painter. I always knew you had it in you, even during your humble beginnings, but this is truly amazing." He waved his arm in an encompassing gesture toward the paintings.

"Thanks," Karla said, her face getting warm.

"Remember how you struggled with abstract paintings at first, how you kept reverting back to naturalistic landscapes?"

"Yes, I do. And I also remember how you splashed paint on the canvas and covered anything that began to look realistic."

Jean Philippe nodded. "I didn't do it to turn you into a purely abstract painter. I just wanted you to explore the unknown, push your boundaries a little. And you sure did.

"I love the way you kept your original passion for landscapes but went on developing them, and how you integrated the other elements, human figures with their grief and passion as well as their joy." He pointed to the painting of the nude woman in the lake, whose face expressed pain.

Jean Philippe stopped and started to cough. "Excuse me." He reached into his pocket and pulled out a vial of pills, and popped one into his mouth. He went over to Luc and asked him for a glass of water. "Sorry about that."

"Are you all right?" Karla asked him.

"Yes, don't worry. I'm getting over a cold. Anyway ..." Jean Philippe took a deep breath. "What I wanted to say, you truly found yourself and your own style."

"Thank you. A lot of it I owe to you. Without you—"

Jean Philippe shook his head. "No, Karla. I may have helped you out of a tight spot once, but this ..." He pointed at the paintings. "This you did on your own. You went far beyond anything I could teach you."

"You exaggerate, Jean Philippe."

"No, I don't." He peered at her with a serious face. "Don't underestimate your strengths. You have to accept your genius as well as keep in mind that this isn't the end. You can always take it to the next level. Never stop learning and experimenting. Once you begin to rest on your laurels, then you begin to die as an artist. But I don't think this is a danger for you. You're much too modest when it comes to your art. Celebrate a little and then get back to work." He gently touched her arm.

Karla felt a knot in her throat. Hearing him talk with so much conviction about her development as a painter brought back memories of that transformative time in Florence, the confusion, the pain, and the exaltation as he helped her break through and produce one of the first paintings she was truly proud of.

Jean Philippe coughed again. "Would you mind a cup of coffee or tea? I'm getting a little tired. We've done quite a bit of driving the past couple of days. I saw a coffee shop down at the lake on my way here." Jean Philippe looked at his watch. "We have about forty minutes until Micaela comes by."

"Oh, so I guess Andreas won only half the bet," Karla blurted out, then laughed. She blushed as she explained to Jean Philippe that Andreas had suspected he would show up by himself.

"Your husband must think I'm nothing but a playboy." Jean Philippe flashed a quick smile, then said in a quiet, serious voice: "Well, in a way he's right—not about being a playboy, but about wanting to be alone with you for a while."

Karla was surprised at the change of mood. Jean Philippe, who just a minute ago was so enthusiastic, looked tired and sad. Down at the lake, his spirits picked up again. He told Karla proudly that he and Micaela had two grandchildren and a third on the way, and he looked with great interest at the photos of Laura and Tonio Karla showed him.

The sun had dispersed the last of the fog and mist, and it was warm enough to sit outside on the sheltered patio. As they were waiting for their order, Karla sighed. "Andreas told me that your wife knows about what happened between us in Florence. I feel really bad. I'm surprised she was so nice to me yesterday."

Jean Philippe shook his head and smiled. "Don't worry. I told her a long time ago. She was upset and angry at first. We went through a difficult time, but she has forgiven me. She was mainly angry at me, thinking that I took advantage of a young girl."

"But that wasn't true, Jean Philippe. I was the one who ... who approached you."

"It doesn't matter, Karla. Micaela knows that I care about you, both as a person and as an artist. Things have happened in our lives that may have made us a little more open-minded about love and compassion." He put his hand on hers. "She's not angry at you."

The waiter brought an espresso for Karla and a cup of tea for Jean Philippe. Karla was surprised that Jean Philippe drank tea. In Florence he had always ordered the strongest of espressos. She was equally surprised that she hadn't seen him smoke once. Probably because of his cold. Not seeing him play with his packet of cigarettes seemed unusual and odd to her.

"Have you stopped smoking?"

Jean Philippe quietly stirred his tea, then looked up at her. "Yes, strict doctor's order." He took a sip of tea, then coughed again. "I finally stopped, unfortunately a little too late.

"Karla, I wanted to meet you alone this morning not because I had any improper intentions, as Andreas might have thought. Rather, so I could tell you something. Unfortunately, something very unpleasant."

Karla was overcome by a feeling of dread. Ever since she had seen Jean Philippe at the gallery again, she had had the feeling that something was wrong with him. His apparent frailty and the coughing made her think he was either sick or recovering from an illness.

"This isn't just a simple cold, is it? What's wrong with you, Jean Philippe?" she asked, her voice unsteady.

He took her hand in his and looked at her tenderly. "I hate to do this to you and spoil our reunion, but ... Karla, I'm a very sick man. I was diagnosed with lung cancer a few weeks ago. Unfortunately, it's one of the more aggressive types of cancer, and it's spreading quite rapidly. According to the doctors, I have about three to five months left to live … if I'm lucky."

"No, that can't be," Karla said quietly, as if talking to herself.

"Unfortunately, it's true. Well, it's not such a big surprise, is it? My heavy smoking, the fact that I've lived in polluted cities all my life—it finally caught up with me."

"But don't they have treatments? Surely, there must be something the doctors can do? They have all these new methods these days."

"Karla, this cancer is terminal."

"But you can't just give up. You have to fight it."

"This is youth speaking." Jean Philippe smiled. "Believe me, we've looked at all the options carefully. Yes, there are treatments, very unpleasant ones, which could prolong life a little, but at great cost. No, I've decided against it, and Micaela and my children agree. The only treatments I get are those that alleviate the pain and the discomfort. I'd rather have a few months of decent life left to do some things I still want to do and then leave quietly, or at least as quietly as possible. That's why we're taking this vacation. We're going to France to visit whatever family and friends I still have. And finally, I want to see and say good-bye to the people who are dearest to my heart, you being one of them.

"Don't be sad, Karla." He put his hand on hers again, as tears filled her eyes. "We all have to die sometime. I know it sounds like a platitude, but it's true. I've had a long and fulfilling life. I got to do what I liked most, which is paint and teach, and I've been able to help a few people. I have a lovely wife, I was able to see my children grow up, and I was even able to enjoy a few grandchildren. I feel very grateful. Sure, I'd like it to go on for a few more years, but sometimes we just don't have that option."

"It must be so hard for Micaela and your daughters." Karla's head was still spinning from the news.

"Yes, that's true. In fact, it's more difficult for them than it is for me. Micaela is a strong woman. She'll be all right, and fortunately, we're very close to our children, and they'll help her get over it."

"Oh, Jean Philippe." Karla sighed. "What terrible news. Here I am, finally able to see you again, and now ... Are you afraid of dying? I'm sorry ..."

"That's all right, that's what we're talking about. I don't see why people shun the topic so much. I'm a little afraid of the pain, but there's morphine and other things. I don't think I'm afraid of dying, but then I don't know for sure. I'll let you know once I've gone through with it." His eyes showed the familiar humorous spark.

"I can't believe you're still joking." Karla managed a weak smile. "God, Jean Philippe, I'm going to miss you. I mean, it sounds kind of strange—we haven't seen each other in years—but I always knew that you were around somewhere and I once in a while got news from you through Silvia. Somehow, I was in touch with you. All those years, whenever I was stuck with my painting, I thought of you and it helped me."

He put his hand on hers. "Karla. You don't need me anymore. You're doing perfectly fine on your own. And if you really get desperate ... I may still be around somewhere, at least in spirit. Just watch for signs." He chuckled. "When you suddenly see something on your canvas that you didn't put there, it may be a message from the other side."

Karla managed a weak smile. "Remember the funny paintings we did together in Florence?"

"Oh yes, I remember." His eyes lit up. "I remember a lot of things from that time. I have a whole list of memories of you. I remember the first week and the half-eaten apple."

"Please cross that off your list."

"I remember how little you always ate because you were nervous being with me. I remember the trouble you had with

423

Andreas, and look how it's turned out. You're married and have two beautiful children. I remember how you slowly lost your fear of painting and how much your artwork improved." He took her hand in his. "I remember that night and how beautiful and wild you were. I can tell you still know how to blush." He smiled and let go of her hand. "See, there's plenty to remember and be grateful for."

Karla nodded. She looked down at her hands, trying to hold back her tears. "I still can't believe it," she sobbed.

Karla thought she had gotten over Jean Philippe years before. But now that she sat across from him and again felt his care and compassion, she realized that he would be another loved one she would have to add to the many losses in her life. There were so many questions she still had, things she wanted to share with him, but she couldn't formulate a coherent thought. Soon, it would be too late. He would be gone, and this time forever. It broke her heart. She struggled for words, but none came, and all she could do was put her head on her arms and cry. She felt Jean Philippe's hand on her back as the sobs shook her body. He waited quietly, as he had done in Florence when she had broken down before.

When she finally managed to stop sobbing and lifted her head, she saw that Jean Philippe had tears in his eyes.

"I'm so sorry to make you feel bad," he said.

Karla shook her head. "You shouldn't be sorry for my sake."

"Karla, I wish I didn't have to do this. But if I hadn't told you, you would've found out from someone else, and that would've been worse, don't you think so?"

"Yes, of course." Karla took a deep breath. "It's just so sudden ... and so final. I wish ... I don't know what I wish for. I mean, you're the one who is dying, and here I am making you feel sorry for me."

"That's all right. I'd rather feel sorry for someone else than being pitied myself." Jean Philippe took another sip of tea, trying to suppress a cough. "I think—and this may sound strange to you—it's easier to go through the process myself than for those who have to watch me go through it.

"I know I don't have much time left, so I try to use it wisely. Sure, I have had my dark hours, particularly when I first found out, and I know there will be difficult times ahead of me. I'm not kidding myself. But I feel strangely composed ... calm ... even happy. It's odd." He gave a pensive smile. "I'm going through every moment I still remember of my life, taking stock. I am getting rid of negative, confusing, and unsettling things, and keeping the ones worth keeping. It's like cleaning house. It's a very liberating task." He paused. "Your love and friendship are one of the treasures I keep."

Karla nodded, pressing her hand to her mouth, stifling a sob.

"Don't cry," Jean Philippe said and patted her arm.

Karla took a deep breath and shook her head. "Remember you said the same thing when we last said good-bye?"

"Yes, I remember." He pulled her toward him and hugged her. "I said something else, as well. Remember? ... I love you, Karla."

"I love you, too." Hugging him, Karla realized again how thin and frail he had become.

"But we should get back. Micaela probably thinks we eloped." Jean Philippe's eyes twinkled as he tried to lighten the mood. "And Karla, don't forget to check your canvas once in a while."

Back at the gallery, Jean Philippe's wife was waiting. Jean Philippe kissed her. "Sorry we're late. Let me take care of the paintings, and then we'll leave."

"I didn't even thank you for buying my paintings," Karla said. "I'm really grateful."

"Don't mention it. I had a difficult time deciding which ones to get. They're all so good. I'll keep them for a while, until ... and then I'll put them in my gallery. Unfortunately, I can't take them with me." He shrugged and walked over to Luc.

When Karla faced Micaela, she saw the whole tragedy of Jean Philippe's illness in her eyes. "I'm so sorry. I don't even know what to say."

"I know," Micaela said. "Sometimes I still can't believe it."

They were both quiet for a while. Karla looked down at the floor, trying to pluck up courage. When she finally spoke, her voice trembled. "Micaela, I want to apologize for what I did in Florence. I fell in love, and I practically threw myself at him. It really wasn't his fault."

To Karla's surprise, Micaela smiled. "You're very kind, trying to shoulder the whole blame, but you don't convince me. He knew what he was doing. He was old enough to know better. But I accept your apology. I put it behind me a long time ago."

"Thanks. You're very generous." Micaela's magnanimity made Karla feel ashamed.

"Karla, what difference does it make now anyway, what happened ten years ago in Florence? I can't possibly begrudge him his feelings of love. I know he loves me, I don't need reassurance. Love is all he has left now, isn't it?"

Karla walked back to the hotel as though in a trance. She almost missed the entrance and decided she needed to be alone for a while before confronting Andreas. She went to the coffee shop and ordered a cup of chamomile tea to calm her frazzled nerves. While sipping her tea, she realized that Andreas was exactly the person she needed right then. The whole morning, with its disturbing news, had thrown her so much off kilter that only his love for her could help her regain her balance. She left the rest of the tea and went up to their room.

Andreas had just come back from a walk. Karla put down her purse and sat on the bed. He gave her a probing look, and seeing her swollen face, he came over and sat next to her.

"Oh no. What happened? Was she there? Was she angry with you?" He put his arm on her shoulder.

Karla shook her head. "No, that's not it. I apologized, and she was very gracious." She put her face into her hands.

"Then what?" He sounded alarmed.

Karla burst into tears. "I'm sorry. I just got some bad news. Jean Philippe is dying. He has lung cancer. He has only a few more months to live."

"God. How shocking." Andreas hugged her. "That must be terrible for his family. Lung cancer? Was he a smoker?"

"Yes." Karla nodded.

"And you're losing a dear friend. I know. It's okay to cry."

On the train home the following day, Karla tried to be cheerful. She felt bad that their vacation together had ended in a flood of tears on her part, and above all, tears for another man. It was unfair to Andreas, yet he had been so supportive.

Andreas was sitting opposite her, scanning the landscape, yawning off and on.

"Didn't you sleep well last night?" Karla asked him.

He shook his head. "I had a hard time falling asleep, and I kept waking up."

Karla wondered if he worried about her, about their relationship. He didn't need to. The moment Karla had finally accepted her love for Jean Philippe, she had also realized that, no matter how deeply she felt for him, it was Andreas who was her life's true companion. He was the one with whom she shared the ups and downs of her artist's career as well as her daily life and the care for their children, with all its joys and problems, its irritation, and its passionate moments. Jean Philippe continued to be her muse, her inspiration, but it was Andreas who nourished and sustained her. Should she ever lose him, she wouldn't just grieve, she would be devastated, unable to bear it. "No!"

Andreas looked at her, puzzled, and Karla realized she had said it out loud. "I'm sorry." She got up and sat next to him and wrapped her arms around him. "Promise me you'll never leave me."

He hugged her. "I'm not intending to. What brought that on?"

"I just couldn't bear losing you."

"You mean ... like Jean Philippe?"

"Yes. ... No, not like him. I'm sad about him, but if you ... if I lost you, I'd kill myself."

"No, you wouldn't. Don't say such things. You'd have to take care of Laura and Tonio."

"Just promise," Karla said.

"Karla, I'm going to try very hard not to die of lung cancer. But I really don't have the power over life and death."

"I know." Karla sighed. "Just hold me."

Chapter 62

On a cool day a few weeks later, Karla received the announcement in the mail that Jean Philippe had died. There was a short personal note from Micaela telling her that he was buried in Siena. She also invited Karla and Andreas to visit her, should they ever be in Florence or nearby.

Karla left the note and announcement on the kitchen table for Andreas to read, and went outside to sit under the chestnut tree on the granite bench Andreas had once called the Wailing Bench. She wasn't as upset as when she first heard of Jean Philippe's illness. She had been prepared and was waiting for the news of his passing. Now, she just felt sad that the man who had at one time been such an important presence in her life had simply disappeared.

Andreas, who was taking a break from working, came outside. "I read the note. At least he didn't have to suffer very long. I guess that's all you can say at such a moment. Are you all right?"

"Yes." Karla nodded. A breeze of cool air flowed into the yard, shaking the leaves on the trees. "It's cool today, it might rain." She scanned a bank of dark clouds that was forming in the northern sky.

"I'm sorry." Andreas put his arm around her.

"She invited us," Karla said.

"I know. She sure is a very generous person."

A week later, the postman delivered another envelope and two packages from Siena. There was a short letter from Micaela.

Dear Karla,

I'm in the process of taking care of Jean Philippe's estate. I'm sending you by separate mail two items of his possessions he wanted you to have. I am trying to adjust to my new life, and it's a slow process. I hope you are doing well.

Kind regards,

Micaela

"Gee, I wonder what's in here." Karla lifted the packages and turned them around. "I can't imagine what Jean Philippe is giving me."

"I bet these are paintings," Andreas said.

He was right. Karla opened the smaller package. It contained a painting of Jean Philippe's she had admired in his gallery. When she opened the second package, she got a shock. It was the picture that had won first prize in Florence.

"This doesn't make sense." Karla shook her head. "This painting was sold. I got the money and the information from the gallery where it was exhibited. Why? Unless ..."

Inside the package was an envelope with her name on it. She opened it up and pulled out a letter.

Dear Karla,

When you get this, I'll be gone—to a better place, as some people claim. I have to say, though, the place I spent sixty-five years of my life was pretty good already. So if the next stage is even better, well, what else could I wish for?

Since I am in the process of redoing my will, I made you the beneficiary of two paintings, one of mine, in which you expressed an interest, and the one you painted. Yes, I know, you'll be surprised; I can already see your shocked face. I have to admit, I played a little trick on you. I am sure you remember how much I enjoyed pulling your leg once in a while.

When I saw your painting for sale in the gallery of the organization who had sponsored the contest, I bought it for myself. I just couldn't bear the thought of someone else owning it. I hope you'll forgive me the little ruse.

Now, I would like you to have it back, to sell again if you want to or to keep for yourself. I am sure Silvia would be much honored to have it in her gallery. Take care of yourself.

Love always,

Jean Philippe

"This is your painting," Andreas said, startled. He lifted the picture up.

"Yes, it is." Karla handed him the letter. "Jean Philippe bought it."

"Wow, what a surprise." He put the picture on the mantelpiece above the fireplace, so he could look at it more closely. "I guess I take back some of the unsavory remarks I made about him. That was very generous to buy it and then let you have it again. Now, you have the painting and the money."

"That's not right, I would've given it to him for free. I can't believe he paid all that money for it."

"Well, you may be a great painter, but you sure are a lousy businesswoman. Give it away for free? No way."

"I'm certainly not going to sell it again. No, this painting stays here. If Silvia wants it, she can put it up in her gallery, but it's not for sale."

"I think that's a good idea," Andreas agreed. "I bet she'll love it."

It was Sunday. The children were playing outside with a few friends. Karla had started a new painting the day before and was getting ready to continue working at it. She mixed the paints, and when she was about to begin, she noticed three small, round blue shapes at the bottom right-hand corner of the canvas. They had not been there the day before, and she certainly hadn't put them there. She thought of Jean Philippe and the hints he had dropped about strange figures on her canvas.

"This is nonsense," she said to herself. "There must be a logical explanation for this." She bent down to check out the forms more carefully, lightly touching them with her finger. The paint was still a little wet. When she smelled it, she smiled. *Finger paints?* She went outside and called Tonio.

He came running up to her, but when she led him into her studio, he stopped at the door.

"Did you do this?" Karla pointed at the blue shapes.

Tonio shook his head and put two fingers into his mouth, a familiar sign of embarrassment. *He is as bad a liar as I am,* Karla thought, amused.

"Tell me the truth." She pulled him toward her. "I am not going to scold you, but I need to know. Did you paint this?" Tonio nodded hesitantly. Karla gave him a hug. "Tonio, you almost made Mama believe in magic. Don't do this anymore. If you want to paint, I can give you your own canvas."

After the little culprit was dismissed, Karla looked at the forms again. They were almost perfect round shapes, and reminded her of the smiling and weeping grapes Jean Philippe and she used to paint. *Strange. Tonio had never messed with my paintings before.*

"Okay, Jean Philippe, I got your message." Karla chuckled.

"Who are you talking to?" Andreas, walking by her studio, stopped at the door and looked inside.

"Nobody. I'm talking to myself."

Andreas shook his head and walked on. Karla picked up a thin brush, dipped it in yellow paint, and painted two smiling faces and one weeping face on the three round shapes.

Chapter 63

All Souls' Day in late fall was a holiday when people honored their relatives and family members who had died. It was believed that on this day the dead and living were united once again for a short time. In the Catholic South of Switzerland in particular, people decorated the graves of their loved ones. Somber grayish cemeteries came to life with flowers, decorations, even food and drink.

Andreas and Karla, together with their children, followed the tradition of visiting the graves of their family members and friends. The day before, they had been to the cemetery in Bellinzona to put flowers on the graves of Karla's grandparents. Today, they were honoring Karla's mother, who was buried in the local cemetery.

Karla put a basket of grapes, apples, oranges, and a bouquet of lilies on her mother's grave. Lena, Luigi, and their children had decorated their grandparents' plots with an arrangement of red and white carnations and pine twigs. Several of the villagers were standing around, exchanging stories about the dead or simply chatting and admiring the elaborate display of flowers, ribbons, and even a few bottles of Merlot del Ticino.

Gabriela, the owner of the small grocery store, invited them all to a snack of salami, dried beef, bread, and wine at the store. As the wine flowed, the mood, which had never been exactly contemplative, became more and more jovial. Some raised their glasses toward the sky, toasting their departed, who they assumed had made it to heaven rather than to the less desirable inferno.

After most of the people had left to return to work or go home to prepare lunch, Andreas and Karla sat on the stone bench at the cemetery. Laura and Tonio were busy inspecting the graves, reading the names and inscriptions on the tombstones. They were particularly interested in the few stones their father had carved. After a while, they got bored and went to play with a few of their friends from across the street.

"I think our children may have a more intimate and natural relationship to death and dying than most kids because of the kind of work you do," Karla said. "I don't know of any other children who enjoy visiting cemeteries as much as Laura does."

"That's true," Andreas agreed. "She told me a few days ago that she, too, wants to make stones for the 'dead people.' Perhaps we'll have another stonemason in the family." He put his arm around Karla. "Do you realize this is the place where it all started?"

"Actually, it started when you almost ran me over with your car." Karla gave him an impish smile. "Remember?"

"Yes, but I think it was here where it truly began, where destiny gave us a chance to start new," Andreas said. "After I drove away, I started to feel sorry that I yelled at you. How stupid could I be? Here I meet this beautiful, sexy woman, who draws these amazing pictures, and all I can do is blow up at her. I didn't even have a chance to look at your drawings more closely.

Anyway, I figured that was the end of it, and I could've kicked myself."

"Yeah, I know what you mean. I wondered why a handsome hunk like you could be such a jerk. And yet, I couldn't stop thinking about you." Karla shook her head.

"Looks like it was the 'dead people' who managed to bring us together." Andreas chuckled. "The dead people and your paintings at the opening. That's when I was convinced I wanted to meet you again."

"Isn't it amazing?" Karla wrinkled her forehead. "If my mother hadn't been killed in that car accident years ago, I probably wouldn't have been at the cemetery that day."

"And if Paulo hadn't died, I wouldn't have been here putting up his gravestone, and we may never again have run into each other." Andreas picked up a pebble and turned it in his hand, examining it. It was a striated gray stone with specks of white. "We can take it further back. If your mother and Arturo hadn't been careless that night, you wouldn't even exist and I wouldn't have met you. And if my mother and my father hadn't engaged in that obviously doomed relationship, I wouldn't be here and ... well, you know the rest."

"You mean to say that our existence and the existence of our children is the result of people dying and couples being foolish and careless?" Karla laughed.

"Yeah, somehow," Andreas said. "Sounds like a miracle."

They watched an old man with a hat and cane walk by. It was one of the village elders. "I'll soon need one of those." He smiled and pointed at one of the gravestones with his cane.

"Oh, no, Giuseppe," Andreas called back. "I'm too busy right now. You'll have to wait a few more years."

The old man waved. Andreas and Karla watched as he limped on carefully, his cane tapping the cobblestone street.

Karla took a deep breath, and leaned her head against Andreas's shoulder and closed her eyes. "It's not so bad." Her voice sounded dreamy. "Lying here, I mean, after you die. At least we'd be together and have all our friends around us."

Andreas snickered. "Some kind of party of the dead? Well, for right now I could think of a few more attractive places to lie with you."

He put his arm around Karla. She brushed her hand through the tangle of hair on his forehead. His face was serious now, and in his intense verdigris eyes she saw again what had attracted her to him in the first place—his intensity, his zest for life, and the ardor with which he pursued his art. Attraction and passion had been the initial fuel that sparked their relationship, but it had been compassion and warmth and the willingness to learn to live with each other's frailties, with the occasional jousts and turmoil, that had sustained them.

As Karla tasted Andreas's kiss and inhaled his scent, she heard the light scratching of the chestnut leaves rubbing against one another in the breeze, and then a voice.

"Mama, Papa." Laura rolled her eyes as she and Tonio came walking toward them. "Are you two smooching again?"

"Yes, we are," Andreas said. "Have you finished playing and looking at gravestones?"

Tonio nodded. "I am hungry."

"Well, in that case we better go and eat another one of Aunt Maria and Grandma Emilia's sinfully huge All Souls' Day meals." Andreas tousled Tonio's hair.

Later that afternoon Karla was searching through her paintings in the storage room when she came across the unfinished picture she had started years before. She picked it up and looked at it again with a sigh. Determined either to finish it or to get rid of it, she dragged it out and put it on her easel.

She stood back and examined it, wondering why she had had such a hard time with it. Now, she understood. She had wanted to portray the pain and grief she had felt at the time, but the painting didn't do that at all. The pain was suppressed, not expressed.

The woman in the painting was a shadowy figure who turned her back to the sun, covering her face with her hands. She stood at the edge of the canvas, as if she wanted to step out of it. She was hiding from life and, with it, from love. The painting was a reflection of Karla's younger self.

After Karla had lost her mother, she had wrapped herself in a protective cocoon of "not feeling too much, not loving too deeply." Andreas, with his often lumbering ways, but with insistence, love, and passion, had been able to pierce that shell and reach into her heart. And there was pain, but also the promise of healing and new life, a process that was ongoing, and probably would be for the rest of her days.

Karla took a deep breath, dipped the brush into white paint, and slathered it on the canvas. After it was dry, she would paint the woman again, in the middle of the canvas, with her face exposed and a bright yellow sun, the sun at its hottest, at the upper right-hand corner.

Acknowledgements

The creation of a book is not just the work of one author. Many wonderful friends have contributed to this novel. My gratitude and appreciation goes to the following people: first and foremost to Scott Nicholson, author and editor, for his careful editing, his invaluable critique, and for his ongoing support; to Susan Deming for the beautiful cover design, her encouragement, and for her help with everything related to art; to the Teale Street Sculpture Studio in Culver City, California, for answering my questions about stone work and sculpting; to Bente, Heinz, and Christina Kirner for their enthusiasm, support, and for catching typos and other blunders; to Diane Busch and Jeanie Lauer-Van Dam for reading early versions of the manuscript and for their invaluable comments; to my nephew, Rico Spiegel, my nieces Claudia Spiegel-Calderón and Eveline Spiegel and their families, for keeping me going; and last but not least to my friends and families in Switzerland, the United States, and Peru for believing in me and for their support.

Christa Polkinhorn, originally from Switzerland, lives and works as writer and translator in the Los Angeles area in California. She divides her time between the United States and Switzerland and has strong ties to both countries. She is the author of six novels and a collection of poems. Her travels and her interest in foreign cultures inform her work and her novels take place in several countries. Aside from writing and traveling, she is an avid reader and a lover of the arts, dark chocolate, and red wine. She can be reached by email at cpolkinhorn@msn.com or you can visit her at her website www.christa-polkinhorn.com.

www.ingramcontent.com/pod-product-compliance
Lightning Source LLC
Chambersburg PA
CBHW020650110726
47901CB00001B/120